Blazing passion . . .

In one sweep he had Brenda in his arms, his lips fully possessing her in a fiery kiss. He held her against his chest, lowering her to the thick mattress of furs and cedar boughs spread on rush mats on the ground.

A wildness surged through Brenda, her mind swirling with a strange headiness. A warning was flashing inside her consciousness but as he kissed her more passionately, her back now against the softness of the furs, his hard, lean body spread atop hers, she lost all ability to reason as to what was right or wrong.

"Please don't," she softly cried. "Striped Eagle, please don't do this . . ."

Striped Eagle brushed another soft kiss against her lips, then cupped her cheek with the palm of a hand. "My heart is lonely," he said huskily. "*You* are lonely. Let us be as one, *Nee-bin-gee-zis*."

Dear Reader:

Since the publication of my first sensual Indian romance in 1983, I have received thousands of letters requesting more. I am pleased to announce that this book, *Savage Surrender*, is the first in a series of sensual Indian romances to be published by The Berkley Publishing Group. As now planned, two books will be published a year, set in as many major tribes across the country as possible!

My goal in each of these books is to give you, the reader, authentic details of each tribe's customs (carefully researched by me), as well as stories filled with passion and true romance.

I am very enthusiastic about this new Indian series. I hope you will read and enjoy them all!

My Warmest Regards,

Cassie Edwards

Savage Surrender

CASSIE EDWARDS

CHARTER BOOKS, NEW YORK

SAVAGE SURRENDER

A Charter Book/published by arrangement with
the author

PRINTING HISTORY
Charter edition/September 1987

ISBN: 0-441-05384-X

Charter Books are published by The Berkley Publishing Group,
200 Madison Avenue, New York, New York 10016.
The name ''Charter'' and the ''C'' logo are trademarks
belonging to Charter Communications, Inc.
PRINTED IN THE UNITED STATES OF AMERICA

10 9 8 7 6 5 4 3 2 1

I lovingly dedicate *Savage Surrender* to my late, dear poet grandmother, Hannah Lenore Cline, who taught me the importance of chasing dreams. I have found my dreams, in my family, and in writing, as did my grandmother whose beautiful poetry is still very much alive inside my heart.

Like the leaves that fall around us
  In autumn's fading hours,
Are the traitor's smiles, that darken
  When the cloud of sorrow lowers;
And though many such we've known, love,
  Too prone, alas, to range,
We both can speak of one love
  Which time can never change.

—Charles Jefferys

AUTHOR'S NOTE

Savage Surrender unfolds among the beautiful Minnesota hills and woods where the Sioux, Ojibwa and white settlers often roamed and clashed. The Ojibwa, whose gentle ways form the background of this romance, claim a long history. After defeating the Fox Indians of Wisconsin in the early 1700s, in a battle for control over wild rice beds, the Ojibwa turned westward to face the more warlike Sioux. Eventually the Sioux succumbed to the hordes of Ojibwa, who then dispersed into bands which ranged over the lake country of northern Minnesota, becoming one of the state's largest tribes.

Though warlike when necessary, the Ojibwa were primarily a gentle people. By driving out the sometimes-savage Sioux and least palatable settlers from the East, this tribe helped open up the state to future development. *Savage Surrender* is set against the growing conflict between Sioux and Ojibwa and the less scrupulous white man, a battlefield rendered powerless in the blazing fires of love . . .

One

❧ ❧

May 1840
Minnesota

The rose tinge of the setting sun had faded in the western sky, leaving the moon a sliver of white as darkness fell like a black cloak over the valley. Smoke spiraled peacefully from a chimney on a log cabin positioned between the smooth waters of the Mississippi River and a field of freshly planted crops. Inside the cabin, as the fire cast golden shadows from the hearth, the aroma of freshly baked bread cooling on the table and coffee brewing over the coals of the fireplace made the atmosphere even more cozy.

Brenda Denise Pfleugger lay before the fire on an oval braided rug, her chin resting in the palms of her hands. She listened contentedly as her mother read poetry aloud by candlelight, the family's entertainment each evening. The day had been long, the work grueling, Brenda having divided her time equally between helping both her mother and father.

But she never complained. She was proud of how her

father described her of late. She could hear his deep-pitched voice saying that she was indeed a young pioneer woman with an attitude of self-reliance, commitment, and courage, qualities that proved assets in this wilderness called Minnesota.

Brenda was proud of her German heritage, her grandfather having emigrated from Germany to Illinois all those many years ago. He, of northern European descent, had found the rich tallgrass prairies to his liking and had homesteaded near a medium-size glacial lake.

Brenda's father had inherited his father's adventurous nature and had left Illinois behind to move on, himself hungering for a new way of life, a . . . new . . . land . . .

Straightening the folds of her faded cotton dress, the white collar of which framed her long and delicate neck, Brenda shifted to a sitting position. The glow from the fire captured the blonde streaks, bleached there by the sun, woven into her waist-length, fiery red hair. At her present age of seventeen she had blossomed into a ravishing young lady with exquisite curves in the right places. She was tall, and her eyes were widely set and so blue they sometimes appeared transparent, feathered by thick, curving lashes. Her nose was straight, her lips sensually full.

Letting her gaze move slowly about, she was reminded of her recent restlessness. The house in which she lived was nothing more than a log cabin, its walls mellow now with flickering light from the fireplace of clay and stone. It was a small one-room shelter, the cracks between the logs filled with a mud and straw plaster; buckskin hung over the windows and at the door.

The furnishings were sparse, but adequate for sleeping and eating. The cabin had been built, log by log, by all four members of the Pfleugger family, even including five-year-old Tommie. It had been a labor of love and Brenda was glad to be a part of such a family that looked forward to all tomorrows. So many of the settlers in this Minnesota land saw only as far as the end of the day and the edge of their clearing, as if in their minds they were imprisoned. They feared the red-skinned Indian *and* evil white men as well . . .

But Brenda feared nothing and no one. It was her restless nights now filled with strange longings that troubled her more than not . . .

It always seemed to begin when she saw her mother and father creep into their bed to snuggle. The low embers of the fire seemed to cast an almost mystical glow on the two people clasped in a lover's embrace each evening, with nothing to separate their bed from those of their two children.

Even when Brenda turned her eyes away it was the sweet murmurings exchanged between her mother and father that made her realize that her restless moods were surely because she desired to be wooed by a man.

But so far none had appealed to her. Her mother had told her that when the right man came along, she would know it. Nature would give her all the right signs. It would be in the way her body reacted. She had even told Brenda that it could happen at any time now. She was of the proper age to get these strange cravings and desires and not to be afraid of them. They were God-given, put there ever since Eve had offered Adam the apple at the beginning of time.

Her mother had also told her to feel free to love openly, to never let shame stand in the way of what could be the most beautiful moment in her life . . . that moment she would share with the man she loved. Sometimes life could be so short. Grasp what happiness she could find . . . when she could find it.

Her mother had seen many die of cholera and other terrible diseases along the trail, even before some of the women had reached child-bearing age . . .

"Brenda has stars in her eyes again," Brenda's brother

Tommie suddenly blurted, leaning his small, square face into hers. "Sis? Are you there? Mama's through readin' poetry. It's time to go to bed."

Feeling heat rise to her cheeks, Brenda fluttered her lashes nervously as she found Tommie's golden-brown eyes close to hers. "What? What did you say?" she asked, laughing softly.

Tommie lifted a tiny shoulder into a shrug as he stepped away from her. "It's time to go to bed," he said, sitting down on the floor to slip his shoes off. "But I think you're *already* in a dream world, Sis. You're sure actin' funny lately."

Brenda rose quickly to her feet, glancing from her mother to her father who were sitting opposite one another at the dinner table. Her father, Harrison, was looking back at her with his cool blue eyes twinkling over the rim of his tin cup as he sipped his coffee. Her mother, Carole, was smiling as she placed a ribbon used as a bookmark in the volume of poems.

"Now, now, Tommie," Carole softly scolded. "Leave your sister alone. She's a right to her dreams, be they night or *day* dreams. Now you just get on to bed, son. I'll come and say prayers with you in a minute."

"Oh, all right," Tommie sighed, ambling toward his bed.

Brenda smiled a silent thank-you to her mother, then took a hairbrush from the fireplace mantel. In even strokes she began brushing her hair, making it shine into a lustrous red satin glow.

"Guess things are a mite borin' for you out here in the wilderness, eh, Brenda?" Harrison asked, scraping his chair back from the table. When he rose to his full six-foot height he had to stoop to keep from grazing his head against the open beams of the room. "It ain't nothin' like Chicago, is it, daughter?"

"No. Not at all," Brenda sullenly agreed.

Then, realizing her tone of voice, she quickly added, "But I understand why we're here. Papa, the challenge of a new land is also exciting to *me*."

"There's more to life than land for a girl your age," Harrison grumbled. Two long steps took him to the hearth. He squatted and wrung his hands in the heat of the fire, staring down into the flames. "Farms are too widespread here for you to meet a likely prospect for a husband. So far the only available gentlemen for my daughter are soldiers. And most we've become acquainted with are damn corrupt."

Brenda rested the hairbrush in the palm of her hand. She had heard the bitterness in her father's words. She could see the hate etched across his face with the mere mention of soldiers, a hatred that had aged him beyond his years. His face, beaten brown by the wind and sun, was furrowed with wrinkles, his hair which had been black upon first arrival to this new land was now thinning and gray.

How many more times would the Pfleugger family be forced by gunpoint to move onward? Twice already they had been made to leave the land they had worked so hard to clear, forced to move downriver. Always after they had broken sod with back-breaking energy, drained the pot-holes, and planted grain, the corrupt Major Joseph Partain had led his troops from Fort Snelling to drive the Pfleugger family out. Major Partain had always used the same reason for this evacuation, saying they had made residence on land set aside for the military. They were only squatters. They had no rights . . .

Seeing her father filled with such embittered hatred, Brenda wondered how many more times her father could be humiliated. She as well as her father knew that the major timed his appearance to occur after the land had been tamed. Then he would swoop down and wrest it away. Brenda knew that the time was now ripe for the major to make his unscheduled debut. The land was cleared, the cabin was built, the crops were planted . . .

Carole moved to Harrison's side. Looking frail, her hair silvering even at her young age of forty, she encircled her husband's waist. "Let's not talk about soldiers tonight," she softly urged, the fire's reflection making her dark eyes flash a golden color. "Let's give a blessin' for what we have, darlin'. We will *always* have each other. No matter what, we'll always have each other."

Harrison turned and placed his strong arms about Carole and drew her into his embrace. He nestled his nose into her hair scented with perfumed soap, the last of the bars from Chicago. "You are all that's good in this world," he said hoarsely. "God a'mighty, if anything should ever happen to you—"

Carole leaned away from him and placed a long tapered finger to his lips, silencing him, and hopefully his worries for the moment. "Shh," she murmured. "I'll always be here for you. Always."

Harrison's insides were gripped with an even deeper resentment of the soldiers as he felt the coarseness of his wife's skin, once so smooth. The soldiers had caused his wife's work to triple since they had to build three separate cabins in so short a time.

Taking her hand away from his mouth, he gently kissed its palm, forcing a good-hearted laugh. In his ocean-blue eyes there was a sudden gleam of mischief. "Before we call it a day, what say we place a little dream dust on the fire?" he said, looking over at Brenda and winking. "Would you like that, pretty daughter?"

"I'd love it, Papa," Brenda said, smiling devotedly at him, feeling way less than seventeen at this moment. She knelt down on her knees by the hearth and watched her father scoop a handful of poplar-stump punk from a small brass scuttle and cast it into the coals, then watched as the flames leapt from emerald to blue.

"It's almost mystical," Brenda sighed, hating it when

the fire fluttered and shifted in its coals as the colors faded away.

Harrison laid two walnut splits against the backlog of the fireplace. "Now's time to continue dreamin' in *bed*," he said, tossing Brenda an easy smile, then casting a look of promise toward his wife who had bent to snuff out the candle on the table.

But a sudden noise outside the cabin made Carole straighten her back stiffly, her eyes narrowing in a frightened, pained squint as she peered intensely toward the deerskin wavering in the cool breeze of night at the door.

"No," Carole gasped, placing a fist to her mouth. "Not again." Her eyes glinted in the dying firelight, beseeching her husband. "Harrison, please tell me it's . . . not . . . going to happen again?"

Brenda tensed, now hearing the loud roar of hoofbeats drawing closer outside the cabin. Her heart skipped a beat, having expected the unfolding scene, yet hoping that this time they would be left in peace.

"Damn them," Harrison said, his face flaming red with anger. "There surely ain't one hones' man among those at Fort Snelling or else my past complaints about what's happened to us ain't reached anybody's ears who gives a damn about we settlers. I thought a fort was built to *protect*. Well, by damn, I've had enough. I'll damn well protect *myself* and my *family* if nobody else will."

He grabbed his flintlock pistol from its leather sheath, flinging it to Carole, then fetching another one for Brenda before he armed himself with a rifle. "This time I intend to fight for what's right and for what's *mine*," he growled. "I aim to stop that bastard Major Partain. I don't even have to look outside to know it's him again."

Brenda's insides were cold, her knees trembling, yet she had known all along that this was her father's intention should he be threatened again by the corrupt soldiers. The pistol was heavy in her hand, almost as heavy as the ache in her heart as she watched her brother Tommie bolt from the bed, his eyes filled with excitement since he was too young to truly understand the dangers.

"Give me a firearm!" Tommie shouted. "I want to shoot me a soldier!"

Carole placed her pistol on the dinner table and knelt to embrace Tommie, tears sparkling in her eyes. "Son, oh, son . . ." she sobbed.

"Wife, ready yourself with the pistol," Harrison shouted. "Tommie, get back to bed. This'll be over soon. The soldiers'll ride away once they see they've failed this time to frighten us away."

Carole led Tommie to bed and covered him up to his chin with a patchwork quilt, then again armed herself with the pistol.

Brenda watched with wide eyes as her father went to the door and threw aside the buckskin. She took position beside a window with her mother on the other side. Each lifted a corner of the buckskin and peered out. The moon now glowed higher in the sky, illuminating the empty saddles of the horses below.

Brenda's eyes frantically searched for the men, then she emitted a low gasp when she glimpsed men dressed not in uniforms but in buckskin slipping silently through the wilderness shadows, their long rifles poised to fire.

Now that she could make out the lead man's facial features there was no denying who was posing a threat to the Pfleugger family. His face had already been etched into Brenda's consciousness and she knew that Major Partain was again making a nighttime visit to the Pfleugger settlement.

She was again seeing his thick, black eyebrows bushy over his eyes matching his black shock of hair, the crook of his nose, the half smile playing on his thin lips, and his powerful build. But tonight he was masquerading in buckskin, as though they were not soldiers at all but a party of renegade Indians.

"The sonofabitch," Harrison grumbled. "Who does he think he's foolin' with that garb?"

He cupped a hand over his mouth and shouted. "You ain't foolin' me none," he called. "Major Partain, I know it's you. And I aim to fight you, every inch of the way. I ain't givin' up this strip of land I've settled on like I have in the past. Either you ride away on your damn horses or get some lead in those damn thick skulls of yours!"

Carole's eyes swept over the dark figures in the night, counting too many for Harrison to be able to stand behind his harsh threats. If there was going to be gunfire, she knew only too well who would be the loser . . .

"Harrison," she harshly whispered, "I'm afraid."

"They're only bluffin'." Harrison laughed sourly. "You'll see. There'll be no cause for any gunfire."

A voice rang out in the night, determined, cold and flat. "Old man!" Major Partain shouted. "Why not just agree to move on? There's no need for bloodshed. Move along peaceful-like and I'll forget you threatened me and my men. Agreed?"

Harrison's face twisted in a grimace and then his jaw tightened, his eyes becoming angry slits. "Damn it, Major Partain, you know I've been pushed around for the last time," he shouted back. "And if you don't back away and leave us be I won't stop at just seekin' help from Fort Snelling. I'll go clean to the top! I'll seek help from President Van Buren! He should know there's such scum as you in charge of his proud fort on the banks of the Mississippi!"

"Now you know I can't let that happen, don't you?" Major Partain shouted back, in a needling tone of voice. "Pfleugger, I'll give you just one more chance. Show me your gun peacefully. Throw it outside, on the ground, so's I can see it. This is the only way you *and* your family are going to walk out of that damned cabin alive.''

"Why you . . ." Harrison snarled, lifting his rifle, taking aim, the shine of the fire golden on its long barrel . . .

Out of the corner of her eye Brenda saw her brother, Tommie, scooting a wooden chair to the window. She knew in an instant why. His curiosity to see the excitement had again drawn him from the bed. As she turned to stop him a shot rang out loud and clear and Brenda stood, mortified, as Tommie's body jerked then crumpled to the floor at her feet with a look of complete shock scalded into his face, his chest a bloody pool.

No sounds could escape from between Brenda's lips, so disbelieving was she of what she had just witnessed. She stood frozen in place, hearing her mother's screams, yet still seeing the lifeless form of her brother and the look locked on his tiny face.

And then there was a volley of gunfire. Brenda's senses returned, instinct causing her to drop to the floor, watching as her heart was tearing in shreds as first her mother was hit by musketballs and shot, and then her beloved father.

The true moment of realization of what she had just seen hit her like a blast of arctic air on her face, sending the icy currents of remorse to the pit of her stomach. She crawled from her mother to her father, checking for a pulsebeat. Numb, she recoiled when finding none at either's wrists.

Tears blinded her eyes and a knot formed inside her throat, choking her when she became keenly aware of the unnatural quiet outside the cabin. Should the soldiers come searching and find her alive, her fate would be far worse than that parceled out to her parents and brother. Their sudden deaths were a disguised blessing. She on the other hand would be at the mercy of these men who were most surely far worse than any savage Indian!

Panic-stricken, she began crawling to the back of the cabin where a window temptingly awaited her. It was her only way of escape. Her hope was that the soldiers hadn't felt a need to surround the cabin, since they knew how few occupants were housed there, having spotted them from the front line of the windows.

If she could crawl from the window and run into the forest, she could perhaps hide until the next day, when she might be able to go and seek help from another settler. She feared the forest and its darkness. Yet she had no other choice . . .

Breathing hard, perspiration lacing her brow, Brenda finally reached the window. Lifting the buckskin covering, she managed to climb through the opening then began running blindly through the woods until her side ached and her throat was dry, and her legs felt as though they would not carry her another inch.

Puffing, she stopped and stared around her. The woods appeared to be a blue and purple jungle, the haunting twisted limbs of giant oaks swaying in the breeze. She heard the far-off baying of a wolf and the screech of an owl.

Again she tried to see ahead of her but it was so dark she could scarcely make out the outline of her hands, the canopy of trees above her head so thick the beams of the moonlight were colored gray. As the wind blew, the tree-tops responded with strange whispering noises. The night air was steeped in chill and flavored with the decaying odor of fallen leaves and forest-cured grass.

Then she caught the whiff of smoke. She lifted her nose and inhaled again and again. She tensed and turned, looking in the direction from whence she had just come. Her eyes widened and her insides moved in a sick quiver when she saw identifiable shimmerings of orange through the trees which could only be caused by some large fire.

"Oh, no," she softly cried, clasping her hands over her mouth as a bitterness rose inside her throat, realizing that this fire had to be . . . the . . . log cabin she had just escaped from!

"Mama . . . Papa . . . Tommie . . ." she cried. "No . . . no . . ."

But knowing it was true, that the demon major had not only killed her family but also burned the cabin which sheltered the lifeless bodies, she turned her eyes away and cried until there were no more tears left to wet her eyes.

And then her mind cleared. She knew that she was in more danger than ever before should Major Partain realize that she was alive. She alone could spread the word of what he was doing to the settlers. She could report him as the vicious murderer that he was!

She slowly turned and looked in the direction of the fire again. A crooked grin spread across her tear-blotched face. "He probably won't even check the ruins for survivors," she whispered. "He probably thinks he killed *all* of us. If so, I am safe, at least for a little while. At least to make my escape."

Her smile fading, sadness too heavy in her heart to be glad about anything, Brenda turned. In a daze she hurried deeper into the forest. She knew that Indians were close by . . . the Dakota and the Ojibwa. But she knew nothing of either Indian, except to sorely fear them . . .

Two

Wraiths of river mist drifted like silvery ghosts away from the river, now shadowing the riverbank in a dreamlike veil. On the horizon the first flood of light cascaded in orange shimmers, intermixing with shreds of black streaked across the sky. A birch-bark canoe was moving down the broad fluid avenue of the Mississippi, its paddles rising and sinking in the water, dripping, flashing in the early morning light.

The lone Indian in the canoe swung the paddles at a more powerful pace, thrusting the canoe ahead toward the rising sun, feeling totally at peace with himself, enjoying this, one of his chosen ways to commune with nature. He inhaled the pure sweetness of the cedar and pinewood fragrance of the forest as it drifted lazily across the feathery spume of the canoe's bow. The sky was now azure from horizon to horizon, the fog having melted away into another promising day of May.

The Indian's keen, penetrating eyes were drawn to the shore. White sycamore branches broke the dense green foliage of the towering hardwood forest; bluebirds and finches flitted about. A grazing doe's dark eyes challenged the Indian's for a moment, then it fled in surefooted leaps up a bluff covered with ferns.

His muscles knotting and rippling, sharply defining his leanness, the Indian rowed onward. The morning sunlight modeled the hard, sharp bones of his handsome, bronzed face greased with the deer tallow he always applied before he canoed in a brisk wind to keep him warm and protect his skin.

His bare, copper chest gleamed. The sleek, black hair that cascaded to his shoulders was held in place by a colorful, beaded headband that displayed a striped eagle feather secured at the back of his head.

He was attired in a breechcloth and tight, fringed leggings extending from the ankles almost to the hip and held in place by a thong tied to the belt. A band made of woven beadwork with a long fringe of yarn was also tied below the knees. Beautifully beaded moccasins graced his feet.

Again he inhaled to draw in scents, curving his finely defined lips into an easy smile. It was at times like this that all duties of a future chief were placed in the farthest recesses of his mind. He could even cast aside the strain between him and his chieftain father, who insisted he, the next chief-in-line, take a woman as a wife. His father frowned upon this inability to choose.

But this son of a chief, himself called by the proud name of Striped Eagle, had not bothered to tell a father who had two wives that it was important for *him* to have only one, one who would fulfill *all* the needs of his heart without having *two* squaws who were in constant conflict over who pleased the chief the most while sharing his skins and blankets at night . . .

"*Ay-uh*," he whispered. "*Nay-mi-no-mun-gi*. I am young still. I shall still take my time in choosing a wife. Then when I do, it will be *ah-pah-nay*. *Ay-uh*, forever."

A heron with its sharply pointed bill that seemed to extend right into its eyes rose gracefully with slow, flopping wingbeats from the shadowy banks of the river to skim along the water in front of the canoe. Then it settled down again, to stalk along the shore in a stately stride, silent and alone.

Striped Eagle lifted his paddles from the water, tensing, believing the sudden appearance of such a great bird could only be an omen of some sort. But was it meant to be good . . . or bad . . . ?

In slow, even moves he again stroked the paddles through the water but this time in the direction of the shore where he beached the craft. He would now travel a distance by foot, less of a target in the forest than he was in the canoe. He would search for anything that might be there to pose a threat. He would search and destroy if the need arose to do so.

A shrill cacophony of birdcalls and cicadas penetrated the leafy walls all about Brenda, startling her into a sudden rude awakening. Huddled beneath a towering elm, she trembled as she studied the forest encasing her, her flight having ended here the previous night after she had become too weary and disoriented to move onward.

The calves of her legs ached even now, chilled and cramped by the coolness of the night air, and her head throbbed from the intensity of her crying off and on throughout the night. Her dress clung damply to her, wet from the morning dew; her hair hung in loose fragments of red, silken threads about her shoulders.

Leaning up on an elbow she squinted, now able to make out the twinkling of the waters of the Mississippi. And then her gaze moved farther down the shore. In her mind's eye she was remembering just how she happened to be there, again reliving the horrors of the gunfire, the orange of the fire's reflection . . .

Scooting up into a sitting position, Brenda held her face in her hands. Her shoulders softly shook as she again began weeping. She felt empty, totally alone, bereaved by the loss of her family. She didn't believe she could go on. And how could she? She now knew that she was . . . totally *lost*.

She didn't know in which direction to go to find sympathy and help. It was important to her to see to it that the corrupt Major Partain be harshly punished. He *had* to pay for what he had done to her family! But she also knew that she had to be cautious about who she chose to tell. Would she be able to distinguish one corrupt person from another?

Striped Eagle moved stealthily through the forest, never straying too far from the shine of the river where he had left his canoe. With his rifle clasped in his right hand, his jaw set, he went on as a hunter would do, his moccasined feet the footsteps of the panther, so silent were they as they touched the pressed leaves and deeply piled pine needles beneath the canopy of trees.

And then a sound caused him to freeze. His eyes narrowed in wonder as he separated this sound of sobs from those of the birdcalls all about him.

"*Ah-way-nish-ah-ow*?" he whispered, then again snaked forward with soft steps, but this time in a purposeful direction. The soft sobs speared his heart, drawing him to the person in pain. And he surmised that it must be an *ee-quay,* for only women cried . . .

Bending his back, Striped Eagle stepped behind a cover of brush and peered through its foliage, seeing a white woman. She was no longer crying, but instead walking toward the banks of the river. The spirits that had warned him by way of the sudden appearance of the heron had wanted him to find this white woman. He had to find out why and never having seen a white woman alone before, and curious as to why she was bare of companions, he straightened his back and stepped into the clearing. Watching her, his eyes were drawn to her splendid mass of hair which seemed to burn like a flame in the sunlight.

Then his gaze lowered, seeing how her gracefulness was accentuated by the gentle sway of her hips and in the way she held her delicate neck and tiny, straight shoulders.

He had yet to look upon her face but he knew that she must be lovely, and hungering to know how beautiful, he began walking behind her, again so silently not even he could hear his own footsteps.

Having the need to freshen up before venturing on her way, and her parched throat crying out for water, Brenda knelt down beside the river. As she bent to lower her hands into the water she watched a leaf tumble from a tree to meet its murky reflection in the river's surface. As it touched the water the reflection broke apart in tiny ripples that radiated out to meet another reflection . . . an Indian . . .

Recoiling, she craned her head around to look up into the face of a tall, lithe Indian. His glittering dark eyes were not absolutely black, but burnished with a tinge of hazel.

At first glance of the Indian her immediate impulse was to jump to her feet and run, but she knew she was too close to retreat, for his legs were much longer than hers. Instead, she resolved to meet the Indian's threat with a bold front.

Though afraid, she was keenly aware of his handsomeness . . . his copper face displaying high cheekbones, a long nose, and lips that were perfectly shaped, as though molded by a great sculptor.

He was deep-chested with a wide breadth of shoulders, his torso and thighs solid and compact. He stood unselfconsciously in his shockingly brief breechcloth, his leggings fringed, his moccasins beaded. He displayed dignity in his stance as he stared back at her, his eyes seeming to burn strangely through her.

Brenda's knees were trembling as she pushed herself slowly up from the ground, resolved to mask her fright from this Indian. She felt it was important to behave bravely though she was dying a million deaths inside, even though her first impression of him was anything but that which she would have expected when standing eye to eye with a bronzed savage.

The way his dark eyes continued to burn into hers caused her pulse to race and a strange sort of aching, sweet pain between her thighs. She wasn't so frightened that she wasn't capable of recalling the nights alone in her bed when her mind had wandered to fantasies of being with a man and experiencing almost the same sort of stirrings when feeling lips on hers in her wildest dreams . . .

A pink flush stole from her neck upward as she wondered how she could let her mind roam so ridiculously when the very next moments of her life depended upon her rational behavior.

"Why do you stand there looking at me so? What do you want of me?" she finally blurted, straightening her shoulders, defying the Indian with a lifted chin and steady stare. She became more unnerved when he shifted his gaze and raked her up and down.

Yet the gentleness radiating from him was causing her insides to take on a strange mushiness, for she was getting the distinct feeling that she just might be . . . safe . . . with this . . . Indian. Though he clasped a rifle in one hand, he was not aiming it at her and when he again let his gaze rest on her face and he began to smile, it was a smile that resembled the sunlight breaking a path through threatening dark thunderclouds in the heavens. It was the most pleasant sight she had ever witnessed, burning a path of sudden desire clean through to her heart.

Striped Eagle placed a fist to his breast. "*Nee-may-nan-dum-wah-bum-eh-nawn,*" he said in a deep voice that touched Brenda's soul with warmth. "Are you in trouble?

While watching earlier I saw you crying. Striped Eagle
will help you. Do you need to be led back to your family?
Are you *gee-wah-nee-toon*? It is easy to lose one's way in
the forest.''

Striped Eagle's heart was speaking a strange message to
him. It was telling him that this woman was different from
all others he had ever met and that he desired her, though
she was white. The sunlight bathed her face in a soft
reflective glow, silhouetting her long, delicate neck. The
sweet smell of her eddied around his face . . . the whiff of
roses found growing wild in the woods? Her wide-set eyes
feathered by thick, curving lashes were lucidly blue, as
though reflections of the day's lovely, clear sky.

His fingers itched to touch the fiery color of her hair,
yet he did not want to alarm her with any sudden movements. It was not expected of a white woman to trust a
man with reddish-copper skin. Unlike his gentle tribes of
Ojibwa, the snakelike Dakota had taken many as hostages,
even forced them to bear them children and live with them.

It was not Striped Eagle's way to force a woman, not
even a white woman. But should he win her fairly, *then*
his possession of her could not be questioned.

Brenda took a step backwards, gasping. "You . . . speak
some English?" she asked incredulously. "And you're
offering . . . to . . . help me?"

An amused smile touched Striped Eagle's lips. "*Ay-uh*,
Striped Eagle speaks some of the white man's tongue."
He nodded. "White fur traders carry the white man's
language into my village. The language is simple. It is
easily learned."

He looked more deeply into her eyes. "And, yes, Striped
Eagle offers help," he added.

Brenda smiled nervously back at him, letting her shoulders relax. This Indian had obviously had much contact
with the white people and showed some respect for them.
And the way his eyes continued to speak silently to her as

no other man before him made her feel doubly safe enough. She only hoped she wasn't trusting too soon. She had heard so many say that the only good Indian was a dead Indian.

A small shudder engulfed her for thinking such a sordid thought. She couldn't envision this beautiful Indian as anything but alive. His eagerness for life seemed to radiate from his pores. His eagerness to please had been revealed in the friendly tone of his voice.

"I do need assistance," Brenda said in a rush of words. She lowered her eyes, swallowing hard, having not yet spoken the tragedy of her family aloud. To speak it made it real and she so wanted to believe it had all been just a bad dream . . . a nightmare from which she would soon awaken.

Striped Eagle sensed the sadness in the white woman again. He could see it in the way she had dropped her eyes. Daring to touch her he placed a forefinger to her chin and lifted it, now revealing to him a pale, vulnerable face, one which displayed tear-streaked eyes and quivering lips. Her sadness speared him again, touching his heart as the sound of her sobbing form had done before.

Brenda's wondering eyes met his. In their dark depths she saw a softness never expected to be found in an Indian, so many settlers having called the redskins by the name *savage*. What she was finding in this man was anything *but* . . .

"*Ah-neen-ay-szhee-way-bee-zee-en*?" he said thickly. "Do you cry because you are lost? Or are you lost because something has happened to your family? I sense you have fled something ugly. Am I right?"

Brenda's heart ached at the thought of what she *had* fled from. She covered her mouth with a hand and harshly whispered her answer to him. "Yes," she said. "My family . . . they are . . . now all dead."

Again she lowered her eyes, grief overcoming her as

tears streamed from her eyes. When she felt the strength of his arms enclose her and then felt the hardness of his chest against her cheek as she was so easily made to draw comfort from this Indian, she was neither surprised nor alarmed. She melted as though meant to be in his embrace and wetted his skin with the hot splash of her tears.

"Weep fully, beautiful one," Striped Eagle said, dropping his rifle to the ground. "Cry, my little *Nee-bin-gee-zis*."

His calling her beautiful and by some other strange Indian name drew Brenda from his arms, again composed and rational. She was letting this something which had flowed between her and the handsome Indian grow too quickly. She still must remember that he was Indian . . . she was white. It wasn't as though she had run across a friendly, sympathetic white man in the wilderness who was ready to help her. This was an Indian, *an Indian*!

"I'm sorry for showing my emotions so openly," Brenda said, sniffling. She wove her fingers through her hair, combing it back from her face. "But I still would appreciate any help you might give me. You see, I am quite lost." She paused, then gave him a cautious gaze. "You called me by a name. What did you say? I haven't yet spoken my name to you."

"Striped Eagle called you by a name given you by me because of the fiery flame of your hair," Striped Eagle said firmly. Since she had already let him touch her, he lifted a hand to her hair and his insides trembled sensuously when feeling the utter silken texture of it, nothing like that of the Indian squaws in his village. Their hair was coarse and dark, and rarely caught the sun. "Your hair is the color of the summer sun. So I choose to call you by the name Summer Sun which when spoken in my tongue of the Ojibwa translates to *Nee-bin-gee-zis*. I hope you are pleased with my choice of Indian name for you."

A blush stung Brenda's cheeks. "But my name is Brenda. Brenda Denise Pfleugger," she said, laughing softly, not at all offended that he had called her by an Indian name, even touched by his gesture of total friendship. "And you have called yourself by the name of Striped Eagle? Am I right?"

Striped Eagle squared his shoulders proudly. "*Ay-uh*," he said in a sort of grunt.

"And what did you just say in . . . Ojibwa?" she asked, now at least glad to know which Indian she was in the presence of, though she still didn't know the difference in behavior between the two neighboring tribes of Indians, the Dakota and the Ojibwa.

She only desperately hoped that all Ojibwa were as friendly and cordial as this Indian. She desperately hoped that he wasn't tricking her. It was known that many Indians had formed an alliance with the white men at Fort Snelling, trading furs for supplies for the Indians. Could this Indian be friendly with Major Partain? Just in case, Brenda must be careful with her words. But hadn't she already told him her name?

"In my proud tongue of Ojibwa *ay-uh* means yes," Striped Eagle said, stooping to pick up his rifle. His eyes shifted to the sun, then back to Brenda. "Come. You can go to my village with me. We will share food and talk. You can tell me about this thing that is tearing you apart inside. Then you can sleep. No harm will come to you in my village of Ojibwa."

Brenda studied him guardedly as he turned and began walking in long strides away from her. Trust? Should she? Yet she had no choice *but* to. And didn't her intrigue of him give her cause to follow?

Lifting the hem of her dress she began running after him.

Three

The water's surface created a hissing silvery froth against the canoe's birch-bark sides as Striped Eagle made a turn in the river, now sending his canoe down a tributary unknown to Brenda. The canoe slipped along smoothly, rising and sinking with the waves. With soft furs covering the floor of the canoe where she sat, Brenda clutched the sides of the vessel, scarcely breathing. She began watching from side to side, feeling as though the narrow banks of this river might swallow the canoe *and* its occupants whole with its fingers of twisted vines and low tree limbs reaching out across the river.

The late afternoon sun stabbed at an angle through the leaves of the trees, dappling the water with sparks of shimmering, golden light. A black bear on a fishing expedition paused to look up, so close Brenda knew that if she reached her hand out she could touch the great beast of the forest.

She breathed more easily when the canoe sailed past the bear, but then she began to worry about how the shadows of the forest were deepening. Night would soon be upon her and Striped Eagle and they had yet to rest since they had begun their journey by canoe earlier in the day.

The gnawing in her stomach from hunger, and the burn on her face were evidence of having been on the Mississippi River for way too long in the sun.

But now that the Mississippi had been left behind, just how much farther would Striped Eagle travel before reaching his village? Brenda was not only hungry, she was weary from the canoe trip as well as her constant remembrances of how she had lost her family.

Bitterness against Major Partain seethed inside her. Somehow she would get her vengeance. Somehow. Someday . . .

Brenda's gaze was drawn back to Striped Eagle. She had almost memorized his back from having watched him all day as he sat in the middle of the canoe, mastering the currents. Something stirred inside her now, primitive it seemed, as her gaze followed the knotting and rippling of his shoulder and arm muscles. He made even, silent strokes with the oars through the water.

He was a powerful Indian brave, perhaps about twenty-five years of age. His copper skin was smooth, his black hair sleek, his dignity that which warmed her heart.

But Brenda knew that she must refrain from the sort of feelings now plaguing her, though he was the first man to cause them. What had her mother said? That her body would tell her when the right man came along?

Oh, how her body sang to her while in this Indian's presence! To be kissed by him could surely cause her weariness to melt away into a languorous sweetness . . .

Shaking her head, she tried to clear her thoughts of such impossible nonsense. She reached a hand out to touch Striped Eagle, having a need to talk, no words having been exchanged since she and Striped Eagle had entered the canoe.

Barely grazing the tight flesh of his back with the fingertips of her right hand, Brenda then quickly drew her hand away as he cast her a questioning look across his shoulder.

"How much farther must we travel?" she said, feeling clumsy as her hand fluttered to her side, his glittering dark eyes setting her afire inside. "I'm hungry. I'm *tired*."

"*Wi-yee-bah*," he said in his deep voice, not letting up on the swift, silent strokes that plunged them forward, even though the canoe swayed with the slightest movement. "We will reach village of Ojibwa soon."

Brenda smiled weakly. "We've left the Mississippi River behind," she murmured. "On which body of water are we traveling?"

"It is the river White Bear," he said, nodding. "I am of the White Bear band of the Ojibwa. Be patient, *Nee-bin-gee-zis*. Your hunger will be fed as well as your weariness in the peaceful quietness of my wigwam."

Brenda swallowed hard, again wondering about what else she might encounter in the privacy of his wigwam. She was glad that his eyes were again directed ahead, for her face not only felt hot from the day's sun, but also from a creeping blush. She had never been alone with a man besides her father under *any* conditions. And now to be alone, wholly, with a man, under these circumstances? Her body quivered at the thought.

The canoe continued slicing its way through the water, the forest deepening to lilac. The sun was no longer flashing its red needles of light through the foliage of the trees, and darkness was quickly filling the woods except for the fireflies that began winking along the banks of the river. A chorus of countless peeps of frogs echoed all about the canoe.

Shivering in the coolness of the night air embracing her in its dampness, Brenda peered through the darkness as fear scalded her all over. A full day had now passed in her total aloneness. And now she had another night to deal with. Could she . . . ? Would this Indian called Striped

Eagle continue to be so considerate to her and her feelings? Or could she expect . . .

She hugged herself with her arms, shivering even more severely as the coldness seeped into her very bones. Then her eyes became two points of alarm when she spotted a glow of orange ahead, reminiscent of the previous night. Such color, reflecting onto the canopy of trees overhead and even farther, onto the heavens, could be made by only one thing. Fire. Surely the canoe was now drawing near to Striped Eagle's village of Ojibwa . . .

The river seemed to be narrowing so that the trees met and interlaced close above the rushing, muddy water, leaving only enough space for the canoe to pass. Great clusters of vines hung over the water, the dark shadows of branches bent grotesquely from the trees, and so low that Brenda leaned as Striped Eagle leaned, to prevent being knocked from the canoe by a limb.

When Striped Eagle came to where the water frothed, he placed the paddles aside and seized a large, long pole from the bottom of the canoe and forced the canoe through the shallow water by his sheer strength.

And then the river again widened. Striped Eagle sat down and the canoe sped quickly onward, gliding over the dark water to a bend in the river where Brenda saw the great fires pulsating on the ground ahead, each reflecting on separate dome-shaped wigwams.

"*En-dah-yen*," Striped Eagle said, giving her a quick glance from across his shoulder. He then guided his canoe to the banks of the river and just as quickly jumped from it and beached it on a finger of sand alongside many other similar crafts.

Going to Brenda he surprised her by suddenly lifting her up into his arms and carrying her through knee-high water toward the shore. "Welcome to my village of the White Bear band of the Ojibwa," he said thickly, setting her down on land.

The fire danced on Brenda's face, fully lighting her delicate features. Her eyes were wide and her lips trembling.

"Do not fear me or my people," Striped Eagle softly encouraged. "We mean you no harm. We are peaceful. We fight only our enemy, the Dakota."

Though he spoke of peace, Brenda still felt flickers of fear as she looked about her, silently praying that what he said was true. The Indian village appeared peaceful enough, with the semicircle of skin lodges sitting beside the river framed by the dark forest beyond. She had always thought Indians' dwellings were cone-shaped. But these had domed roofs, their sides and roofs made of birch bark.

A cook fire was burning beside each wigwam and on a forked stick on the side away from the smoke a long pole had been propped, from the end of which dangled a hunk of fresh meat on a long cord. Indian squaws were tending the fires, and children ran and played about the wigwams, followed by yapping dogs. Horses grazed near at hand and far afield; a drum beat in a low, slow rhythm somewhere in the distance.

Striped Eagle placed Brenda on the ground, his eyes imploring her as she looked up at him. "*Mah-bee-szhon*," he said, gesturing with a hand toward the village. "Come. I will take you to my dwelling. It is too late to disturb my chieftain father. *Wah-bungh*. We shall meet with him tomorrow."

Brenda's heart thumped wildly inside her, now seeming to beat in cadence with the Indian drums. She had measured his words and now knew with whom she had become acquainted. The son of a powerful Ojibwa chief! One day *he* would be chief. She became even more in awe of him than before.

Half stumbling, her legs weak from sitting immobile in the canoe for so long, Brenda walked alongside Striped Eagle, feeling eyes following her as she went along. The children had stopped playing, the squaws had straightened their backs and lifted their chins, watching Brenda. The fires were casting dancing, ghostlike shadows on the wigwams, while the aroma of cooked meat crept into Brenda's nostrils, making her stomach rumble.

And then she realized something. She hadn't yet seen any other Indian braves in the village besides Striped Eagle. Were they in council? Or did they wait inside their dwellings for their women to serve them food, and then, later, their . . . bodies?

Not wanting to think of the possibilities of being taken by force by this Indian with the face of serenity walking at her side, Brenda brushed the ugly thought from her mind. She focused her thoughts elsewhere, observing the Indian village as Striped Eagle continued leading her around wigwam after wigwam, seemingly heading for the far end of the village.

In the exact center of the circular village, facing west, stood a much larger wigwam than the others. Brenda surmised this must be the chief's wigwam, standing like a giant chief itself, its scarlet and blue and bright yellow painted symbols dimmed by night.

She further noticed that many of the other wigwams were embellished with Indian paintings, their figures grotesque and without parallel in the realm of art. There were others that were not decorated at all.

Striped Eagle stopped and again gestured with a hand. "My dwelling is yours," he grumbled, nodding toward a wigwam that sat back away from the others, in a dense growth of pines and hemlocks. A generous wood supply had been piled high to one side of his dwelling, a pulsating fire was glowing orange on the other. The stripped remains of a rabbit turned on a spit over the fire, filling the night air with a savory aroma; a liquid of some sort brewed in a pot at the edge of the coals.

The night was throbbing with the song of a nightingale somewhere close by. The warmth of the fire caressed

Brenda's flesh as she brushed by it and entered the wigwam when Striped Eagle lifted the deerskin entrance flap. But then she stopped, stunned to find herself face to face with one of the loveliest women she had ever seen, a beautiful Indian maiden.

"*Ay-way-nish-ah-ow*?" the squaw asked, directing her question to Striped Eagle. "Who is she? And why do you bring her here?"

Brenda heard the icy coldness in the maiden's words, saw a deep mistrust in the maiden's scalding dark eyes. Her gaze swept over her, seeing the gentle features of the Indian maiden's bronzed face, cheeks reddened with the juice of the bloodroot, the perfect shape of her nose and lips, the soft curve of her jaw, and her jet black hair hanging in two long braids across her narrow shoulders.

The maiden was attired in a lovely fringed white doeskin dress ornamented with rows of shining white elk teeth and tiny painted shells. Her beaded headband and the strings of beads about her delicate throat snatched the reflection of the flames from the fire built in the firespace at the center of the wigwam, and her bracelets of turquoise and silver spangled as she folded her arms across her chest.

The loveliness of this maiden stabbed with spears of jealousy at Brenda's heart. Then she grew cold inside, realizing just how seeing the maiden in Striped Eagle's wigwam had affected her. How could she let jealousy enter into her thoughts at a time like this? How could it have become a part of her flight? Jealousy . . . for an Indian? It was incredible. It was unbelievable. Had losing her family caused her to lose her mind? She was becoming unrecognizable even to herself . . .

"Do not be *gee-nish-kee-nah-wah*," Striped Eagle growled, scowling toward the maiden. "I have brought the white woman to my wigwam because she needs a friend." He squared his shoulders and placed a fist to his heart.

"Striped Eagle is *nee-gee*. So shall she be to you, *Gee-gee-shayb-wah-bee-go-neens*."

"Striped Eagle, is she to be just a friend?" the maiden spat. "Or is she to mean more to you than that? You know how Father wishes you to take a wife." Her pigtails jumped on her shoulders as she turned and boldly faced Brenda. "Father would not want a white woman to stand beside you once you become chief," she added hotly, then ran from the wigwam.

Striped Eagle went to Brenda and softly clasped her shoulders with his hands. "Morning Flower is temperamental," he chuckled. "My sister worries too much about her brother. Should she have had more than one brother then perhaps I would have been spared her spiteful tongue."

Brenda's insides quivered. A relief she shouldn't be feeling washed through her at discovering the lovely squaw was only Striped Eagle's sister. She smiled weakly up at him. "Sisters always protect brothers," she murmured, almost choking on her words, oh, so missing her brother, Tommie. How could she have protected him? "Please be patient with her."

"You are a generous white woman." Striped Eagle laughed. He eased his hands from her shoulders, then nodded toward a heap of blankets and furs that lay before the fire. "Sit. I will see to it that water is brought to you for bathing. Morning Flower will bring you a dress and then I will share food with you."

"Bath . . . ?" Brenda said in a whisper, recoiling at the thought, even wondering if he would insist on watching her. She couldn't. She *wouldn't*.

"No thank you," she said a little too coldly. "I'm fine. All I would like for now is some food. And I prefer my own dress."

She blinked her eyes nervously. "You see, I would like to go on my way. I need to reach another settler's cabin. I must do it. Soon."

Even then she envisioned the evil Major Partain going from farm to farm, uprooting one family after another, leaving a path of death and destruction behind him.

But surely not. If he was so blatant, surely he would be caught and punished! Or was everyone too frightened to tell?

"A bath will relax you," Striped Eagle said dryly. He turned and moved toward the entrance flap. "A clean dress will enhance your loveliness."

Brenda's mouth went agape and a blush rose to her cheeks. She reached a hand out to Striped Eagle, wanting to stand firm, but he was too swift. He was already gone, leaving her standing alone, feeling alien to herself, and especially so of her surroundings.

Slowly she turned and let her gaze take in the place where she now knew she was to spend a full night. Or even more? Striped Eagle's words tormented her heart . . . words which spoke of his needing a wife. But it was evident to her just what the Indians would think of a white woman being considered as the wife of a future chief. No. He had brought her here out of friendship. Nothing more . . .

She twined her fingers together behind her as she gazed about. The wigwam appeared to be carefully constructed. It was composed of a framework of bent saplings covered with hides and secured with willow twigs, much more spacious than it had looked from the outside. There was even enough room to stand without grazing the rafters.

The firespace was in the middle of the lodge, outlined by logs, the central point of all activity, its gray banner of smoke curling out a ceiling hole. A kettle was suspended over the fire from a tripod of a wooden hook made of chokeberry cord. A short pole was fastened across the smoke hole to allow pieces of meat to dry above the fire.

Buckskin hides lined the walls and artful symbols had been painted on them in bright colors. From what she could gather the paintings took on the designs of the sun, the new moon, the bear, and the eagle.

The air was scented with the perfume of burning sweetgrass upon the embers of the lodge fire. Rush mats covered the ground and woven bags of cedar bark, cooking utensils, and colorful blankets lined the outside wall, as well as all of what appeared to be Striped Eagle's personal belongings: bow and arrow, clothes, and leather pouches cinched by leather strippings.

Brenda was drawn quickly around when she heard soft footsteps sounded behind her. Again she found herself face to face with Striped Eagle's sister. Morning Flower was carrying a wooden basin of water and a snow-white dress was flung across her arm, a flash against the copper of her skin.

"Striped Eagle wants you to have bath, you have bath," Morning Flower said flatly. She knelt and placed the basin of water on the floor beside the fire, now enabling Brenda to see a square of soap and a deerskin cloth floating in it.

Morning Flower held out the dress. "And my dress is now yours," she said, the coldness in her voice and eyes warming. Her lips lifted into a soft smile. Brenda accepted the gift. "Morning Flower sorry for snappy tongue. It is just that my brother's future must be measured very carefully. The color of skin for his mate is important."

"I am not here to become *anyone's* wife," Brenda said quickly. "I am here for only a short while. I must get to my own people. It is only by chance that your brother and I met. He is a kind and generous man, to help me, a complete stranger, in such a way."

"*Ay-uh*, he is kind," Morning Flower murmured, frowning. "I worry about his kindness. Someday it might be misplaced."

With that Brenda was again left suddenly alone. She was filled with renewed wonder at the handsome Indian who would one day be chief. But as she told Morning

Flower, she would soon be gone and Striped Eagle would no longer scintillate her senses. He would be forgotten in her search of vengeance for her family's murder.

Checking the entrance flap, seeing that it was securely in place, Brenda went to stand before the fire, eyeing first the water and then the dress. Somehow she knew that if she didn't take a bath *and* change into the Indian dress, she would never be fed. Though Striped Eagle spoke in a gentle manner, there was a distinct firmness in his words. And without food she wouldn't get far once she left the Indian village.

Brenda began loosening the buttons at the back of her dress.

Four

༄

The doeskin dress grazing her skin like a soft kiss as she drew it over her head, Brenda was glad that she had chosen not to defy Striped Eagle's wishes. The bath had refreshed her, and the dress chosen for her to wear was a welcome change from her cotton dress, which was ripped and torn from her flight through the forest. She lifted her hair and then let it tumble in a fiery red wave down her back, then smoothed the dress down over her hips. It clung to her thighs and curves as if it were a glove.

With heat in her cheeks, intrigued by this way of life she had been so quickly catapulted into, Brenda let her gaze survey the full dress now fitting her snugly. It was of doeskin, but seemed to have been whitened with clay. Trimmed with the milk teeth of elks and with tips of turkey feathers and porcupine quills, it was eyecatching, even one Brenda could be proud to own, should one be given to her to keep.

Barefooted, she stepped closer to the fire, feeling the night air creeping in from beneath the entrance flap. But she turned with a start when a shadow fell over her, once

again looking up into eyes that set her pulse racing, seeing
in them a hint of smoldering fire.

In spasms her eyes lowered. She emitted an embarrassed
gasp when she saw that Striped Eagle had removed all his
clothes, even his headband and eagle feather, everything
except his brief breechcloth. Beneath it Brenda could see
the telltale outline of his magnificence there. The shameful
cravings and desires which swam through her soared. She
turned her eyes quickly away, afraid that he had seen the
way he affected her.

Her mother's words kept haunting her. Every time she
looked into this Indian's eyes, her heart seemed to melt.
She was becoming strangely and strongly aroused by his
nearness, surely in the way a woman becomes aroused
. . . the way her mother described she would feel once she
found the man of her midnight dreams.

She coiled her fingers into tight fists at her sides, confused by her feelings, confused even more by her inability
to control them . . .

Striped Eagle's heart thundered inside him. He had seen
so much in her eyes . . . so much in the way she had
turned away from him to avoid *his*. No other woman had
made him feel this strange weakness that was plaguing him
at the pit of his stomach. No other woman had ever made
him feel as humble.

His gaze took in her loveliness, the way the dress
molded to her exquisite figure. He now saw the full outline
of her breasts, a sight denied him when she had been
clothed in the white woman's dress. Her breasts were ripe
and full, the nipples fully outlined. Her hips were gently
rounded, leading his gaze even lower, where he could see
the triangle of soft down between her thighs pressed against
the clinging material of the dress.

It took all he had not to reach out and touch her. He
looked at her hair, seeing how the firelight flamed in it. It
was as though this flame was burning a path to his heart,

an extension of what he knew she had shown to feel for him.

But he had always been proud of his self-restraint. If he was to be a great chief he was required to be independent, to reject any sort of submission, even the cravings to be with a beautiful *ee-quay* . . .

"Do you feel better now that you have bathed and changed into a more comfortable dress?" Striped Eagle said, moving to squat before the fire, balancing himself on his heels. He clasped his hands together, the whites of his knuckles proof of his restraint.

He looked into the fire instead of at her. "As promised, food will be brought. *Wi-yee-bah.*"

Feeling anything but relaxed, having felt so much being woven between them, Brenda eyed the blankets and furs beside the fire, opposite to where Striped Eagle now squatted. Barely breathing she eased down onto them, tucking her bare feet beneath her.

"The dress *is* lovely," she murmured. "It's so beautifully white."

"White stands for consecration to the Ojibwa," Striped Eagle said, settling down onto the furs beneath him, crossing his legs, sitting tall and straight. "White stands for all things pure."

"That's a beautiful meaning," Brenda said, almost shyly looking at him. "And the dress isn't only lovely . . . I don't think I've ever felt anything as soft against my skin. Thank you, Striped Eagle. I appreciate your kindness."

He unlocked his hands and waved one in the air, still staring into the fire. "*Mee-nee-dee-win,*" he said matter-of-factly. "It is a gift. It is now yours."

Brenda's hands brushed across her thighs, her eyes wide. "I wasn't hinting that it be given to me," she said. "I only wanted you to—"

The entrance flap swayed and then raised as an Indian squaw unfamiliar to Brenda stepped into the wigwam, carrying a large tray of food, while another squaw brought a large wooden pitcher and two wooden cups, all of which were placed on the floor beside Striped Eagle.

Waving the squaws away, Striped Eagle raised his eyes and looked sternly across the fire at Brenda.

"*Mee-gim*," he said flatly. "Come and sit beside me. We will share the meal together."

The growling of Brenda's stomach and the tantalizing aroma of the food wafting across the fire made her not wait for a second invitation. She rushed around the fire and laughed lightly as she sank down on even softer furs beside Striped Eagle.

Looking down at the wooden platter, her eyebrows lifted quizzically, recognizing only what appeared to be a small bowl of honey. But where was the meat? She had seen and smelled it cooking over the outside fire. All that was being offered her was honey and some sort of square cakes.

Striped Eagle could read the expression on her face. He smiled slowly and lifted a pemmican cake and offered it to her. "We must eat lightly before sleeping," he said. "Pemmican cakes and wild honey will fill the empty spaces in your stomach. *Wee-si-nin*. Eat and then you can sleep. Sleep is an escape from sorrow. Tomorrow life will be more generous to you."

Brenda could feel the nagging tremor on her lips that she had become accustomed to since the tragedy of her family. The need to cry was a constant urge for her now.

Clearing her throat nervously and squaring her shoulders she forced herself to smile as she put out a hand, palm side up, toward Striped Eagle. "Yes. Tomorrow *must* be more generous to me," she murmured. "I don't think I could bear another day like today and . . . yesterday."

Brenda was surprised at his having yet to fully question her about her tragedy. But surely he would. Soon. Then what would she say? She must first know if he was a friend to Major Partain!

She took the food offered her, looking down at it, wondering just what it was. He had called it a pemmican cake. She wasn't sure if she truly wanted to test its taste, fearing its ingredients.

Slowly lifting her eyes, she again smiled weakly at Striped Eagle. "Just what is . . . a pemmican cake?" she dared to ask.

"It is made of meat, dried and pounded to a pulp," Striped Eagle said, now offering her the bowl of honey. "It is *o-nee-shee-shin* with wild honey. *Goo-gee-pee-dum*. Taste. Eat. *Nee-bin-gee-zis*, Summer Sun, needs nourishment. This is the best sort of nourishment for a stomach that has been allowed to get too empty."

Brenda could feel her cheeks burn, again recognizing his chosen way to address her. Summer Sun. It was a beautiful name.

But again she had to remind herself just who she was and who she was with. Though there were no tensions between them and Brenda was feeling anything but fear of him, she knew that she must be wary. Perhaps he worked smoothly, drawing her into a web of deceit, planning to take full advantage of her later.

She must learn not to trust too quickly! She was now alone in the world. Her survival depended totally on her abilities to choose who was and was not friend and foe. She had no doubt about Major Partain. But . . . what about this Indian whose eyes commanded respect and a deep liking of him?

Brenda accepted the bowl of honey and placed it on the ground beside her. "What do I do with the pemmican cake? Do I dip it into the honey?" she asked, her stomach again nagging, growling back at her.

"*Ay-uh*," Striped Eagle said, chuckling at her clumsiness, her ignorance of how to eat food which was so natural to the Ojibwa.

He took a pemmican cake from the platter and reached

across Brenda's lap and dunked the cake into the honey.
With honey dripping from the cake, Striped Eagle placed a
hand beneath it, protecting the doeskin dress which so
beautifully outlined Brenda's figure, then took a large bite,
the honey sending a sweet message to his brain.

"This is how it is done," he then said, licking the
sweetness from his lips. He nodded toward the honey. "It
is now your turn. Eat. Enjoy."

Embarrassed, feeling as though Striped Eagle was treat-
ing her as a child who did not know how to eat, Brenda
scowled at him, then let herself enjoy her first bite of the
pemmican cake, rich in flavor that was enhanced by the
honey.

Striped Eagle's eyebrows raised, and he leaned toward
Brenda, anticipating her reaction. "You like?" he said,
his gaze again drawn to her heaving breasts, the doeskin
clinging to them, her nipples fully outlined. He hungered
for her—not pemmican cakes, not honey!

But he knew that to gain her full trust, he must for now
brush manly needs from his mind. He knew the skill of
making a woman want him. This he must do with this
woman, even though she was white. The color of the skin
would be no barrier between them if he could make her
desire him as much . . .

Striped Eagle's eyes gleamed when he saw satisfaction
etched across Brenda's lovely face. "You do enjoy the
meal of the Ojibwa," he said, again straightening his
shoulders, proud of at least this accomplishment. He would
work slowly. He would gain first her trust . . . then her
love.

"It is delicious," Brenda said, eating one whole pemmican cake, accepting a second that was being offered her.
She ate ravenously, watching Striped Eagle pour a sort of
brownish liquid into two wooden bowls. She eyed him
suspiciously as he offered one of these cups to her. Should

she trust him this much? What if this had some sort of potion mixed into it?

But thirst was foremost on her mind now, the pemmican cakes and rich honey too alluring and satisfying.

Taking a cup, she anxiously drank down the liquid, only sensing a minute flavor of tartness. Otherwise it was a pleasant sweet mixture, one that was fulfilling both to her thirst and tastebuds.

"Does the white man hunt through the forests for bee-trees?" Striped Eagle asked, again soaking a pemmican cake with the honey. "The maidens of our village hunt for the bee-trees. We have become fond of the white man's fly."

Brenda placed her empty cup on the ground, her stomach contentedly full. She arranged the skirt of the doeskin dress around her legs as she raised her knees before her to lock her arms about them. "Bee-trees? White man's fly?" she murmured. "I can understand what you are referring to when saying bee-trees. But I don't understand what a white man's fly is."

"A white man's fly is the bee," Striped Eagle chuckled, stretching out beside the fire, leaning back on an elbow. "Long ago the Ojibwa believed that the appearance of bees foretold further invasion by the white man. But we learned quickly that this was wrong. The white man's fly has been good to us. Not evil. Its nectar has filled many an empty stomach on a cold winter day."

He lifted an eyebrow as he gazed intensely at Brenda. "You do not answer me. Does the white man hunt for the bee-trees? Do you enjoy honey?" he persisted.

Brenda hugged her legs, staring into the dancing flames of the fire even as a chill enveloped her as she remembered the many times she had gone with her father to gather honey from the woods. A sadness tore at her heart as she spoke.

"Yes. We like honey," she murmured. "Our house

was always well stocked with wild honey. We kept it in a large trough hewn out of a linden log. We liked to eat it on biscuits. My mama made the . . . best . . . biscuits . . .''

She closed her eyes and turned away so that Striped Eagle could not see the tears sparkling in their corners. She swallowed a strong urge to cry, remembering how it drained her of so much of her strength. She must remain strong to survive!

Striped Eagle rose back to a sitting position, again drawn into her sadness. He reached a hand to her shoulder and clasped it solidly. "*Nee-bin-gee-zis*, again you are sad," he said thickly. "Remember tomorrow. Yesterday— tonight—is so fleeting. In a blink of an eye all sadness will be behind you."

Hearing the concern in his words, feeling the warmth of his touch, Brenda's insides melted. Fear was becoming quickly a stranger to her. How could she fear this Indian when he radiated such a sweet gentleness?

Turning her eyes to his, again she was swept up in a strange desire coiling tightly inside her. His eyes burned into hers, saying what he had yet to speak aloud. If he did, what could she do? She knew that she had wished to be kissed, to be fully touched, by him. And she knew that these feelings were wrong . . .

"I'm all right," she said in a strained whisper. "Truly I am, Striped Eagle." Her body was tense as he kept his hand on her shoulder. Their eyes were locked, her heart hammering, her insides suddenly gone crazed.

"Please?" she finally managed to say. "I am fine. Striped Eagle . . ."

In one sweep he had Brenda in his arms, his lips fully possessing her in a fiery kiss. He held her against his chest, lowering her to the thick mattress of furs and cedar boughs spread on rush mats on the ground.

A wildness surged through Brenda, her mind swirling

with a strange headiness. A warning was flashing inside her consciousness but as he kissed her more passionately, her back now against the softness of the furs, his hard, lean body spread atop hers, she lost all ability to reason as to what was right or wrong. She only wanted to savor this delicious languor he was creating inside her. It was making her momentarily forget, oh, so much that she wished to forget . . .

She trembled as Striped Eagle's hands began moving along her body, awakening in her something that could never be defined with words, it was so beautiful. She strained her hips upward, as though commanded to by his hands as they cupped her buttocks through the softness of the doeskin.

But when she felt the swell of his hardness pressing against her, as though there was no barrier of clothes at all between them, her fear of what this could lead to caused her eyes to fly open and her hands to press against his sleek bare chest.

When his lips left hers, she felt the void, hating him to go, yet she had the need to protest, for if not now, *never* . . .

"Please don't," she softly cried. "Striped Eagle, please don't do this."

Striped Eagle brushed another soft kiss against her lips, then cupped her cheek with the palm of a hand. "My heart is lonely," he said huskily. "*You* are lonely. Let us be as one, *Nee-bin-gee-zis*. Let us cleanse ourselves wholly of our loneliness."

"But I am not lonely in . . . *that* way," Brenda gulped, dropping her head away from him as he lessened his weight on her. "I am lonely for my *family*. Please understand, Striped Eagle. I must be free to go on my way tomorrow. Please do not make me a prisoner in your village. For taking me in such a way you seem to desire *would* be your way of telling me I am no longer free to move about on my own, wouldn't it? Till now, you have treated me with gentleness . . . with respect.''

"You say my way of kissing you is not done with gentleness?" He scowled. "Did I not touch you always with gentleness?''

Brenda lowered her eyes, aching even now for his touch, his kiss, but having to deny herself of both. It wasn't meant for her to love an Indian. They were of two different cultures, two different peoples . . .

"You are very kind," she murmured. "And I will always remember that. But I have to leave your Indian village in the morning. I have much that has to be done.''

"Let Striped Eagle do whatever needs to be done for you," Striped Eagle said, moving away from her. He grasped her elbow and lifted her to a sitting position beside him.

Brenda eyed him speculatively, combing her fingers through her hair. Could she trust him enough to tell him? His suggestion was inviting, yet she knew that even if she *did* confide in him, it would take the white man's voice, not an Indian's, to see that Major Partain and all men like him were dealt with properly. And Brenda didn't want to set the relationship between the Indians and soldiers ablaze. So far there had only been minor skirmishes. No. She had to deal with the major in her own way.

"I appreciate what you have offered," she said, looking away from him, her insides still aquiver from what had flamed between them. "But what must be done must be done by the white man. There is no need for you to become involved.''

"Striped Eagle is already involved because it involves *you*," he said flatly.

Brenda jerked her head around and looked at him, hearing the possessiveness in his words, suddenly fearing it. "My problems are my problems alone," she said dryly.

"I need no one but myself. Please understand this, Striped Eagle."

Striped Eagle's lips curved into a soft, sure smile. He lifted a stick and stirred the coals in the fire. "*Ay-uh*," he chuckled. "*Ay-uh*."

Brenda felt the need to draw Striped Eagle into small talk, at least until the fire dimmed and they retired for the night. Even this thought unnerved her, making her wonder just where he would sleep, where she would be assigned to sleep . . .

"You do speak the white man's tongue so fluently," she blurted, not wanting to think further on what might happen once they stretched out for a night of sleep. Would he truly allow her to just . . . sleep? Or would he insist on continuing what had begun between them? "You made mention of white traders earlier. Did one in particular teach you to speak English?"

"Many of the Ojibwa learned the white man's language from the white traders," Striped Eagle said, crossing his legs, looking steadily into the flames of the fire. "But no one in particular."

Brenda drew her legs beneath her, Indian fashion, her racing mind still suspicious of his possible alliance with Major Partain. Yet how could a man as gentle as he ever become involved with such a man as the evil major?

"I always thought your people would have much hate in your hearts for the intrusion of the white man on land that was always yours before they came," she softly tested.

Striped Eagle's face became solemn, his eyes flat. "*Ay-uh*, the white man did come. They *did* begin taking our land . . . our means of feeding our people. Yet the first time I saw a white man my parents told me that white men were going to live here, that I must not injure them in any way, and that I must have respect for them, because they had always been kind to my parents. I was instructed to respect the white man and so I did. I respect *all* people."

A low grumble arose from deep inside him. "Except, perhaps, for the exception of the thieving Dakota," he growled. "It is easy to go on the warpath against the Dakota who steal our women and horses."

He lifted his shoulders in a casual shrug and he smiled smugly. "When the warpath is needed, we kill or be killed *first*." He laughed softly.

He then looked over at Brenda, his heart swimming with desire as his gaze took in her serene loveliness enhanced by the soft glow of the fire. "But enough talk for the night," he said hoarsely. "It is time for sleep."

He rose to his feet and stalked to a pile of blankets which lay beside the far wall. He chose a blanket and carried it back to Brenda, offering it to her. "This will keep you warm through the long night of darkness," he said. "Take it. Sleep, I will be only a breath away, sleeping beside you."

Brenda's eyes were wide, her pulse racing. She accepted the blanket in her outspread arms, seeing how the background was like new-laid snow, interwoven with symbols colored in the scarlet and russet and gold of autumn leaves and blue of summer skies.

"Thank you," she murmured.

She then watched as he stretched out beside her, placing his bare feet toward the fire. Tense, she sat for a while, then, seeing his eyes peacefully close, she, too, lay down by the fire among the warm robes of animal hides and furs. She scarcely breathed, hearing the steady rhythm of his own even breathing. She drew the soft blanket over her, curling up on her side, her eyes directed toward Striped Eagle, watching him for any movements. But there were none. He did appear to be concentrating only on the need to sleep.

But Brenda couldn't sleep. Her thoughts were too muddled to relax. She was filled with many emotions, most of which confused her. She pinched her eyes together, forcing herself to try to sleep.

Striped Eagle's heart pounded inside him, the restraint this night almost too much to bear. Squaws were the flower of the wigwam and his *ee-quay* who lay so close to him smelled the sweetest of any he had ever sheltered. Ah, how she stirred the coals of his desire . . .

Five

❧

The light of the dim campfire served to accentuate Brenda's loneliness, its flickering shadows writing weird lines on the ceiling and walls of the wigwam. As hard as Brenda had tried, sleep would not come. Even when she closed her eyes she was plagued by heart-wrenching remembrances of the last night spent with her family.

Closing her eyes now, she let the warm feelings of family engulf her: poetry being read by her mother . . . the smell of the freshly baked bread . . . the mischief in her brother's eyes when he had caught her daydreaming of things which shamed her face into a rosy blush.

Her heart ached to hear the familiar pitch of her papa's voice, the touch of his callused hands on her face . . .

A tearful sob broke the silence of the wigwam, Brenda unable to quell what she so sorely felt. She doubled her body into a fetal position and placed a fist to her lips as again she let her pent-up emotions spill free in the form of tears.

And then she felt the tight arms of comfort embrace her. She let Striped Eagle turn her to face him, himself lying on his side, his eyes soft with their understanding of her pain.

"Weep fully, beautiful one," Striped Eagle murmured, weaving his long, lean fingers through her hair, drawing her face into the crook of his arm.

Brenda slowly moved her arms about his powerful back, then clung to him, sobbing against his sleek chest. "I miss them so," she softly cried. "It's so unfair, Striped Eagle. It's . . . so . . . unfair. They're dead. My papa, mama, and brother are *dead*. I must avenge their deaths. I must. I *will*."

"Do you not want to tell me about it? How they died?" Striped Eagle asked, his voice hoarse with emotion.

Brenda wanted to tell him everything, to feel free to confide in him. But she had already said too much. "No. I don't want to talk about it," she sobbed. "It pains . . . me . . . so . . ."

She cried until she could cry no longer. Then, embarrassed, she eased from his arms, looking with tear-soaked lashes up into his eyes. "It seems my tears are endless," she said softly, wiping her eyes with the back of her hand. "You must think me very weak."

"Striped Eagle thinks many things about you," he said thickly. "But weakness is not one of my thoughts. I hear much determination in your words when you talk of your future. I sense that you will make all things right for you and what has been done to your family. Vengeance drives one to strongness. I know. I have felt the same." He chuckled low. "But I have not shed tears when angry. Only *ee-quay* cry."

"*Ee-quay*?" Brenda said, sniffling as she again wiped her eyes with the back of her hand.

"I say the word 'woman' in Ojibwa." He chuckled.

He reached a hand to her face, his own now solemn, his eyes glistening with feeling. "You are all right now?" he asked softly. "You feel as though you might be able to sleep now?"

"Yes. Surely I can." Brenda sighed, feeling the tired

ache in her bones. "I must get rest. I have much ahead of me that must be done."

Striped Eagle offered her the white blanket, nodding toward the skins and furs. "Sleep. But this time I will sleep next to you so that our bodies will touch," he said flatly. "My body will reassure you that you are no longer alone. I will warm your body. You will warm *mine*."

A blush heated Brenda's cheeks. She smiled weakly up at Striped Eagle, yet knew not to argue with him. She had heard the determination in his voice. She could see the command in his eyes. Was this the way it felt to become captive to an Indian? Could an Indian make one captive without even using force? Striped Eagle seemed to have such skills!

Nodding, she crawled onto the softness of the furs. She turned on her side away from him and closed her eyes, trying to forget his nearness. Yet the more she lay there with the hardness of his muscled body curved around hers, the more her heart hammered against her chest. Her fragmented, flickering thoughts burned inside her head, stoked by the heat of his hot breath on her neck.

Even Striped Eagle's scent was strangely pleasant. It was sweet, smoky, and musky, stirring Brenda's inner soul to a passion that threatened to smolder into a raging fire. And when one of his hands brushed against a breast as he casually leaned an arm across her, she tensed and bit her lower lip in frustration. In him, she was forgetting her remorse, but in a way she did not wish to confess.

"*Nee-bin-gee-zis*?" Striped Eagle softly whispered, his hand now fully cupping the breast it had been resting against. "*Gee-zah-gi-ee-nah*?"

Brenda's face flamed, realizing that his Indian words were causing a sweet, painful ache between her thighs, now recognizing it as a woman's feeling of need for a man. Was she going to become a woman in every sense of

the word this night? Was there no escape from these
torturous feelings now that they had begun again?

"Striped Eagle, I don't know what you said, but please,
please move . . . away . . . from me," Brenda said in a
voice unfamiliar to her. It was thick in tone, soaked in
passion. "I must sleep. Only . . . sleep . . ."

His strong arms locked about her, slowly turning her to
face him. "I do not take women by force," he said
huskily. "As I do not take *you*, Summer Sun. You are
willingly going to share more than words with me this
night. You feel it in your heart, this bond which has begun
to form between us. Let yourself go, to fully love. Love
me, Nee-bin-gee-zis."

Brenda's eyes widened in remembrance. Her mother
had said to fully love . . . love openly . . . when her body
spoke to her as it surely was doing now. But would her
mother have approved of an Indian as her first lover? Was
her mother even wise to *give* such advice?

Yet Brenda didn't wish to wonder any more, Striped
Eagle's lips were driving her wild with want, his hands
tantalizing her into sweet response. She arched her neck
backward as he softly kissed her tapered throat, the tip of
an ear, and then her closed eyes.

And when he fully consumed her lips, delicious shivers
of desire pulsed through her. Newer, strange sensations
were born inside her to cause a seeming madness that
engulfed her. She twined her arms about his neck, she
writhed in total ecstasy, feeling his strong thighs against
her legs, his hand again cupping a breast through the
softness of the doeskin.

With a languorous spinning of her head, feeling a seeping warmth inside, Brenda let her hands begin exploring
him, first feeling the taut muscles of his shoulders, and
then lower, across the copper smoothness of his back.

"*Nee-bin-gee-zis*," Striped Eagle said huskily as he
lifted his lips away from her, looking down at her with his

startlingly dark eyes, now two points of heated fire. "Give yourself to me. *Moo-shkee-nay* Fully. Now."

In his voice she heard the command that was already familiar to her. She silently studied his keenly penetrating eyes that were burnished with a tinge of hazel, hypnotized not only by them, but also by the way the soft light of the fire in the firespace framed the hard sharp bones in his bronze face and the set of his sculpted lips. He looked back at her with the same command that she had heard in his voice.

A part of her feared him. A part of her would always . . . love him. He had awakened in her something that she knew she would never find with another man. This, too, ignited her fear, for she knew their paths surely were not meant to cross. Their meeting had been caused by fate. Their parting would be caused by . . .

Brenda's thoughts were brought back to an abrupt halt when Striped Eagle began loosening the ties at the back of her dress, his fingers nimble, his touch leaving a trail of fire. Scarcely breathing, Brenda let him lower the dress, now exposing her bare breasts to his eyes. She sucked in her breath when he lowered his lips to a taut nipple and began gently sucking while his hand cupped and kneaded her flesh.

Her head spinning crazily, Brenda had no power to push him away. It seemed that he had total power over her and she was enjoying this surrender, now a captive of his heart.

And then his mouth lowered over hers, kissing her with a lazy warmth. She was only vaguely aware of the doeskin dress being lowered over her hips and then away from her. Her heart thudded, and her entire body felt like one massive heartbeat as she experienced for the first time a man's bare body touching the flesh of her own. Striped Eagle had somehow managed to remove his scanty breechcloth while he had mesmerized her with his kiss of total passion.

When the hardness of his man's strength probed between her thighs, a bizarre weakness engulfed Brenda, fear intermixed with rapture. His fingers swept down her abdomen in a soft caress, stopping at the junction of her downy hair where his throbbing hardness now lay. While one of his knees parted her legs, his fingers began a teasing, slow caress on the spot Brenda now knew to be the core of her desire.

His head lowered, his lips and tongue teased her taut breasts while he seemingly readied her for what would transpire next: total surrender to him and his needs, now one with her own.

Breathless, Brenda closed her eyes and bit her lower lip, waiting, not letting shame for what she was sharing with this handsome Indian spoil her moment of heaven. She could not deny herself this intense pleasure. It was something so keenly sweet she understood in an instant the love shared between her mama and papa at night while tucked beneath their blankets, only soft murmurings of love away from Brenda in her own troubled bed . . .

Warm tears wetted her cheeks and a smile touched her lips, a headiness causing her to feel what surely must be drunkenness. She wove her fingers through the coarseness of Striped Eagle's hair. She nipped his shoulder with her teeth, softening a cry of pain as he slowly entered her.

His eyes rose to look into hers, hazed over with intense passion as he smiled softly down at her. "It will be *mee-kah-wah-diz-ee*," he said huskily. "Beautiful and enduring. Give in to the pleasure, my Summer Sun. It was destiny that led me to you in the forest. It was an omen, sent by the Great Spirit that sent me from my canoe in search of you. Our union will be blessed by Wenebojo, the spirit who made the world and who created man for woman and taught both the way to share the pleasures of the heart."

"Please don't say any more," Brenda said, gulping

hard. "If you say much more it will break the spell of the moment and I will turn . . . away from you in . . . shame."

"*Ah-gah-dayn-duh-mo-win*: shame is an ugly word," Striped Eagle hissed. "It is not a word to describe our being together. Do not say the word again in my presence. What we have found together is meant to be. I told you that Wenebojo led me to you. Do not say any more against what the Great Spirit commands."

Brenda looked wide-eyed at him, rudely aware of the differences in their beliefs. She had momentarily forgotten anything but what her body had ached for. But now she was, indeed, feeling shame. It was engulfing her fully. Surely she had misinterpreted her mother's meaning when recalling her mother's words to fully, freely love. Surely her mother had meant that this would be done after a preacher's words had been spoken over her chosen one. It was wrong to be here with the Indian . . . to have let him remove her clothes so easily . . . to have let his hands and lips touch her in such a way. She had to get away. Now! Or she might never be able to respect herself again.

Placing the palms of her hands to Striped Eagle's chest she pushed at him. "Striped Eagle, I don't know of this 'great spirit' you call Wenebojo. If he is your god, you surely know that he is not mine." Her face flushed crimson, her eyes lowered. "Mine is surely quite upset with me at this moment. Please . . . please let me up. What I've almost let happen *is* wrong. I can't; I can't."

Striped Eagle framed her face with his hands, directing her eyes to his. "Striped Eagle has never forced a woman. I will not do such a thing even now," he grumbled. "You know that what we have done was shared equally in desire by both of us. So shall this . . ."

He seared her lips with a fiery kiss. He plunged himself deeply inside her, his hands now at her hips, lifting her to meet his thrusts. Brenda winced anew with the brief moment of pain that accompanied his entrance inside her. Her mind filled with a rush of feelings, those which were beautiful outweighing those which were only momentarily painful.

The instant of pain was now changed to a strange, wondrous warmth enveloping her. She sighed against Striped Eagle's lips as he eased them away to burn a trail of kisses to the throbbing tip of a breast.

"Oh, Striped Eagle, I do . . . want . . . this with you," she softly cried, consumed by intense rapture. She writhed as his hardness so wonderfully filled her, his sure strokes setting her senses to soaring as he moved rhythmically within her.

Again he kissed her hungrily, his tongue sweeping between her lips, awakening her every nerve ending, leading her deeper into a world of sensual pleasure. She locked her legs about his hips, running her hands down the tight muscles of his back, marveling at what she had found in the arms of this Indian. No, he was not forcing her. She was willingly falling into an abyss of total ecstasy.

Striped Eagle let his hands explore the curves of her slim, sensuous body, desire swelling inside him. He leaned only a fraction away from her, his eyes taking in the lustrous red of her hair as it lay spread about her oval, pink-cheeked face. She was awesome in her beauty. Her eyes the color of the sky were looking adoringly up at him, her ruby lips shaped into a soft smile. He smiled down at her, then greedily absorbed the sight of the round magnificence of her breasts peaked with brown.

And then he again pressed a hot kiss against her lips, feeling her hunger in her seeking lips against his. He emitted a thick, husky groan as the spiral of pleasure swam through his head, downward, reaching his loins. He thrust harder, then shook with intensity as he felt his love seed spilling out, filling her . . .

Brenda's breath now came in short rasps as she marveled at the beautiful sensation spreading throughout her.

For a moment she was aware only of intense pleasure, blocking out all consciousness but that of her body responding to Striped Eagle's in a thrilling, floating, drifting mindlessness . . .

And then it was over and she lay spent in his arms. She was aware of his thudding heartbeat as his chest pressed against her own. His breath was hot on her cheek, his lips softly grazing the lobe of her ear, sending shivers of pleasure throughout her once more. She caressed the flesh of his back and relaxed beneath him, suddenly content and warm. It was so beautiful to be with him; she now wondered if she could ever live *without* him.

"You are not *nish-ska-diz-ee*?" Striped Eagle said, now leaning away from her to implore her with his piercing dark eyes.

Brenda squinted her eyes and shook her head. "I don't know what you just asked me," she murmured. "You spoke partly in Indian."

Striped Eagle gently brushed a dampened lock of hair back from her cheek. "Striped Eagle asked if you were angry," he said hoarsely. "You were protesting when I sealed your words with a kiss. Are you now sorry I did?"

Brenda smiled weakly up at him. "I should be but strangely I'm not," she murmured. Her gaze moved over his handsomeness, having never felt so close to anyone before in her life. Not even her family . . .

Could such a feeling be wrong? Had she just committed an unpardonable sin?

She looked away from Striped Eagle and closed her eyes, not wanting to let such thoughts spoil what she had shared with this Indian . . . surely the man she would always love . . .

Striped Eagle placed a finger to her chin and turned her face to meet his gentle kiss. He then scooted away from her, handing her the white blanket. "It is now time to sleep," he said, sighing heavily. "Tomorrow will come much too quickly."

He looked at her with heavy eyelids. "You will now stay with Striped Eagle?" he asked thickly. "You have reason to stay?"

Brenda's insides quivered. Shouldn't she have expected him to want her to stay? Yet wasn't she white? What would his people think if he introduced a white woman into his village of Ojibwa . . . a woman intended to stay, to share a wigwam with the next chief of this tribe of Indians?

Looking away from him, not wanting to reveal her sadness over what she knew had to be done, she drew the blanket about her shoulders and stretched out on the skins and furs, facing the fire.

"You do not answer Striped Eagle," he said, leaning to again force her eyes to meet his.

"Striped Eagle, let tomorrow bring what it may," she said softly. She stretched out her hand to cup the smooth copper of his cheek. "But always remember that these moments shared with you were the most beautiful of my life."

Striped Eagle's insides grew cold, knowing that by morning she would be gone. He knew she had vengeance on her mind. And until she had it worked out of her soul he would have to be patient. One day *he* would be the total of her being . . .

Six

The fire in the firespace was only a small flicker of orange. Brenda glanced over at Striped Eagle. Her heart pounded and her stomach felt strangely empty at the thought of what lay ahead of her. But it was necessary to escape from this new imprisonment brought on by this Indian, this imprisonment of the heart. If she waited until morning then it might be too late. Surely if he held her in his arms again she would never want to leave him. But she must, for many reasons.

Striped Eagle's eyes were closed and his breathing was even and shallow, all signs that he was fast asleep. Brenda rose up on an elbow to test him, believing him to surely sleep as lightly as he so soundlessly walked. Should he awaken and find her readying herself for escape, then all her plans of vengeance would be delayed. Possibly even forever . . .

Realizing that he didn't even flinch as she stirred on her bed of furs, Brenda was determined to dress and leave without him knowing it. When he awakened, would he then seek her out? Or would he be so disheartened with her he would not care if she was gone?

She couldn't think about his feelings at this time. The thought of her dead family lay heavy on her heart. Finding someone who would believe what she had to report about Major Partain was now the most important goal in her life.

But again she was nagged about who she could and could not trust. The timing would have to be right. The person would have to be someone who had no connections whatsoever with those who controlled Fort Snelling. Chances were good that those who frequented the fort might even be corrupt.

"Time. It will take time," Brenda thought to herself, stiffening her upper lip in determination. She only hoped that she could somehow keep what had happened to her from happening to anyone else.

Easing the white blanket from atop her, Brenda crept to her feet, keeping an eye on Striped Eagle as she bent to sweep the doeskin dress up from the floor of the wigwam. It would be the easiest and fastest way for her to dress for her getaway. And wouldn't it be a remembrance of the moments shared with Striped Eagle? Somehow it was important to her to keep these memories warm in her heart for she might never again share such bliss with another man. Only Striped Eagle . . . only Striped Eagle . . .

Slipping the dress over her head, fitting it snugly around her hips and then her thighs, Brenda looked about the wigwam for moccasins that might fit her feet. She felt they were the best sort of shoes to wear for moving stealthily through the Indian village to get to the canoes. Though she hadn't manned a canoe before, she knew that to reach civilization as she had always known it, she must get back to the Mississippi River, then follow its currents to, hopefully, another settler's farm sprouting from its banks.

In the dim light of the fire's glowing embers, Brenda spied moccasins placed neatly beside the entrance flap. A slow smile curved her lips. She hadn't seen them there before. Somehow Striped Eagle's sister had slipped them inside the entrance flap for Brenda. Had it been ordered done by Striped Eagle? Or had his sister done it out of the kindness of her own heart?

"Or did she place them there, suggesting I use them for escape?" Brenda worried to herself.

Shrugging, Brenda tiptoed to the entrance flap and slipped her feet into the wells of the moccasins. Then, turning, she took a lingering look at Striped Eagle, warmth filling her at the sight of his peaceful, handsome face, the breadth of his powerful shoulders, and the shine of his bare buttocks turned toward her as he slept on his side.

Now blushing at the sight of his nudity, she flipped her hair about her shoulders and turned her eyes away from him. Quietly, she raised the deerskin entrance flap to peek cautiously outside. She breathed easier, sighing silently with relief. Though it was not all that late, no one stirred. Only the sounds of frogs croaking, horses neighing, and the staccato barking of a dog from somewhere in the village could be heard. The whole village of Ojibwa appeared to be asleep as though obliging her need for a smooth avenue of escape.

Trembling, not knowing what the next few hours would hold, Brenda stepped gingerly from the wigwam. Embers from a few of the outdoor fires about the camp were yet red but furnished no more light than a dull glow which seemed to make the night all the blacker.

Still determined, she started along the route from which she had been brought earlier in the evening by Striped Eagle. Her pulse raced and her throat was dry with her fear of the canoe ride and even more of where it might take her. She knew that the Dakota Indians could be the next to discover her alone. Or might even Major Partain come along and see her riding alone in the canoe before she reached a safe haven?

Nervous beads of sweat sparkled on her brow; her palms were damp as her heart continued to thud. She half ran, weaving her way around one wigwam and then another. The night was ghostly with a queer, luminous darkness. It was like velvet, soft and heavy, yet with a sheen of light so dim, she could just discern the wilderness of thicket.

With every nerve tingling, she continued to run, panting. The distance to the river seemed to be endless. The calves of her legs ached, her throat burned from her ragged breathing. Looking toward the sky, she gave a small thanks to God that the moon had crept from behind a cloud. Beams of soft, pale light fell downward, illuminating her way now that she had left the wigwams behind and was running toward the shine of the river.

She stopped and crouched low behind a forsythia bush deeply colored by golden blooms when a sudden sound erupted from behind her. Chilled with terror she waited, stiff and silent, her eyes wide, watching.

And then she laughed softly as she saw an opossum scampering along the banks of the river, five tiny babies clinging to its back.

Shaking her head, running her fingers through her hair, Brenda inhaled another nervous gulp of breath. She shivered, touched by the cool dampness of the late night. Her arms had goose bumps rising along them, her nose was reddening, and her breath was escaping from between her lips into shrouds of white fog.

She hugged herself for a moment, her teeth now chattering, then pushed relentlessly onward, glad to finally see the line of canoes rocking gently in the waters of White Bear River. As she hurried toward them her eyes searched for the one she knew to be Striped Eagle's. She had spent many hours in this canoe and knew that it was navigable enough. She hoped Striped Eagle would understand.

When she reached the water's edge, she grimaced, realizing that she would have to wade in the knee-deep water to get the canoe pushed away from shore. She was already freezing; after becoming wet, she would be doubly cold!

But she had no choice. To reach the Mississippi River, she must first travel down White Bear River. It was not only the quickest way, but the surest. By foot she could easily get lost, as she had before, when running away from the scene of her family's ruthless murder.

Going to Striped Eagle's canoe she gave it a shove, then splashed into the water herself, guiding the canoe into deeper water. She struggled to get aboard, each time almost toppling the canoe and herself over with the effort.

But finally she managed to hoist herself into the canoe, balancing her weight as the light craft wavered beneath her. Settling herself onto the seat she scanned the floor for the paddles and found them. Pouncing, she picked one up and plopped the spooned end into the water. Groaning with the effort, she finally succeeded in getting herself into the middle of the river, the Ojibwa Indian village now only dark shadows beneath the silver splash of the moonlight.

Looking over her shoulder, Brenda saw the shadowy outline of a mass of trees and spot of inky blackness which told of the location of the farther shore.

Taking wide strokes, Brenda moved down the river, her eyes watching on all sides of her, now at the spot where the banks narrowed and the low limbs threatened to knock her from the canoe, as they did before when she and Striped Eagle had passed this way earlier.

The unaccustomed work soon made her arms ache in agony. She groaned aloud as she bent to complete each stroke. She pushed herself harder, relieved now to be in a wide stretch of water. Her steering clumsy, many times she feared she might be dumped overboard into the freezing abyss of the river.

Finally, a bend in the river took her to her destination . . . to the great body of water she now knew to be the mighty Mississippi. Sighing with relief, she again began maneuvering the canoe onward, fighting currents she had not expected. When she had been with Striped Eagle the waters had seemed calm and manageable. Yet she knew that it had only seemed that way because Striped Eagle had mastered the currents. Her inexperience, however, made even the gentlest current feel like a treacherous whirlpool.

Again a fiery pain ran through her arms as muscles cramped and stiffened. Groaning, Brenda closed her eyes to the pain, pausing from the paddling, pulling her dripping paddles inward. Seeking a moment's rest she began rubbing her arms, letting the canoe drift slowly onward under its own power.

But a sudden loud thump and a jolt to the canoe quickly drew Brenda's eyes open. Her heart lurched as she saw a great piece of timber quickly entangling the canoe in its branches of green glistening leaves. Frustrated, Brenda put out a paddle to push the heavy branch away. Stretching, she continued pushing the limb as the distance widened. But when she tried to draw her paddle back, she discovered that it was stuck!

Angry, she gave the paddle another tug, and when it loosened from the branches much too quickly, her breath caught in her throat, feeling the light craft wavering dangerously beneath her. She flipped the paddle into the air as she felt herself tumbling along with the canoe as it tipped over, throwing her into the cold darkness of the muddy river.

The water sucked at Brenda's moccasined feet, pulling her downward into total darkness. Her lungs ached from the sudden onslaught of water, forcing her to swallow. She kicked and fought to get back to the surface for air.

When she finally broke through the water's surface, she coughed and spewed river water from her throat, looking desperately around her for the tipped canoe.

But it was nowhere to be seen. The current had loosened it from the branch and had swept it away from her. She looked wildly toward shore. A ray of hope shone forth in the form of a gold shimmering light through the trees. A campfire! Someone was camping here!

Her eyes searched further. She caught sight of a flotilla of beached canoes. Her insides tightened. Was she destined again to be forced by circumstances to be among Indians? And were they Ojibwa or Dakota?

But at this moment it didn't seem all that important. If she didn't act quickly she would be swept downriver. She would either drown or die of exposure.

Stiffening her upper lip she was determined to let neither happen. She began swimming toward shore, wincing with each lift of her arms, already painfully heavy from her battle with the paddles.

Yet, having been taught by her father the necessity of knowing how to swim at the young age of two, Brenda's practiced strokes were clean and long, taking her quickly to land. Her fingers finally found the wet grass and the yielding mud of the bank and like a sleek water animal she drew her dripping body out of the river and crouched for a moment, winded. Her clothes were cold and clammy as they clung to her. Her body fighting for warmth, she rose to her full height, wiping her wet hair back from her eyes.

She attempted to straighten the doeskin dress to hang gracefully around her ankles, but in the spill of the moonlight she saw how the wet, clinging dress accentuated the curves of her body, leaving nothing to the imagination should anyone look squarely at her. She gasped, seeing the clear outline of her breasts, even to the crests of each, the nipples straining against the doeskin.

Water dripped from the dress about her ankles; her hair hung in wet red wisps about her shoulders. Droplets of water even clung to the tips of her thick eyelashes.

She blinked her eyes nervously, feeling a sudden desperation seize her as she again realized how well defined she appeared beneath the moonlight. If the campfire she had seen had been built by Indian braves and they saw her like this, she could be in danger of being raped by not only one, but many.

Yet with the chill of the night wind on her, she knew the dangers were doubled if she didn't get close to a fire and dry her wet hair, clothes, and body. She was wet and chilled through. She had no choice but to at least try to seek sympathetic assistance from those who had fires blazing. Perhaps she might even be given dry clothes to wear.

Glancing toward the large canoes beached only a few yards from where she stood, Brenda could see that each was filled with tarpaulin-covered objects. Somehow this didn't seem to be the way an Indian would carry supplies. But if not Indians, who?

And then she remembered having heard tales of French voyageurs who traveled the waters of the Mississippi River. Perhaps these canoes belonged to this sort of men.

If so, what did they carry aboard their canoes along the Mississippi River? Might they be taking ammunition to Fort Snelling? Or might they just be traveling innocently along with their wares for selling to the small communities dotting the banks of the Mississippi? She hoped for the latter.

Shivering almost uncontrollably, tall, wild grass pulling at her legs, the moccasins squishing on her feet with each step, Brenda began creeping toward the light of the fire. The black jungle of trees about her appeared to be of a great age, wearing thin, gray beards, moss, and lichen. Many of the younger shoots, stretched thin in the race for light, had fallen to the winter gales and made awkward barriers across the way. She wove a slow, careful path through the mantle of fern.

A jew's harp faintly buzzed and twanged through the black web of trees. Surely she hadn't come upon Indians. The jew's harp was not an instrument of the Indian. Perhaps it *was* Frenchmen! Either way, however, she felt no safer.

Brenda paused and listened, hearing the laughter of men, fear ebbing its way into her heart, wondering just how *many* men? One was a threat. But many . . . ?

She again shivered, propelled to move onward, hungering for the warmth of the fire against her flesh. When she came to a break in the riverbank forest where small stumps of trees dotted the clearing, she caught her first glimpse of the huge bonfire blazing, its flames leaping upward. A deer carcass was turning on a spit, filling the evening air with its savory aroma. The smell of coffee wafted to the brush where Brenda was now crouching, hiding.

Hugging herself with her arms, she was now close enough to almost touch the men, at least now knowing she had indeed not ventured into an Indian camp. But, again, she felt no relief at her discovery. The hair at the nape of her neck bristled as she counted at least twenty men.

Swallowing hard, almost too frightened now to even move, Brenda's gaze moved slowly about the fire, trying to calculate whether the men would be her friend . . . or her foe. Some were sitting, some standing, some lounging against tree trunks. They were drinking from silver tankards, laughing, exchanging colorful tall tales among themselves.

And then a man bearing a hornpipe stepped into the center of the men. He began playing a jig as the onlookers' feet stomped to the time of the music.

Again Brenda looked from man to man, thinking they appeared friendly enough, their dark eyes merry, their lips curved into smiles below thick mustaches. Their clothes— plaid jackets and dark pants and colorful knitted hats— were clean and neat.

She bent an ear to the conversation, cringing at the realization that the men were speaking French. Brenda had been well educated in Chicago before her father had decided to make the move to this wilderness of Minnesota. She had had a brief course in French and could speak a few words, but surely not enough to carry on a full conversation with a Frenchman. Could she explain her plight to these gentlemen? Should she even attempt to? What if they *did* have dealings with Major Partain?

Her eyes feasted on the fire, feeling an occasional touch of warmth on her face as a breeze carried the heat from the flames her way. Yet she still shivered, the doeskin dress icy cold as it clung to her flesh.

She moved to reposition herself behind the bush, still not brave enough to make her presence known. But in the darkness she failed to spot a rock jutting up through the ground, and she was helpless to regain her balance as she broke through the brush to fall in a heap in view of the men who turned to gape openly at her.

Her heart thundering inside her, Brenda pushed herself up from the ground, eyes wide, searching from face to face. When the stoutest of the men began walking toward her, she recoiled, seeing a gleam in his eyes as he studied her from head to foot.

Stone cold with fear, Brenda looked up at him as he came to stand over her, his legs widespread, a great beak of a nose dominating his face. She flinched when he nervously waved a pair of enormously long arms as he spoke, giving him the look of some sort of strange, flapping, predatory bird. He spoke quickly in French, his bold, black mustache jostling on his upper lip, his eyes flashing.

And then his rattlings stopped, and he smiled crookedly at her. "*Bonjour, mademoiselle,*" he said, placing his fists on his hips. "*Mon Dieu*! Where do you come from?" His eyes flashed amusedly. "And so wet? *Pourquoi*? Why *are* you wet? What has happened to you? Where is your family, *ma petite*?" Again his eyes traveled over her. "But perhaps you do not have family? You wear an Indian squaw's dress. You have been captive? *Mais oui*?"

Brenda's heart skipped a beat, only now realizing the

questions aroused by her attire. How could she explain the
Indian dress without telling all that had happened to her?
She didn't wish to bring Striped Eagle's name into the
conversation and she didn't feel it wise to tell this man and
his friends the full extent of her plight. She now knew not
to trust any of them. She was seeing too much written in
their eyes and in the hungry expressions of their faces. She
knew lust when she saw it. She could almost even feel it
pulsating about her, this need the men had for a woman's
companionship . . .

"How or why I am here is not important," Brenda said,
again hugging herself, trying to ward off as much chill as
she could against the breeze that whipped about her. "What
is important, *monsieur*, is that I need assistance. Can you
help me? I'm freezing in this wet dress. I would like to ask
that you consider taking me to the next settlement up the
Mississippi. That was my destination when the canoe I
stole tipped over."

The Frenchman laughed gruffly. "*Monsieur*?" he
mocked. "So the little one speaks at least one word of
French. That is good. I like that."

He made a sweeping gesture with a hand, motioning
toward the fire. "Let me offer you warmth by our fire, *ma
petite*. And perhaps I can even find you a change of
clothes." He pinched his face into a frown. "I take it you
aren't going to tell me where you got the Indian dress?"
He shrugged casually. "*Très bien*. Very well. It doesn't
matter."

Brenda crept toward the fire, holding her breath. Her
eyes darted from man to man, her knees trembling. When
the same Frenchman spoke again, she jumped, startled by
the grating sound of his voice, then remembered her man-
ners enough to smile weakly up at him as he lumbered
along beside her.

"Pierre Gustave is my name, *mademoiselle*," he said
hoarsely. "I am proud to say I am a French-Canadian

voyageur—a traveler to you. My occupation is that of transporting furs and trade goods for the traders in the area. My men and I trade furs even ourselves. You are in proud company, *ma petite*. We are known wide and far, up and down the waters of the Mississippi and even beyond.''

"How nice," Brenda managed in a whisper. "I appreciate your kindness, Mr. Gustave."

Pierre threw his head back in a roar of laughter. " 'Mister' you call me?'' he shouted. He again looked down at Brenda. "Pierre. *Ma petite*, only call me Pierre." His eyes traveled over her, now in the intense light of the dancing flames of the campfire, his loins tightening at the sight of the full outline of her breasts straining against the wetness of the doeskin.

"And your name?" he asked huskily. "What is your name?"

Brenda felt a blush rising to her cheeks, having felt his eyes exploring her body. Her pulse raced, fear building inside her. "Brenda. Brenda Denise Pfleugger," she murmured.

Then a coldness circled her heart—had she been too loose with her name? What if this Frenchman told Major Partain about having found her? She bit her lower lip in frustration.

"Ah, a beautiful name for a beautiful lady," Pierre said, forcing his eyes straight ahead, over her head. Though he had been denied a woman's flesh for several months now, he would not take advantage of this poor, wet waif. He was a gentleman. His gaze crept about him, seeing the looks in his companions' eyes. He knew they were feeling the same stab of loneliness and he had to make sure it went no further than just thinking about what they would like to do.

He scolded them in a rush of words in French, much too quickly for Brenda to interpret what was being said. But low grunts and grumblings from the circle of men made her guess what the Frenchman had said in his apparent warning. Hopefully, he was going to defend her from what the men so obviously desired. Perhaps he was not only a gentleman, but one she could learn to fully trust?

Pierre again gestured toward the fire. "*Asseyez-vous, s'il vous plaît*. Sit down. Please," he said. "Among my men I will find clothes to at least partially fit you. Then you can change from the wet, uncomfortable clothes you have somehow managed to get from an Indian squaw."

His eyebrows rose, puzzled. "Perhaps you will tell me later how you came to have the squaw's dress? How you happened to be in the position of stealing an Indian's canoe?"

Brenda smiled weakly up at him, then eased down to the ground and huddled close to the fire. Out of the corner of her eye she saw the men still closely watching her. She was glad when the jew's harp that had stopped when she had been discovered now again buzzed and twanged. This seemed to be the reason for the change in the men, directing their full attention away from her. Slowly the men again began gossiping among themselves. And finally Pierre came back to Brenda, holding out to her a pair of breeches and a plaid shirt.

"Go behind the trees," he said flatly. "I will see to it that no one disturbs you while you change into these clothes. And then you can either eat or sleep. I will offer you enough blankets to keep you warm. Tomorrow, at the crack of dawn, we will be moving onward. You will go with us. We will help you find friendly Americans. *Bien*?"

Brenda's insides relaxed. She exhaled a nervous sigh, then smiled warmly at Pierre as she took the clothes from his outstretched arms. "'I thank you, oh, so much," she murmured, moving quickly to her feet. "You are very kind. So very, very kind."

She hurried to the cover of trees and shrubs and quickly

slipped the wet dress over her head, exchanging it for the shirt and breeches, both hanging loosely around her, yet affording warmth and welcome to her body. A drawstring at the waist of the breeches afforded her the opportunity to tighten them. She buttoned the shirt to her throat.

But not wanting to part with the dress she had been given at the Ojibwa camp, she folded it across an arm, and holding her soaked moccasins in a hand she marched back to the fire, now feeling fairly safe, yet not trusting enough to seek help in what she truly wanted. She still didn't know if these Frenchmen dealt personally with Major Partain. She would wait until she was taken to trusting Americans. Then she would get on with what needed to be done.

Seven

⊱∽≺

The campfire now glowing embers, Brenda huddled beneath a heavy blanket, her eyes burning with need of sleep. She had allowed herself to drift off only to startle awake and cast her eyes all about her. She didn't know how long she had been playing this sort of game with sleep, but each time she had closed her eyes, the intervening moments when she started awake seemed to lengthen.

Turning her eyes upward she peered through the dense foliage of the trees. She smiled smugly to herself, seeing the sky lightening, night giving way to the eerie blue light that was morning's harbinger. She had managed thus far to make it through the night untouched. Just a few more hours and she would be safely on her way, hopeful to find someone who would assist her in unveiling Major Partain.

Again feeling the hazy languor of sleep wanting to claim her, Brenda fisted the blanket up to her chin and closed her eyes, this time letting herself drift off into a peaceful sleep. In her dreams she was being embraced by Striped Eagle. Her heart raced as she felt his hands warm on her breast, his thumb and forefinger caressing the stiff peak of her nipple. A sensuous thrill coursed through her as his hand began creeping lower, making the skin of her abdomen ripple with mounting pleasure, his fingers setting each place he touched anew on fire.

Brenda's eyes opened wildly. It hadn't been a dream at all! Hands inside the shirt she now wore were touching and fondling a breast. It hadn't been Striped Eagle's hands claiming her flesh—it was a Frenchman!

Knocking the man's callused hand away, Brenda scurried to her feet, screaming. She stumbled backward as the leering Frenchman, one with a pointed chin and sunken-in cheeks, began inching his way toward her, his hands lowering his breeches, readying to free his swollen-manliness to rape her.

"No!" Brenda shouted. "Stay away from me!"

Out of the corner of her eye she caught a sudden movement. She placed her hands to her throat as the stout Frenchman, Pierre, rushed to her assistance, grabbing the other Frenchman by the throat, shaking him. She leaned an ear toward the two men now exchanging angry words in French, understanding only a few of their words.

She recoiled when Pierre gave the other Frenchman a shove, knocking him to the ground, and pinning him there with a foot. "We are gentlemen! We behave honorably toward women!" Pierre shouted. "When I promise this lady that I will look after her then do not make me a liar by assaulting her!"

A keen relief flooded Brenda's senses; she was truly safe as long as Pierre was there to protect her. Her shoulders slumped as she exhaled nervously, sighing heavily. She tucked the shirt back inside her breeches, shuddering with the thought of the man's hands so possessively touching her body. Combing her fingers through her hair, she watched Pierre go about the camp, nudging the men to a full awakening, grumbling to each, flailing his long arms in the air as he cursed first one man and then another.

"We must be on our way!" he shouted. "Do you not

see the pale light in the sky? We've many miles to travel today!''

Pierre lumbered toward Brenda, his dark eyebrows pinched over his eyes as he frowned toward her. "*Avez-vous bien dormi*?'' he asked, now towering over her as he stood before her.

"*Monsieur*, I slept very well, thank you,'' Brenda lied. She cast her eyes downward, her face hot with a blush. "I must again thank you. That man. He gave me quite a fright.''

She cringed when she felt Pierre's broad hands frame her face, lifting it to direct her eyes into his. "It is hard for these men to see such a beautiful mademoiselle without at least wanting to touch her,'' he said hoarsely. "We travel many miles between women. You are lucky only one of my men dared a touch of your lovely flesh. If they had all decided to, I couldn't have truly stopped them, you know.''

Brenda's eyelashes fluttered. "Please help me,'' she softly pleaded. "Perhaps you can see to my safe arrival to Mendota? I thought much about it through the night. I know that Mendota can't be too far away upriver.''

Pierre's eyes took on a different sort of cast as they narrowed. "Mendota?'' he grumbled, arching an eyebrow. "We'll see, *ma petite*. We'll see.'' He dropped his hands to his sides, letting his studious gaze travel over Brenda. He took in her loveliness. He would like her for himself, but he had other plans for her. He had gained her trust just to be able to . . .

"The canoes are ready!'' a Frenchman shouted from the river, interrupting Pierre's train of thought. "You say you want to travel many miles? *Très bien. Venez*! Bring the lady and let us be on our way, Pierre!''

Pierre gave Brenda a strange sort of scowl. "We must now leave,'' he said gruffly. "Go to the canoes.''

"Yes, sir,'' Brenda said, nodding. She slipped the soft moccasins onto her feet and reached for the doeskin dress and hurried to the river. The heavily laden canoes nuzzled the rocky beach with their pointed prows. The bank of the river was lighting with reflections of the orange sunrise, the crowns of the huge trees capturing the orange splash of color as though a painter had touched their tips with the magic of his brush.

A Frenchman helped Brenda into a canoe while she watched, wonderingly, as one of the canoes was pulling out in the direction opposite to that which was planned for the others. Brenda had to wonder why, but she would not question anyone about anything yet. She would wait until she was safely at Mendota. Then she would choose Americans to whom she could confide. Not Frenchmen.

Brenda's gaze swept the makeshift wharf, now able to make out what was in the canoes as the tarpaulins were peeled back, the men checking their cargo. Brenda could see bundles of furs, grain sacks, powder kegs, and stacks of rifles gleaming in the morning light.

And then Brenda's gaze quickly shifted to Pierre as he positioned himself in the same canoe in which she sat, realizing this was to be the lead vessel. He waved his long arms and shouted. "*Tout droit*! Cast off!" he said. "Let us make many miles today!"

The tarpaulins were refixed hurriedly, leaving a few powder kegs uncovered. The rifles had been handed out to each of the men, loaded and primed, ready for anyone who might be a threat to their voyage down the river.

Clutching tightly the sides of the canoe, Brenda sat numbly quiet as the men positioned themselves and rowed the canoes away from shore. The rowers swung the oars deeper and the canoes thrust ahead, the convoy now sweeping down the middle of the river in single file.

Pierre sat on a powder keg, keeping his eyes trained on the riverbank, penetrating the foliage. It was always best to keep his canoes traveling in midchannel. The width of the river itself was the best defense against any Indian ambush.

Pierre squinted harder, knowing the importance of detecting any movement right away. Yet his thoughts were on the American lady who sat only a few feet away from him. When the canoes would glide on past Mendota, what would her reaction be? But, of course, she would quickly understand that she had been lied to. And then later, what would her reaction be to what he had planned for her?

Casting her a half glance over his shoulder he smiled to himself. Yes, she was worth many furs! The trade would be well worth it. He could get a piece of woman flesh for himself later, when his price paid would be much lower. He wanted this lady to be prime stock when he traded her. Surely she was a virgin. This made her worth much more than those harlots who lifted their skirts for any price offered them.

"*Mademoiselle, avez-vous bien dormi*?" he suddenly repeated. "Did you keep warm as well as sleep comfortably beneath the blankets I offered you?"

Brenda had been watching Pierre and had seen a strange sort of look flash in his eyes. She felt the beginning of an instinctual mistrust growing in her. If he took her to Mendota she would be surprised!

"I was quite warm and, as I told you before, I slept quite well all night," she said flatly, again lying. Even now her chest ached and her temples throbbed with the need of a full night's sleep. "Do not worry yourself on my behalf, *monsieur*."

"Pierre to you, my beautiful lady." Pierre laughed. "Why do you always forget? I would like to be addressed as Pierre by all lovely ladies."

"I feel more comfortable, *monsieur*, when calling you anything but your first name," Brenda said dryly, flipping her hair back from her shoulders.

"*Mon Dieu!*" he exclaimed, his dark eyes twinkling. "I thought we were friends."

"We shall see about that," Brenda said softly, her eyes scanning the shore for any signs of habitation. So far she had seen no cabins. Only forest. How far was she even now from where she had left her own? Would she ever be able to return, to give her family a proper burial.

The image of the burning cabin stung her heart as though thousands of bees were inside her, mad to be set free. She knew that even when she returned to the spot where she had left her parents, the graves that she would make would be barren. The cabin itself was the true grave for her family.

She hung her head at the thought, glistening tears escaping from the corners of her eyes even as she fought the urge to cry. But she was so lonely. She was so alone in the world . . .

The canoes moved in a windless stillness, the sun now high in the sky. Brenda's stomach ached from hunger and her mouth was parched from thirst. She gave Pierre a questioning glance, now realizing that these men probably ate only once a day, their evening meal. She had now also to fight this hunger nagging at her insides as well as the loneliness, leaving little room for fear.

Now the canoes traveled against a fast current, the men groaning as they worked the oars, whipping them up, then down. The water spewing over the sides of the canoe was refreshing to Brenda. She tipped her chin upward and closed her eyes to the breeze as it brushed past her face and lifted her hair from her shoulders. She could feel the forward surge of the canoe each time the men stroked their oars in unison.

The splashing of the oars rising and falling became hypnotic in their sounds, lulling Brenda almost to sleep. She was brought suddenly awake when sounds of shouting from the shore broke through the monotonous sounds of travel to which she was just becoming accustomed.

With eyes wide, her heart pounding excitedly, Brenda looked toward shore to see wharves packed with men loading and unloading boats. The buildings of the town were square and blue in the hard afternoon light. Chimneys on the houses dotting the banks of the river emitted puffs of smoke. A stockade fence in the distance revealed a fort, made for retreat should the Indians decide to attack.

"Mendota!" Brenda cried. "It *must* be Mendota."

Then her insides grew cold as she quickly realized that none of these canoes of their convoy were turning in the direction of the small settlement. Her eyes grew wild when she clearly understood that Pierre's intentions toward her weren't friendly or honorable after all! He had lied to her! He wasn't going to set her free at Mendota. He probably wasn't going to set her free . . . *ever*. All along he had been playing a cruel game with her. He was most surely saving her for himself, later, when he could have her totally alone, to ravage her . . .

Setting her jaw firmly, Brenda glared at Pierre as their eyes locked. "You tricked me," she hissed. "You never intended to take me to Mendota at all."

She rose shakily to her feet. She would jump overboard and swim to freedom. That was her only choice. But Pierre was too quick for her. He took a wide lunge and grabbed her by the waist, dragging her down, crashing her against the bottom of the canoe, momentarily dazing her as her head hit against the edge of the seat.

And then she was aware of hands on her wrists. "*Asseyez-vous, s'il vous plaît,*" Pierre growled, now placing her firmly back on the seat. "You will sit there like a nice lady, no? Do not try to jump overboard again. My men would enjoy jumping in after you." He laughed, his eyes gleaming into hers. "And after they get you I would this time not stop the games they would like to play with you.''

Brenda breathed hard, her pulse racing. "You are despicable," she hissed. "You are not even *human*."

Pierre shrugged nonchalantly. "*Oui*. I have been called many things by many women. It does not matter any longer to Pierre what *you* call me. You will soon be gone from my sight, no longer a bother to me at *all*."

Paling, Brenda leaned forward. "What do you mean?" she gasped. "What do you intend to do with me?"

Laughing boisterously, Pierre repositioned himself more comfortably in the canoe. "You will see," he said. "*Oui*, you will see."

"You must tell me," Brenda softly cried. "I cannot bear much of this any longer!"

Pierre's eyebrows forked. "You want to know?" He chuckled. "Then I will tell you. *Ma petite*, surely you realize that you are something to be bargained for more than anything else that I carry in my convoy of canoes. I will sell you to whomever offers me the most. *Comprenez*?"

Brenda stared disbelievingly at this man who had at one time been her only hope. But now? He surely was the devil in disguise!

She turned her eyes away from him, looking over her shoulder and at the wharves along the shore being left quickly behind. Numb, she watched as even they were taken from her sight. She didn't dare to venture in her mind what the next several hours would bring her. She closed her eyes, envisioning Striped Eagle and his handsome strength, wishing that he could somehow find and rescue her. But even if he did, she knew that she would again find means to leave him. It was as though life had become one large trap for her, ensnaring her deeper, moment by moment.

Eight

❧❧❧

The canoes again beached, Brenda sat beside a great camp-fire, clinging to the doeskin dress as though it could become a lifeline. The fields and forests had deepened to lilac, the westerly contours of the sky flushed red-gold by the setting sun. Hunting parties had been sent out and had returned and fresh meat was broiling, dripping fat into the flames over which it hung, its smell causing Brenda's stomach to ache unmercifully.

A barrel of rum had been taken from one of the canoes and opened, tankards filled to the brim now being passed around from man to man. Brenda tensed, watching the men, knowing that if they consumed much alcoholic beverage, the danger of again being assaulted was great. Though Pierre had said that he wanted her kept virginal for whomever he planned to trade her to, several of his men together could overpower him, to do as they pleased, when they pleased.

Rocking softly on her legs bent beneath her, Brenda closed her eyes and let her mind drift, her heart aching when she recalled the very moment she had given up her virginity. In Striped Eagle's arms it had been a moment of sheer bliss. In another man's arms, it would surely be as bad as burning in the pits of hell.

"So you are relaxed, *ma petite*?" Pierre said, kneeling on a knee beside Brenda. "Soon you will have food to feed that hunger you have so bravely kept yourself from complaining about. You are a woman of steel. *Oui*?"

His wicked laughter and the vile stench of him, reeking of perspiration from lack of a bath intermingled with the aroma of rum, drew Brenda quickly from her reverie. She pinched her lips and eyes into an angry scowl and refused to answer him. She was remembering him calling himself "honorable." He was anything *but*. He was nothing but a liar . . . a thoroughly deceitful Frenchman!

Pierre flailed a hand at the air, his eyes twinkling. "So you do not wish to speak to me?" he chuckled. "Très bien. Very well. We will see how long you keep your silence when I trade you for many, many valuable furs."

He rose to his full height, throwing his head back in a hearty laugh, then nodded to one of his men as he was handed a tankard of ale. He tipped the tankard to his lips and drank the liquid in fast, loud gulps. Handing the one-handled drinking vessel back to the man, Pierre rudely hiccoughed and wiped his mouth dry with the back of a hand. He then lumbered toward the river, standing quietly as he looked, squint-eyed, down its long avenue of water bordered by a rose-tinge from the continuing lowering sun.

Brenda clasped the doeskin dress, knowing that Pierre was undoubtedly watching for the one to whom he planned to trade her. Who could she expect? Would it be a white man wanting female companionship? Could it even be Major Partain? Buying female flesh in such a way seemed to be the sort of despicable thing Major Partain might do. If he could shoot people in cold blood and burn their remains, he was capable of anything.

Shivering with the thought, Brenda scooted closer to the fire. She focused her eyes on the dripping meat, unable to stop her mouth from watering. She had never been so hungry. Weakness was troubling her, caused by her hunger combined with sheer exhaustion from the traumatic experiences she had undergone. Would it ever end? Could she ever expect to live a normal life again? Weren't there any decent men left in the world? Surely her father wasn't the only man who knew how to be kind, loving . . .

The face of Striped Eagle materialized in Brenda's mind's eye. She was recalling the kindness of *his* eyes, recalling his gentleness. How could she forget those qualities about *him*? He had treated her as kindly as her father, yet in a much different way. His way of loving her had been that kind only shared between a man and woman in love. Yes, how could she have let herself forget?

A commotion at the riverbank caught Brenda's attention. Though dusk was nigh, there was no denying who Brenda saw walking tall and square-shouldered alongside Pierre toward the campfire. Brenda's heart fluttered at the sight of Striped Eagle, his chin tilted upward, his jaw and lips set tautly as his eyes met and held Brenda's.

"Striped Eagle," she gasped, placing a hand to her mouth. In one glance she had caught his bare copper chest, his fancy, fringed leggings, breechcloth flapping in the wind, his beaded moccasins and headband, and the eagle feather in a loop at the back of his hair. Across his nose was painted one red and blue stripe, and his high cheekbones were tinged white. He wore a stern expression and his footsteps were determined, as were his corded shoulder muscles and his fist doubled to his side. In the other he clutched a long-barreled rifle.

Too stunned to rise to meet him, Brenda's vision now settled on an array of Ojibwa Indian braves following along behind Striped Eagle, their arms heavy-laden with many furs and hides. Something tugged at her heart. The man who was buying her was Striped Eagle!

Striped Eagle took two more wide strides then stood

over Brenda, his eyes burning hotly into hers. "*Nee-bin-gee-zis, gah-ween-nee-nee-sis-ey-tos-say-non,*" he said, lifting the rifle into the air as he spoke. "You are costing my people many valuable furs. *Mah-bee-szhon.* I now take you back to my village. This time you stay. This vengeance you seek gets you into too much trouble."

His dark eyes traveled over her, an eyebrow lifting when seeing her attired in a man's breeches and shirt. Then his eyes settled on the doeskin dress and how she clung to it. A slow smile curved his lips, happy that the Ojibwa dress meant so much to her that though she was dressed in such a strange way, she still preferred to keep the dress she had been given.

"So it was you who gave this beautiful lady the doeskin dress," Pierre chuckled, moving to Striped Eagle's side. "I knew if I sent that one canoe of men away from the convoy to question around the Indian villages, I would find the right one." He lifted his lips into a sneer as he looked down at Brenda. "Perhaps I was wrong to believe you were a virgin. Surely this Indian . . ."

In a blur of sudden movement, Striped Eagle had cast his rifle aside and was lifting Pierre from the ground as he held firmly onto Pierre's shoulders. It was as though Pierre was a mere sack of potatoes to Striped Eagle instead of a muscled, stocky Frenchman.

"*Mee-eewh!*" Striped Eagle growled. "You are lucky I have come to your campsite in peace, Frenchman. And because I have, you do not speak disrespectfully to my woman. *Gee-nee-see-do-tum?*"

"Yes. I . . . understand . . ." Pierre said, out of the corner of his eyes seeing the fierce expressions in the eyes of Striped Eagle's warriors. "I meant no . . . disrespect, Striped Eagle."

Striped Eagle loosened his hands and let Pierre stumble back to the ground. As he stooped to pick up his rifle he kept his eye on Pierre. Then he turned his gaze to Brenda.

"*Mah-bee-szhon*," he growled, nodding toward her. "You are now mine. I paid for you fairly with many of my people's furs and animal hides. You will now come with me back to my village. You *will* cast thoughts of vengeance aside! You are now my woman. You are mine . . . *ah-pah-nay*, forever."

Brenda's eyes widened, her breathing now shallow, her face pale. "Yours?" she gasped, her fingers trembling as she clutched to the doeskin dress. "Striped Eagle—"

Striped Eagle reached out, taking her by a wrist, urging her gently from the ground. "Do not argue," he said flatly, his brown eyes almost black with intensity. "Or would you rather I leave you with this Frenchman? Do you enjoy his company?"

He dropped her hand away from her, his eyes now twinkling amusedly. He lifted his shoulder into a casual shrug, turning. He began walking away from her, yet barely breathing as he listened for her footsteps behind him. He knew her quite well sensuously—did he otherwise? Did his declaration of possession frighten her? He knew her determination to avenge her family's deaths. Yet he also knew that it was the Americans she would seek this help from, not Frenchmen. These Frenchmen in whose company she was now reeked of the white man's poison, liquor, as well as body odor. Surely she would be glad to be away from such an unpleasant group, to be with Striped Eagle and his proud Ojibwa warriors . . .

Brenda was stunned to almost total numbness by Striped Eagle's attitude. First he says that she is totally his, even pays for her, and then he so easily walks away from her, as though he didn't care at all. She was seeing the complexity of his personality. Or was he just tormenting her? Did he truly care about her?

But she knew that he did. She knew the value of the furs and hides that he had parted with on her behalf. Yet to say that this trade made her totally his? How dare he! She could not be bought and paid for as if she were a barrel of rum.

But this was not the time to argue *that* point. The fact was that he had come for her and had rescued her from this vile group of Frenchmen. This was the second time he had rescued her and she owed him much for his kindness. But she did not owe him her life!

Afraid now that Striped Eagle might change his mind and go on without her, Brenda began running after him. She tensed and set her jaw firmly when she heard Pierre laughing behind her.

"*Au revoir, ma petite,*" he said. "Perhaps we will meet again? Yes?"

Her nerves bristling Brenda stopped and turned on a heel to glare at Pierre. "*Monsieur,* I most certainly hope not," she said flatly. She lifted her chin haughtily as she turned and again began following Striped Eagle in hasty steps. But she stiffened once more at Pierre's sarcastic remarks.

"*Mademoiselle,* how you choose a savage Indian over a Frenchman is something that will always puzzle me," Pierre laughed. "*Je me suis trompé* when thinking you special. *Oui,* I made a mistake. No white woman with a thread of decency in her would choose an Indian's bed over a Frenchman's."

Brenda's eyes widened as she watched Striped Eagle stop and turn to stare angrily at Pierre over her shoulder. She placed a hand to her mouth and gasped as she watched Striped Eagle toss his rifle aside and rush to Pierre to wrestle him to the ground. Striped Eagle's warriors surrounded the remaining, gaping Frenchmen, their rifles poised as Striped Eagle spoke into Pierre's face, now drained of all its color.

"Again you belittle my woman and now even the Ojibwa," Striped Eagle growled. Striped Eagle knocked Pierre's knit hat from his head and intertwined his fingers in the Frenchman's dark hair and yanked. "A Frenchman's scalp could decorate my dwelling quite appropriately. One more time I have to warn you about your loose tongue and your scalp will be loosened and will become *mine*."

"*Très bien*," Pierre mumbled, his eyes wild with fear. "*Je me suis trompé*. I will be more careful with words, Striped Eagle. I am sorry. I apologize."

Striped Eagle yanked harder. "Apologies. You Frenchmen are quick with apologies," he grumbled. "But it is what you *do* that matters. No more warnings, Frenchman. *Gee-nee-see-do-tum?* My warriors outnumber yours. Always. Remember that."

"*Oui, oui*," Pierre said in a harsh whisper. "Now just take your white woman and leave. You have paid for her; she *is* yours. I never want to see her again. That is a fact, Striped Eagle. I will not be a threat to her at all. Nor to *you*."

"*Ah-neen-ay-kee-do-yen?*" Striped Eagle laughed, sarcasm thick in his words. "You think you are a threat, ever, to me and my people? *Gah-ween-wee-kay!* You are never a threat to anyone. Especially my woman. My warriors will be watching you. You so much as draw near my woman, you will all be shot and fed to the bears."

With that, Striped Eagle jerked his fingers free from the Frenchman's hair. He rose quickly to his feet, turning to look at Brenda, his heart hammering against his chest on seeing her meekness, the look of wonder in her eyes as she looked back at him. In wide strides he went to her and stood momentarily over her, again looking into her eyes, as though looking into her soul.

"It is time to go, Summer Sun," he said flatly. "Too much time already has been wasted on these Frenchmen."

He took her roughly by a wrist and began half dragging her toward the beached canoes, his moccasined feet moving soundlessly through the knee-high grass, his wide stride almost too much for Brenda to keep up with.

"Striped Eagle," Brenda pleaded, panting for breath, her knees almost buckling from her hungry weakness. "Please. I can't walk as fast as you. And I'm so weak. I haven't eaten . . ."

Striped Eagle gave her a sideways glance, his brow furrowed into a frown. "*Nee-bin-gee-zis* should learn her lesson well this time," he grumbled. "Twice I have rescued you. Both times you have been in need of food. Maybe next time I let you *starve*."

A flush of heat rose to Brenda's cheeks, anger swelling inside her. "I never asked you to save me, nor have I begged you for food," she snapped. "Nor will I *now*."

"You speak boldly. But do you want to test your words?" Striped Eagle chuckled as he led her to one of the many beached Ojibwa canoes at the riverside. "Though food is plenty in my canoe, do you wish not to eat any?"

Night had fallen in its total darkness, the moon silvering everything it touched, mirroring the canoe in the river as it gently swayed back and forth with the rhythm of the water's gentle movements. Brenda clung to the doeskin dress as Striped Eagle lifted her into his arms and carried her to the canoe, sitting her down on a soft cushion of furs on the seat. The canoe shook and quivered as Striped Eagle put his weight into it. Positioning himself in the middle, he reached beneath the seat for a leather pouch, its drawstring drawn closed.

"Do you wish to feed your hunger?" Striped Eagle said, smiling devilishly over at Brenda. "Or do you wish to feed your stubbornness by refusing the food I am about to offer you?"

Brenda's stomach ached as she anxiously watched Striped Eagle remove food from the pouch. Though what he offered her was sparse, at least it *was* food!

Smiling weakly up at him, she accepted the parched kernels of corn. "Thank you," she whispered. "I do appreciate what you continue to do for me."

Then her shoulders squared and her chin lifted. "But that does not mean I accept what you said about you now owning me. No one *owns* me. I cannot be your woman. I am *not* your woman, Striped Eagle. And I will prove this to you. I will escape again."

Striped Eagle returned her smile, signaling private amusement. He twisted back around and took his paddles and dipped them in the water, soon guiding the canoe far from shore, following the rippling shine of the moon's beams down the Mississippi River. Though his beautiful captive vowed never to accept what he knew now to be true—that she was his, totally his—in time he knew that she would cease fighting this truth. He *had* won her fairly. She would have to be made to understand this was the way of the Ojibwa.

Nine

It seemed as though Brenda hadn't ever left the Indian village once she was back inside Striped Eagle's wigwam. Her skin warming beside the fire in the firespace, she watched Striped Eagle place his rifle against the far wall, then turn and give her a heavy-lashed look, one that confused Brenda. She was reading anger in his eyes' depths, yet it was intermixed with the same gentleness she was growing accustomed to seeing whenever his gaze touched her.

Brenda shifted her feet nervously, still clutching the doeskin dress. "Striped Eagle, why are you looking at me in such a strange way?" she suddenly blurted. "When you look at me in that way I feel as a child, waiting to be scolded by a parent. Surely you understand why I left your Ojibwa village . . . why I stole your canoe in my escape. I told you—"

Striped Eagle raised a fist into the air, his interruption of her words cold and snappish. *"Mee-eewh,"* he said. "I do not wish to hear any more about why you chose not to stay with me. I chose to let you leave, hoping that at the last minute your decision would be to stay with me. You chose not to. But you are here *now*. That is enough.''

He dropped his hand to his side, his eyes shifting to the doeskin dress doubled in Brenda's arms. ''You keep Ojibwa dress with you while you flee in my canoe? That is good. That tells me enough of your feelings. You will get a *new* dress to take place of the one that has been soiled by Frenchman's stench. My sister will give you a more beautiful dress. It will be decorated with more beads and shells. It is one that you will also be too proud to ever leave behind.''

''And I *will* leave again,'' Brenda said, stiffening her upper lip. ''You surely only jested when you said that I was now your woman. Striped Eagle, I cannot stay here with you. I *won't*.''

''You *are* my woman,'' Striped Eagle said, taking two wide steps which made him tower over Brenda. He cupped her chin with the palm of a hand. ''As I am now your *ee-nee-nee*.''

Brenda's insides spread with warmth, his nearness, his touch drowning her as her passion crescendoed. ''If you just called yourself my husband, you are wrong,'' she said, her voice weakening. ''In the white man's world a marriage is not performed so simply. It is not done by just *saying* it is done.''

''*Gah-ween*. No. I do not call myself your husband,'' Striped Eagle grumbled. ''I call myself your *man*.''

His copper brow furrowed into a frown. ''And what I did was not *simply* done,'' he added. ''I paid for you with many furs and hides. You call that simple? Nothing Striped Eagle does is simple. I do everything with strength . . . with determination . . . with much thought put into my decisions.''

''Yes. I'm sure you do,'' Brenda said, so desirous of him her skin was pulsing where Striped Eagle's fingers touched.

"And, my woman, when we become man and wife, the whole village of Ojibwa will share in the moment," Striped Eagle said softly. "There will be a celebration of celebrations . . . a feast of feasts. It is I who is to be the next chief of the White Bear band of the Ojibwa. Even now I command respect from my people, as now I command respect from *you*."

Striped Eagle swept his arms about Brenda and drew her next to him, the abruptness causing her to drop the doeskin dress to the bulrush mats beside her. Her insides melted as Striped Eagle's lips crushed down upon hers, kissing her hotly, passionately, his tongue seeking entrance into her mouth.

Brenda was able to forget that she was in his arms because it was his command that she do so. Being there only seemed right, as though somewhere, written on scrolls of time, their lives were meant to intertwine, a timeless love, as nobody else had shared before them. The proof was in the magic of his kiss and the way she so wantonly responded. With him strange new sensations had been born inside her. Her answering heat and excitement were alarming. She felt vibrant, glowing . . .

Striped Eagle's fingers went to the buttons of the man's shirt that lay like a cruel wall between her and the bare flesh of his chest. He wished to feel the rose-tipped nipples of her breasts pressed against him. The ache in his loins was proof of where else he so desired to feel her. His heart was like a throbbing flame, scorching him.

Moving his lips only a fraction away from hers, Striped Eagle spoke against the softness of her cheek. "We must celebrate your return," he whispered, his fingers now at the last button of the shirt. He could hear her breaths coming in short rasps, could feel the pulsebeat growing more rapid at the hollow of her throat as he pressed his lips there, gently kissing her.

When he fully cupped a breast with the pressure of his

hand, Brenda moaned and sucked in her breath. Surely
nothing could be so sweet . . . so dear . . . as the way he
touched her, arousing her to the core. Somewhere down
deep inside her there was a little cry of denial, telling her
to push him away, not let him take her again sexually.
Each time he did, she *would* become more his. She couldn't
allow it! She . . . couldn't . . .

When he lowered his lips to the taut, throbbing nipple of
her breast, all was removed from her senses except the
pleasure building inside her. The soft cry of internal denial
was swept away by a wild current of desire. She trembled
sensually as his hands created fires along her flesh as he
lowered the breeches away from her, leaving her only in
the soft moccasins.

And then through what seemed to be a sort of haze over
her eyes she watched as he stood before her and ceremoni-
ously disrobed, revealing to her eyes the readiness of his
man's desire, the reflection of the fire in the firespace
coloring it a pale gold.

"Do you not hunger for me, as I do for you?" Striped
Eagle said huskily, his eyes feasting on her pink, silken
body, her hair a mass of red silk tumbling across her
shoulders and down her back, brushing her waistline. He
locked his eyes on hers. "You are so silent. Is this because
you are filled with passion of the heart? Say it is so,
Nee-bin-gee-zis." His hands molded over each of her breasts.
"Tell me there will never be another to touch your heart as
I have the power to do. Tell me that you are mine. Totally
mine."

Brenda's pulse raced, the pressure of his hands on her
breasts turning her to molten lava inside. She felt the
command not only in his touch, but heard it in his voice.
She *was* his captive. In every way . . .

"Striped Eagle, is it truly so necessary to hear me say
. . . those things?" she whispered, not wanting to give

herself so wholly to him as he wished. Tomorrow she would be gone . . .

Striped Eagle eased his hands away from her breasts, placing them gently on her shoulders. He began urging her to the furs spread out beside the fire. *"Gah-ween,"* he murmured. "No. Just speak with your body, my love. Let it reveal all your emotions to me. Words will come later." His lips grazed a breast as he lowered her to the furs. *"Gee-dah-gee-ee-goo.* Much, much later."

Shifting his body above hers, Striped Eagle let his hands begin discovering the tempting contours of her body anew, his eyes smoke black with passion. He ran his fingers over her narrow waist, her invitingly rounded hips, and then left a trail of fire as he sent quivering touches to the core of her womanhood.

Brenda let out a low gasp as she felt his fingers slowly caress her love mound, the calluses of his fingers causing a friction that pleased her more than if they were rose-petal smooth. Limp, a building pleasure enveloping her, she opened her legs to him, then emitted a guttural moan when he plunged a lone finger inside her, where she now welcomed the thrusts, slowly, almost meditatingly so.

And then his lips fully possessed her as he kissed her with pressing hunger, his tongue probing her secret places, sending something akin to a flash of lightning tingling through her. She felt the warmth building into a maddening heat, swirling downward from her brain to where his finger still taunted her into mindlessness.

And then she sighed against his cheek as his lips left hers, feeling his man's strength replacing his finger, rhythmic in his movements as he pleasured her as never before, his steel arms enfolding her, his hard, muscled body against hers.

"Gee-zah-gi-ee-nah?" Striped Eagle murmured, his hands smoothing wild sprays of her hair back from her flushed face.

Brenda licked her lips and swallowed hard, her body one massive heartbeat, consumed by this Indian who could intoxicate her even with his eyes. "You know that I do not understand your language," she sighed, marveling at how he could concentrate on speaking to her while continuing to send her to paradise with his blissful thrusts inside her.

Striped Eagle lowered his mouth to a nipple and flicked a tongue about its taut tip. "Striped Eagle asks if you love me," he said huskily, again mesmerizing her with his passion-dark eyes. "Now is the time for words, my love. Let me hear you say it. *Ah-szhee-gwah*."

Smothered whole, sensuously trembling, her senses now reeling in drunken pleasure as she felt herself tumbling into the abyss of fulfillment, Brenda closed her eyes and shook her head. "Yes. Yes. I . . . love you," she whispered. "Oh, Lord, I love . . . you . . . totally."

She realized that she had just fully surrendered herself to him for the second time. Yet she was glad. She knew that she could only be a whole woman with him. The fact that his skin was of a different color meant nothing to her. The fact that their cultures were from opposite realms of reality did not matter. But, oh Lord, how could she leave this behind? Yet she must . . .

"You must say yes in the Ojibwa tongue," Striped Eagle said, his hands scoring her flesh as they moved delicately from the base of her throat downward.

Brenda's skin rippled as his fingers touched her and her hips arched when she felt them encase her buttocks, digging into her flesh to lift her higher, making his swift strokes inside her more accessible.

"Striped Eagle will be your teacher in many ways," he said huskily. "I first taught you how to make love. Now I teach you how to speak all over again. You will speak Ojibwa. I will teach you one word at a time."

Brenda smiled questioningly up at him. "But now?"

she murmured, her brow feeling feverish from the building passion. "Striped Eagle, please . . ."

Striped Eagle's body became quiet. His largeness lay inside her, the walls about his man's strength pulsing with pleasure, begging for him to continue. "The Ojibwa learns restraint as a child," he said flatly. "So shall *you*, my love. Do you not feel the pleasure mounting even now as you anticipate the release of my love seed inside your womb? Waiting enhances the pleasure. So while enjoying the waiting you will say yes in Ojibwa."

Brenda's eyebrows raised in utter surprise. And then his words sank in: he had said "your womb." It hadn't occurred to her to worry about becoming with child. When she was with him all thoughts of anything but need of him were swept from her mind as though by waves on an ocean carrying the tide away from the shore.

She tensed and pressed her hands against his solid chest. "Striped Eagle, I don't want to learn any Ojibwa words," she suddenly said, her eyes now wild. "I don't want to be here. Let me go."

She squirmed, but she was locked beneath the steel frame of his body. "I must be insane to have ever let myself enjoy this time with you. I should have worried about . . . the consequences."

Her face colored with a blush, her eyes cast downward, now fully understanding what the union between her and any man could bring. A child! And with an Indian, it would be a half-breed child! Though she was in love with the man no matter the color of his skin, couldn't a child born into this world as a result of their union be branded for life? The child *would* be a half-breed. The cruelties of people would cause such a child to live a life of suffering, not truly knowing where he belonged.

Striped Eagle's eyes darkened, his jaw tight. He took her wrists and held them into the softness of the furs and his brow furrowed. *"Gah-ween-nee-nee-sis-eh-tos-say-non,"* he growled. "How can I understand you? First you say you love me, and then you fight this love. Is learning the words of the Ojibwa so distasteful to you that you push me away, deny me the pleasure of hearing you speak in Ojibwa? Or are you someone I do not know at all? Are you a tease? Do you enjoy playing games with me . . . an Ojibwa brave? Is it because of the color of my skin?" His fingers tightened on her wrists. "Tell me, *Nee-bin-gee-zis*. Reveal to me what your heart is saying to you. Tell me *ah-szhee-gway*. Tell me *now*."

Brenda cried out as his fingers tightened about her wrists. She glowered up at him. "Do you honestly think that I would behave in this way only because you wished to teach me how to say yes to you?" she softly cried. "Striped Eagle, you even accuse me of being a tease. Both times you are wrong, both times. I was only made aware of what I was letting myself do when you . . . when you made mention of . . . uh . . ."

A blush rose to her cheeks. She turned her eyes away from him, not wanting to admit to him that her worries were now of having a child by him. Shame engulfed her, she who so loved the color of his skin. But not everyone did. Indians were hated by most white men and women. Indians were branded as savages, no matter how peaceful they proved themselves to be. Too many homes had been burned. Too many women had been raped, killed.

But she now knew, from what she had learned from Striped Eagle, that it was the Dakota, not the Ojibwa, who did this in this land called Minnesota. But not everyone knew it. She had found out by means much different than most . . .

"Speak your mind, woman," Striped Eagle said, his tone softening when he saw she was torn with feelings. He released her wrists and placed a forefinger to her chin, slowly turning her face around so their eyes could meet. "When with Striped Eagle, open your heart and mind.

You can open your innermost thoughts and feelings. Feeling about you as I do, everything you say will be tested first, then quickly understood. For it is with my heart that I have taken you as my woman.''

Brenda drew a ragged breath, Striped Eagle's dark, stormy eyes now peaceful with the tenderness he offered her. He lowered his lips to hers, kissing her wonderingly, draining her of all troubled emotions. His kiss smothered her muted outcry, his hands warm and gentle on her breasts, again kneading them into heated points of fire.

And then his lips moved downward, his warm breath stirring shivers where he kissed anew, now enveloping a breast with his tongue, licking flames into the flesh there.

His eyes were passion-filled as he looked at her. ''Do you still wish that I leave you alone?'' he asked, his voice husky, his hands now caressing her pulsing core, awakening renewed ardor inside her. ''Tell me that you do not wish to share the next moments of fire with me, *Nee-bin-gee-zis*. Tell me that your body does not respond to my touch . . . to my lips. Tell me you can forget that momentary question in your mind that wondered about our bodies fusing into one. Tell me, Summer Sun. Tell me.''

Desire swelling inside her, Brenda knew she could no longer deny either of them the culmination of what his touch had promised. The fear of becoming with child shrank to a soft memory at the far recesses of her mind, replaced quickly with the intoxication of these moments of bliss shared with the man she loved.

''Just love me,'' she whispered, her hands wandering eagerly over the expanse of his coppery, sleekly muscled chest, her lips moving to the hard crests of his nipples, her teeth nipping, teasing.

Striped Eagle groaned longingly, feeling the coals of his inner self again ignited, the warmth touching him all over, flaming his desire for her even higher. He felt the walls of her love cave become wet and enticing, tightening about his man's strength that filled her, urging his thrusts to become even harder.

"Until you, my heart was lonely, my spirit cried," he whispered against her cheek. "Striped Eagle is glad that you listened with the ears of your heart and looked beyond your doubts with the eyes of your soul, my love. The squaw is the flower of the wigwam. Be my squaw . . ."

Brenda bit her lower lip, hearing the sincerity with which he spoke. She felt deceitful, knowing that she must again leave him. But wouldn't he also if his life was now destined to seek vengeance for the taking of those he loved? She would have to make him understand somehow.

"All I can say is that I *do* love you," she murmured, clinging, devouring his nearness, the beautiful scent of his body. "Let that be enough for now, Striped Eagle. Let knowing that be enough . . ."

"Striped Eagle will never have enough of you," he said softly, his eyes piercing hers before he crushed her lips beneath his.

His movements inside her grew more determined. Brenda's breath was coming in short rasps and her head was spinning with delight as she felt the pleasure mounting, higher . . . higher . . . higher . . . then grow into a storm of effervescence bursting forth throughout her. She pressed her hips upward, taking from him every moment of bliss that he could give her. She tingled when his hands cupped and squeezed her breasts as she felt his body arching then trembling with the same intense passion that she had just experienced.

And then they lay breathing hard in one another's arms, their bodies glistening pearlike in the fire's glow, perspiration beading their skin.

"*Mee-kah-wah-diz-ee,*" Striped Eagle said, leaning away from her to rest on his side beside her. "You were surely sent to me by the Great Spirit. No woman has ever made me feel so much.'' He reached a hand to her face and cupped her chin. ''None ever will again.''

Brenda turned to her side, fully at peace with herself, finding it so easy not to think about what losses had befallen her, or what lay ahead for her to do. This moment with Striped Eagle was to be savored, placed in her treasure house of memories, always to be drawn from when she was forced to part from him.

''Before me was there someone you did call special, Striped Eagle?'' she dared to ask, her eyelashes fluttering nervously, almost afraid to hear the answer.

Striped Eagle rose to his feet and offered her a hand. ''Come. We will take a walk beside the river and talk,'' he said thickly. ''I will acquaint you with some aspects of my life. You acquaint me with some of *yours*.''

Brenda laughed nervously as she clasped his hand and rose to her feet, her eyes now timidly raking over him, drinking in his beauty. ''But we are not dressed for a walk,'' she said. ''Can't we just talk here, by the fire?''

''You wish for a fire? I will build you a fire. By the river,'' he said, reaching for two blankets. He placed one about her shoulders, then slung one around his own. ''These are appropriate enough for such a walk. This time of night the Ojibwa people are seeking their own pleasures in the privacy of their wigwams. We will have privacy of our own to do as we wish outside *our* wigwam.''

His emphasis on the possessive word made Brenda tense, knowing that he still did claim her as his, and perhaps always would. But be that as it may, she wouldn't argue with him again about such a claim. Perhaps it was even better not to try to convince him of what she must do. Again she must just slip off into the night when he was asleep. But this time she must be more careful of whom she would ask for help. She must fend for herself totally, until she was certain she had found someone she could wholly trust.

"A walk by the river sounds lovely," she agreed. "But no fire is needed. The blanket is warm and so is your arm should you choose to place it about me."

She smiled seductively up at him, feeling deceitful, knowing that going to the river with Striped Eagle was for another purpose. She hoped this would give her the opportunity to look at the canoes, choose in silence which she would steal. And this time she must be more careful. The memory of being dumped into the icy waters of the Mississippi lingered in her mind. The remembrance of the vile Frenchmen stung her consciousness, making her recoil at the thought of the Frenchman's hands on her breasts while she had been dreaming of Striped Eagle!

Striped Eagle swept his arm beneath the blanket she clutched about her and eased it about her tiny tapered waist. He drew her to his side, their hips touching through their blankets, and began guiding her from the wigwam. Striped Eagle tilted his head toward the forest. "Do you hear it?" he murmured. "The voice of the *koko-koko*, the wise owl of the forest?"

His eyes penetrated the forest, the branches tossing and cracking overhead almost in a groan. "And do you see the *wah-wah-taysee,* the little fireflies lighting their little candles?" he added. "It is a night of peace. It is a night made for love."

He looked up at the moon. "It is *zah-gee-bah-gah-gee-zis*. The time of the Budding Moon," he softly added.

Drawing Brenda even closer, Striped Eagle guided her through the sleeping village, the outdoor fires now burning low, an occasional dog bounding toward Brenda, sniffing her moccasined feet.

And then the riverbank was reached, the wide stretch of water flowered with stars, the moon's beam a shimmer of white making a path down the center of the river.

Easing Brenda onto a soft bed of moss, Striped Eagle sat down beside her. The air was fresh and cool, tinged

with the aroma of pine and cedar. In the north a shooting
star blazed an arrow of light across the heavens; the birch
canoes rocked gently in the water, the paddles resting
against the sides inside them.

Guilt splashed through Brenda as she studied the canoes, knowing that at this moment Striped Eagle was
wholly trusting her. He had given *her* no reason to do
anything but trust him. It shamed her that she was not
returning his kindness. But she had her life and he had his.

Remembering her momentary fears while in the wigwam, Brenda's hand moved slowly to her abdomen. What
if there *would* be a child? Oh, what would she—

"In the white man's dwelling, I hear there is only one
wife," Striped Eagle said, interrupting Brenda's train of
thought. "Is that true, *Nee-bin-gee-zis*? Did your father
have only one wife? Did you have only one mother to look
after you?"

Brenda turned her head with a start, staring wide-eyed at
Striped Eagle. "There is always only one wife for a white
man," she said guardedly. Her insides rippled strangely,
knowing that he asked her this because it seemed strange
to him. Did his people's custom call for something quite
different? Could *he* possibly one day have more than one
wife? Jealousy tore at her gut even though she knew she
had no right to feel this way.

"Polygamy is practiced among my people only among
hunters, chiefs, and medicine men who can support several
families," Striped Eagle said matter-of-factly. "My father
had three wives. He now has none. My true mother died
many moons ago. Because of his failing health, my father
banished his other wives from his dwelling."

Brenda's insides turned cold, envisioning Striped Eagle
with several wives, one for each night. "And you will one
day be chief," she murmured. "Does that mean that you,
too, will have more than one wife?"

Striped Eagle chuckled low, then, choosing to delay his

answer, changed the subject. "You will one day meet my father, Chief Growling Bear." Again he chuckled. "Does not the name sound fierce? But it does not match the personality of my father. He is a man of wisdom as well as kindness. He is as gentle as the breeze now touching your face. His wives . . . his people . . . will attest to that."

Brenda knew when she was being toyed with. She went along with his little game, not forcing answers from him that he didn't wish to give until he chose to.

"I would enjoy meeting your father," she said, picking up a pebble and tossing it into the water. She watched as the star's reflections broke apart and melted away.

"One day you will meet him," Striped Eagle repeated, letting the blanket drop from his shoulders to lay about his naked waist. "But he left today. He has gone to meet with the other bands of Ojibwa, close to the Saint Croix River, those who call themselves the Saint Croix band of the Chippewa. He has left me in charge until his return."

He swelled his chest out and squared his shoulders. "I accept the duty proudly. One day I will be a proud chief."

Brenda let her blanket drop from around her shoulders as well, enjoying the cool breeze against her flesh still hot from their intense lovemaking. Her breasts shone in the moonlight. She could feel Striped Eagle's eyes capture them in a visual caress.

"You said that your father had gone to meet with Ojibwa, yet you called them the Chippewa," she said, trembling when Striped Eagle gently circled a breast with the sureness of a hand. "Are the Objibwa called by two names?"

"*Ay-uh,*" Striped Eagle grumbled, a scowl furrowing his brow. "Some choose to be called Chippewa. Some choose to be called Ojibwa. It doesn't matter. It means the same thing in the Ojibwa language."

His eyes took on a faraway cast. "As the Dakota are called the Sioux by the Great White Father in Washington, so is Chippewa the only name called our tribe by the Great White Father in Washington, in treaties and other negotiations," he said thickly. "But it will never be adopted by us, the White Bear band of Ojibwa, or *a-nicina-be*—original or first man."

"So your band of Ojibwa has thus far succeeded in avoiding having to sell your land to the white man?" Brenda asked softly, knowing that so many Indians had sold their land after being pressured to do so.

"*Gah-ween*," Striped Eagle said flatly. "No. And we never *shall*."

Brenda couldn't hold back her most important question any longer. It was nagging at her consciousness, this need to know whether or not Striped Eagle would one day choose one, two, or more wives, though she doubted if she would ever see him again after tomorrow, to even know for sure.

"Striped Eagle, I must know," she said, drawing up to her bare knees before him, the moss like a silken sponge beneath them. "Will you have one or more wives?"

Striped Eagle's heart thundered against his ribs, seeing her skin of velvet within his reach, her eyes eager with the question that he hoped she would ask.

"You say the white man has only one wife?" he said thickly, placing his hands on her waist, drawing her closer to him.

"Yes . . ."

"Say *ay-uh*," he interrupted. "That will be saying yes in Ojibwa. It will be your first lesson in the language of my people."

Brenda leaned into him, moving from her knees to straddle him, her legs about his waist, her breasts barely grazing the flesh of his chest.

"*Ay-uh*." She giggled. "Now that I have proven a good student, give me an answer, Striped Eagle, or I will think you are afraid to tell me."

"You say the white man has only one wife," he said, running his hands down the smooth line of her spine. "That is the way it is to be in *my* wigwam. I want only one wife. I want my heart to be wholly hers."

He framed her face between his hands, urging her lips close to his. "I want my heart to be wholly *yours*."

Brenda melted against him, their lips on fire with renewed passion. When Striped Eagle placed his hands beneath the soft curves of her buttocks and urged her onto his risen manhood, she rocked and swayed with him.

Her hands clung to his sinewy shoulders, her neck arched backward, her spirit soaring, forgetting the coming hour when she would again bid him a silent good-bye while he peacefully slept. There was only now . . . only now . . .

Ten

❧ ❧

Brenda woke with a start. She glanced about, momentarily lost, still feeling as though she should awaken in the coziness of her own bed, in her own cabin. She still expected to see her mother already up, kneading the dough for the day's bread, and her brother Tommie snuggled still asleep in his own bed, their father having risen before daybreak to begin his daily chores out of doors.

A painful ache crept through her heart, again rudely reminded of her loss. She rose up on an elbow, seeing the flames in the firespace tinting everything in the wigwam with a soft, golden glow, this, too, becoming familiar to her. She had spent only two nights in this wigwam yet it seemed as though she had spent many more: its walls had been witness to so much already shared between her and Striped Eagle.

Her heart lurched. She moved quickly to a sitting position, looking around her for Striped Eagle. But only the indented impression of his magnificent body in the plush furs spread out on the bulrush mats lay witness to his having been at her side.

Smoothing her hands over this outline of his body,

Brenda could so recall the blissful wonder of his lovemaking. He was a skilled lover. Surely he was as skilled in everything he did. One day he would become chief of this band of Ojibwa . . . and he would most surely rule his people as none had before him.

Then Brenda paled, somber at the recall of what she had planned while Striped Eagle soundly slept! She wasn't supposed to have slept so soundly herself. She had planned to make her escape before the morning light awakened the entire village of the Ojibwa. But now she didn't dare try to escape; Striped Eagle could be near, watching! It seemed he had only let her go that other time to teach her that she was not capable of fending for herself!

Scowling, Brenda rose quickly to her feet, now thinking that Striped Eagle had planned this well. He was most surely guarding his wigwam, waiting for her to try to escape. This time he would block her path! She was a virtual prisoner of this Indian.

Stooping to pick up the man's breeches and shirt, defying him even in choosing the white man's clothes over the Indian's, she hurried into them.

"I'll show him," she whispered. "I shall escape out the back way even if I have to remove many birch-bark mats in the wall to make a hole for escape. He cannot, he will not, keep me from doing what must be done."

Her gaze settled on a white object spread out on the bulrush mats beside the entrance flap. Her heart felt a warmth encase it, seeing that Striped Eagle had placed a new doeskin dress there for her. And as her eyes studied the beautiful dress studded with beads of resplendent colors significantly the green earth, the blue sky, and the yellow of the sun, she recalled his having said that this new offering of dress would be even more beautiful than the last, and he had been right.

Brenda went to the dress and picked it up, knowing that

she so badly wanted to claim it as hers. Any gift from Striped Eagle she would always cherish. She placed the soft dress to her cheek, closing her eyes, again swept up into the world of Striped Eagle and what he had begun to mean to her.

Yet she forced herself from her moment of reverie. At this moment in time anger must take precedence over any other concerns. She would not let this Indian dictate her life in any way. She had to be free to search for a way to destroy Major Partain. And she had to be sure she didn't implicate Striped Eagle in these plans. She still felt the same as before. She didn't want to be the cause of trouble between the Indian and the white man. Her troubles were her own, no one else's . . .

Voices sounding now outside the wigwam made Brenda tense. She listened, recognizing Striped Eagle's deep, resonant tone of voice without understanding what he was saying. He was not only speaking in the Ojibwa language, he was also speaking too softly for her to have heard *had* he been using words familiar to her.

Her eyes widened when she heard Striped Eagle begin to scatter a few English words among the Ojibwa, her heart skipping a beat when she thought she heard the mention of Major Partain!

Her heart throbbing against her ribs, she crept stealthily to the closed entrance flap and placed her ear close to it. Her arms clutched the new doeskin dress to her breast as she continued to listen, now fully understanding Striped Eagle as he issued low commands to his braves.

"The sun will soon be rising. The silver moccasins of dawn will soon be changing to beaded ones of a wild rose tint," Striped Eagle said smoothly. "We will then plead with the fire of the sun to give us strength and life and health. We will ask the great spirit Wenebojo to help us in our fight against this Major Partain who has many times threatened our land."

"Major Partain must be dealt with. He has sided with the area lumbermen and has helped to raise a dam across White Bear River. It is not right that he does this thing. This dam is located on our land," Striped Eagle continued. "We ride today! This evil major cannot be allowed to place this dam across White Bear River! It will endanger our wild rice beds. We must take action. This day!"

Brenda began to tremble with her discovery. Not only did *she* hate Major Partain, but Striped Eagle and his people hated the major as much—maybe even *more* than she did. Striped Eagle was even now speaking with angry words of revenge!

As she listened, Brenda's mind began to conjure up ways to get her own revenge at the same time Striped Eagle got *his*, knowing that she would not be the cause of any harm that might come from this battle between the white man and the Indian because Striped Eagle was making plans of his own without knowledge of her own experiences with the major. Striped Eagle had already made up his mind to take action against the blackhearted Major Partain for his *own* reasons.

Wondering how she might approach Striped Eagle to ask if she could accompany him on his mission of vengeance, she cast aside all plans of escaping from the Ojibwa village this morning. She did not want to escape now; she wanted to become one with the Indians this day!

Bending to place the doeskin dress on the bulrush mats, Brenda then quietly lifted the entrance flap and inched her way outside into the coming daylight. A misty morning fog reached from the banks of White Bear River to blend with smoke spiraling from the peaked holes of the wigwams in one white shroud covering the Indian village.

Brenda's eyes sought and found the outline of Striped Eagle silhouetted against the backdrop of a bonfire. His back was to her, his fists resting on his hips, his legs widespread. She took in his majestic mien, his stolid dignity, his inscrutable self-poise.

His voice of authority was reaching at least twenty braves crowded in a close circle about him, all observing him intently, all buckskin-clad and well armed with bows and arrows, some also bearing rifles whose barrels were reflecting ominously in the firelight.

Standing in the shadows, Brenda continued to listen, wondering just how she should approach Striped Eagle to ask if she could travel with him and his braves on this mission. The thought of an actual battle caused goose bumps to rise on her flesh. Could she even do it?

Her papa had taught her to ride a horse but had never taught her to fight, only how to aim a pistol and fire it at empty bottles lined up on a fence.

The only time she had been given a pistol to use against another human being had been the fateful night that was tattooed into her memory.

She closed her eyes, the remembrances flooding her senses, yet glad this time that she was experiencing the ugliness all over again. It inflamed her hatred of the major even more. It gave her the courage to help in any way she could that might lead to the corrupt major's demise!

She wanted the opportunity to be the one who fired the fatal shot that would snuff out the major's life. She wanted to stand over his body and gloat, hoping to make her future free from guilt for not having been able to defend her family any more than she had. She hadn't even fired a first shot before she had fled from the death scene. She hadn't been able to keep her brother from being murdered right before her eyes!

A tearful sob tore from her insides, a sound reverberating through the cold morning air, touching Striped Eagle's trained ears.

Turning abruptly on a heel, he peered through the semi-darkness and saw Brenda standing outside the entrance flap of his wigwam, tears shining on her face, the firelight turning the tears golden as it reflected from them.

The yellow fire in Striped Eagle's eyes burned savagely as he again let them move over her, seeing her attired in the Frenchman's clothes instead of the doeskin dress that he had laid out for her to find.

Seeing her crying, seeing her dressed in such a way, confused him. And why was she standing there in the shadows, listening, while he instructed his men of their morning duties?

Ay-uh, she was a complex personality, this, his white woman.

Two swift steps took Striped Eagle to Brenda. He clasped his hands to her shoulders, his eyes imploring her as she gazed with nervous, blinking eyes up at him.

"Andi-dush-ay-uh-szhi-on-nee-gee?" he grumbled. "Where do you think you are going?"

His gaze again swept over her. "Why are you dressed in such a way?" His brow furrowed into a frown. "You must burn the Frenchman's clothes. If not, I will burn them for you."

He nodded toward the entrance flap. *"Mah-szhon.* Go and remove the ugly clothes. You wear doeskin dress. Then you wait for my return. Striped Eagle will return soon. I will expect you to be here, waiting."

A slow smile teased at his lips. "You have seen what happens when you try to make your way alone in the canoe and by foot. It was not meant for a woman to travel alone." He squared his shoulders. "Only men travel alone. Remember that, my woman."

Brenda wanted to lash out at him, defend all women, protest that women could be as strong, as knowledgeable of the world as a man. But she needed to use a different tactic than venomous words with Striped Eagle this morning. She had to convince him that she was capable of traveling with him. She must finally disclose to him who had killed her family. Only then would he understand why she must go with him. Surely Indians knew well the meaning of vengeance. So much had been taken from them since the arrival of the white man. Surely he would see that her need of vengeance was no less than his.

"I won't leave while you're gone, Striped Eagle," she finally said. "I can promise you that. I—"

Striped Eagle smiled smugly. "*O-nee-shee-shin.* Good," he said, interrupting. "You listen well, Summer Sun. That makes me glad."

Frustration building inside her, Brenda grasped his hands and eased them from her shoulders. "I listen well to you," she said softly. "Now you listen well to *me*. Please hear what I say and weigh your decision of what I will ask you very carefully inside your heart. What I ask of you means very much to me, Striped Eagle. Please try to understand. Please don't deny me what I ask of you."

His eyebrows forking, Striped Eagle looked upon her pale, vulnerable face, again taken by her beguiling, flashing eyes. He, at this moment, knew that it would be hard to deny her anything. Their moments of shared pleasure were not that long ago behind him. He still felt the fire of passion that even now was smoldering in his loins.

Summer Sun's splendid mass of hair was like a flame in the early morning sunlight; her eyes, like deep, cold water, touched his very soul each time he looked upon her anew. She had robbed him of his heart and he had parted with it willingly . . .

"What is it that you wish to ask of me?" he said after her rush of words trailed away. He folded his arms across his wide breadth of copper chest. "Speak now. My men await my further instructions. We must travel soon."

"I know," Brenda said, anxiously nodding. "And I want to go *with* you." The palms of her hands had become damp in anticipation of hearing the answer she feared he would give.

But if he didn't agree to let her go with him, she would follow behind, on her own. It would be much simpler than searching for an honest white man to do the deed for her.

And even if she found someone to tell her troubles to, how could she be truly assured that Major Partain had been properly dealt with? On the other hand, if *she* pulled the trigger, she would *know* that the deed was done.

Striped Eagle was taken aback by her suggestion. A look of disbelief was quickly replaced by a quiet amusement revealed in the twinkling of his dark eyes.

"You? You wish to travel with Striped Eagle and his braves?" he said, chuckling low. "*Nee-bin-gee-zis,* why would you? I do not understand. You do not know anything about the Ojibwa and his fight for survival. Or is asking to ride alongside us on our proud steeds a way that you wish to prove to me that your commitment to me and my people is true, is strong?"

A slow blush rose to Brenda's cheeks, her eyes lowered, hating to reveal the total selfishness of her request.

Yet it wasn't truly selfish! She wasn't doing it for herself, but for her papa, mama, Tommie!

Jerking her chin up in a haughty tilt, she looked Striped Eagle straight in the eye. "No. It is not for you I want to do this thing," she said dryly, flinching as a wounded look flashed across his handsome face. "It is for my *family*. It is for *myself*. I must have this opportunity to join you in your vengeance against Major Partain. For, you see, Striped Eagle, he is the man responsible for my family's deaths."

Striped Eagle's breath was momentarily stolen from him in his surprise. So the white man could have the same enemy as the Ojibwa? This major who boasted of being so powerful in the white community was, in truth, hated by them? He actually turned on the white man himself and ravaged and killed his own kind? It seemed that this white man was even more disgraceful in his actions than the dreaded Dakota!

His jaw tightened, his eyes again hinted of fire. "We travel by horseback to do this deed," he said thickly. "Do you have such skills?"

Brenda was stunned by this question when she had expected an immediate refusal. She stuttered when she responded. "Yes, I have such skills," she said. "My papa taught me to ride a horse when I was quite small."

Striped Eagle knit his brow. "It is not usual for a squaw to ride with the Ojibwa braves against the white man," he growled. "But a white woman?"

His gaze raked over her. "Yet it *would* be a way to know that you did not escape my village while I am gone," he said thoughtfully.

He nodded, reaching to take her hands in his. *"Ay-uh,"* he said, smiling mischievously down at her. "*Nee-bin-gee-zis* can go with Striped Eagle."

Again his eyes focused on her attire. "But first you will change into the clothes of the Ojibwa. You will wear fringed leggings and dress of the squaw."

His hands released hers. He wove his fingers through her hair. "Your hair shall be woven to hang into one long, flaming braid down your back. To fight Ojibwa battles with the Ojibwa, you must *look* Ojibwa!"

The word *battle* caused a coldness to wash through Brenda's veins. She tilted her head sideways, studying Striped Eagle's expression, seeing so much hidden beneath his smug smile. Why *was* he so eager to let her ride into battle with his braves? Didn't he fear for her life? Surely he cared enough to worry that she might not survive such a battle. *She* was now plagued by such a worry. Perhaps she had made this decision to ride alongside Striped Eagle in haste.

But to see Major Partain die would be worth any sacrifice she would have to make.

She looked up into Striped Eagle's eyes, knowing that there was one thing she did not want to have to sacrifice. Striped Eagle. If he were to die, a part of her would die with him, of that she was certain.

Eleven

❧ ❧

On a proud steed, a dappled gray gelding, Brenda moved
alongside Striped Eagle in the serene silence of the stately
Norway pines. Her hair was woven into one long braid
down her back. She was dressed in the lovely doeskin
dress and matching fringed leggings, moccasins soft and
warm on her feet dangling on each side of the horse, bare
of stirrups since no saddle had been offered her. Blankets
had sufficed, bright in their colors.

The air was fresh and cool, smelling of lake water and
pines; forest spider webs glittered and clung between blooming forsythia bushes. Clusters of wintergreen berries showed
red against their glossy green leaves nestling in the fallen,
browned pine needles, the sun's rays now barely over the
treetops, pulsing and glowing, tongues of flame among the
towering trees.

Brenda cast Striped Eagle a sideways glance, his smoldering brown eyes flat this day, his jaw tight. A huge bow
was slung across his shoulder, a quiver of arrows at his
back. A rifle was sheathed in a leather gun sling on Striped
Eagle's white stallion, jostling at the side of Striped Eagle's right leg.

Striped Eagle wore his hair straight to his shoulders, bear grease having been worked into it to make it smoothly shine; his beaded headband displayed its usual gray striped eagle feather. A black stripe had been painted across the bridge of his nose and a dot of red at each of his high cheekbones.

He was attired in only a breechcloth and moccasins, his corded muscles rippling at his shoulders and at the powerful thighs of his legs.

Brenda's gaze settled on the small tomahawk thrust into the waist of his breechcloth. She had never seen him carry one before. She gulped hard. Was he planning to scalp the soldiers?

But she couldn't imagine it. He was not the sort to do such a thing. He most surely was not the savage most thought the Indians to be!

Striped Eagle, dressed as sparsely as the proud braves following their leader, was unnerving to Brenda. They were all dressed scantily in breechcloths and sported a various assortment of weapons.

She forced her eyes straight ahead, reminding herself that she had chosen to be with the Ojibwa. She mustn't question their way of dressing, even though she had been forced to wear the Ojibwa attire.

Gazing downward, her eyes touched the lovely dress, truly adoring it, relishing the feel of its softness against her flesh. She truly didn't mind having been forced to wear the dress. In truth, it felt warm and snug against her skin, and accented her curves as no other garb had . . .

Lifting her chin, Brenda again focused her eyes straight ahead, this time pride for who she was flooding her insides pleasantly. Her gelding snorted steam from its wide, rigid nostrils into the cool morning air, its hooves squishing in the sodden ground of the forest.

Its wind-flung mane and tail resembled wings as it moved now into a clearing which stretched out momentarily into a lush meadow starred with wild, gold-faced daisies and goldenrod. The brilliant yellows of the flowers made Brenda feel as though she were traveling in a field of sun.

The sky was now an emerald blue overhead, only an occasional puffy white cloud disturbing its tranquility. The breeze carried the bittersweet smells of the wildflowers to Brenda's nose, the sun now touching her face warm and welcomed.

Following Striped Eagle's lead, she urged her gelding into a canter across the meadow, the fringes of her white doeskin dress skipping in the wind, her long red braid blowing back from her shoulders.

Brenda rode alongside Striped Eagle into a copse, splashing through a shallow brook, then galloped up the slope of a small knoll where knee-high grass blew green and wild, giving her a full view of White Bear Lake and the makeshift dam built of logs and brush which stretched across a narrow channel.

Anxious, hoping to soon have her revenge, her insides quivered as her gaze scanned the scene below, looking for signs of Major Partain's soldiers. Then, seeing no one, a numbness enveloped her. There was only a beaver scampering along the highest peak of the dam.

With questioning eyes, Brenda looked toward Striped Eagle. "There's no one here," she said thickly. "Striped Eagle, surely they found out you were coming."

Striped Eagle removed the tomahawk from the waist of his breechcloth. He waved it in the air, shouting at his braves. *"Awn-go-toon! Gee-szhee-dee-nay!"*

Brenda's eyes widened as she watched the braves directing their horses down the incline, rushing toward the dam. What were they going to do? There were no soldiers to fight, but the Indians' expressions were fierce, their eyes ablaze!

Then she turned her gaze slowly to Striped Eagle, finding him sternly regarding her. She wavered beneath his steady stare, squirming on the horse's back. "Striped Eagle, I don't understand any of this," she finally blurted. "What did you order your braves to do? There is no one to *fight*."

"*Gah-ween*. No. There are no soldiers to disturb what must be done," Striped Eagle stated flatly, lowering the tomahawk to rest the blunt end on the thigh of his right leg. "The dam must be destroyed. All of it. When the soldiers dare to build it again, my braves will destroy it again."

A slow flush crept up Brenda's neck, and upward, to scald her cheeks. "You knew all along there would be no soldiers here?" she gasped. "You didn't plan to fight them? Only destroy the dam "

"*Ay-uh*," Striped Eagle said, nodding. "It is the peaceful way. None of my braves' lives will be lost."

He thrust a fist to his heart. "But the white soldier, the evil, scheming Major Partain, will know the meaning behind what has been done here. He will know that the Ojibwa's heart speaks in a peaceful way, that it is the Ojibwa who have decided not to use the voice of the rifle to show that we will not stand by and watch our wild rice beds ruined by the white man. But in time, if the major doesn't understand the peaceful message given here, we will have to relay the message by other means."

"Then all along you knew that the soldiers wouldn't be here?" Brenda asked, gripping the reins more securely, so tight they bit into the flesh of her hands.

Striped Eagle's eyes lost some of their fire and a slow smile curved his lips. "You think Striped Eagle would let his woman accompany him on a mission if gunfire was expected?" he said, edging his white stallion closer to her gelding. "You think your life means so little to me? Summer Sun, you surely do not know the depth of my feelings for you."

Brenda's eyelashes fluttered nervously, hearing the strain in his voice as his smile faded. "I *had* wondered about it, why you were so easy to agree to my accompanying you," she said, giving Striped Eagle a half smile, her lips quivering. She felt torn by feelings, disappointment uppermost. It seemed that revenge wasn't that easily achieved.

Her gaze moved to the activity at the dam, seeing the Ojibwa braves hacking their tomahawks into the many limbs and caked mud interwoven together to block the flow of water.

"All along you planned to only do *this*?" she repeated, yet now recalling that she hadn't actually heard Striped Eagle refer to a battle with the soldiers when he had given instructions to his braves about the full day's plans.

But how could she have known? After all, he had spoken in Ojibwa! She had only thought that when he mentioned fighting . . . it was to be done while in the presence of the soldiers. She had never had reason to think otherwise.

"Summer Sun knows the Ojibwa always seek the peaceful solution first," Striped Eagle said, his eyes narrowing as he looked toward the activity at the dam. "And it is now that I must join my braves." He gave Brenda a sideways glance. "You seek vengeance? *Mah-bee-szhon*. Come. Join me in the way I have chosen to seek mine."

Frustrated, Brenda looked first at the dam, then at Striped Eagle. "This will only be temporary, you know," she said, her disgruntled mood showing in the tone of her voice. "The dam will be built back."

Striped Eagle lifted a shoulder into a casual shrug. "Perhaps," he mumbled. "Striped Eagle will worry about that when it happens. Right now I will receive much pleasure in what I am about to do."

Brenda eased up on the reins, watching Striped Eagle lead his stallion down the slope of land, then dismounting at the banks of the river. She further watched as he began chopping limbs away from the dam, his copper skin soon shining with sweat, glossy as satin.

The sight of the muscles cording and flexing with each of his movements caused Brenda's heart to race. And when he glanced up at her, momentarily locking eyes with her, she felt as though he had looked clean into her soul, sending soft whispers of consciousness through her, knowing what he expected of her . . . his woman . . .

Like a puppet on an invisible string following the guidance of her master, Brenda pressed her heels to the flanks of her gelding and eased the horse down the incline, then dismounted. With her eyes still on Striped Eagle she moved toward him, the moccasins she wore soaking up moisture from the dew-dampened grass.

When she reached the riverbank she became almost breathless when Striped Eagle offered her a tomahawk. "You join my braves," he said flatly. "You also help remove the hated dam?"

Feeling the flow of emotion exchanged between them, Brenda nodded and accepted the tomahawk, the handle strangely cold against her flesh. She had read of Indian massacres and how this instrument had been wielded. Imagining this very tomahawk being used in such a way caused shivers to ride her spine. She didn't even want to look closely at it for fear of seeing dried blood where the blade and wooden handle met. If it hadn't been entirely washed off . . . ?

Shaking her head to clear her thoughts of such gruesomeness she smiled weakly up at Striped Eagle. "Yes. I will help you," she said. "I will enjoy helping. Anything I can do against Major Partain I will."

Striped Eagle placed a hand to her elbow and helped her down the rocky embankment. They exchanged smiles, then together began chopping and pulling the twisted limbs away from the dam. The sun was now hot, pulsing overhead. Brenda's brow was beaded with perspiration, her throat dry.

But she would not slacken her movements. She wanted to show Striped Eagle that she was strong, that she had muscles, developed while helping her father build three log cabins and planting three separate gardens in three years. Even now the sun-bleached streaks woven into the red plaits of her hair attested to her many days of working in the sun alongside her beloved father. She was proud to have such moments to treasure. She was happy now to be able to share such moments with Striped Eagle, the man she loved . . . would *always* love.

Casting him a sideways glance, seeing the sweat trickling down his handsome face, she wondered what he would do when on the morrow he would find her gone again. She knew that she would still have to seek vengeance in her own way. If she stayed with Striped Eagle, she would never achieve what she so sorely needed. A peaceful solution to her problem was *not* her chosen way. She would never rest until she knew that Major Partain had paid fully for what he had done to her family. And the only way was to see him dead.

Thinking of Major Partain and her hate of him was cause for Brenda to cut away at the dam more vigorously. She breathed hard. Her arms ached, and she realized they hadn't had the required time to rest after her torturous paddling of Striped Eagle's canoe.

Yes, she was strong, perhaps more than most women her age, but she was also learning that she wasn't *that* strong. It was becoming harder to arc back the tomahawk. Her eyes became cloudy as spirals of sweat rolled down into them. Her feet were soaked as water trickled over the partly dismantled dam.

And then Striped Eagle suddenly grabbed her by the waist and lifted her into his arms to hoist her to the riverbank, just as the force of the water being held at bay suddenly sprang free and frothed over the dam, loosening the rest of the limbs and carrying debris along with its forceful fountain of water.

Loud whoops and shouts arose from the Ojibwa braves who stood in the path of the water, welcoming its splash on their bodies. Joy was etched on their faces, victory marked in their eyes.

"It is done," Striped Eagle said thickly, holding Brenda closely to his chest. His gaze met hers. "*Nee-bin-gee-zis,* my Summer Sun, it is done. Thank you for joining the Ojibwa in their fight against the evil white man. The spirits will reward you for this."

Brenda clung to his neck, the smell of him spicy in its fragrance. Adoringly she looked up at him. "I need no rewards," she murmured. "You know it was for my own selfish reasons that I did this, Striped Eagle."

"You may think so," he said hoarsely. "But I have to believe you also did it out of respect for my people. And for this I will take you back to my village by way of a different route. You will see a place sacred to all Ojibwa. Striped Eagle has never taken a white man or woman to this place. It is my way of showing you just how much I love and trust you."

Intrigued and touched by his words, Brenda lowered her lashes. She already knew how much he cared for her. But after tomorrow, would he still?

Twelve

The horses continued to lope. Brenda was becoming weary from the long ride, her leg muscles aching so miserably she felt as though she couldn't go any farther. Striped Eagle led them along the course of streams as they zigzagged among the trees. The sunlight was creeping through the forest ceiling like gold velveteen streamers; the air was of a crisp freshness as a sweet breeze swept through the pines.

Brenda squirmed on the horse, casting Striped Eagle a frown that changed into a soft smile as he looked back at her with his own smile of warmth, his eyes telling her what he didn't need to say aloud. She could see not only love for her in them but also pride. She knew that he loved her, was proud of her, yet she knew that she might not be worthy of either feeling. Yes, tomorrow she would again steal his canoe and bid him a silent good-bye . . .

"Ah-neen-ay-szhee-way-bee-zee-en?" Striped Eagle suddenly said, his smile fading.

Brenda's thick eyelashes fluttered and her smile weakened; he was disturbed about something. But she could not guess why. "Striped Eagle, please speak in English to me," she said, her fingers slacking on the horse's reins, sore from having grasped them for so long. "Why are you frowning at me? Only a moment ago you were smiling."

Striped Eagle edged his mount close to hers. "In Chippewa I asked what was wrong with you," he said, a hand reaching to touch the soft curve of her cheek. "First you frown, then you smile. Summer Sun, do you not wish to be with me? Do you not wish to go with me to the sacred quarry?"

Brenda's flesh quivered sensuously beneath his touch, then her back straightened when he mentioned a sacred quarry. "Sacred quarry?" she said, her eyes wide. "That's where you're taking me? Striped Eagle, what *is* this sacred quarry?"

"You will soon see," Striped Eagle said, dropping his hand away from her. His brow furrowed into a deeper frown. "Striped Eagle has never shown the quarry to any white man or woman before. I have told you this. Do you not see the importance in this, my *Nee-bin-gee-zis*?"

Brenda avoided his steady stare by looking away from him. "Yes, I recall," she murmured. "And I *do* feel honored. But do I deserve such an honor?"

Her gaze quickly returned to him, her insides flushing hot as her eyes swept over him, seeing his broad, muscled shoulders, his proud, straight back, the tilt of his chin. His handsomeness always sent a rapturous glow through her, his dark eyes hypnotizing as they burned into hers.

"Summer Sun, only you truly know the answer to that question," Striped Eagle said dryly. He flicked his reins and spurred his steed a few yards ahead, the bright colors of his headband weaving an almost hypnotic pattern in the air as he rose and fell in rhythm with his stallion.

Brenda clutched her reins fiercely and nudged her knees into the gelding's sides, hurrying on after Striped Eagle, wondering if he had read her thoughts of the coming morning. He did seem to have skills that no white man had. So often, even, his eyes seemed to penetrate clearly into her soul . . .

White sycamore branches and fuzzy-looking, pale flower catkins of cottonwoods broke the dense green foliage of the towering hardwood forest. Distant tanagers and jays flickered like orange and blue sparks against the backdrop of green.

And then, suddenly, before Brenda lay an open meadow bordering a ring of thicket and tall trees, its long grass waving warm and ruddy under the blazing sky.

Striped Eagle reined in his horse, turning to wait for Brenda, his breechcloth skipping in the breeze, his skin a smooth bronze shining beneath the sun. His eyes were smoldering as he watched her so skillfully ride the gelding, the pink of her face, the blue of her eyes touching his heart, making it race. He knew her so well, or did he? She was a woman of many moods. He had to wonder if all white women were as complex. Or was it only his woman? She was special in so many ways . . .

Brenda saw the look in Striped Eagle's eyes as he watched her approach. Why did he always have to study her so closely? It was as though each time he did he turned another page of a book, learning more and more about her the more that he read.

Would she ever have the abilities to study and know him as well?

Smiling softly, she reined her horse next to his. "Are we about there?" she murmured, beads of sweat again pearling on her brow.

The softness of the buckskin dress clung to her body, revealing all her curves; the moccasins on her feet were still damp from her time in the river when she had joined in to loosen the tree limbs from the dam. She knew that if she looked down at the dress she would see many dirt smudges. She knew that she must even have such smudges on her face. But of course Striped Eagle was looking past such things. He most surely was seeing her as he desired her. She could tell by the flame in his eyes . . .

"You are anxious?" Striped Eagle asked, a slow smile lifting his lips.

Brenda didn't want to reveal the true cause of her anxiousness, that she mainly wanted to stop and rest. Yet her curiosity to see the sacred quarry increased with each added moment. Why would a quarry be sacred to the Ojibwa?

But she was aware of how so many of their daily activities centered around a belief in spiritual beings. This was a part of the Indian culture she knew she could never understand as surely as Striped Eagle wouldn't understand her own beliefs . . . her belief in one God who ruled over all.

"Yes. I'm anxious," she said, flicking perspiration from her brow with the sweep of a hand. "And I appreciate you trusting me so much, Striped Eagle. I truly do."

"One day my woman will know all reasons behind everything the Ojibwa do," he said thickly. He gestured with a hand. "*Mah-bee-szhon*. Come. I will now show you."

Her gelding fell into step beside Striped Eagle's stallion, and Brenda's eyes searched all about her, watching for any signs of the quarry.

And then, suddenly, they were there, looking down into a great, wide pit, its walls like the crumbling ruins of an ancient, moated castle, red walls standing sentinel over a rugged piece of landscape.

Gasping, Brenda looked at the cliffs and stones covered with ancient carvings. At its base, under overhanging sycamores, maples, and walnuts, a deer stood on the banks of the lazy waters of a creek; a turkey vulture soared overhead. Deep pits had been dug into the ground, supported on all sides by timber.

"What *is* this place?" she asked, inching her gelding

closer to the edge of the quarry, her eyes again taking in the redness of the stone, the hieroglyphics carved onto its surface, the accumulation of many tribes over many years.

It was impressive, to the point where even Brenda could feel an eeriness about her, as though spirits were looking down upon her and Striped Eagle. For the first time she couldn't help but feel tugged into believing in Striped Eagle's spirits, for she was silently praying that they approved of her presence!

"This is the sacred quarry I told you about," Striped Eagle said simply. "It is from this quarry that the Ojibwa remove the red pipestone for making peace pipes. The pipe is the Ojibwa's 'Secret to Happiness.' It is a 'good heart maker.' With the pipe the Ojibwa seals his councils. No white man has been allowed to reach this area. The stone is sacred, given to our people by the Great Spirit, Wenebojo."

Brenda's eyes measured the circumference of the quarry's opening. "It is so huge," she said. "It's so . . . lovely, Striped Eagle. The carvings. What do they say?"

"It is the story of the beginning of time," Striped Eagle said, squaring his shoulders. "My people read this like you read this thing that you call Bible."

Brenda jerked her head toward Striped Eagle. "You know of the Bible?" she gasped. "Striped Eagle, you know so much of the white man's culture. Sometimes I'm amazed at how much you know."

Brenda leaned toward Striped Eagle. "Tell me more about the quarry," she said, squinting her eyes against the slanting rays of the sun. "That is, if you don't mind. I would like to learn of your ways, as you have learned of the ways of the white people."

"The quarry has a spirit of its own and sometimes speaks with a voice of thunder," Striped Eagle said, happy that she was showing a sincere interest in his beliefs. "Striped Eagle and the Ojibwa fear that the white man might try to take the quarry away from us, steal our

precious pipestone. This is why no white man must ever
know of its existence. But if they did, the voice of thunder
would frighten them away."

"Voice of thunder?" Brenda asked. "What do you
mean?"

"The spirits. When angered, they are the voices," Striped
Eagle said, his eyes stormy.

"You feel so strongly, yet you trust to bring me *here*?"
Brenda said softly, the trust he felt for her again tugging
her consciousness. If he knew what she had planned—that
she would again be among the white man, most probably
the next day—he would curse the word *trust*, even omit it
from his vocabulary.

"Your trust has been earned," Striped Eagle said, swinging his horse around, headed away from the quarry. "And
now we must go." His gaze shifted upward, seeing the
angle of the sun. "The sun is moving quickly this day.
Before the moon replaces the sun in the sky, I wish to
share another private place of mine with you, Summer
Sun."

"Oh? Is it a place also sacred to you?" Brenda said,
reining her horse around, urging it into a trot alongside
Striped Eagle's.

Striped Eagle's eyes twinkled as he looked over at
Brenda. "Before the moon silvers the trees it will be
sacred to both you *and* me." He chuckled. "It will be a
place that will remain special inside our hearts, my lovely
woman."

Brenda felt a rush of warmth radiate upward, only imagining what he now had on his mind. The look in his eyes,
the way his gaze was now sweeping over her, made her
blush. She could already feel the pressure of his body
against hers, and the thought was welcome . . .

In silence, Brenda and Striped Eagle traveled over a
meadow dotted with wild daisies, the buzz of bees a low
hum in the air. And then they reentered the denseness of

the forest, ducking to avoid low tree limbs, through air tinged with a musky fragrance.

Again Brenda was becoming aware of her achy bones, her legs seemingly glued to the horse's back as she swayed with its every hoofbeat against the brown pine needles of the forest floor.

"Striped Eagle, I'm not sure I can continue much farther," Brenda sighed, hating to show any signs of weakness. "And we still have to travel back to the village this day. How can I? Already my bottom feels numb from the long ride." She placed a hand to her face and leaned her cheek into it. "I need to *rest*."

"We don't have much farther to go," he said, moving steadily onward. "And then you will have your required rest."

His amused look and the pleasant gleam in his eyes spoke of something besides rest. It bespoke unleashed passion. Brenda wasn't sure if she could return such passion this time. How could her leg muscles even relax to invite him atop her . . . ?

Her face turned crimson as she realized where her thoughts always seemed to take her while in this handsome Indian's presence. Had she no shame? Oh, what would her papa think if he knew what an immoral daughter he had raised!

The passing remembrance of her father made her sit more upright on the horse and her fingers tighten on the reins. Somehow . . . someday . . . she *would* get her revenge! She knew not how . . . but in time . . . she *would*!

The splashing of water ahead drew Brenda's thoughts back to the present. She gave Striped Eagle a questioning stare, then peered through the cover of trees to see a great waterfall and its silver splash of water as it tumbled effervescently over boulders of rock downward. Mountains of wild pink roses pressed against the outline of the waterfall. As if by magic, pines sprang monstrous and green from the very sides of the boulders!

"We are almost there," Striped Eagle said, giving Brenda a slow smile. "It is a place I call paradise."

Brenda was more amazed the closer they moved to the splash of water. And when they reached the banks that overlooked the transparent water below, she found the sight dizzying in its utter loveliness. The lake appeared translucent and deep, fish swimming like sunbeams beneath its surface. Moss agate, so called because of the moss at the heart of the stone, rolled up and down with the water.

Small dogtooth violets, pale-blue bird's foot, moccasin flowers, and trailing arbutus decorated the ground about them. And along the shore a covey of partridges were feeding on pigeon berries, filling their crops until their breasts looked lopsided.

Then, suddenly, the partridges sensed the presence of humans, rising on a great whirring of wings, fast and low, disappearing into the tall pines.

Brenda felt Striped Eagle's eyes on her, drawing her to turn to meet his steady gaze. As though under a spell she watched as he dismounted his stallion and went to her, lifting her from her gelding, pulling her into his embrace.

His lips were demanding on hers as he locked his fingers together behind her neck and held her fixed in place. Breathless, feeling the usual spin inside her head that his kisses always caused, Brenda leaned into his taut body, and at once became aware of the manhood pressed into her abdomen where her satiny-soft dress acted as a flimsy shield.

Feverish, Brenda let her hands rove over the tightness of his rippled shoulder muscles, then lower, down his back, where his breechcloth was a barrier between her searching hands and the sleek outline of his buttocks.

Daringly, her fingers crept inside the breechcloth. She became drunk with the feel of him, the tightness of his curved buttocks. The smell of him was a smoky sweet-ness, musky to the taste as he continued to kiss her with passion's fire.

And then Striped Eagle's lips left Brenda's and his fingers worked to peel the buckskin dress from her shoulders.

"Striped Eagle, here . . . ?" Brenda said in a whisper, already feeling the touch of the breeze on the bare tips of her breasts.

Her eyes darted about her, again taking in the steep valley slope where the land plunged suddenly away into the lake below. A small bird hung like a star overhead. On the opposite side of the waterfall nothing moved, only wind-blown ripples chasing through the trees.

"We are quite *gee-nay-ta*," Striped Eagle said huskily. "We are alone except for the forest animals, birds, and the spirits. None will disturb our loveplay, Summer Sun."

"But what if one of your braves would pass by here on his way to the quarry?" Brenda persisted, yet quivering when Striped Eagle leaned a kiss to the taut tip of her exposed breast while his hands continued to slip the dress down over her hips.

"Do not worry so. This is a secret place of mine," Striped Eagle said. "I always swim in peace. So shall *we*."

Brenda's breath caught in her throat, again looking down at the lake, quite a distance below where she and Striped Eagle now stood. "But *how*?" she murmured. "The water is . . . is too far down below. Striped Eagle—"

Striped Eagle placed a finger to her lips, sealing them of further words. "Your father taught you the skills of riding a horse," he said softly. "So I am sure he also taught you the skills of swimming. When my canoe tipped you into the water on your morning escape from my village of Ojibwa, you had to swim to safety, did you not?"

"Yes . . ." she murmured.

"Then so shall you swim this day with me, Summer

Sun," he said simply, easing her dress down and away from her. One by one he lifted her feet and removed her moccasins.

"But, Striped Eagle, it is so far . . ." Brenda persisted, pleading with her eyes.

Striped Eagle ignored her pleas, instead unbraided her hair. When it cascaded free and long down her back, the sun shone onto it, smoldering like trapped fire.

"Now we shall dive together into the river," Striped Eagle said, stepping out of his breechcloth and then his moccasins. In one swift movement he had his headband removed and placed aside, then had Brenda's hand clasped in his as he guided her to the very edge of the cliff.

Brenda's heart pounded out her fear as it thudded against her ribs. Her eyes were wide as she looked downward along the waterfall splashing into the lake below.

She looked up into Striped Eagle's eyes. "But, Striped Eagle, I doubt if I *can* swim if I survive the plunge," she said, gulping hard. "I am so tired from the long, tedious ride. I don't think I am up to it—"

"You dive when I dive," he said flatly. "You will see how the water soon fades the ache in your bones. It is warm, as though warmed over the coals of my firespace. It will caress you, and then I will further teach you ways of making love."

Brenda looked over her shoulder at the grazing horses and then back at Striped Eagle. "But once we dive into the lake how can we return here?" she persisted. "Striped Eagle, it is so *far*. Striped Eagle—"

"You will dive. *Now*," Striped Eagle said, arching his back to fall into a graceful dive.

Brenda momentarily watched as he moved gracefully downward. Knowing that she must follow his lead, Brenda ducked her head, placed her hands together over her head, and leaned forward. Soon she felt the wind brushing against her face as she also plummeted downward.

Thirteen

The plunge into the water was gentle, as though the water itself had been a soft bed of feathers, cradling Brenda. Swept softly downward to the inner depths of this gentleness, Brenda opened her eyes and saw Striped Eagle swimming toward her through the clear opalescence of the water. His body was a sleek copper streak, his eyes inviting dark pools.

Straightening her body, Brenda began swimming toward Striped Eagle, their fingers soon intertwining. Brenda's body felt weightless, and her soreness was forgotten as if dissolved in the water.

Yet her mind wasn't as peaceful, for in it she was already experiencing the searing, scorching flames he usually ignited, setting her on fire with passion and love that he so genuinely offered.

Lips sought lips, body sought body as Striped Eagle drew Brenda into his embrace. As he kissed her he guided her up to the water's surface, then locked his arms about her as he drew the soft crests of her breasts against his chest.

''My love . . .'' Brenda whispered, wrapping a leg

about him, now swimming alongside him as though they were one being in body and in soul.

Striped Eagle's fingers twined through her hair, urging her mouth to his. "Talk will come later, my Summer Sun," he said thickly. "For now just let me love you . . . fully love you."

The water was warm, fueled by the radiant beams from the pulsing sun, the touch of Striped Eagle's lips a heated flame as he cupped one of Brenda's breasts and eased his lips over it, sucking it to a hard point.

Brenda had no need to tread water for Striped Eagle was doing it for them both, skillfully holding her while swimming with her, taking her to a shallower spot of the pool where he could stand on the soft, sandy bottom. Then he lifted her, positioning her legs about his waist, and in one stroke slipped his hardness up inside of her.

Brenda trembled in ecstasy, her eyes closed, marveling at how he so masterfully filled her. And when he began his eager thrusts, she threw her head back and closed her eyes, forgetting everything but the rapture she was again sharing with the man she loved. She wouldn't think about when and why she would leave him. There was only now . . . only now . . .

Her hands clung to his sinewy shoulders. She lifted her hips with each of his movements inside her, helping him to reach farther into her. His lips pressed a kiss at the hollow of her throat; his fingers sought and found her breasts, molding them, his thumbs circling the tender nipples, teasing them into ever harder peaks.

Consumed by her need of him, Brenda let her gaze meet Striped Eagle's eyes, dark and stormy as they scrutinized her. Their lips were drawn together in a sultry kiss, their tongues dancing together, fanning the flames to a scorching intensity.

"I so love you," Brenda murmured, moving her lips to

the sleek copper of his cheek. She sent passionate kisses
along his jawline, his high cheekbones, his eyes, closing
them.

And then Striped Eagle returned the tender kisses as he
first kissed the lobes of her ears, the tiny tip of her nose,
and the delicate line of her cheekbones, all the while
keeping a steady rhythm of strokes inside her.

"My woman," he murmured huskily. "Forever my
woman . . ."

The sun was becoming softer in its touch as it lowered
behind the tall pines. The waterfall's splash became cooler,
the songs of the birds softening as they settled in their
nests for the evening.

But Striped Eagle and Brenda were oblivious to anything but the rapturous pleasure of the joining of their
bodies. They rocked and swayed together in the water,
their skin gleaming with wetness. Their low moans of
delight were echoing from shore to shore.

As Brenda felt the pleasure building, she writhed in
response and Striped Eagle increased his thrusts. She clung
to his rock hardness and gave herself up to the rapture, her
body quaking with the tremors as the desire swelled and
surfaced, scalding her all over with an exquisite wildfire.

Panting, now descending from her pinnacle of pleasure,
Brenda placed her head on Striped Eagle's shoulder, waiting for him to reach his own release. She kissed his neck,
ran her fingernails up and down his back, smiled when she
felt his body stiffen, knowing that his release was also
near.

Striped Eagle was blinded with passion's fire. He held
Brenda as though in a vise as he plunged himself harder
inside her, feeling her silken softness encasing his hardness in a bondage he both relished and strained against.

His muscles corded, his breathing hard, he lay his head
upon Brenda's breast and emitted a groan as he trembled
in his own intense pleasure's abandon . . .

And then the world was silent except for the splashing of the waterfall, the breeze having fallen with the dusk, leaving not so much as a sigh among the trees. The moon seemed drawn toward the earth, brushing long shadows on everything it touched.

Striped Eagle eased Brenda away from him. He framed her face with his hands and drew her lips to his and softly kissed her.

And then he swept her fully into his arms and carried her to the mossy banks of the shore and spread her out on her back, where he leaned down over her and began worshiping her with the soft touch of his lips.

Brenda closed her eyes, barely breathing, feeling as though she surely must have died and was now in heaven, for never had she felt so at peace with herself, with the world. Striped Eagle's lips were causing her to become languorous, his hands weaving passion into her heart all over again. They had just *been* to heaven and back. Could they again . . . so soon . . . ?

Striped Eagle's fingers began burning a path across Brenda's flesh, beginning at the tiny taper of her neck, moving lower . . . lower . . . lower. They traced the outlines of her breasts while his tongue flicked across one stiffened nipple and then the other, drawing a sensuous, lazy moan from somewhere deep inside Brenda as she slowly moved her head back and forth on the soft pillow of moss.

Striped Eagle's fingers moved stealthily lower, drawing circles on her abdomen, causing her skin to ripple from the pleasure. And when his tongue followed the path of his fingers, intermixed with warm kisses, Brenda clenched her own fingers into tight fists, hardly able to stand the desire building inside her. He had ways to arouse her that she never knew existed—she would soon surely burst into a million pieces of sunshine if he continued!

Striped Eagle's lips and fingers moved still lower. He caressed her inner thighs and then nudged her legs apart and delicately placed a kiss at the core of her womanhood, causing Brenda's eyes to fly wide open to look down at him, stunned. But as his tongue flicked along her flesh there, causing a mindlessness to grab hold, she trembled with this new way of receiving pleasure and again closed her eyes in joy.

Striped Eagle's heart pounded against his ribs, thinking it could surely be heard, like a drum beating in rhythm with dancers at a celebration. But being with her in such a way was causing him to again lose control of what he had always prided himself on: the power to give pleasure while he restrained himself. At times this was necessary. But now? He felt powerless in this white woman's presence, as though *she* had the power to rule *him* and his every need and desire. With her, everything was different! Surely it was because he truly loved her; he had never felt the same emotions before with any other woman. But she was clearly made for this pleasure, not for worry. He was going to enjoy . . . fully enjoy . . .

Placing his hands beneath the softness of her buttocks he lifted her closer to his lips. Kissing her, worshiping her in such a way, he could feel her body quake. He could hear her moan. He, too, moaned, knowing that he was nearing the point of no return.

One last time he sucked her womanhood between his teeth, gently nipping it, then rose above her, holding her face between his hands, and plunged his hardness inside her. At first his strokes were slow, then they increased in speed, causing beads of pearly sweat to shine on his brow.

He smiled down at Brenda, seeing the glassy haze in her eyes as she smiled back at him. "*Nee-bin-gee-zis,*" he said huskily. "My Summer Sun. My love."

His lips bore down upon hers in a scorching kiss, his

lean, sinewy buttocks moving, his hands burning her flesh as he kneaded her breasts.

And then he wrapped his arms about her and drew her against his hard body in a torrid embrace, plunging harder into her, their moans fusing as they again were consumed by the fires of their passion . . .

Still trembling, still breathless, Brenda clung to Striped Eagle as he buried his face in her cleavage, breathing hard. Her heart still pounded, yet a great calm was filling her. She knew peace only in the arms of her loved one. Was vengeance even all that important to her? Wasn't Striped Eagle the total of her being now?

Yet flashes of remembrance of that fateful night when the evil major had taken her loved ones' lives again plagued her. All she had to do was close her eyes to see the terrible look on her brother's face the very moment he had been shot. She could still even hear the screams of her mother . . . the raging gunfire exploding all about her as her mother and father crumpled to the floor . . . .

Turning her face away, a soft sob broke from her lips, reaching Striped Eagle's ears. He rose away from her, looking down at the tears streaking her cheeks, the moonlight now filling the heavens and all that it reached beneath it, silvering the tears as they continued to roll from Brenda's eyes.

Striped Eagle placed a hand to the side of Brenda's face that was turned away from him and urged her to look at him. "Why do you cry?" he asked thickly. "Did I love you too fiercely? Summer Sun, I loved you with all feelings powerful *for* you. If I hurt you, I am sorry."

Brenda sniffled, seeing so much written on his face, most of which was the love he spoke so openly to her. She reached out a hand and softly touched his cheek. "No. You did not hurt me, Striped Eagle," she murmured. "It is as before. When I am feeling content . . . peaceful . . .

when I think I am forgetting that horrible night of not so long ago, the remembrances are again there, hurting me so deeply I cannot refrain from crying.''

She leaned up and laced her arms about his neck, pressing her cheek against his. "I am sorry if I ruined the moment for you." She sighed. "I just can't seem to help these feelings that rob me of my moments with you. It is still all so fresh in my mind."

A low sob tore from her throat, causing her body to shake. "I so miss them, Striped Eagle," she cried softly. "Even with you, loving you so much, I miss them. Will it ever get easier, this missing them?"

Striped Eagle smoothed his fingers through her hair, then caressed her back. "This love for family is only right," he said softly. "I, too, love mine as much. My sister and my father are most important to me. But one day, *ay-uh*, the burden on your heart will lessen. You will see, my Summer Sun. You will see. Just let me help you along the way. Let my love for you help erase the hurt, the torment you are feeling because of your loss."

His lips found hers in a gentle kiss, his hands cupping her breasts. Again he felt his need for her rising.

Spreading her on the soft moss he again let his lips worship her body, hearing her intake of breath when his tongue touched her most sensitive spots. His tongue flicked at her breasts, his fingers entered her from below, feeling the tight confines of her love canal, feeling it pulsing warmly against his fingers as she cried out as she reached another pinnacle of release.

But knowing that he must prove to himself that he still had power over his feelings, he leaned away from her, taking her hand, urging her to her feet before him.

"We must return to my village of Ojibwa," he said hoarsely. "My father returns on the morrow. I will proudly present my woman to my father."

Brenda was awed by how he had again caused her to

experience a moment of bliss; she felt almost insatiable while with him. Yet his mention of his father sobered her much too quickly. Would it bring shame upon Striped Eagle if she again ran away from him, especially if he was planning to introduce her to his father?

And why *was* he anxious to introduce her? She was remembering Morning Flower's words about how their father felt about Striped Eagle marrying out of the Ojibwa tribe of Indians. No white woman would be welcome! Surely Striped Eagle understood this. Yet was his love for her so strong he would even defy his chieftain father?

Feeling cornered, not wanting to hurt Striped Eagle, she lowered her eyes, not knowing how she could do this to him. But she must . . .

"Summer Sun?" Striped Eagle said, sensing her suddenly distant attitude. "Do you not wish to have council with my father? Do you not wish to be shown off as my future wife?"

Brenda's gaze flew upward. The night seemed to have been trapped in Striped Eagle's dark eyes, so intensely dark were they.

"Your . . . wife . . . ?" she murmured, pretending she hadn't already known of his intentions. Oh, how could she turn her back on him . . . on what he was offering her? The thought of a lifetime with him and what they shared together filled her heart.

But to live a life as an Indian . . . ? It would be hard enough without the hate of his father and sister to contend with! And *children*, should they have any—would it be fair to bring children into the world when a child of their union could be branded a half-breed? And Brenda still had to avenge her family's deaths. She could only accomplish this on her own. She knew this. Oh, how she knew this!

Striped Eagle wove his fingers through her hair, his gaze traveling over her, touching her all over. *"Wi-yee-bah,"* he whispered. "Soon you will be my wife."

Again his eyes locked on hers. *"Gee-zah-gi-ee-nay?"* he said hoarsely. "Do you truly love me? You will be my wife, won't you? We will bring to my village of Ojibwa a celebration of celebrations. My love, there will never be such a celebration again. My people . . . my father's people . . . will love you."

Brenda's eyes squinted. "Striped Eagle, you know that I love you," she said softly. "But your culture and mine are so . . . so different. Surely it wouldn't work."

Striped Eagle's brow furrowed in a deep frown. He clutched her shoulders. "We will make it work," he said flatly. His eyes moved to the sky, then back to Brenda. "The moon now silvers a path to my village. *Mah-bee-szhon.* Come. Let us now go."

Recalling the ache in her bones after the long journey to the dam and then the quarry, Brenda winced with the realization that she had the same journey to make again without having had enough rest. This time given her had been spent in loving, this, too, draining her of her energies.

Her gaze moved to the waterfall and then the cliff from which she had made her half-hearted dive. She turned questioning eyes to Striped Eagle, then her breath was stolen from her when he suddenly drew her fully up into his arms and began carrying her up the incline until they reached the grazing horses.

When Striped Eagle placed Brenda on her feet and she began dressing, she again questioned him with her eyes, unashamed to see him standing nude before her, now drawing on his breechcloth. She hated to admit that she felt she couldn't make the journey again so soon. He looked to her to be strong, to be venturesome. Yet she truly doubted if she could stay on the horse again for such a lengthy time as that required to return to his village.

"Striped Eagle, I just can't," she blurted, the doeskin

dress fluttering down over her hips as she drew it over her head.

Striped Eagle placed his headband on his head, straightening his hair to lay neatly beneath it. "What do you mean? What do you talk about when you say you can't?" he said, taking a step toward her. He placed his hands on his hips. "You refuse to become my wife? Is that what you are saying? Do I have to *force* you, Summer Sun?"

Hearing the flatness in his tone of voice and his use of the word "force," Brenda's heart fluttered. She straightened her shoulders and lifted her chin, placing her hands on her hips.

"So you would force me to become your wife, would you?" she snapped angrily. "Striped Eagle, I thought you were a man of gentle ways. You even once told me that you never force a woman. Would you now? I don't think it would be all that easy to make me become your wife if I wouldn't want to."

Hearing her anger, seeing the flash of her eyes, took Striped Eagle aback. He never expected her to continue defying him. His jaw tightened. He turned his back to her, folding his arms across his chest, looking down at the glaze of water below him. No woman should be allowed to defy Striped Eagle, the next chief in line of the White Bear band of Ojibwa.

Yet she was right! He would never force her. When they loved . . . when they became man and wife . . . it would have to be by mutual agreement. If she wished to turn her back on him, he would let her go. Perhaps he had been wrong to let his heart be fooled by her!

Seeing the hurt on his face and deep in his eyes before he turned away from her, Brenda's anger wavered, her heart leading her to softly touch the corded muscles of his shoulder.

"I'm sorry," she murmured. "Lord, Striped Eagle, I'm

sorry. I don't want to hurt you. I . . . love you. I love you more than life itself. Please don't be angry with me.''

Striped Eagle turned on a heel, his eyes devouring her, again seeing the silvery shine of tears in her eyes. He drew her into his embrace, snuggling his nose into the depths of her hair. ''Then what is it that you don't wish to do?'' he said thickly.

''I was speaking of having to travel back to your village,'' she murmured, pressing her cheek against his chest. ''I don't think I can, Striped Eagle. It is so far. I'm not sure if I have the strength.''

''You will be using my strength,'' Striped Eagle said, smiling down at her as he leaned away from her. He kissed the tip of her nose. ''You will ride on my horse with me. You will sleep in my arms as we travel back to the village of Ojibwa.''

Brenda's eyes widened. ''Sleep . . . in your arms?'' she said with a shallow gasp. She smiled crookedly. ''Striped Eagle, I—''

Striped Eagle placed a forefinger to her lips, sealing them of further words. ''Do as I say, Summer Sun. I, too, see the importance of not tiring you. You must be fresh to meet with my father. I want him to see you in your full radiant loveliness.''

He nodded toward her leggings and moccasins. ''Fully dress. Then we shall go,'' he said, fitting his feet into his own moccasins.

Brenda did as he bade, mesmerized by his tenderness, his true concern for her welfare. And after she was fully clothed and he had led the two horses toward her, she went to him and let him lift her onto his proud steed. She watched as he tied the reins of the horse she had traveled on to his own, then moved onto the horse behind her.

''Move into my arms. Sleep against my chest,'' Striped Eagle said, positioning her on his lap, his arm anchoring her there. ''Sleep, my love . . .''

Brenda snuggled, feeling perfectly content. She was only half aware of the horse's movements as it cantered away from the waterfall. She closed her eyes and sighed, trying once more to figure out a way to leave Striped Eagle without hurting him. Surely there was a way . . .

Fourteen

In a daze, hardly remembering the long night spent on Striped Eagle's proud steed cradled in Striped Eagle's arms, riding in the moon-bright air, Brenda was now in Striped Eagle's wigwam, preparing herself for the meeting with his father.

Having been back at Striped Eagle's village for only a short time, Brenda had not been given the opportunity needed for her escape. Now she had another full day to wait. She feared this waiting would only continue to complicate matters, yet she had no choice but to accept fate as it was handed to her. Was it her destiny to spend forever with Striped Eagle and his people? After today, how would she feel about her planned escape? Would she even *want* to?

Her skin tingled where Striped Eagle's fingers grazed her naked back as he proudly plaited her hair in a braid, to hang sleek and long down her shoulders. If she closed her eyes she could still feel his lips on her body, kissing her so boldly where even now she pulsed with the need of him. He had awakened in her such delicious feelings, she hungered for them both day and night. Could she truly exist without him and his skills at pleasuring her?

She was suddenly gripped with the fear that she acted almost like a whore, one whose life was measured by how many men she could bed and take payment for in one day.

But she calmed herself, knowing that when she was with Striped Eagle in such a sensuous way it was not wrong. They loved one another. Their love was pure . . . decent. And to think that she had to leave such a love behind.

Oh, she must be mad!

Yet there *was* his family and how they disapproved of her. She couldn't win, no matter what she did!

"Summer Sun, you are deep in thought," Striped Eagle said, turning her to face him. He tilted her chin upward with the light touch of his forefinger. "Did the journey tire you? Did you not sleep cozily enough in my arms?"

Brenda's eyes wavered beneath his close scrutiny. She couldn't reveal her tumultuous feelings. He would never understand. Never!

"It is not every day a woman is introduced to a powerful Ojibwa chief," she murmured, her face flushing at the thought. "And he is not only a powerful Indian chief, he is also your *father*," she blurted, easing away from Striped Eagle to drop to her knees before the fire in the firespace.

Her doeskin dress had been replaced by another, sparkling clean, white as snow, resplendent with colorful beads in designs of the rainbow about the low neckline and the hem of the skirt. Fringed leggings fit her tapered legs snugly and new moccasins soft as silk clung to her feet.

Her cheeks shone cherry red from berry-juice face paint; silver bracelets jangled on her arms. She felt as though she must look lovely. She could see images of this loveliness in the way Striped Eagle had looked at her.

Yet she could not shake her uneasiness, feeling as though she was tricking Striped Eagle, for she was going to do his bidding . . . meet his father . . . but, shortly after that, she was going to sneak away from his wigwam like a thief in the night.

Yes. She felt like a thief, stealing first Striped Eagle's heart, and then his pride!

She bit her lower lip in frustration, then shivered with ecstasy as Striped Eagle encircled her waist and urged her back to her feet and into his embrace.

"My father is a kind man," Striped Eagle murmured, his eyes heavy-laden with emotion as he gazed down at her face, studying each and every feature, as he had done so many times before. Ah, how her blue eyes touched his heart! How the flame of her hair ignited his desire! Without her, it would be no life at all.

Brenda set her hand to his face and cupped his cheek. "If he is like you, *ay-uh,* my love, he is gentle," she said softly. "*Ay-uh,* so gentle."

Striped Eagle's eyes took on a sparkle. His lips curved into an eager smile. "My Summer Sun has spoken in Ojibwa," he said proudly. "You remembered what I taught you. You said 'yes' in *Ojibwa.* Striped Eagle proud."

Brenda's face colored. She lowered her eyes. "Yes. I remembered." She laughed, a soft laugh that touched Striped Eagle as though she had kissed him.

"Your love is true. It is true," Striped Eagle said, crushing his lips down upon hers, kissing her hard and long, then drawing away from her and composing himself. He tilted his chin, reached to straighten his headband, and checked to see if his eagle feather was in place.

"It is time to go," he said gruffly. "My father must not be made to wait."

Brenda's insides quivered with fear. It had been easy to become drawn into liking Striped Eagle . . . even into loving him. He had a way about him that had made it impossible not to. Surely his father couldn't be the same. How could any other Indian equal Striped Eagle in gentleness and kindness? Wasn't he this way toward her because he had fallen in love with her? His father would probably *hate* her! There had been too much evidence that no white woman would ever be accepted into the tribe as a wife to the next chief in line. Morning Flower had proved this in her behavior toward Brenda.

Brenda could feel it now . . . the way her insides had turned cold beneath Morning Flower's look of hate . . . mistrust. And wasn't Brenda going to be displayed to Chief Growling Bear as a future wife? She couldn't explain to the chief that no real promises had been made to Striped Eagle. It would disgrace Striped Eagle in his father's eyes.

Oh, how trapped she felt! She was trapped between loving and wanting Striped Eagle and the fear of this very desire!

Her knees rubbery weak, Brenda nodded a silent thank-you to Striped Eagle as he lifted the entrance flap. Stepping outside, she again entered the world of the Ojibwa. Through the air an insectival hum was heard as gaily clad figures darted about the village, women bent upon their daily tasks. Some carried great loads of wood on their backs, bringing them into the camp from the forest. Some carried water from the river while others were cooking over the outdoor fires.

Still others were sitting about on colorful blankets before the outdoor fires working on their beadwork of a most bewitching order, meanwhile watching their papooses, fastened completely in their wooden, beaded-covered cradles with only their heads protruding. The cradles were hung from a lodge pole or the bough of a tree, rattles and bells playing in the breeze for the babys' amusement.

A noisy, gleeful group of children were playing with their dolls and dogs while elderly men were sitting about puffing on their pipes. Their squinted, fading eyes followed Brenda and Striped Eagle as they made their way toward the centermost point in the village, where the chief's wigwam stood in its magnificence, larger and greater than all other wigwams encircling it.

In the morning sunlight the bright paintings on the chief's wigwam seemed to come to life, as though the birds should suddenly begin flapping their great wings to fly from the sides of the wigwam. The summer sun painted in brilliant golds seemed to pulsate and the blues of the sky were so real one would expect a sudden puff of a cloud to skip across its horizon.

But Brenda's focus was on something else. Morning Flower had stepped quickly up to the chief's wigwam and was glaring first at Striped Eagle and then at Brenda, her arms folded across her chest. Brenda was again aware of Morning Flower's loveliness, this day attired in a beautiful doeskin dress with lovely beads carved out of bone and painted with dyes hanging gracefully at her slender neck, her breasts magnificently filling out the dress where it fell to reveal their top curves.

Her long, braided black hair was blowing back from her shoulders and the silver bracelets at her wrists chimed rhythmically in the wind. Her beaded headband and necklaces snatched the reflection of the flames from an outdoor fire close by.

But the scowl across Morning Flower's face detracted from her exquisite facial features, and Brenda knew why she was angry. She dreaded even more than before having to enter the chief's wigwam.

Striped Eagle placed an arm about Brenda's waist as they stopped only a few footsteps away from Morning Flower and where she stood blocking the entrance flap which led inside Chief Growling Bear's wigwam.

"My sister, do you also have business with father this morning?" he said, smiling softly down at her. "And if you do, is it that which troubles you? Your lovely face is void of a smile, *Gee-gee-shayb-wah-bee-go-neens*. Why is that?"

"Morning Flower is not here for private conference with father. I am here for *you*, my brother," she said flatly. "Morning Flower not mind giving dresses to white woman but I mind white woman taking *you*, Striped Eagle. The white woman is why I am here. *You* are why I am here. Surely you are not serious about introducing her to father. You know his feelings, Striped Eagle. You know he has not been very well. I see his strength fading as each day passes. The voyage with the Saint Croix band of the Chippewa has weakened him. Do you also wish to add to this weakness by angering him? Why do you insist on annoying him with such foolishness as this white woman?"

Striped Eagle's eyes blazed angrily at Morning Flower. His jaw tightened. His words came out in a low hiss. "My sister, when did you choose to become my keeper?" he said, doubling a fist at his side. "Now step aside. I wish to pass. So shall Summer Sun."

"You do not listen with your heart this morning, big brother," Morning Flower said, her shoulders squaring. "Does this white woman blind you to what is important to the Ojibwa? Has she stolen your senses as well as your heart?"

"It is none of your concern," Striped Eagle growled, staring into Morning Flower's face. "It is my decision what my future holds for me. If I feel I can rule the Ojibwa better with a white woman by my side, so be it."

He waved a hand in the air. "Step aside, Morning Flower," he grumbled. "You and your words are not needed here. Go back to your wigwam and do as is expected of you. Perform your duties as a woman of the Ojibwa."

Morning Flower's lips curved into a slight smile and her eyes shone a sudden wickedness in their depths. She took a step toward Brenda and softly touched her cheek. "And will this white woman perform the duties of the Ojibwa woman as well?'' she mocked. ''Will she carry wood from the forest? Will she plant the seeds? Will she even accept a child with the skin not of her coloring? Or will she disappoint you in all of these things, Striped Eagle, should she become your wife?''

Brenda flinched and stepped out of Morning Flower's reach, feeling as if she were on the auction block, being bidded for. She wanted to lash out at both Morning Flower *and* Striped Eagle, tell them that she was a person with her own decisions to make. No one would make them for her, not even Striped Eagle!

But she kept silent, again knowing that she might shame Striped Eagle should she be so outspoken in another's presence. She knew the importance of keeping his pride intact. He was this band of Indians' future chief. He must be treated as such.

Yet his sister most certainly lacked the respect due her brother! How could Striped Eagle let his sister be so openly disagreeable to him?

But, of course, Brenda understood. It was Striped Eagle's way—his gentleness, not wanting to injure anyone's feelings. And this being his only sister, he surely had learned long ago to tolerate, even accept her tongue!

Striped Eagle clasped Morning Flower's shoulders and gave her an easy shake. *''Mee-eewh!''* he spat. ''That is quite enough for this morning, my sister with the spiteful tongue. I could even ask the same with a spiteful tongue. You choose your mate. I choose mine. Now I do not wish to hear any more about it. Do you understand?''

''Mee-goo-ga-yay-ay-nayn-da-man,'' Morning Flower murmured, reaching a hand to Striped Eagle's cheek. ''It is only that I fear for the future of our people. I fear for *your* happiness.''

Striped Eagle's expression softened. He drew Morning Flower into his arms and gave her a gentle hug. ''Little one, you worry too much about too many things," he said thickly. "Why not let your brother do the worrying? Your heart would sing much prettier songs."

Morning Flower cast Brenda a half glance. "My heart sometimes gets out of tune," she said, trying to look apologetic. "But it is for only a moment."

Striped Eagle eased her out of his arms and looked toward Brenda, seeing how vulnerable she looked, having been forced to witness again a brother and sister bicker when she most surely was tied in knots over meeting his father. He took her hand and squeezed it.

"Let us now go and bid my father a cheerful good morning," he said softly. "I am sure he has been amused again by hearing his daughter and son and their usual playful banterings."

Brenda's eyebrows forked. She had found the banterings neither playful nor amusing, being herself the object of such amusement.

Morning Flower lifted the entrance flap and began to step inside but was stopped when Striped Eagle placed a hand on her wrist. "What do you think you are doing?" he growled.

"Is it not a time of family in our father's dwelling?" Morning Flower asked, her voice light and feathery, her eyes innocently wide.

Speaking down into Morning Flower's face, he said, "It is a time for my woman. She soon will be family."

Morning Flower's eyes and her attitude did not waver. "Father has just returned from his journey, you from *yours*," she said softly. "Morning Flower missed you *both*. Please let me be with you, Striped Eagle. I will say nothing, do nothing, to disturb you *or* your chosen woman. Please?"

Striped Eagle shook his head in silent annoyance. Yet he always found it hard to refuse his sister anything, remembering how she, too, had been raised without a true mother, having only him to confide in when she became troubled.

He gestured with a hand. *"Been-dee-gen,"* he said hoarsely. "My little one, enter and share." He gave her a quick frown. "But hold your tongue. If not, your brother will carry you—forcefully—from the wigwam. Do you understand?"

Morning Flower placed a hand to her mouth, giggling behind it. *"Ay-uh,"* she said. "You have done it before. You *are* a man of your word." She crossed her heart with her fingers. "I cross my heart, big brother. I will keep my opinions to myself. I will only sit by and enjoy being with you. You are gone so often from the village. When you are here, I hunger for your nearness."

"That is the way of sisters," Striped Eagle said, sighing. He smiled warmly at Brenda. Then his smile faded, seeing a wounded look in her tender blue eyes. He didn't have to ask why she looked so forlorn. He could only imagine that she was thinking of her small brother and how she had behaved sisterly toward him.

Placing an arm about her waist, feeling her sadness yet unable to lessen it for her, he led Brenda into the wigwam behind Morning Flower.

Green ash and juniper were stacked high on the fire to purify the air with their smoke. The flames from the fire reflected a golden glow upon a figure sitting cross-legged beside the firespace as though a solitary pine on a lonely hill crest. Chief Growling Bear had the bearing and dignity of a royal prince, a Roman cast to his face, the keen penetration of his eyes and the breadth of his shoulders displaying his dignity well.

His hair hung in long, loose black folds about his broad and unbending shoulders, a breechcloth his only mode of attire, his face as seamless as the leather of polished but worn boots. His legs were sinewy, his cheeks sunken; his mouth was very wide, thin-lipped, and severe. There was a gray cast to the copper skin of his face, the only evidence of his ill health.

A rest was made with supports like an easel. A lattice-work of slender willow rods passed down the front, which was covered by a long strip of moose hide. Against this the chief now rested, obviously occupying the place of honor in this, his private wigwam.

Filling his long pipe with tobacco from a beaded sack at his side, the chief's eyes followed Brenda as she was urged to sit down on a cushion of furs opposite him. Holding his long-stemmed calumet pipe decorated with duck feathers, he lit it with a coal from the fire, then placed the pipe to his mouth and puffed on it, drawing the rich, pungent tobacco smoke into his mouth.

His eyes remained flat as he carefully scrutinized Brenda, seeing in her a rare loveliness. Her eyes were crisply blue, as the waters of the White Bear River on a summer day; her hair seemed to have been colored by the sun, its red hue reminiscent of the sun itself.

His gaze swept lower, seeing how her breasts strained against the inside of the doeskin dress, calling up in him a long-lost twinge of desire he once felt as a young man.

Ay-uh, Chief Growling Bear could understand well his son's attraction for this woman. But the fact remained that she was *white*. How could Striped Eagle have let her so easily steal his heart? Hadn't Striped Eagle been taught the art of restraint well enough?

But, inside, Chief Growling Bear knew how easily the heart betrayed a man. It was this weakness of the heart that had caused many an Ojibwa brave to fall prey to the needs of the flesh . . .

Chief Growling Bear's thoughts strayed to the first time he had seen a white woman. It had been the first time the white woman had seen an Ojibwa. She had even dared to step up to him and rub her hands against the flesh of his arm to see if his beautiful copper coloring would rub off!

He had, in turn, touched the gold of her hair, wondering how the normal, lovely color of black had faded—he had never seen any other color hair!

It hadn't taken long for the white man and the Ojibwa to be able to laugh about this kind of misunderstanding, and Chief Growling Bear even now gloried in the fact that from his earliest days he had never fought the white man, his life having only seen a long series of conflicts with other Indian nations. Before the white man ever placed his foot upon Indian soil, Chief Growling Bear's days had been filled with the struggles of warding off the blows of hostile tribes who sought the women and the horses of his own people. This thing with his son seemed simple enough to cope with in comparison!

Passing his pipe over to Striped Eagle who was now sitting beside Brenda, Chief Growling Bear nodded. "And so we have council this morning with white woman in our midst?" he said, his speech sparkling and eloquent, his face wearing a mask of serenity. "Why *is* that, Striped Eagle?"

He paused and glanced over at Morning Flower who had seated herself beside the fire and had taken up her basketry. "And even you join the council this morning, Morning Flower?" he said, eyeing her closely, seeing how she glanced guardedly at the white woman occasionally.

Morning Flower's lashes lowered, almost humble in the presence of her powerful chieftain father. "*Ay-uh,*" she murmured. "You have been gone. Striped Eagle has been gone. I have missed you both."

Chief Growling Bear's gaze moved slowly back to Striped Eagle. "The white man, Major Partain, is doing his ugly deeds again, I hear," he mumbled. "But the dam is now destroyed, Striped Eagle?"

Striped Eagle drew the tobacco smoke into his mouth then returned the pipe to his father, blowing the smoke into the air. "*Ay-uh,*" he said, nodding. "The dam is no more." He gave Brenda a proud smile. "And Summer Sun did her part. She also helped to tear away the tangled branches of the dam. She has proved her loyalty to the Ojibwa. She has proved her loyalty to *me*."

A slow blush rose onto Brenda's cheeks as she saw she was again being closely scrutinized by not only Chief Growling Bear but also Morning Flower. She cast her eyes downward, feeling ill-deserved of any praise Striped Eagle handed her way. She was in the end going to betray him. He would hate her forever! Oh, how could she learn to live with such a hate?

Chief Growling Bear again drew long puffs from his pipe, now looking sternly at Striped Eagle. "Tell me what is in your heart, my son," he said thickly, the tobacco smoke wafting slowly in the close confines of the wigwam.

"I wish to seek your approval of my chosen woman," Striped Eagle said, straightening his shoulders, sitting more erect as his eyes did not waver under the steady gaze of his father. "I have come for not only your approval but also your blessing."

Brenda bit her lower lip in frustration. She was getting more entangled in her web of deceit by the moment. Her heart ached for Striped Eagle, but she was honor-bound to avenge her family's deaths. Yet, since she had let this thing go this far with Striped Eagle, how *could* she back down? It was going to be harder than ever now to flee in the night . . .

"Why is it that my son, the next chief in line, feels any responsibility for this white woman?" Chief Growling Bear said in a low growl. "There are other white families in the area. Why does she not go to them for help?"

Brenda wanted to scream out that that was what she had attempted many times! But she had always ended up back in this village of Ojibwa! Having come here, she had been led into a sweet love affair with Striped Eagle, yet this was not all there was in life. She had to convince herself of this. With him life would be even more complicated than living alone, even without family.

But she could not voice this opinion aloud to Striped Eagle's chieftain father. It was not the right time to say *anything* aloud. This thing today was between father and son. She only happened to be the issue between father and son, although she would rather be anything but.

Her insides melted when Striped Eagle placed an arm possessively about her waist, and all thoughts fled for an instant.

"Father, you know that I speak of more than simply protecting Summer Sun. I wish to have her as my—"

Chief Growling Bear interrupted Striped Eagle. "More than once you have called this white woman by an Ojibwa name. So you have gone this far already with her, my son, to give her an Ojibwa name?"

Striped Eagle's lips narrowed and his eyes flashed, but he knew he had to hold his temper at bay in respect to his father. But it seemed that his father was going to make Summer Sun prove her worth to the Ojibwa more than once in order to fully accept her.

"*Ay-uh*, she has been given a name appropriate for any woman who becomes a part of the Ojibwa family," he said hoarsely.

His arm tightened about her waist, his gaze traveling over her. "Do you not see how well she wears the clothes of the Ojibwa? Do you not see how her hair is braided? She even wears the touch of berry juice on her cheeks."

His tone softened. "Is she not beautiful, father?"

Chief Growling Bear tapped the tobacco from his pipe and rose straight and tall, towering over those still sitting. "My son, give yourself time with this woman," he said flatly. "Give yourself time to see if she speaks with one heart and one tongue."

He gestured with his hand. "Now leave me. I must rest. My journey was long from the Saint Croix village of the

Chippewa," he murmured. "My eyes are weary as well as my bones. We will talk again. *Wi-yee-bah.* Soon, my son."

Striped Eagle placed a hand at Brenda's elbow and urged her from the floor. "*Ay-uh,* father," he said flatly. "It *will* be soon. *Gee-mah-gi-ung-ah-shig-wah.* We must have this same council again *tomorrow.*"

Chief Growling Bear nodded. "*Ay-uh.* If you wish. *Wah-bungh.*"

Hours later, Striped Eagle retrieved Brenda from the wigwam of a female tribe elder who had been teaching her the Ojibwa method of tanning hides and grinding grain, while Striped Eagle and other males in the tribe had gone hunting for the afternoon.

Brenda was ushered from the wigwam into the dewy mist of falling night. She walked numbly beside Striped Eagle, hearing the small sounds of night; the sleepy melody of the cricket, the shivery voice of the screech owl, the lullaby croon of the river where a bullfrog cried at the rising moon.

She walked beside him until they were again in his wigwam where shaggy darkness was stealing, catlike, around the dwelling, creeping inside to lie in the far corners where the firelight failed to reach.

The ghostlike, dim interior of the wigwam seemed to reflect Brenda's own feelings: anything but serene. She hadn't asked for the approval of the great chief, but having not been given it made her feel less than worthy to be in the company of this handsome brave, the man she loved.

When Striped Eagle drew her around and into his arms, his eyes dark with emotion, she didn't know what to say to him. She now felt as though she had failed him in more than one way.

Fifteen

Striped Eagle's night-black eyes held a hint of amusement as he looked down at Brenda. Brenda arched an eyebrow, having seen nothing amusing in their council with Chief Growling Bear.

"Striped Eagle, why are you looking at me like that?" she asked, feeling uneasy beneath this strange, close scrutiny while he held her at arm's length. "Are you angry with me because I was not accepted by your father?"

"You think you were not approved?" Striped Eagle said, chuckling low. He swept a hand to her hair and began skillfully unbraiding it. "Summer Sun, my father approves. He sees you as *I* see you: desirable. Did you not see it in his eyes as he looked at you? Did you not see the sparkle? Your presence made him come to life again, reliving his days as a youth wishing to take his first young bride."

Embarrassed, she looked away from him, relieved that Striped Eagle at least thought she was worthy in his father's eyes. But she knew better. She knew that she would never be accepted. What his father had accepted was that she was, perhaps, lovely. But that was not what *he* was looking for in a wife for his son! Surely Striped Eagle knew this; he just wouldn't admit to a truth that could cause a strain between father and son. Surely he was hoping for more tomorrow.

She wouldn't allow that to happen. The strain would be less between father and son if she were *gone*, not giving them an opportunity to argue over her. Yes, leaving was going to be much easier now. In a sense, she was doing it for Striped Eagle.

Brenda trembled as she watched Striped Eagle begin to remove her leggings and moccasins. And then he again began working with her hair until she felt it loose and free, then spilling over her shoulders to tumble down her back in a spill of red. Warm shivers stirred along her flesh as he drew her lips closer . . . closer . . . then kissed her with thoroughly intoxicating intensity.

Drawn to him and the love that could not be denied, she twined her arms about his neck and returned the kiss, tingling even more when his hand sought the swell of her breast through the sleek doeskin dress. Brenda moaned softly as he kneaded her breast while his other hand made a heated path up her leg, past her thigh, to the junction of her long, slim legs.

Her heart thundering, Brenda eased her legs apart and let his hand fully cup her softness where pulsated her passion, again hungering to be fed. She arched this softness more fully against his hand, then shuddered with pleasure as she felt a finger slip easily inside her, skillful . . . gentle . . . probing.

"My woman, again you are the flower of my wigwam," Striped Eagle said, lowering her to the soft furs beside the simmering fire in the firespace. "Let me show you how Striped Eagle thanks you."

"Striped Eagle, you don't—" Brenda began, but she was silenced by his kiss, feeling his hunger in the seeking pressure of his lips. She surrendered to the hands now lowering her dress to her waist. Her insides melted as he molded her breasts, his thumbs and forefingers kneading and drawing the nipples into tautness.

And then Brenda felt a sensuous tremor as he knelt down over her and scooted her dress down and away from her. Without shame, she let her fingers wander to the straps of his breechcloth and smiled seductively up at him as she began lowering it until it was drawn away from him.

Brenda's eyes kept locked on Striped Eagle's, knowing that if she looked downward, she would see the powerful strength of his manhood, ready again to take her to the soaring, mysterious realms of fulfillment. She needed no more arousing, which is what looking at him would cause.

Gently he positioned himself fully over her. In one thrust his hardness was inside her, stroking . . . smoothly stroking, moving rhythmically within her. Brenda lifted her legs about him, locking them together. She arched her hips, consumed by a spreading, raging heat.

She drew a ragged breath as again his lips sought her mouth in a sweet and hungry kiss, the power of his body driving her to unimagined bliss. She felt drugged, reveling in the exquisite sensations overtaking her.

Twining her arms about his neck, Brenda clung to Striped Eagle, his lips still pressed hard against hers, his hands again teasing her taut breasts. She inhaled the smell of him, the pleasant, sweet, smoke-musky smell of him. Her heart seemed to melt into his, loving him . . . always loving him . . .

Striped Eagle could feel the pleasure mounting, as though a rope coiled, tighter . . . tighter inside his loins. He swept his hands to her hair and wove his fingers through it as the firelight starred it. His lips worshiped her, raining kisses along the soft, gentle curve of her jaw to the tiny tip of her nose and then to her thick lashes. Pressing his lips he closed her eyes, then sent feathery kisses along one of her ears, and then the other, nibbling on her earlobes until she laughed softly of her pleasure.

"Neen-ee-quay," he whispered, lowering his lips to a breast, flicking his tongue about its throbbing tip. *"Gee-zah-gi-ee-nah?"*

Brenda was floating, thrill-bound. She was only half aware that he had spoken to her. She was too near to reaching the wild, exuberant passion that she sought to respond.

Instead, she pressed her lips against his throat, her fingernails traveling along the tight muscles of his shoulders. She could feel his body stiffening. She could hear his breathing becoming more rapid. She knew him and the way he made love well enough now to know that he was going to join her in her moment of total release.

"I . . . love . . . you . . ." she said barely aloud as she clung to him, lifting her hips to receive him fully, soaring now above herself. When he plunged harder and emitted a throaty groan, she knew that he had just experienced the height of wild pleasure to match her own. Again they had become one . . .

Completely spent, Striped Eagle gave Brenda a fleeting kiss then crept away from her to lie by her side. His hand traced the outline of her breasts, his eyes feasting on her serene loveliness.

"Striped Eagle does make you happy?" he murmured, brushing some loose strands of hair back from her eyes. "Your pleasure matched my own?"

"Ay-uh," Brenda murmured, gazing over at him, seeing how the flickering light of the low-burning fire magnified the handsomeness of his bronze face and deepened the color of his smoldering eyes.

Her eyes lowered to take in his sinewy, gleaming body, the breadth of his shoulders, his solid and compact torso and thighs. His long muscles knotted and rippled, sharply defined by his leanness as he raised a leg to place it familiarly on one of hers in a welcome gesture of possessiveness.

"You speak the word of the Ojibwa well," Striped Eagle chuckled. "Like I said, you are a good pupil. But I've so much, much more to teach you. *Gee-nee-see-do-tum*?"

Brenda leaned up on an elbow, shaking her hair to tumble down her back. "My darling, I am always eager to learn," she said softly. "But . . ."

Striped Eagle saw the wavering of her eyes and understood only too well why. He knew of her determination to avenge her family's death. He silenced her further words with a forefinger.

"No buts," he growled. "That is a foolish word. Do not use it in my presence, Summer Sun."

Brenda lowered her lashes. She now knew that he expected her to try and escape. How would he try to keep her from it *this* time?

Breathing shallowly, she watched him rise to his feet to draw on his breechcloth. She then watched, wide-eyed, as he gathered up the doeskin dress he had just discarded from her and began walking away with it toward the entrance flap.

"What are you going to do with the dress?" she asked, rising to a sitting position.

When he turned and looked at her, it was a fierce look, one that turned her insides cold. "You will not leave my dwelling tonight once I am peacefully asleep," he mumbled. "Without a dress you will go nowhere."

Brenda gasped, speechless. As Striped Eagle raised the entrance flap and stepped outside, the cool evening breeze touched Brenda's body like a cold hand. Goose bumps rose on her flesh. She shivered. Looking down at herself in her total nudity she was rudely awakened to what she had so willingly participated in with Striped Eagle. His now refusing to return her clothes to her made her feel a true captive for the first time.

Frustrated, anger welling inside her, Brenda grabbed one of the furs on which she had just made love and clasped it around her shoulders. She scooted closer to the firespace, trembling. Her eyes stung with tears as she stared hopelessly into the dying embers of the fire, at this moment hating Striped Eagle as she never thought herself capable. She did not want to be this kind of prisoner. Before, her secret plan had always made her feel free, independent, no matter what Striped Eagle did. But now? What was she going to do? He was determined not to let her go, no matter *what*.

Her eyes sparkled, a renewed determination causing her jaw to tighten: he would not hold her here, even *this* night. She would find clothes to wear, somehow!

Letting her gaze range slowly about the wigwam, hope rose inside her. In a dark corner of the dwelling she saw a neat pile of Striped Eagle's fringe bordered clothes. Though they would probably almost swallow her whole in their largeness, they offered her the only hope.

She glanced over her shoulder at the entrance flap. If she hurried she could get some of Striped Eagle's clothes hidden beneath the bear skin; while he slept she would *still* make her escape. She would leave the village looking like the rest of the Ojibwa. Striped Eagle's braves might even think she was him in the blackness of night if they saw her leave. The outdoor fires had a way of distorting one's stature by its ghostly waverings.

With a nervous heartbeat, Brenda let the protective fur fall away from her shoulders as she crawled on her knees to Striped Eagle's clothes. Her fingers trembled as she sorted through them until she found what seemed to her an appropriate pair of fringed buckskin trousers and shirt. Feeling the thief that she was, she even removed a beaded headband and moccasins from his personal belongings.

And then, afraid Striped Eagle might return and catch her, she hugged his clothes to her and hurried back to where she had been before he had made his surprise departure. She carefully and quickly raised the furs and hides and placed her small bundle of clothes snugly beneath them.

Then, chilled by her own planned deceit of the man she loved, she again drew the fur about her shoulders and waited beside the fire for his return. She felt totally empty, a void of torn desires. Why couldn't life be easier, not so full of complications? Why couldn't she have just fallen in love with a white man and gotten married? That would be so much simpler than battling these feelings inside her for Striped Eagle. She had to wonder: if not for his father and his feelings for her, what *then*? Could she give up her way of life for Striped Eagle? Would she?

She frowned, picking up a twig with which to stir the fire's embers. What sort of life *did* she have in the first place? What *was* there to give up? She had lost her parents. She had lost everything in life that meant anything to her. She had nothing, except for Striped Eagle's love. And she was running from it. Oh, what more could she expect of life, except to be loved, totally loved?

The cool breeze suddenly lifting her hair to touch the nape of her neck was proof that Striped Eagle had returned. Brenda tensed, hoping he wouldn't step on the furs beneath which were hidden her means of escape!

Brenda glanced sideways at Striped Eagle as he took wide steps to stand on the opposite side of the fire from her. He spread blankets and furs for the night, still having said nothing to her since his return. Quietly she watched him, wondering why he was so silent. She hadn't given him cause to be angry. He had only *surmised* that she would again attempt escape.

Yet he knew her well, and knew her intentions even before quizzing her, and forcing her to deny or confirm his assumptions.

Yes, he did know her so well and thus had cause to be angry with her. They had again made passionate love . . . he had introduced her to his father . . . and she was still planning to leave him.

Oh, Lord, she was going to shame him. But she had no choice . . .

Striped Eagle turned and gave her a soft smile, his anger seeming to have faded into the wind. He offered her a hand. *"Mah-bee-szhon,"* he said thickly. "Come. We now sleep. You will sleep by my side, Summer Sun."

Brenda smiled weakly back at him as he came to her and eased the bear fur from about her shoulders. She trembled like a limb swaying in a soft breeze as he lowered a kiss first to one breast and then the other, his hands tracing the softness of her flesh as though discovering her anew.

Sucking in her breath when his fingers once more broached the forbidden triangle of her thighs and tangled them into the softness there, she closed her eyes to the ecstasy building inside her, willing herself to fight it. This ever-present craving, desire, for Striped Eagle was surely going to be the cause of her demise! But she could not help herself. She wanted this. She wanted *him*. He was again rendering her mindless, banishing all sense of logic and right.

Brenda's breath came in short rasps as Striped Eagle spread her legs and she found his lips kissing a hot path downward, stopping where his fingers had just been.

When he began pleasuring her in this new, strange way he had introduced her to, her body again threatened to betray her. But he suddenly stopped. He rose to his feet and swept her fully into his arms.

"Sleep is what you need most, my woman," he said

huskily, carrying her to the pallet he had prepared for them.

Brenda's face was aflame with shame, realizing that she had allowed herself to be taken to a peak of pleasure and left there. "Striped Eagle, if sleep was most prominent on your mind, why did you just . . . ?" she said, her words trailing off, unable to be so bold as to ask why he hadn't finished what he had started with her.

"This aroused passion will linger in your mind throughout the night," he said thickly, spreading her gently on the soft fur cushions. "You will not dream of escape. You will dream of *Striped Eagle* and what we will share tomorrow when the grass still sparkles with dew."

Again his hands traveled over her body, so surely, yet with a devastating gentleness. He gazed down upon Brenda, smiling. "Tomorrow, my Summer Sun," he whispered. *"Wah-bungh."*

Brenda's body shivered beneath his touch, but she was glad when he placed a blanket of bright colors atop her. And when he positioned himself beside her, their feet facing the firespace, she only glanced over at him, smiling awkwardly when she found him still gazing openly at her.

"Good night," she murmured, quickly turning to her other side, placing her back to him. She could not let herself relax. She must stay awake. Her eyes stared straight ahead as though propped open, even though they burned and itched with want of sleep. She could feel her heart nervously pounding, her palms damp with perspiration.

Moving her head a fraction to one side she listened to Striped Eagle's breathing, wondering if he was still looking at her, or if he felt comfortable enough with having discarded her clothes to let himself fall into a restful sleep.

Brenda smiled to herself, hearing his breathing grow relaxed, seemingly on the verge of sleep. So many nights in the close spaces of her family's cabin she had listened to each of the members of her household falling to sleep while she lay restless and unable to.

She knew that if she turned and looked at Striped Eagle his eyes would be closed. But perhaps it was too soon to get up and dress in his clothes. She had to make sure . . .

Brenda jumped as if a shot had been fired when one of Striped Eagle's hands suddenly flopped over on her, resting casually on her left breast left uncovered by the blanket. He wasn't asleep after all! And now was he ready again to explore her body with his hands?

She barely breathed as she watched for his hand to begin toying with her breast, but it still dangled lifelessly across her. She smiled to herself, realizing that his hand was there by accident, having been tossed there in his sleep as he had turned on his side, his body now surely facing hers.

"Dare I?" she whispered, speaking as though saying a prayer as she looked toward the ceiling of the wigwam. "Is it too soon?"

But anxious to get this ordeal over with she reached a hand to his and gently lifted it, turning quietly as she did so, then lay his hand on the blankets beside him.

Moving to her knees, Brenda leaned to look down into Striped Eagle's face and watch his eyes, waiting for the lids to flicker open. But when they didn't she knew that she was in luck. He was most certainly asleep. And she must move quickly; no more quietly than quickly! Should he find her again in the throes of escape, she had no idea what to expect of him! She didn't want to take that chance . . .

Crawling around the firespace, Brenda stealthily removed the hidden clothes and began slipping into them, all the while keeping her eyes on Striped Eagle for any signs of movement. Once the breeches and shirt were on she eyed the moccasins, frowning. They were almost twice as large as her feet! She would most surely stumble if she tried to wear them, but she couldn't move shoeless through the village and forest. One sharp rock piercing her foot would undoubtedly cause her to scream out, and she couldn't afford that this night!

Looking about her, she found some loose straw beneath the bulrush mats. With deft fingers she stuffed it into the toes of the moccasins. Then, smiling triumphantly, she slipped her feet into the moccasins and wiggled her toes, seeing that this would do until she found someone who would help her out of this dilemma begun those many nights ago, when her family had been unmercifully slain!

Now eyeing the headband, Brenda's hands went to her hair. If she was to look like an Indian moving through the village, she must plait her hair.

Hurriedly, she made two braids to hang down her back. She slipped the headband on, then wondered about her face. She must find a way to darken it . . .

Her gaze lit on the firespace. The ashes! Surely she could scoop some of the cooled ashes and put them on her face as if they were a layer of powder. Though most unpleasant, it would at least get her safely away from the village!

Determined, she applied the ashes to her face. Feeling as ready as she could be, she stopped and again looked toward Striped Eagle. Her heart ached, already missing him. She reached a hand out toward him, wanting one last touch of his gorgeous, copper skin.

But that one touch could awaken him! She must hurry onward. Though he hadn't known it at the time, they had said their good-byes in a special way. And this time Brenda believed the good-bye was forever.

Her insides knotted, finding it hard to take that first footstep toward the entrance flap. She choked back a sob, still gazing longingly down at Striped Eagle. "I've got to do it," she whispered in an unheard apology. "For many reasons I must do it . . ."

Turning on a heel, she fled from the wigwam, tears

burning her eyes, a knot in her throat threatening to choke her. She stepped out into a moon-splashed night, the many outdoor fires casting dancing shadows on the outside walls of the wigwams. The sound of a flute in the distance added to an almost overwhelming atmosphere of melancholy romance that made Brenda momentarily pause.

Suddenly, voices coming close startled her into remembering how she was dressed and why. She must make her way to the river to again steal a canoe. This was the only way. Her destination was Mendota once more. Her chances of reaching the village were much greater by herself. Hopefully, by this time tomorrow she would be telling someone about Major Partain and he would soon be rightfully dealt with.

Sixteen

Brenda stirred on the floor of the canoe, sore and cold. She was trying to throw off the web of languor holding her captive. Rubbing the sleep from her eyes, she could feel herself being rocked, recollections of her past once again stealing through her. If she let herself believe it, she was a small child again. She was on her mother's lap on a rocking chair, being sung a lullaby in rhythm with the chair as it creaked slowly back and forth before the lazy warmth of a fire dancing in the family fireplace.

But the air about her broke the reverie. It was steeped in chill, causing her to shiver, wide awake. Her eyes darted about her, seeing the sides of the canoe, the paddles resting on each side of her, and the sky lightening to blue overhead.

Something grabbed Brenda at the pit of her stomach, again making her aware of where she truly was . . . and why. She had successfully stolen another Ojibwa canoe and had made her escape from Striped Eagle's village. But in the darkness she had lost her way, having guided the canoe up an unfamiliar tributary, the Mississippi elusive to her this time.

Pushing herself up on an elbow, careful not to tip the canoe, Brenda wondered how long she had been drifting. She had fought the urge to sleep until her eyes would not stay open any longer. She had feared falling asleep in the canoe, but she finally gave in, utter exhaustion overtaking even the need for safety. If the canoe had snagged in brush and had tipped . . . ?

Shuddering at the thought, emitting a soft prayer of thanksgiving to God that she was still afloat and *alive*, Brenda peered through the softness of morning. A cottony fog was lifting from the river's edge, revealing to her that she wasn't too far from shore. Though lost and in danger, she couldn't help but marvel at the wild splendor which walled the river that lay basking quietly in the cool sunlight and shadows of the early morning.

The shoreline was thick with new green cattails and watercress. Mud hens and several other kinds of waterfowl were swooping down to settle in little clusters, waiting for unwary fish, a great blue heron dominant over all, spearing chubs.

Muskrats were feeding; the air was rich with the scent of cedar; a deer drinking thirstily darted nimbly away into the thickness of Norway pines.

Moaning from weariness and aching muscles, Brenda rose up to settle herself on the seat in the middle of the canoe. Fear of what lay ahead was like a throb deep within her chest where her heart pounded. She looked up both forks of the river, wondering which way she must travel, so disoriented she couldn't discern from which direction she had come.

"Striped Eagle was right," she whispered. "It seems that I cannot take care of myself. I am lost . . . as never before."

But not only wanting to find civilization as she had always known it, but to also prove Striped Eagle wrong, Brenda forced herself to reach for the dreaded paddles and, placing them in the water, she began urging the canoe through the sun-splashed water. There had to be someone out there to help her. There *had* to be . . .

Holding her chin high, straightening her back, she stroked harder with the paddles, but too soon breathless, had to again stop. She was realizing just how long it had been since she had eaten. She was becoming weaker by the minute. She was thirsty . . .

Balancing herself in the canoe, she cautiously leaned over its edge to cup her hands into the water to sip the badly needed liquid. Her reflection shining back at her made her recoil with a start.

Then she was able to laugh, taking another long look in the cool mirror of the river, seeing the blackness of her face. She had forgotten that she had placed the ash on her face before leaving Striped Eagle's wigwam. Her hands went to her hair, touching the braids. Strange . . . she *did* look Indian. In her heart she ached for an Indian . . . her lover . . . her only love.

Suddenly Brenda became aware of sounds behind her. Without looking she recognized the splash of many paddles in water. Her insides went numbly cold when she turned around to see many canoes manned by Indians heading toward her.

The Indians quite close now, Brenda's eyes quickly searched their faces, hoping above all else to see the one Indian she could trust. But her hopes waned when she didn't recognize any of them. If these were Ojibwa searching for her, Striped Eagle would be in the lead canoe.

Fear gripped her. If these were not Ojibwa braves, there was only one other possibility: Dakota. Knowing that much depended on a brave front, Brenda repositioned herself in the middle of the seat of the canoe and straightened her back. She folded her arms stubbornly across her chest and tilted her chin, her pulse racing as the canoes began circling around her, the dark eyes of the Indians glittering cold as they took in this strange sight.

She stubbornly met their icy stares, staring back at them in return. She did not see any distinctive differences between these Indians and the Ojibwa and was beginning to think that perhaps she had been wrong. But when the largest of the canoes pulled alongside her and the most powerful-looking of the Indians, attired in a heavily beaded and fringed shirt and leggings, with a headband displaying two eagle feathers and his face painted with red and yellow, scrutinized her, she began again to lose hope.

While all of the people of Striped Eagle's village were able to communicate in part in English, this Indian who now boldly faced her was speaking in sign language and an occasional low grunt wherever the word Dakota was voiced to her in broken English.

Almost afraid to breathe, yet retaining her stubborn stance of crossed arms and tilted chin, Brenda watched the Indian perform his way of speaking as he motioned with his hands and arms. Brenda, who had studied a book on Indian sign language before traveling from Illinois, quietly translated some of the words to herself.

Her eyes followed the fingers of both of the Indian's hands as they became slightly curved, and began making downward motions from the top of his head to his shoulders, as if combing long hair. She knew this word well. He had just said "woman" to her. It was apparent to her that upon first sight of her he had thought her to be a man. Her insides quivered. Her disguise had worked well until now. Now that he had gotten a closer look at her face, however, he had seen her tiny facial features and surely even recognized the fact that she had spread firespace ash across them. She was wondering if he found this amusing or puzzling.

Brenda further watched as he pointed to her with his right thumb, recognizing this to mean "you" in Indian.

Her spine stiffened and fear grabbed her when she quickly understood his next word as he closed his fists and placed his right hand over his left at the wrists as if they were bound together. She knew that she had just been told that she was now his captive.

The Indian then nodded his head and crooked the index finger of his right hand and motioned toward his body, instructing her to follow him and his braves.

Swallowing hard, her face scalding with the fear building in her, Brenda saw no other choice than to act out the word "yes" back to him. She placed her right hand even with her shoulder, her index finger pointing straight up, her thumb pressing on her second finger, then quickly dropped her hand downward, closing her index finger over the end of her thumb.

She grimaced when a smug smile lifted the Indian's narrow lips as he paddled quickly away from her and began leading the way for the rest of the canoes filled with Indians, Brenda's caught in the middle of the many.

With each stroke of the paddles, Brenda's heart cried out for Striped Eagle. Perhaps she deserved this fate, having deceived the one Indian who cared whether she lived or died. But now? What would her purpose be to *these* Indians? She had heard that white women were made hard-working slaves for some. Was this to be her destiny? To live with Indians . . . not the Ojibwa, but the *Dakota*?

Half bowing her head, perspiration pearling on her brow from the exertion of the continued paddling and the ensuing weakness from the hours passing without food, Brenda felt the desperate need to cry.

But she would not show such a weakness to these Indians whose eyes seemed to bore holes through her as they watched from one canoe and then another. The lead canoe was the only canoe that was now ignoring her presence, but the Indian who had initially confronted her knew that it did not matter. She had no way of escaping from this fortress of Indian braves accompanying her, flanking her canoe's sides and following along behind her.

She was surely doomed. Perhaps the upcoming hours of her life would be her last . . .

Again recalling the importance of behaving as brave as possible, Brenda straightened her shoulders and lifted her chin, flipping her braids to hang down her back. With determination she made the paddles obey the orders of her arms, though each stroke was now like a painful stab in her shoulders. She kept her eyes straight ahead, ignoring the Indians, pretending she was still alone, in hopes of finding someone who could help her. If she pretended, surely she could remain sane!

The sun was high overhead when Brenda caught her first sight of life besides animals and birds at the banks of the river. She tensed when she saw copper-skinned children wandering in the spotted shade of the forest along the riverbank, picking wild strawberries and raspberries, dogs yapping at their feet.

And then her gaze captured the full setting of the Indian village, seeing for the first time the true difference between the Ojibwa and how she knew them and the way they lived, and these Indians she was sure to be forced to become acquainted with, the Dakota.

In a clearing spread along the shining waters of the river, in the light of the glaring sun, she saw a village of tepees instead of the wigwams she had become accustomed to in the village of the Ojibwa. This village was shaped in a great horseshoe, all cone-shaped tepees facing east, offering the traditional welcome to the spirit of the rising sun. The skins of the tepees were painted with brilliant colors in geometric designs, and the smoke of the outdoor cook fires spiraled away into the air.

Brenda tensed as she watched the many canoes about her now being beached on spits of rocks and sand, the Indian who was still acting as the leader now at her canoe,

pulling it alongside his, then beaching it. In an instant he
had grabbed her by a wrist and was dragging her from the
canoe. Her knees scraped the pebbled beach as she tripped
and fell. They throbbed as did her wrists when the Indian
forced her back to her feet.

Again in Indian sign language the Indian told her to
follow him and his braves as they began making their way
toward the village of tepees, and then into its midst,
moving in the direction of a much larger lodge at the
center. This lodge, different than the cone-shaped dwellings, was square and bark-covered.

In the near distance Brenda could see women with
babies in cradle boards on their backs working in the
fields. And closer still Brenda could see women pounding
dried kernels of corn into meal within a hollowed-out tree
stump.

Pots made of bark hung over the heat of the fire but not
too near the flames to burn them. The mingled aromas of
boiling squash, beans, and corn and meat rising from them
caused Brenda's stomach to growl in hunger. Her knees
were fast becoming rubbery from her growing weakness,
and she wondered just how long she would now have to go
before being offered any sort of nourishment. Perhaps
these Indians wouldn't even offer her food. What if they
would make her suffer by starving her to death? She had
read horrible tales of how some Indians practiced the art of
torture. Were the Dakota among these who enjoyed such a
pastime? Brenda groaned to herself, knowing that she was
soon to find out.

Striped Eagle's dark, fathomless eyes, his anger reflecting in them, flashed inside Brenda's mind, making her
wince. Was he, at this very moment, thinking about her?
Would he come in search of her? Or would he be so angry
with her he would not care about what happened to her this
time?

If she closed her eyes she could still see him sleeping so

peacefully . . . so trustingly . . . moments before she again fled into the night, a flight she still believed was necessary to achieve her goal.

But would she ever see Striped Eagle again under any conditions? Oh, how she prayed that she would!

Half stumbling, Brenda followed alongside the Indian brave who had taken full possession of her. Casting him a brief glance, she saw that he was perhaps the same age as Striped Eagle, as stately tall, as erect in posture and stance. His face was masterfully sculpted, yet not as handsome or as stirring to Brenda as Striped Eagle's. The thought of what night might bring made her insides curl with dread.

The Indian gave her a hard stare, as though he had read her thoughts, then began communicating with her in sign language as they approached the largest dwelling in the village. As far as she could gather he was about to introduce her to the chief of this tribe of Indians. And when he touched the right side of his chest with his closed right hand several times, making her realize he had spoken the word "father" to her, she knew that again she was in the presence of the son of a chief.

Licking her parched lips, her face dry from the irritating firespace ash still coating her, Brenda found it hard to take the remaining steps required to reach the Indian chief's dwelling. Though her eyes were hazy from weakness, she could now make out a stolid figure sitting on a colorful blanket beside the entrance flap of the dwelling.

When his eyes raised and met hers, Brenda's fear rose inside her heart, for she could see in their depths a coldness, the same that she had seen in his son's. She knew that she was looked upon with anything but kindness. It was more than likely that she would be seen as a source of amusement for any who cared to use her as such, then discarded . . .

Brenda's gaze wavered beneath the chief's silent, close appraisal of her. Now that she was standing before him, she saw that before her arrival he had been polishing arrow shafts by passing them through holes drilled in a thin, flat rock.

He was clad in the rich Indian raiment of his tribe, gray wolfskin, otterskin smooth and dark like the velvet of moss, myriads of ermine tails glistening white in the sunlight, and glimmering beads from necklace to moccasins. He had the appearance of some god of the forest!

As he placed his arrow shafts aside and stood to tower over her, Brenda saw that he was flaunting a headdress made from a crest of eagle feathers tipped with orange and crimson tassels that must have floated in many a sky, bound into his scalplock and hanging down his spine. The strenuous war career of this noted chief had ploughed deep furrows and written serious lines in his copper-colored face.

Yet he didn't seem old enough to have such an aged appearance. Brenda could only surmise that this Indian chief must have fought many a battle in the prime of his youth. Wounds and scars and battles rushed age upon any man, even a great chief of any Indian nation.

The chief and his son embraced, then stepped apart, talking in the Dakota tongue, which made Brenda become more uneasy by the minute. She could feel the presence of the many Dakota warriors behind her. She could hear the silence in the village, herself now the center of attention.

When the chief's son turned abruptly and faced her, Brenda shifted her feet nervously, trying to read the expression in his eyes to see whether she was going to be treated gently . . . or roughly.

The chief's son swept his gaze over her and gestured with a hand. He began speaking to her with his hands once more. She frowned when she could not decipher what he was trying to communicate to her. It was not a word that she understood in sign language.

Again he spoke with his hands. He folded the fingers of

his left hand over his palm and pushed the fingers of his right hand under them to indicate puckered moccasins.

But again Brenda could not understand. She took a step backward, frustrated. Surprise then lighted up her eyes when she heard him say the word "Ojibwa" and again gestured toward her attire, snickering low as though mocking her clothes.

Brenda's eyes widened. She placed her hands to the tail of the fringed shirt and held it away from her. "Ojibwa?" she murmured, at last understanding why someone would laugh at her. Striped Eagle's clothes hung on her like a sack. Then she suddenly recalled the ash on her face. "Yes. These are Ojibwa. Are you friends with the Ojibwa?" Though she had chosen to flee the Ojibwa village, she hungered to be back there, safe, *alive* . . .

When the chief's son's brow furrowed into a frown, Brenda acted out the word "yes" in sign language, then again repeated the word "Ojibwa" and acted out the word "friend" in sign language.

She barely breathed when she saw his face darken with a deeper frown. When he spoke this time, the word "enemy" was quite distinct. A shiver coursed through Brenda. Striped Eagle was an enemy to these Dakota Indians. If Striped Eagle came looking for her, she would be the cause of bloodshed between these two factions. She knew that he would fight to the death. He had said that his wars had been fought with Indians, not white men.

Yet he had talked of making peaceful efforts with the Dakota in recent years. Would he forget his peaceful ways now? Had she forced him to? Would he welcome the fight, or would he hate her for causing it?

It occurred to her that her appearance into his life could cause him to become involved in wars with both the Dakota *and* the white man.

Yes, in the end, he would surely hate her. If she even lived long enough to become a target of such hate . . .

"Chief Walking Hawk," the chief's son said, motioning toward his father. He doubled a fist and placed it to his chest. "Cloud Rising," he grumbled. "Me called Cloud Rising.

"You?" he said, gesturing with a hand.

"You wish to know my name?" Brenda murmured, wondering why he had, up to now, spoke to her in sign language. Surely it had been a test of her abilities . . . her skills . . . in ways of communicating. Well, she would show him *and* his chieftain father! She would speak in Ojibwa, thankful now, in more ways than one, that Striped Eagle's lessons were branded in her mind.

"*Nee-bin-gee-zis*," she said firmly, gesturing toward herself with a hand. "My name is *Nee-bin-gee-zis*."

Fear once more entered her heart when noting both Indians' faces again draw into fretful frowns. It came to her suddenly that since the Dakota and Ojibwa were enemies, it wasn't wise to show her alliance to the Ojibwa. She ran the risk of being treated as if she, too, were a member of that enemy tribe.

Again she felt helpless, oh, so alone. Her shoulders slumped. Her head was becoming light, hunger now seeming to pervade all her senses. She teetered momentarily before being drawn back to her full height when she heard a commotion at the riverbank.

Swinging around, she saw the cause. It seemed impossible, yet the sight must be real, for relief flooded her. Striped Eagle! He was arriving by way of canoe along with many of his braves! He had searched and found her! He had cared enough not to give up on her. Oh, how *could* he love her so much when she had been nothing but trouble and disgrace for him from the very beginning?

Brenda's first instinct was to run to him but she wasn't given the chance. Rough hands grasped her wrist and guided her into the chief's large dwelling, cutting off any means of rescue.

Stumbling, desperation seizing her, knowing this was her only chance, she began clawing at Cloud Rising. "Let me go!" she screamed. "You can't hold me here. You can't!"

Callused hands quickly covered her mouth. Cloud Rising glared down at her, his eyes dark with warning. He spat many words to her in his Dakota tongue, then thrust a wad of deerskin into her mouth, then just as quickly had her hands secured behind her. Tossing her to the floor he bound her legs at her ankles and left her in the darkness as he went outside to join his chieftain father.

Brenda's heart thudded against her ribs. She strained her eyes, trying to see about her. But the fire in the firespace was not lighted. She could only see the edging of light about the deerskin flap at the doorway. But she could hear. Her ears were met with the sound of Striped Eagle's voice booming over everyone else's.

Then a cold, quiet panic seized her. She scarcely breathed, waiting for the first sounds of fighting to erupt outside this dreaded Indian dwelling where she so helplessly sat . . .

Seventeen

Brenda was huddled in the darkness, unable to scream, but relieved that thus far no fighting had broken out among the Indians. She struggled to get to her knees. She must get outside. If Striped Eagle and the Dakota could even remain civil to one another, the Dakota chief and his son would lie about her being there. Hadn't they quickly whisked her away to hide her? They surely had more planned for her than to release her to another red man! Her only hope was to make her presence known.

But perhaps Striped Eagle already knew that she was there. She could still hear the stormy quality of each of his words, though most were unintelligible to her. He was speaking in his full Ojibwa dialect as he shouted to the Dakota.

Brenda winced, wondering just how much of this verbal abuse the Dakota would take before lashing back. Would gunfire be their response? She must hurry. She must get outside for Striped Eagle to see her, before it was too late . . .

Her knees burned like fire as the sharp ends of the bulrush mats that she now scooted across pierced her buckskin leggings. She groaned as her muscles began to ache with the effort, the bindings at both her ankles and wrists cutting unmercifully into her flesh.

Her throat was dry, the buckskin wad stuffed into her mouth having absorbed the normal saliva flow, leaving her none with which to properly swallow. If she didn't get it removed from her mouth soon, she would choke to death!

Her brow damp with perspiration, she moved closer and closer to the closed entrance flap; possible freedom was only a few heartbeats away. Her pulse raced as she calculated Striped Eagle's proximity by his voice. She guessed him to be standing a few feet outside this central dwelling of the Dakota village. His voice boomed so like thunder as he questioned and probed.

Grunting with her continued effort, Brenda's knees took her to the entrance flap, but just as she reached it, a spike from the bulrush mat pierced the flesh of Brenda's knee. The wad in her mouth muffled her cry as she lost her balance and found herself tumbling forward and through the flap, landing face down. A pair of beaded moccasins appeared just beneath her nose as she twisted on the ground outside the hut, a huddled mass of bound ankles and wrists. She lifted her gaze upward, recoiling at the anger she saw flashing in Striped Eagle's eyes as he stood there glaring down at her.

Though her mouth hardly afforded her the chance, Brenda managed a crooked smile as she looked up at him. She didn't know if all his anger was directed now at her and her flight from him and the Ojibwa village. Or was some of this stormy darkness in his eyes still directed toward the Indians who had made her a hidden prisoner, the obvious proof—her bound and gagged form—now lying in the dirt?

She found herself perplexed. Why hadn't the Dakota received Striped Eagle more fiercely? They were enemies! Why hadn't Striped Eagle stormed the village with his braves? Would his choice of a more peaceful way prove best in the end, after all? Did the Dakota, too, hunger for such a peaceful solution to their problems?

Striped Eagle glared down at Brenda, folding his arms angrily across his chest. "*Weh-go-nen-dush-wi-szhis-chee-gay-yen?*" he grumbled. "What do you plan to do now, Summer Sun? Did I not tell you that you were not able to care for yourself in the wilds of this Minnesota land? You leave my village again . . . you in *trouble* again."

His eyes narrowed and his jaw tightened as he looked from her bound ankles to her wrists, and then to the buckskin stoppering her mouth. His gut twisted with hate of the Dakota for having treated her so roughly. His heart pulsed with anger at her for having made him come into the Dakota camp to rescue her. She was not only costing him many valuable furs, but also portions of his pride as well.

Brenda tried to talk as she managed to scoot herself to a sitting position, but the sounds coming from her were nothing but garble through the obtrusive buckskin that was becoming more frustrating with each added minute.

She challenged Striped Eagle with an angry stare. How could he stand there and let his anger prevent him from fully realizing how she was suffering in her bondage, humbled, it seemed, at his feet?

Or was that how he now saw her, a humbled prisoner, one he perhaps didn't even want now that the Dakota had touched her?

Yet he was there, wasn't he? He had certainly come for her. Again she would find herself in the Ojibwa village. Again she would have to flee.

Her gaze moved to Striped Eagle's many braves as they began arriving in the Dakota camp, their arms burdened with massive weights of furs and hides. She understood in a flash why the Dakota had received Striped Eagle into their village so civilly. Her cheeks burned with the sudden knowledge of exactly why Striped Eagle was so furious. It wasn't only because she had left his village. It was also because he was having to *pay* for her again! She had cost him so much already and she continued to cost him! Would he ever forgive her?

Or was he silently enjoying this, thinking that this time when he bought and paid for her, she could not possibly argue this ownership to which he would again lay claim?

Beneath his burning eyes, Brenda squirmed. Was he also enjoying making her wait to be released from her bonds? He apparently believed the longer she was at his *or* the Dakota's mercy, the humbler she would be, and would be eager to accept whatever fate was handed her. He would expect her to eagerly become his wife, forget her plans of vengeance, to accept only *him* as her prime objective in life.

Anger rose inside Brenda as the moments mounted. She could feel tension building among the waiting Indians, none saying anything to the other. It seemed to be a battle of silence!

To Brenda it seemed that the Ojibwa had *many* ways to fight the enemy. She was at least glad, though, that this way—not the bloody confrontation that she might have expected—had been chosen today. But the longer Brenda lay at Striped Eagle's feet, the more alarmed she became. Just how long would Chief Walking Hawk allow Striped Eagle to stay in his village, no matter how many gifts he offered in exchange for this white woman?

Striped Eagle suddenly bent to a knee and removed first the bonds at Brenda's wrists and then her ankles. When he placed a hand to the buckskin in her mouth, their eyes met and within his Brenda could see the same gentleness that had at first attracted her to him.

He then drew the buckskin gently from her mouth, giving Cloud Rising an ugly glance. Tearing the heart from Cloud Rising's chest would not be enough in pay-

ment for what he had done to his Summer Sun. If not for
the necessity of protecting her while in the Dakota camp,
Striped Eagle would have received much pleasure in claiming many Dakota scalps. It had been many sunrises and
sunsets since such a trophy had been received in his village
of Ojibwa!

The White Bear band of Ojibwa had fought many a
battle with the Dakota tribes. They had even forced some
tribes of Dakota to leave Minnesota when they had shown
that their lives were ruled by how many horses and Ojibwa
women they could steal and brag about! Perhaps one day
even *this* tribe of Dakota would be forced to leave this land
of honey and trees!

When Striped Eagle had received word from one of his
Ojibwa scouts that Summer Sun had been taken captive by
the Dakota, Striped Eagle had at first thought to again
show the Dakota who was the strongest of them, but his
woman's safety had ruled his heart and mind, leading him
to this more peaceful solution. Now, seeing his Summer
Sun so humbled at his feet, he knew that he had made the
right decision, at least for now . . .

A slow smile lifted Striped Eagle's lips, his gaze taking
in the blackness of Brenda's face and the looseness of the
outfit she had stolen from his personal belongings. The
Dakota had surely thought they were abducting an Ojibwa
brave when they had at first seen her.

Ay-uh, she could have looked Ojibwa from a distance.
His woman was smart in some ways, *gah-ween-nee-tah-
gee-gi-do-see*, dumb in others. She still had much to learn
before becoming his wife . . .

With her mouth now free from the gag, Brenda wiped
the back of her hand across her lips, finding them so dry
they were scaly. She coughed when saliva began to trickle
down the back of her throat and she inhaled deeply, relieved to fill her lungs freely with the air that had been all
but cut off by the buckskin wad.

Striped Eagle placed his hands on Brenda's waist and urged her to her feet to stand beside him. He felt her teeter and gave her more support by slipping his arm about her waist, fixing her in place.

With his chin held proudly high he glared from Chief Walking Hawk to Cloud Rising. After this brief staring match, he spoke words in Ojibwa to them, telling them that the next time the Dakota should be more careful whom they chose to take captive. If there was a next time . . . if the Dakota chose to take his *Nee-bin-gee-zis* captive . . . he would not come in peace bearing gifts for exchange! He would speak with the thunder of his rifle! His tomahawk would move swiftly and he would return home with its blade the color of the setting sun. Do not tempt him *or* the White Bear band of the Ojibwa. Patience was becoming a virtue unfamiliar to them all.

Brenda watched as Striped Eagle's braves began placing the furs and hides at the feet of Chief Walking Hawk and Cloud Rising until an abundant display of many colors and shapes lay there in a heap as if live animals.

Striped Eagle nodded to his braves when their chores were completed, and they silently obeyed the command that hadn't even been required to be voiced aloud, returning to their canoes with Brenda and Striped Eagle now following along behind them.

Brenda's insides were quivering. She truly wondered if Chief Walking Hawk and his son would stand by and let her leave with the Ojibwa. It appeared as though Striped Eagle had the upper hand. Was it because there were more Ojibwa than Dakota? Or did the Dakota see a fierceness in Striped Eagle that he had never exhibited to her?

This man she loved surely had many hidden talents, perhaps some not even yet tapped! She had to wonder just how he now planned to treat her once he took her back to his village. She hoped he would not show her a side to him

that she had not yet seen . . . a side that could cause her to
be frightened of him . . .

Now stumbling along beside Striped Eagle, again made
aware of her hunger by the weakness of her knees and the
total emptiness of her stomach, Brenda was glad when
they finally reached the beached canoes. She was even
more relieved when Striped Eagle did the gentlemanly
thing and lifted her into his arms and carried her through
knee-high water to his canoe, placing her gently on a seat
covered with soft, comfortable furs.

Her head even fuzzy now from hunger, Brenda squinted
her eyes against the brilliant rays of the sun. Cupping her
hand over her brow as a visor, she watched Striped Eagle
shout commands to his braves until they were all in the
water, shoving away from the shore lined with gaping
Dakota Indians.

Grasping the sides of the canoe, Brenda was only half
aware of the canoe rising and sinking with the waves as it
slipped smoothly along in the water. She glanced at Striped
Eagle's straight, perfect back facing her and the corded
muscles of his powerful arms and shoulders as his paddles
struck the water in unison.

Lethargy was seeping in and she wondered if she might
even faint from hunger. She had never been one to with-
stand going long without eating, and this was surely the
longest she had gone without food. The other times when
Striped Eagle had rescued her he had offered her food just
in time to save her from the strange spell that seemed cast
over her. Should she faint . . .

The last thing Brenda felt was the impact of her body as
she crumpled into the canoe, her hand grazing Striped
Eagle's back as she tried to reach out for him. The rest
was total blackness.

Eighteen

Brenda awakened to a gentle, wet softness on her brow. Her eyes fluttered open to see Striped Eagle closely watching her. Fully awake now, she was aware of being cradled in his arms, her head resting on his lap, and that he was gently washing her face with a soft buckskin cloth.

Putting a hand to her brow, Brenda blinked her eyes. "Where am I? What happened?" she said in a shallow whisper.

Her gaze moved quickly to the embankment where she saw Striped Eagle's canoe beached, now aware that she and Striped Eagle were completely alone, for she saw no other canoes or Ojibwa braves in viewing range.

Her gaze moved back to Striped Eagle, seeing the moodiness of his deep, dark eyes as he still closely watched her, his jaw set firmly, his lips unsmiling.

"Striped Eagle, say something," Brenda said, easing the buckskin cloth away from her face. "Tell me what happened."

Her nose caught the smell of something cooking, and her eyes turned to follow the scent. Not far from where she lay cradled in Striped Eagle's arms a fire burned in a pit in the ground over which a cooked rabbit hung, dripping its greases into the flames beneath it. To the edge of the fire a small pot had been positioned, steam spiraling from its boiling contents.

Brenda's stomach erupted with hunger cramps as the scent of the food tantalized her nostrils. She again turned her gaze back to Striped Eagle, now recalling what had happened. She must have fainted! Hunger had never so plagued her as it did now!

"*Gee-bah-kay-day-nah*?" Striped Eagle suddenly said, breaking his silence. "Again Striped Eagle must rescue, then feed you? Summer Sun, do you never learn what dangers await you when away from the village of the Ojibwa? *Ah-neen-ay-szhee-way-bee-zee-en*? Do you even wish to see blood spilled on your behalf?"

Brenda eased away from his lap to sit at his side, dizzy still from her need to eat. A moment of blackness swept before her eyes. She rubbed them, feeling herself teetering.

"I . . . must . . . eat . . ." she murmured. "Arguing with you, Striped Eagle, is the last thing I want to do."

"*Ga-gway-day-bway*?" he spat angrily, tossing the buckskin cloth aside. "Argue? You do not wish to argue, yet you continue to defy me? Summer Sun, you cannot have it both ways."

He rose angrily to his feet and moved quiet-footed to the fire. In one jerk he took the rabbit from over the flames and was tearing a leg away from it. In still angered movements he handed the cooked meat to Brenda.

"Eat. Give your body nourishment required to make your senses return to what is right and wrong," he said flatly.

He nodded toward the pot of boiling greens. "You will then eat the greens plucked and cooked for you. They will give you even more strength."

He pointed toward a clump of grass. "Over there I have found a nest of wild *mi-see-says*, turkey eggs. I will cook them for you next if your hunger is not yet fed enough after what I have prepared for you.''

Brenda eagerly took the cooked meat and sank her teeth into it, relishing its savory juices as they ran through her teeth and over her tongue. As the meat left a trail of warmth on its path downward to her stomach, she was already beginning to feel the lethargy leaving her.

Her gaze went to the clump of grass, where she now spotted the nest of wild turkey eggs, dirty white with reddish spots. Her father had always prided himself in finding those prized eggs. There it goes again, she thought; reminders of her father, mother, and brother were again paining her, arising constantly from even the most innocent of sources!

She ate more ravenously, needing to forget everything but fueling her body for what lay ahead . . .

Striped Eagle went back to Brenda and knelt on his haunches before her. ''So do you feel your strength returning?'' he said thickly.

Brenda nodded anxiously as she took another bite of the rabbit. ''Yes. And I am always given cause to thank you,'' she murmured. ''You are so kind, Striped Eagle, to always be there when I need you, when I deserve less from you.''

''*Ay-uh*, this is true,'' Striped Eagle grumbled, his brow creasing into a heavy frown. ''How is it that you cannot let your heart only include *me*? Why must I always be put into the position of having to come after you when you should know the importance of staying in the Ojibwa village, where you will be safe and looked after? Do not my words of my feelings for you reach your heart?''

Brenda sighed heavily. ''I have told you so many times why I do what I do,'' she said, then resumed nibbling on the rabbit bone until all meat was stripped from it. She tossed the bone aside, her shoulders relaxing with her newfound strength.

Striped Eagle placed a forefinger to her chin and began

tracing a path upward. "You even chose to deceive the Ojibwa by trying to *look* Ojibwa," he said hoarsely. "You even attempted changing the color of your skin to fool my people as you stole away from my wigwam as I trustingly slept."

Brenda's eyes became wide, his touch sending ripples of fire across her flesh. "*Ay-uh*," she murmured. "I did that. I had no . . . other choice. Please try to understand."

Striped Eagle smiled at her use of the Ojibwa word, then his face grew somber. "My father has been spared the fact of your leaving," he said, now framing her face between his hands. "My father would have thought me weak to let you leave me in such a way. I have ordered my braves to keep the truth from him. So now you must return with me. Make things right in the eyes of my father, Summer Sun. It is not easy for a son to deceive a chieftain father. In my own eyes I have become a disgrace to my father not only for my weakness of loving you but also for not being able to keep you loyal to me, the man who has already asked for approval of you from my chieftain father."

Brenda swallowed hard, again feeling trapped. She wanted to make things right for Striped Eagle, yet she still had her own task to set things right for herself! How could she achieve both? Yes, it was a web ensnaring her, drawing more tightly about her with each breath she took.

"You say your father has been spared hearing of my leaving," she said, lowering her eyes. "Striped Eagle, the truth is that he would be glad I was gone should he be told. You know he doesn't favor me for your wife."

Her gaze moved slowly upward. She leaned her face into the palm of his hand, relishing the touch of his flesh against hers, relishing this moment with him. These moments could so quickly become a thing of the past. If what she had planned was achieved, these moments *would* be . . .

"My father accepts what he knows is truth," Striped

Eagle said, taking Brenda's hands, urging her to her feet before him. "He knows that I am from his same mold, and that I am wise and will be a wise leader of our people. He only displays hardness about you as a last attempt to dissuade me from loving you. He *would* rather an Ojibwa maiden be at my side when I rule our people. It is his wish . . . but one that will not be fulfilled by me. He understands this now and he accepts."

Striped Eagle drew Brenda into his embrace. "You must return with me and let me prove to you that I am right," he said thickly. "We will again have council with my father. Not today. But *wah-bung*. Tomorrow will be soon enough. The remainder of this day will give my father just one more day of added rest which he needs. His health is worsening. One day he will part from us and travel the road of the hereafter."

Brenda felt a tremor engulf Striped Eagle with his talk of his father's passing away. She slipped her arms about his waist and pressed her cheek against his bare chest. Feeling the rapid beat of his heart against her flesh, and feeling the hardness of his arm muscles tightening more intensely about her, she was compelled to look up into his face, feeling as though he had commanded her to do it without having said a first word.

"Striped Eagle . . .?" she whispered, watching his lips slowly lowering to hers.

And then she was consumed by his fiery kiss, his body pressed hard into hers, melting, blending them together as though one. It was as if he had fed her only to consume her!

But she wanted it. While in his arms it was so easy to cast aside all worries, all demands that she made of herself because of her family's death. The only drive within her at this moment was to cling to him, Striped Eagle at this moment her sole lifeline.

Bending Brenda as he kissed her, Striped Eagle urged

her to the ground beside the low embers of the fire. A thick carpet of grass became their bed, the canopy of trees overhead their roof. Only rivulets of the sun lowering in the sky wove their way through the leaves of the trees like streamers of golden satin, the songbirds filling the air with their tremulous songs. Sturgeon splashed in the waters of the river; frogs croaked.

Striped Eagle's deft fingers were unbraiding Brenda's hair as his lips nibbled on the lobe of her ear, his breath hot and sensuous against the gentle curve of her neck.

The rapture building inside Brenda was stealing from her mind all thought of what she had just gone through . . . the Dakota . . . the fainting spell from her lack of food. The only thing that lingered with her was the gentleness with which Striped Eagle continued to treat and care for her.

She bent her head back as Striped Eagle's lips kissed the hollow of her throat, her hair now loose and free. His fingers twined through the red tresses and guided her face to meet his lips as his mouth closed over hers.

Striped Eagle kissed her with a lazy warmth that sent a message of ecstasy to Brenda's heart. Her hands explored the taut muscles of his bare shoulders, then traced the soft skin downward until her thumbs and forefingers met on each of his silky nipples. She gently squeezed and heard Striped Eagle's quick intake of breath.

And then Striped Eagle leaned away from her, his eyes twinkling devilishly as he slowly began to remove the clothes from Brenda that were in truth his own.

"We will delay our arrival back to my village until after the moon colors the treetops with its silver magic," he said thickly. "We will make love here, eat some more, make love again, then leave. *Gee-mee-nwayn-dum*, my Summer Sun. Enjoy. Time is too fleeting when we are together. We must make every moment count."

His mouth was soft and passionate as he again kissed

her. With a hand he took one of hers and guided it to his breechcloth. He did not have to tell her what to do next. All times past he had been a good teacher, she an avid pupil. She knew to remove his breechcloth and to expect his man's strength to be fully alive, swollen with desire for her, soon to carry her to that world of sheer bliss.

Her face flushed crimson, her heart soaring, Brenda lowered his breechcloth from around his hips. And then he moved her hands away and instead took it upon himself to lower his own scanty attire.

With eyes a mixture of ice and fire he looked at her as he positioned himself over her. She looked adoringly up at him and voiced a soft moan of pleasure as he lowered himself and his fullness entered her to begin its masterful strokes.

At first he was slow . . . gentle. And then the ice in his eyes melted and the fire within them grew to heated flames as he thrust harder . . . harder. His hands cupped her buttocks, his fingers imprinting their softness. She lifted her hips to meet his eager strokes inside her. He urged her legs about him; she locked her ankles together behind him.

Breathless, feeling herself floating, a mindlessness she always welcomed, Brenda clung in a torrid embrace with Striped Eagle while again his lips paid homage to hers.

His hands skillfully molded her breasts, kneading them, their nipples growing hard against the palms of his hands. As though willed to, his lips lowered and moved from breast to breast, his tongue inflicting a delicious tingling first in one, then the other.

His lips again devoured Brenda's mouth, his tongue a heated sword impaling her as it pressed between her lips. The intoxication of their moving bodies transferred pleasure from one to the other. Brenda trembled in an intense release of pleasure, and Striped Eagle followed with his own.

And too soon they unlocked their bodies, spent, panting. Brenda marveled at Striped Eagle's ability to manipulate her mind as well as her body. Only a few hours ago she had been a captive of the Dakota and now she was again Striped Eagle's captive in every way.

Flipping her hair behind her shoulders, Brenda rose to a sitting position, eluding Striped Eagle's intense, steady stare, knowing that he was trying to read her thoughts, troubled as they were.

Feeling no shame for her nudity, knowing that even with clothes on Striped Eagle knew her every dip and curve, Brenda brought her knees to her chest and stared into the flames of the fire, too soon again a part of the real world of confused thoughts . . . of being pulled in many directions . . . of wanting Striped Eagle, yet fearing this desire.

She shuddered when the breeze touched her flesh with a sudden coldness, the wind appearing to have switched to the north. When Striped Eagle moved to her side with a blanket he had brought with them from the canoe when first making this momentary camp, and placed it about her shoulders, she welcomed it, smiling weakly up at him.

"What is now troubling you?" Striped Eagle said, sitting beside her, placing his arm about her waist. "Your face has the look of sadness. We have just shared the most beautiful moments that can be shared between man and woman. You should have the look of contentment, my Summer Sun."

"Striped Eagle, everything can't be solved by making love," Brenda murmured, casting him a sideways glance. "I still have much to do that you still do not understand." She hung her head, slowly shaking it. "What am I to do? You'll *never* understand."

"It is time to return to my village," Striped Eagle said suddenly. "Now, Summer Sun." He rose to his feet and pointed to her clothes. "Dress. We go."

"Striped Eagle, you didn't hear what I just said," Brenda

put in, her voice strained. "I have much to do. I *can't* return to your village. Please escort me to a white settlement. Take me to Mendota."

Striped Eagle said nothing more. He went and stood beside the canoe, waiting for Brenda.

Angry, Brenda glared at him, then hurried into her clothes. She had no choice but to do as he commanded. But later she would show him. She would not be held captive by anyone. She would be more careful next time. She was beginning to know the ups and downs of being alone in this desolate land called Minnesota . . .

Nineteen

Standing angrily in Striped Eagle's wigwam, still attired in his loose-fitting clothes, Brenda refused to look his way. They had only just arrived back at his village. Brenda could hardly believe that she was even *there*. It seemed that her life moved in circles, the central point of her existence now always the village of the Ojibwa. Was it truly her destiny to be there? Was it meant to be from the day of her conception that her family would be slain, so that she would be a part of the Ojibwa way of life? It was beginning to seem that every time she fled from the village she was defying fate. If not, why did she always end up back at the village?

"So you are again *nish-ska-diz-ee-win*," Striped Eagle said, settling onto his haunches before the firespace. He began placing wood on the dying embers of the fire, himself attired in only a breechcloth and moccasins, his headband and eagle feather.

"You pout like an *ah-bee-no-gee*, Summer Sun," he added.

Brenda folded her arms across her chest. She turned on a heel and glared at Striped Eagle. "I don't know what

you just said and I don't *care*," she fumed. "Striped
Eagle, when will this end? I must be allowed to go on to
Mendota. I must find someone trustworthy to tell about the
evil deeds of Major Partain."

Striped Eagle rose quickly to his feet. He clasped Brenda's shoulders. "Striped Eagle say you are again angry
and that you are pouting like an *infant*," he grumbled.
"Are you not happy that I rescued you from the Dakota?
You seemed happy enough last night while we were making love."

Brenda shook her head in frustration. "You know that
you have ways of making me forget everything but being
with you," she murmured. She implored him with her
eyes. "And, yes, I'm glad you came to the camp of the
Dakota. And I have thanked you. But, please, let me go
on my way now. If you truly loved me you would even
take me to the village of the white man."

"You think I would ever give you up so easily?" he
scolded. "Proof has been shown that I will not."

Brenda winced as she fought free of his fingers, her skin
still stinging, his clasp had been so fierce. She challenged
Striped Eagle with a stare. "Yes, I have been shown many
times your persistence to have me here," she snapped
back angrily.

"It is *best* for you, Summer Sun."

Brenda's shoulders slumped from despair. "Striped Eagle, I'm sorry for sounding so ungrateful." She sighed.
"It's just that I have my own idea of what is best for me. I
must be given a chance to make things right for my
family."

The flames from the fire cast golden fire in Striped
Eagle's eyes. "It is this Major Partain who causes your
mind to stray from Striped Eagle," he growled. "Major
Partain must be dealt with by *me*. Then, Summer Sun, it
would be interesting to see what your excuse would be to
leave my village of Ojibwa."

Knowing what the outcome of a battle between Striped Eagle and Major Partain would be, a quiet panic seized Brenda. She had spoken out against Major Partain one time too many in the presence of Striped Eagle. She had not wanted to stir his anger so against the major, did not want Striped Eagle to become involved. Should his people suffer because of her tendency to air her feelings she would never forgive herself!

She eyed the entrance flap. She must escape. Once and for all she must leave Striped Eagle's village. It was the only way to keep him from becoming involved with her vengeance against Major Partain.

Inching her way toward the entrance flap, knowing the chances were nil that she would be allowed to leave, Brenda knew she must make a last attempt at proving to Striped Eagle that she did not want his further interferences in her life. Though a part of her heart would be severed should she never see him again, it was a risk she must take to ensure peace for his people and his community.

Striped Eagle's eyebrows forked as he saw her moving toward the entrance flap. Had nothing he said touched her heart? Was it to be the same all over again, she stubbornly refusing to accept the fact that she was his . . . totally his?

His jaw set firmly, his eyes angrily gleaming, he took a quick step toward her and grabbed her by the wrist. "*Andi-dush-ay-ah-szhi-on-nee-gee*?" he hissed. "Where do you think you are going? Do you truly think I will *let* you leave? *Gah-ween-wee-kah.* Never! Twice I have paid many furs for you. Three times I have rescued you. The need to do so again will not arise!"

Brenda trembled with anger, her face flaming. "Striped Eagle, I will not beg," she said in a strained voice. "But I do demand to be given my freedom. Now!"

"Must I be forced to bind your ankles and wrists as did the Dakota?" Striped Eagle said icily.

Brenda gasped, her eyes wide. "You wōuldn't . . ." she said in a near whisper.

"*Ay-uh*. It would be done," Striped Eagle said, his voice flat, his eyes inscrutable. "Do not force me. It would not be pleasant for you to be fed by my sister. She would not enjoy giving you your daily baths."

Brenda placed a hand to her mouth. She paled. "Striped Eagle, no . . ." She gasped.

Morning Flower's voice outside the wigwam seemed timely as she spoke Striped Eagle's name.

"Striped Eagle, let me enter. I must speak with you," Morning Flower said anxiously. "I saw you arrive in the village. You don't know about the dam that is again built across the White Bear River. Word has only just been brought to me by a friend, to pass it on to you. Striped Eagle, do you hear me?"

Brenda's breath caught in her throat as she glanced from the closed entrance flap to Striped Eagle. "Major Partain . . ." she said, her voice trailing off as she saw a look of hate enter Striped Eagle's eyes.

"Today I will rid the earth of that evil man for both you *and* me," he growled. He threw the entrance flap open and nodded toward Morning Flower. "*Mah-bee-szhon*. Morning Flower, come and stay with Summer Sun. While I am gone, see that she does not leave the village again. See that she does not leave my *dwelling*."

Brenda took a shaky step backward as Morning Flower entered the wigwam looking wide-eyed and innocent, her loveliness enhanced today by what appeared to be a shine in her dark eyes, contrasting so against the white of her doeskin dress. Surely this shine in her eyes wasn't caused by the duty just assigned her. Though Morning Flower had tried to show her brother that she would attempt to accept Brenda, Brenda suspected that Morning Flower still anything but approved of her being there. So what sort of mischief could cause this difference in Morning Flower's appearance?

But Brenda had more to worry about than Morning Flower. Brenda's happiness was in jeopardy! To be left with Morning Flower guarding her like a prisoner would demean any relationship she had shared with Striped Eagle! How could Striped Eagle do this to her? He was giving her cause upon cause to hate him. Surely he knew this! Or did he even care anymore since she had continued to betray him?

"Better yet," Striped Eagle said, stroking his chin contemplatively, "she must be bound." His eyes gleamed down into Brenda's as he saw her expression of disbelief. "One woman guarding another is not enough. My woman knows too well the art of escape."

Morning Flower stepped into the wigwam, appearing complaisant to Striped Eagle's every request. In truth, she was deceiving her brother. But in the end, it would be best for their Ojibwa tribe. With Summer Sun gone, truly gone this time, having gone to her own kind of people, Striped Eagle could get back to the important things in life . . . allegiance to *his* people. The fact that he might hate Morning Flower for lying to him would have to be dealt with later. At times, lies were important . . .

Brenda barely breathed, feeling trapped between Striped Eagle and Morning Flower as they blocked her way of escape through the entrance flap. She squared her shoulders and glared at Striped Eagle. "How could I ever have loved you?" she said, hating it when her voice broke with emotion. "Striped Eagle, you are *inhuman* if you bind my ankles and wrists. How *can* you?"

Striped Eagle moved to a knee and drew two strands of leather from his belongings. "Striped Eagle can no longer trust you," he said thickly. He gave her a sideways glance. "This is the only way I can be assured that you will be here when I return. And when I return you will have no true need to leave,'' he said, his voice weakening with gentleness. He stroked her chin softly and continued. ''When I return I will bear news that Major Partain is no longer a problem for you. I will do what should have been done long ago. I will *kill* him. He will make it easy should he again be building a dam across White Bear River. He has received our peaceful warning. The Ojibwa wild rice beds must be protected.''

In quick movements he had Brenda's hands, holding them both in the largeness of one of his while with his other he began wrapping the leather bindings about her wrists.

Brenda was stunned into speechlessness. She glanced from Striped Eagle to his sister, wondering why Morning Flower wasn't protesting as she usually did when seeing Striped Eagle's determination to keep Brenda there. With Striped Eagle actually making her a prisoner, Brenda would have thought Morning Flower would say *something*.

Yet Morning Flower still stood by, silently watching, with that same strange, mischievous look in her eyes, as though she was up to something, but only Lord knew *what*.

Then Brenda's numbness faded. She was forced to sit down beside the fire on a thick layer of furs and blankets so that her ankles could be bound. She hadn't struggled with Striped Eagle. She had known that to do so would be useless. Her only hope was that as soon as he left, Morning Flower could be encouraged to free her . . .

''Striped Eagle, I shall never forgive you for this,'' Brenda blurted. ''How *could* you? You have always said that you never force a woman. I would have hoped that meant in every way. Do you intend to keep me in bondage forever, Striped Eagle? Do you?''

His deft fingers coiling the leather strips into a knot, yet making sure they weren't so tight that they would cut into Brenda's flesh, Striped Eagle ignored Brenda's question. He had to believe that this *would* be the only time required to imprison her in such a way. When he returned he would prove to her that she was rid of the evil major, giving her a peaceful mind and heart, no longer tortured with the need for revenge.

Even if Striped Eagle had to return to the village of the Ojibwa with a scalp for his proof, he would do it for his woman. Then let the white soldiers come! He had chosen the peaceful way because that had been the way of the Ojibwa for many moons now and because it was what his father desired.

But if the soldiers made the first move and came to his village, then his father would steel himself to fight! He would even proudly shout out the commands to his warriors! In his father's eyes Striped Eagle had seen a longing for the fight. His father just hadn't spoken of this need from the heart . . .

Frustrated, her pride wounded, Brenda pleaded with Striped Eagle with her wide eyes, wondering why he was now so suddenly silent. "Striped Eagle, surely you know the wrong in doing this," she said, his eyes now locked on hers as he crouched before her, his duty complete. "If you truly loved me, you couldn't leave me like this. You could be gone for *hours*."

"*Ay-uh*," he finally said. "This is why Morning Flower will be here. She will feed you. She will make you comfortable."

Brenda laughed scornfully. "Comfortable?" she cried, holding her bound wrists up before his eyes. "You call this comfortable? By evening my wrists will be raw from these leather bindings." Her gaze moved to her ankles. "The blood flow to my feet will be impaired." Her gaze moved back to meet his. "I am already miserable, Striped Eagle. And I . . . hate you. Hate you . . ."

Her voice broke with those last words, her eyes lowered. She flinched when he reached a hand to caress her face. "Summer Sun can never hate Striped Eagle," he said quietly. "You know I do this out of love."

He placed a forefinger beneath her chin and forced her eyes upward to meet his steely gaze. "If you would promise not to flee my village again I would remove the bonds," he said softly. "It is that simple, Summer Sun. It is that simple."

Brenda's eyes blazed, her lips pressed together into a grim line. She knew she could not agree to those terms and she stubbornly refused to say anything to him.

His shoulders lifting in a casual shrug, Striped Eagle rose to his feet. "*Gee-mah-gi-on-ah-shig-wah*," he said, arming himself with his bow and arrow and gripping his rifle in his right hand. "Striped Eagle must leave now." He gave Morning Flower a stern look. "Little sister, my woman is not to leave this dwelling. Do you understand? You stay with her until my return."

Morning Flower nodded, guilt plaguing her. Knowing that Striped Eagle would most surely hate her when he discovered her deceit, she rushed to his arms and tightly embraced him. "Striped Eagle, I love you so," she cried softly. "Always remember that, my brother. Besides father, you have always been the most important person in my life."

Striped Eagle eased his free arm about his sister's tiny waist. But feeling the anxiousness in Morning Flower's hug and hearing it lace her voice, Striped Eagle's eyebrows forked. Knowing what he was about to do, did she fear for his life, or was it something else? There seemed to be a different sort of desperation about her mood. He had to wonder why.

He eased Morning Flower from his arms. He studied her face for a moment, seeing much written in the wavering of her eyes, the quivering of her lips. "What are you not telling me, Morning Flower?" he asked flatly. "You are not yourself. Do I have cause to believe you are not being altogether truthful to me? You act as one who has guilt heavy in her heart. Why is this, Morning Flower?''

Morning Flower winced, having feared that Striped Eagle, in his wisdom, would see her uneasiness, even feel it as she sped into his arms. She couldn't tell him that his Summer Sun would be gone upon his return home!

Oh, there was so much she could not tell him. There were so many feelings tearing her apart! Yet what she was doing was right. One day he would surely understand. When he would have a beautiful Ojibwa maiden ruling at his side he would understand and thank Morning Flower!

Truly believing this, Morning Flower squared her shoulders and defied Striped Eagle's accusing eyes. ''You are wrong,'' she said dryly. ''There is nothing that I have to tell you except that which I have already said. You must go. You must see to Ojibwa business this morning, my brother. I will see to your woman.''

Brenda quietly struggled against the bonds at her wrists, suddenly aware that Striped Eagle didn't trust his sister. Brenda now knew that she shouldn't, either. She must not depend on Morning Flower for anything. She must manage to wrest her wrists free!

The leather bindings cut into her flesh painfully, causing her to cease her struggles. When Striped Eagle went to the entrance flap and raised it, then stopped to give her a lingering tear-dampened gaze, she turned her eyes away.

Her spine grew stiff as she listened to him now outside his wigwam shouting orders to his braves. He, at this moment, was someone she neither understood nor knew. To her he had become the savage she had never thought him to be.

Twenty

Brenda scowled at Morning Flower, her wrists and ankles aching and raw from having struggled to get free. Determined to not let Morning Flower see that she felt utterly defeated, a thoroughly unwilling captive, Brenda kept her shoulders squared and her chin lifted, but her resolve was weakening as she occasionally glanced at Morning Flower. She was sitting just outside the opened entrance flap of the wigwam, preparing skins. Morning Flower had used a stone to scrape the hair from the remains of a deer and was now smearing the skin with the deer's brains.

"How can you do that?" Brenda suddenly blurted. "It is so . . . so inhuman."

Morning Flower cast Brenda a smug smile. "And you are the woman my brother chose to be his wife? You could never learn all that is required of an Ojibwa wife." She laughed softly. "Do you not know the importance of using the deer's brains on its skin? It is to make it soft. Later when it is clean and dry and soft as velvet I will cut it up into leggings."

Again laughing, Morning Flower continued her task.

"*Ay-uh*, it is wrong that you are here," she said. "It is best that you will soon be gone."

Brenda's eyes widened. "Gone? What do you mean . . . gone?" she challenged. "How can I? Your brother has made sure I won't leave." She lifted her bound wrists and gestured with them for Morning Flower to see. "How can I go anywhere with bound wrists and ankles? Striped Eagle has even ordered you to stand guard over me. There is no way I can escape this time, Morning Flower."

Morning Flower's eyes were gleaming as she again looked Brenda's way. "Morning Flower only pretend to watch you for brother," she said flatly. "Soon you *will* be gone. You shall see, white woman with the hair of flame. Soon you shall see."

Brenda shook her head, becoming more confused with each turn of their conversation. "How?" she murmured. "How is it that I will be gone? How do you *know* it?"

But at this, Morning Flower became silent, ignoring Brenda's further questions. She placed the skins aside that she was preparing and washed her hands in a wooden basin filled with water. She went back into Striped Eagle's dwelling and settled down onto the furs close to Brenda and began her beading.

"The Ojibwa women have many tasks assigned them," Morning Flower went on as if nothing was amiss. "They carry wood, plant seed, bear children and raise them, and they make dyes from berry juices and roots with which to paint designs upon their husbands' arrowheads and hunting knives. We spend many hours painting new symbols upon our dwellings."

Brenda sighed deeply as she listened to Morning Flower ramble on and on, and she suspected Morning Flower was passing the time away in an attempt to keep Brenda's mind from her predicament.

"Did you not know that red represents the sun, stone, and forms of animals?" Morning Flower said, stringing one bead and then another. "Blue represents heaven, winds, water, and thunder. Yellow represents sunshine . . ."

Morning Flower glanced at the entranceway nervously, relieved when she heard the thunder of hooves and knew that Striped Eagle had left. Now she could carry out her plan. It would be some time before Striped Eagle discovered anything and returned.

Her heart pounding, on the verge of being more daring today than ever before in her life, Morning Flower dropped her string of beads to the floor. She went to Brenda and knelt before her, her fingers trembling as she began loosening the leather bindings at Brenda's ankles.

"What are you doing . . . ?" Brenda gasped. She had wanted to ask Morning Flower to release her, but she never thought she would, and didn't even dream of bothering to ask. And now? Why would Morning Flower do it of her own volition? Was it a trick? What could Morning Flower's plans be for her once she *did* release her? Brenda didn't trust her. She was surprised that Striped Eagle had, in light of how Morning Flower had felt about Brenda from the very beginning.

Brenda grimaced when Morning Flower ignored her question and began working with the bonds at her wrists, the leather strips having already fallen away from her ankles. She rubbed her raw, aching wrists when they became free. "Why are you doing this?" she persisted, speaking guardedly.

"You want to leave village?" Morning Flower finally said. "You *leave*. Morning Flower *take* you. By canoe we go far, quickly."

"But, Striped Eagle . . ." Brenda protested, still not believing that Morning Flower's intentions were so good, or that she would go against the commands of her brother to do her a kindness. "He—"

"You will be gone when he returns," Morning Flower

said matter-of-factly. "You will never return. You will be at white man's community, *happy*."

Morning Flower took Brenda off guard by thrusting a buckskin dress into her arms. Only when she slapped a sheathed knife into Brenda's hand did she know the determination of Morning Flower.

"Dress is for you," Morning Flower said flatly. "It makes travel more simple than those over-big clothes of my brother's you now are wearing."

"And the knife?" Brenda cautiously questioned.

"You defend yourself," Morning Flower spat. "Do not be taken so easily by Dakota again so that my brother has to rescue you!"

"Oh, I see," Brenda said sarcastically. "It is not so much for my protection as it is for *yours*. You are doing everything possible to make sure I do not become involved in your life—*or* Striped Eagle's."

"That is so," Morning Flower said, placing her hands defiantly on her hips.

"What did you do to get Striped Eagle away from the village so that you could do this?" Brenda asked, quickly changing clothes, not wanting to miss this opportunity at hand. "And that you would even deceive him to help me surprises me."

Morning Flower's eyes grew glassy with hate. She spoke into Brenda's face. "Again I tell you. I do nothing for you," she hissed. "I do it for my *people*."

"Yes. For your people." Brenda sighed, placing the knife on her leg beneath the skirt of her dress. "But what about Striped Eagle? What about *him*?"

"My brother is always first in my mind," Morning Flower said, turning her eyes away from Brenda to look sullenly down into the fire. She was already dreading Striped Eagle's scolding. If he did not forgive her, she would forever pay for her deceit with his total silence after his scalding words had scorched and torn her heart apart.

"You didn't say, Morning Flower, how you made sure Striped Eagle would not be here so that you would be free to release me," Brenda said, combing her fingers through her lustrous red hair. "I knew you were too anxious to agree to watch me when Striped Eagle asked you to. I saw something in your expression that didn't ring true. Striped Eagle would have seen it also had he not been so angry and anxious to leave to get to Major Partain's dam."

Brenda stepped around, blocking Morning Flower's view of the fire. "What did you do? What did you say, Morning Flower, to get Striped Eagle to leave you alone with me?" she persisted.

Morning Flower's eyes wavered as she met Brenda's questioning gaze. "If you must know, there is no dam this morning," she said weakly. "There is no Major Partain building a dam. It was the only way to get Striped Eagle to leave the village for the length of time required to take you away with me. By the time Striped Eagle returns, you and I will be many miles upriver."

Brenda took a startled step backward, her eyes wide. "You lied to Striped Eagle?" she gasped. "You went this far to be sure that I wouldn't be Striped Eagle's woman?"

"*Ay-uh*," Morning Flower said, inwardly quaking when she again imagined Striped Eagle's reaction once he found out the truth. Hopefully, in time he would forgive her and come to know that what she did was for his benefit. "When I saw my brother return with you again to our village, I had to think quickly of a way to get you away from him. It was then that I knew that if it was to be done, finally done, *I* would have to do it."

Seizing the opportunity at hand, foolish even to be worrying about Striped Eagle's deceit, Brenda inched toward the entranceway. "Then let us go, Morning Flower," she murmured. "You are right to do this. It *is* best. For *everyone*."

"You follow," Morning Flower whispered, creeping

stealthily past Brenda. "No one must see us. News would spread much too quickly to my brother."

She ushered Brenda out of the wigwam and led her behind first one wigwam and then another, carefully avoiding being seen. When they finally reached Morning Flower's canoe and Brenda was safely inside it, Morning Flower hurriedly pushed the canoe from the shore and jumped into it herself. She maneuvered with the paddles and soon had the canoe moving down the river, staying close to the shoreline until beyond possible observation by any in the village of the White Bear band of the Ojibwa.

Then Morning Flower turned and glanced at Brenda over her shoulder from her position in the middle of the canoe, only momentarily resting her paddles. "Soon you will be in white community," she stated flatly. "Never again will you trouble my brother's heart!"

Brenda's insides quivered, wondering at Morning Flower's words. She was so vindictive. Could Morning Flower be trusted to take her to safety? Or could Morning Flower be planning to take her to an isolated spot along the river and abandon her?

But Brenda did not want to think of such possibilities. She wanted to believe that she would finally be able to point an accusing finger at Major Partain.

But never see Striped Eagle again . . . ? Now that she was close to what she thought she desired most in the world, she felt torn. Could she bear denying him to herself in making vengeance her choice . . . over him?

Clutching the sides of the canoe, Brenda watched the trees pass by her along the shore, feeling strangely empty when she should be feeling victory near. Soon she might finally have her revenge. But the thought still plagued her: had she also lost the man she would always love?

Many miles had been traveled. The sun was lowering in the sky, the forest darkening with shadows as Morning

Flower finally guided the canoe to shore. Moving lightly, as though weightless as a feather, she jumped from the vessel into knee-high water and stood holding the rocking canoe, looking harshly at Brenda.

"You now leave canoe," she said quickly. "You walk rest of the way. Morning Flower return to village of Ojibwa."

Brenda frowned as she looked into the distance, seeing nothing but trees. Her feelings of mistrust assailed her. "But I see no town," she said, her voice strained. She looked down the fluid avenue of the Mississippi River. "In no direction do I see any signs of life." She gave Morning Flower an angry stare. "You *have* tricked me, haven't you? You've brought me nowhere. I should have known better than to trust you even for one minute!"

"Leave canoe. Now," Morning Flower said, showing no emotion in her voice. "You go one way. I go another. That is the way it must be. You wanted to escape my brother's village. You have escaped. Woman with the hair of flame, do not expect any more than that from sister of next chief in line."

Brenda leaned with the wobbling canoe as she moved to her feet. Her lips set in a narrow line, she jumped down into the water, cringing when its coldness seeped through her moccasins and dress, touching her legs and feet like clutching, icy fingers.

"I hope you lose your way back to your village," Brenda snapped angrily, splashing toward shore. "I hope you have to spend a full night alone in the forest, as I know I am about to do, thanks to you!"

A mischievous smile touched Morning Flower's lips as she eased herself back into the canoe, purposely neglecting to tell Brenda that only over the hill and through the forest ahead she would find the town of Mendota. Morning Flower was enjoying this moment of torment too much to ease the white woman's mind. Hadn't the white woman caused Morning Flower nothing but aggravation since their first introduction? She was only paying her back in kind!

With skill learned from childhood, Morning Flower stroked her paddles through the water and was soon back in midstream, heading toward the sinking sun. Though she had the wrath of her brother to contend with upon her return to the village, what she had just done was right, she knew. She would gladly pay the penalty if it meant that this white woman would no longer plague her brother's life.

Smiling, she lifted the paddles in rhythmic strokes, not looking behind her, Brenda Pfleugger already a distant memory.

Brenda stood with her hands on her hips, following Morning Flower's canoe with her eyes until it was only a speck in the water in the distance. Then she swung around and began assessing this new dilemma in which she found herself. Which way should she travel? Did it make any difference?

Seeing how the land sloped upward where a break in the trees could be seen ahead, Brenda chose that route to travel. With determined steps she made her way onward.

Twenty-one

Fearing nightfall, Brenda made her way breathlessly up the steep incline toward the clearing. Birds scattered in the trees overhead, her presence frightening them from their evening nesting rituals. Her heart carried an ache within it now, for she was free, yet still a captive. Again she was a prisoner of dread. She had so hoped that what she had to do would soon be put behind her. If Morning Flower had only spoken truth instead of lies by saying she would take her to a white community, then everything would be going as planned.

But Brenda had been wrong to trust someone who so terribly disliked her. In truth, Striped Eagle had become the only one she could trust. Everything he did in her behalf was done with sincerity. Even today, when he had bound her, it had been done with only her welfare in mind.

Her thoughts returned with bitterness to Morning Flower, wondering what her reception would be upon returning to the Indian village. Would a brother banish a sister from the tribe because of her deceit? Or would Striped Eagle exhibit his customary gentleness and easily forgive her?

"Will he forgive *me*, should we chance meeting again?"
she worried aloud.

Then, knowing the dangers of being alone in the forest,
Brenda cast all thoughts but self and her need for revenge
from her mind and hurried her steps even faster, the calves
of her legs aching as she pushed her way on up the hill.

And then, finally, she reached its crest and was able to
see the distant vista. She was awestruck to discover that the
city of Mendota lay just below her, spread peacefully
alongside the silver reflections of the Mississippi River.
While in the canoe, searching in vain, she had not seen the
bend of the river which had hid Mendota beyond its snakelike curves.

Brenda's heart thundered wildly, her destination reached
. . . and, perhaps, her revenge near! Had Morning Flower
known that she had been near civilization when she had
chosen this spot at which to leave Brenda? Or had it been
by chance?

"It doesn't matter which! I am *here*!" Brenda cried
softly, joyously beaming.

Her hair shimmering in brilliant reds as the cool evening
breeze caressed it, Brenda stood for a moment to get her
bearings before venturing onward. In the green river valley
below, the rooftops of the village of Mendota were catching the last orange rays of the setting sun. Some roofs
were thatched and some were made of split-wood shakes.
Smoke spiraled lazily from the chimneys; dogs barked.

The streets were lined with businesses displaying gray
false fronts. Horses and buggies trundled along the dirt
streets, but most activity seemed to center about the wharves,
where men moved to and from moored sloops with their
single masts, fore-and-aft rigs, and single jibs.

From this vantage point, Brenda could hear a player
piano with its sharp, high notes tinkling boisterously from
a saloon. Loud guffaws echoed from its swinging doors,
making her tense. She was suddenly aware of what could

lay before her. It could be hard to find someone who would sympathize with her. Everyone was driven in their own way by life's fateful turns. Her problems could look less than important to those she might approach to seek help from. She might even be ignored, except for the fact that she was a woman. Most women were not ignored by men, especially those who had more than kindness on their minds.

Such a thought made a chill race across Brenda's flesh. The dangers she might be facing could be worse than any she had faced before. Yet she must do what she must. Major Partain had been a part of her nightmares for too many nights. He *must* be dealt with, no matter the risk!

Determined, she continued onward, now half running down the hill, from this point on not wagering what might become of her. Life had become a gamble. She knew that some gamblers won . . . some lost. She did know one thing for sure. She was becoming weary of this thing that ate away at her gut; revenge, when spoken, left a bitter taste on the tip of her tongue!

Her brow creased into a frown. Things in life had never been simple and were not easy now. There were many complications along the way, but it was in her power to erase one from her life. Major Partain. And it must be done, *now*.

When she reached level land she walked beneath the canopy of green trees, then splashed through a stream, completely wetting her moccasins and the hem of her dress. She moved endlessly onward, now through a grove of cottonwoods, finally coming to another clearing that stretched out into the outer limits of Mendota.

Fear and excitement fused inside Brenda. Her pulse raced; her face was flushed. She looked up the busy street that was so near her, seeing many lone horsemen. Could any truly be trusted? Thinking about approaching someone in the city for help had been easy, but actually doing it was another matter.

Having the need to first rest somewhere unnoticed, to get her breath and bolster the courage to do the deed so long planned, Brenda centered her attention on two buildings closest to her. She would find refuge between them to fully compose herself, where an alley lay deep in their shadows. She had to look calm and sure of herself when she approached anyone for assistance. No one should be able to sense her fear. And she must concentrate on the tactics to first test this man she would choose for sharing her confidences, to see what his feelings were for Major Partain.

When the right, trustworthy man was found, she would spill out the truth of what had happened to her parents and brother.

Hopefully, she would find the right man soon. She could not bear to think of having to carry this burden around with her for another night! And the longer Major Partain was allowed to run free, the longer innocent people would suffer because of him!

Moving stealthily into the city, watching for any suspicious attention on all sides of her, Brenda was glad to finally reach the buildings where she would find some sort of peace before rushing herself into another potential stormy situation.

Nervous perspiration beading her brow, she moved deeper into the shadows, back where she could assure herself full privacy. But the sound of an approaching wagon from somewhere close behind her made Brenda turn with a start. Her spine stiffened when she saw that a covered wagon pulled by a team of two horses had entered the alley and was moving toward her, with barely enough space between the buildings for the wagon to squeeze through.

Then Brenda's gaze settled on the driver of the wagon.

Though it was fast growing dusk, she could see well enough that this man had only one eye. A scar stretched across his face where the other eye should have been. He was stocky, attired in bright clothes: a colorful flowered-decorated shirt with flaring, long sleeves, and bright red breeches banded at the waist by an even brighter red sash.

His hair was black and brushed his shoulders. Gold hoop earrings hung from his earlobes. His complexion was ruddy, his nose bulbous. And as he grew closer, Brenda could see a half smile lifting his lips and that his one lone, gray eye appeared bottomless, raking over her, as though he had been without a woman for too lengthy a spell. Brenda shivered at the implicit danger she was in.

This sense of threat building inside her, Brenda began inching her way backward. She had been wrong to seek the dark shadows between the buildings. She would surely be much safer out on the streets than here, where this evil-looking man could have his way with her should he choose to!

Clumsily she moved backward, her eyes riveted in place, watching his every movement as he led his team of horses toward her.

Then, breathless from fear, her knees weak, Brenda turned and began to run, only now realizing just how far from the street she had come to seek her moment of privacy. Her eyes wild, her throat dry, she ran faster.

But hearing the continuing rattle of the wheels of the wagon and the steady clip-clop of the horses behind her, she knew that he was still not far behind. He had nowhere else to go but forward in these tight confines! Nor did *she*. Hopefully he didn't have what she dreaded on his mind. But she couldn't take that chance. He had looked at her as a man does when he had only evil thoughts on his mind!

Lifting the skirt of her dress, baring her knees, she ran harder . . . harder. Her breath was coming in shorter gasps and her side ached. Now, with the street so near, she began to doubt she could even reach it. Her legs felt as though they might buckle beneath her at any moment! Could this truly be happening . . . was she to become a victim . . . again? How many more times could she find the courage to face such trauma? Even now she felt that all was lost to her, possibly forever . . .

She looked toward the heavens, tears sparkling in her eyes. "Lord, please let me be wrong," she softly prayed. "Let me be wrong about this man. Let him just pass on by me. Let my fears be unfounded!"

Suddenly she was aware that she didn't hear the horses or the wagon. The man had stopped. Did that mean . . . ?

Brenda didn't have time to turn around to see why all was quiet behind her. An arm suddenly encircled her waist. Her heart skipped a beat as panic rose inside her. She was so frightened no scream would surface. It was as though her throat was frozen!

Twisted around by force, now feeling fingers on her shoulders digging into her flesh, Brenda was made to look into the face of the leering, one-eyed man. She had been right to fear him, to run from him. He wouldn't be holding her so brusquely if he didn't have something horrible in mind for her!

Her arms flailing, Brenda struggled to get free. She kicked aimlessly at the man, the skirt of her dress tangling with her movements to lessen the blows against the hard flesh of his legs.

"Let me go!" she was finally able to scream, her voice mercifully back. "What do you want of me? Let . . . me . . . go . . . !"

"It ain't every day I find me a waif lurkin' in the alleys of Mendota," the man chuckled, his voice low and gruff. "Now ain't I lucky? Just what I needed. A pretty lady to keep me company for a while."

Brenda looked frantically around her, hoping someone would pass by to discover her plight. But there was no one

within seeing or hearing range. She was trapped. The
worst of her fears had come to pass. Luck would have it
that if there was an evil man close by, she would attract
him to her!

Anger replacing the fear that had robbed her of her
senses, Brenda knew that if she didn't fight for her survival, no one would. She was alone, by choice, wasn't
she? She had gambled and again she had lost.

Her hands free, Brenda swept them quickly down and
formed her fingers into claws. She sank them into the flesh
of his face, pleased when he emitted a loud yowl of pain
and by instinct released her.

Wheeling around, Brenda began running again. She was
blinded by her flying hair. She ran her fingers through the
wild tresses and struggled to get them from her eyes. The
tail of her dress was an encumbrance, twisting and circling
about her legs.

Cursing beneath her breath she tripped, falling with a
jolt against the hard, rain-starved ground, momentarily
dazed as her head hit the earth.

Lying there, shaking her head, Brenda was only half
aware of movement beside her. And then suddenly rough
hands were on her wrists, forcing her back to her feet. The
one-eyed man stood before her, blood-streaked welts rising
on his clawed face.

When he growled and doubled a fist to hit her in the
jaw, the pain was only momentary, for a blackness rushing
before her eyes enveloped her in unconsciousness. She
wasn't even aware when the man swept her up into his
arms and carried her to his covered wagon.

Twenty-two

Striped Eagle stood motionless, staring disbelievingly where he had been told a dam was being built across the White Bear River. His insides were numb. There was no evidence of a dam there, *ever*. He had been lied to, and by his sister. Never had she lied to him before. Why would she now?

Straightening his back, he emitted a soft cry, startling his braves who were still on horseback behind him. He could only guess why his sister had lied to him. It was to steer him away from the village because of Summer Sun. Morning Flower had never approved of her, no matter how she had tried to pretend that she did. Telling him falsely about the dam had been a ploy to get him away from the village so that Morning Flower could release Summer Sun, possibly even lead his woman from the village herself.

"She has betrayed me!" he shouted, lifting a fist toward the sky. "Morning Flower, *gah-ween-nee-nee-sis-eh-tos-say-non*!"

Then he lowered his fist, his heart flaming with anger. He quickly mounted his stallion. "*Mah-szhon!*" he shouted to his braves. "We must return to our village. *Wee-weeb!* Quickly!"

Wheeling his horse around, he thundered away from the river, filled with pain at this betrayal.

His heart heavy, anger and hurt fusing inside him because of his sister's deceit, Striped Eagle rode at a steady lope on his white stallion, the fires of his village reflecting orange onto the black velvet cover of the sky only a short distance ahead. Without even returning to his wigwam he knew he would not find Brenda there.

Bitter, Striped Eagle's thoughts returned to Morning Flower and how she had so sweetly promised to make sure Summer Sun didn't escape again from his dwelling, all along knowing that she would even help Summer Sun to do so. That had to be the only reason his sister had led him astray, lied about the dam having again been built. To have the chance to rid the village of the Ojibwa of the beautiful white woman and the threat she posed to his people as seen in Morning Flower's eyes. Did his sister hate Summer Sun so much that she felt the need to lie to her own brother? It was something Striped Eagle may never understand!

His braves following close behind him, Striped Eagle dug his heels into the flanks of his stallion. "*Aiee,*" he shouted, urging his steed onward.

He held his chin high although he felt shamed by his sister's behavior. It would look most disrespectful in the eyes of the other Ojibwa braves, a sister's deceit of her brother . . . a brother who would one day reign as chief!

Yet how does one punish a sister for such behavior? It was not in Striped Eagle's heart to make an example of his very own sister! Somehow he would think of a way . . . somehow he would see that she would make amends to Striped Eagle so that he would not lose face!

A mournful sound echoing through the forest ahead

made Striped Eagle jerk his reins to draw his steed to a sudden halt. "*No-gee-shkan!*" he shouted, raising a hand into the air, commanding his braves to rein to a halt.

With trained ears, he listened in the direction of the sound, now recognizing the sound that was so mournful it made the hair at the nape of Striped Eagle's neck rise. He lowered his hand and cast a nervous glance over his shoulder, studying the faces of his followers. They had also heard. Fear was etched onto their faces, as it was engraved into Striped Eagle's heart.

"*Way-nen-dush-win-ah-ow?*" he said, receiving no substantial reply, only a quivering of grunts traveling from man to man, blending into one worrisome sound.

Turning his head to peer straight ahead, Striped Eagle listened again. His pulse began to race, *ay-uh*, recognizing the wails of the Ojibwa who cried in mournful cadence with the steady beat of drums, both sounds reverberating around Striped Eagle. Such sounds were only made when someone of great importance had died in the village, to show respect for the loss of someone so powerful . . .

The pit of Striped Eagle's stomach felt suddenly hollow, knowing that such mourning would take place should a *chief* die!

Again he looked over his shoulder, checking from man to man, seeing a wariness in each of his braves' eyes. "*Neen gee-bah-bah?*" he said in a strained voice.

When heads nodded, agreeing that it most surely was his father being mourned, Striped Eagle quickly turned his eyes away. He feared that the sudden tears wetting the corners of his eyes might be reflected beneath the rays of the moon, disclosing his weakness. He had to show much courage at a time such as this. His people would expect it of him. If his father was truly dead, Striped Eagle was even now chief of his people!

Raising his eyes to the sky, he spoke a silent prayer to the Great Spirit, Wenebojo, to look after him in this time of great sorrow. He asked for Wenebojo to give him the wisdom he sorely needed. He must have strength. For he had loved his father boundlessly, the great chief—the great *man*—that he had been! It was going to take much guidance for Striped Eagle to be as knowledgeable in ruling his people!

The continuing wails speared Striped Eagle's heart painfully. Too much time had been wasted in meditating. His father was waiting. It was his duty to go to him and prepare him for his long journey to the hereafter. His father was past this life and all its troubles. He had been blessed with the kiss of death. It was now for the living to adjust to his loss. It was always the living who suffered in death . . .

Striped Eagle raised a fist into the air. "*Aiee!*" he shouted. "*Bee-mee-nee-szhah*! We must hurry, my brothers!"

The wind brushing past his face was cold, but Striped Eagle did not feel it. The leather reins held so tightly within his grip were cutting his flesh, but he did not feel this either. He felt a strange numbness he had never felt before, but he had never lost a father before. Losing a father was the same as losing part of a son's own self! It was up to Striped Eagle to acquire his father's better traits, in a sense *become* his father. Only by doing so could Striped Eagle feel whole again . . . become as one with the memory of his dearly departed father.

Urging his horse to thunder onward, Striped Eagle leaned low over its thick, flying mane. He squinted his eyes and pressed his lips tightly together, now so close to his village that the wails were so piercing they seemed to tear pieces of his heart away!

When he reached the outermost edges of the village he wheeled his horse to a sudden stop, commanding his braves to follow his lead. Dismounting, Striped Eagle secured his reins to the lower limb of a maple tree, then went by foot into the village, past wigwams and blazing outdoor fires.

Out of the corner of his eye he saw his people, men, women and children alike, falling into step behind him, shrouded beneath white blankets signifying the white trail of the stars whither the Ojibwa felt their loved one had gone.

No words were spoken to Striped Eagle. The wailing had even ceased, the drums silenced. He held his head high, walking solemnly onward.

As Striped Eagle reached his father's dwelling, the light of the outdoor fire played on the colorful designs painted on the wigwam. The eyes of the large thunderbird appeared alive, as though following Striped Eagle as he stepped up to the closed entrance flap which separated him from the reality of death.

Only a quick glance was sent toward his own wigwam, knowing to go there would be to find it empty. It was not time to dwell on why. Duties of a son, of a *chief*, were now precedent over all else.

Needing added strength, Striped Eagle stepped closer to the entrance flap and raised his eyes to the heavens. Silently, he again asked for strength . . . for courage . . . for guidance. His father awaited his full attention, and then his people . . .

A total peacefulness settling over him, Striped Eagle smiled to himself, feeling as though Wenebojo had heard his pitiful plea. He felt strong. He felt as though his burden of sadness had been momentarily eased. He silently thanked Wenebojo for the respect shown him from this mighty spirit, now also understanding that Wenebojo already approved of his status as chief.

With squared shoulders and uplifted head, Striped Eagle stepped into his father's dwelling. One glance about him showed that Morning Flower was not there. This was proof that she was, as he had expected, not in the village.

If she was, she would be at her father's side, mourning, drawing comfort from his nearness for just a while longer, before he was laid to rest beside his descendants in the burial ground of the White Bear band of the Ojibwa.

Knowing of his sister's betrayal no longer weighed heavy on Striped Eagle's heart. No thought of how to punish plagued him. Upon her return, it would be punishment enough for her to find that her father had taken his final breaths of life while she had not been there to comfort him, as daughters were meant to do. In time Striped Eagle would put things right after what Morning Flower had done. He would go after his Summer Sun. She would never leave him again. When she found that he was a great chief how could she turn her back to being his princess?

Shaking off thoughts that were not proper at this time, Striped Eagle stepped further into the large dwelling and peered through a haze of smoke swirling from rocks heating in the firespace. The fragrance of medicinal herbs, spread across the rocks where the fire could not reach them, lay heavy about him, purifying the air.

The smoke dissipating in the draft caused by the lifted entrance flap, Striped Eagle got his first glance of his father, lying peacefully quiet atop a raised platform at the far end of the wigwam, a robe of white encasing his body, only open at his face for viewing. A knot twisted in Striped Eagle's gut. He emitted a low cry of remorseful pain as he went to kneel beside his father whose face reflected in a death mask of a smile the gentleness of the life he spent.

"*Gee-bah-bah*," Striped Eagle said in a choked whisper, humbly bowing his head. "*Ah-nish-min-eh-wah*? Do you leave your son so ill prepared? No chief will ever be as great as you."

Striped Eagle's spine stiffened when the mournful wails again began in cadence with the drumbeats outside his father's dwelling. He knew what must be done: it was up to him to prepare his father for burial. And then Striped Eagle would wait a while for his sister's return for the burial rites to begin. He would wait the full night and the next day. But no longer. His father could not begin his long journey to the hereafter until placed in his grave with his feet toward the west, the direction of the departed spirit's journey.

Another choked sob rose from Striped Eagle's throat as he recalled the times spent with his father, learning the customs of their people. His father had talked of death, of burial. His father had said that the land of the departed spirits was not of necessity toward the west, but somewhere as though in *space* . . .

Striped Eagle's father had said there was day and night in that place, but that during the day there was absolute silence. When night came the drums were beaten at some particular spot and the spirits assembled from all directions and danced during the entire night, dispersing at daybreak.

His father's words would forever be with Striped Eagle to guide him. And it seemed strange that Striped Eagle would be following the burial rite instructions taught by his father who had known even then that his son would one day be using these teachings to ready him for the grave. As one day Striped Eagle would also teach a son . . .

A momentary thought of Summer Sun flashed across his consciousness. A son by her; a daughter . . .

Knowing this was not the time to let his thoughts wander from duties to a father, Striped Eagle looked about him, seeing that the maidens of the village had already brought the necessary articles for preparing his father's body. Again he looked down at his father. With trembling fingers, he removed the blanket from his father's body to bare a massive chest and squared, proud shoulders. Even in death Chief Growling Bear embodied power and greatness. He would walk proudly among his departed loved ones, still the greatest of them all!

Attired in only his breechcloth, his own muscles reflecting a copper sheen beneath the glow of the fire in the firespace, Striped Eagle shifted a basin of oiled water close to his father and began washing him gently.

When this was done Striped Eagle neatly braided his father's hair, then dressed the body in his father's most elaborately decorated shirt and breeches, both of which displayed a great quantity of every sort of beadwork, now catching the light of the fire in them.

And then was added his father's headdress of many feathers, placed neatly beneath his head with the feathers about his face, boldly bright . . . boldly poignant . . .

And then Striped Eagle placed a round spot of brown fungus on each of his father's cheeks, and over this painted a horizontal line of vermilion. He painted his father's moccasins brown, and drew brown streaks on his blanket.

Finally, his father's body was fully arrayed and ready to join the dance of the ghosts in the land of the hereafter.

With this done, Striped Eagle rose to his feet and began moving about the dwelling, gathering together those articles of his father's which had been particularly valued by him in life. He chose his father's pipe and tobacco pouch, and placed these close to his father's face so that the aroma of the tobacco would forever please him.

And because his father had been a great hunter Striped Eagle placed his father's rifle beside him as well as his bow and quiver of arrows.

Striped Eagle eyed the heavy birch-bark sheets awaiting him to be wrapped about his father after his people had paid their last respects to their departed chief. That would make everything final. Striped Eagle was glad that his sister had momentarily strayed, causing the burial services to be delayed. It gave Striped Eagle more time alone with his father before the final farewell.

Settling down on his haunches beside his father, Striped Eagle clasped his hands together before him. The plaintive wails continuing outside the wigwam were proof of the love the White Bear band of the Ojibwa had for their departed chief. Striped Eagle was glad. But he did not wail. He was a person of strength. But he *could* cry. Crying was silent. Bowing his head, rocking back and forth on his haunches, he let the tears cool his flushed cheeks.

In a self-induced trance Striped Eagle had sat vigil beside his father throughout the night. Only when he finally heard a soft voice speaking behind him did he respond to his surroundings. Morning Flower had returned home. It was her voice reaching beyond that wall of controlled inducement.

Moving lithely to his feet, Striped Eagle turned and found Morning Flower pleading with him with the deep pools of her dark eyes. It was not in him to scold her for her bad behavior, although seeing her reminded him of his Summer Sun and of her absence in his wigwam at a time when he sorely needed her comfort. As he had guessed, Morning Flower was suffering enough, having been greeted back into the village of the Ojibwa by news of her father's death.

Tears silvering her cheeks, Morning Flower looked past Striped Eagle to Chief Growling Bear. She placed a fist to her lips and sobbed, then again beseeched Striped Eagle with her weeping eyes.

"*Gee-bah-bah*," she softly cried. "Father is dead, Striped Eagle. He is *dead*. When? How long?" She threw herself into Striped Eagle's arms. "Morning Flower so ashamed, Striped Eagle. Morning Flower should have been here. First I shame you, then father . . ."

Striped Eagle was showing restraint learned as a child by not asking about Summer Sun; where she might be,

who she was with, if she was all right. These questions
would come later, after his silent mourning was a thing of
the past. He had to forget Summer Sun for many days
now, days requiring him to depart to some desolate hillside
to meditate with the spirits during the time when his
father's spirit would be on its long journey to the hereafter.

Easing Morning Flower away from him, Striped Eagle
gently clasped her shoulders with his hands. "It is not the
time to dwell on concerns of self," he grumbled. "It is
time to do what is required to see to Father's burial,
Morning Flower." His brow furrowed into a frown. "Are
you of sound mind for doing this thing? Can you place
your tears behind you? A departed chief's daughter must be
as strong as was the chief." He leaned closer to her. "A
chief's sister must be as strong as her chieftain brother.
Make me proud, Morning Flower. Set an example for all
our people to see."

Morning Flower lifted her chin and looked deeply into
Striped Eagle's eyes. A soft smile touched her lips. "My
brother is now chief," she murmured. "Morning Flower
will do what new chief commands."

In her white doeskin dress, delicate and soft, Morning
Flower slipped from Striped Eagle's grasp. Still watching
his eyes she bent before the firespace and swept her fingers
into the cooled ashes at the edges, then again stood and
began applying the black ash to Striped Eagle's face in the
symbol required for a man in deep mourning.

When this was completed, his face completely black,
Striped Eagle turned Morning Flower around, placing her
back to him, and began unbraiding her hair. This was
proof of *her* mourning.

After the hair was unbraided Striped Eagle greased it
with deer tallow until it shone, then tied the hair back with
a thong and let it hang straight and long down her back.

Morning Flower turned and obediently stood while Striped
Eagle placed narrow strips of braided buckskin about her

neck and waist, then let her place the same on him, both required to wear these during their period of mourning.

Striped Eagle's and Morning Flower's eyes met and held as Striped Eagle drew her into his arms. "Be *zongh-gee-day-ay*, my sister," he murmured. "Bravery is needed at this time."

Softly sobbing, closing her eyes as she pressed her cheek against Striped Eagle's chest, she gathered strength from his words as well as his arms. "*Ay-uh*," she whispered. "Morning Flower is brave. Morning Flower ready for the burial rites."

"Then it shall begin. Take your place at father's side, Morning Flower," Striped Eagle said, stepping away from her.

Nodding, Morning Flower stepped up to the platform and fell to her knees beside her father. Clasping her hands in her lap she gazed upon a face of gladness, pleased that her father was happy, not sad, to face his long journey. She was only half aware of the mourners now entering the dwelling one at a time. She barely heard the low chants and the rattles of the shaman as he now performed his rituals over her father's lifeless body. Little did she notice the voices speaking low to her father, wishing him well, as his warriors knelt at his side, speaking with extreme rapidity.

As though in a trance, Morning Flower had to be led away from her father after everyone had gone. Striped Eagle and she were again alone in the wigwam and Striped Eagle had already wrapped their father in very heavy birch bark tied with basswood cord, his valued articles wrapped with him.

"It is now time for the burial," Striped Eagle said, praying she would be strong enough for this part of the ritual. Together they must carry their father to his final resting place. As frail as she was he only hoped she had the muscle to do this last chore for her father.

"*Ay-uh*, Striped Eagle," she said, humbly lowering her eyes. "*Ay-uh*."

Striped Eagle positioned himself at the head of his father, Morning Flower at his feet. As though the departed chief was as light as a feather, they moved from the wigwam, carrying him. The mourners of the village followed along after them. After Chief Growling Bear had been placed in his shallow grave and covered by many birch-bark coverings, Morning Flower did the requisite dance around the grave and then it was over.

Sadly, Morning Flower returned to her wigwam. Striped Eagle went to Chief Growling Bear's two prized horses. Knowing that his father's spirit required it, his horses needed to assist him on his long journey, Striped Eagle did not flinch when he killed them and placed their two heads toward the east, fastening their tails on a scaffold toward the west.

Standing over his father's grave, Striped Eagle raised his arms to the sky, spreading his fingers. "It is done, my father," he cried. "May your journey be safe. *Wee-wee-bee-tahn*! Go in peace, my beloved father!"

Without a word of good-bye, knowing that everyone knew what was required of him, Striped Eagle left the village, searching for the proper hillside on which to spend his days fasting and communing with the spirits. He would sit amid cloud, sunshine, and storm, with bowed head, in solemn silence.

Twenty-three

Stirring from her unconscious state, Brenda heard voices that sounded as though they were being spoken from the depths of a well. She shook her head, trying to clear her muddled senses, now understanding why the voices sounded so hollow. It was because her head was throbbing so unmercifully. And the more she awakened the more alert she became to the pain in her jaw and the rawness of her wrists and ankles. She understood why her jaw ached. She was just recalling the one-eyed man and the fact that he had hit her! But her wrists? Her ankles?

Blinking her eyes nervously, now fully awake, Brenda found the source of her pain. She tried to move her wrists, then her ankles, only to discover that they were bound. Again she was a captive! The one-eyed man must have abducted her!

Scooting into a sitting position, Brenda squinted her eyes, trying to see through the darkness that spread out on all sides of her. The only light she could see seeped in at the bottom of what must be a door a few yards away from her.

Sniffing, she smelled an unpleasant odor. Its aroma was something similar to yeast. Or was it whiskey? She gathered that she had been put in some sort of storage room, and on the floor, for the hardness pressed into her thighs as though giant fingers grasped her.

Squirming, trying to reposition herself on the floor, Brenda heard the voices of men coming from an outer room. Her heartbeat grew erratic for a moment as she recognized one of the voices. She couldn't be mistaken. She had heard his voice not only in her nightmares, but also in real life. She would never forget the times he had ordered her father from the land her father had toiled over.

Brenda grew numb with fear. She could never be mistaken about Major Partain's voice. It *was* he! He was in the next room. But how, why? Had she been taken to Fort Snelling?

But it didn't matter where she was. What mattered most was that if Major Partain saw her, he would most surely recognize her. And if he did, she was doomed!

Frantically working at the strips of leather at her wrists, Brenda only managed to make her flesh burn even more. In her struggles, her elbow accidentally grazed against something, knocking it onto the floor beside her.

She grimaced as glass shattered, its sound ringing in her ears, knowing that not only had *she* heard it, but undoubtedly the one-eyed man and Major Partain as well.

Their voices suddenly lulled to low murmurings in the other room, Brenda awaited the inevitable: the door opening. Trembling, barely breathing, she watched the door, her eyes wide. When the door finally opened with a jerk and she saw the silhouette of two men standing against the light in the outer room, Brenda began inching her way backward. From having been forced to stay in the dark room for so long, the brightness of the light shining through the open door almost blinded her. And she was quite aware of the light now illuminating her face, giving Major Partain a full view of who was being held captive.

"So this is the plaything you were tellin' me about, eh?" Major Partain said, kneading his chin contemplatively. His eyebrows arched. "Hmm. Pig's Eye, seems something mighty familiar about 'er. Do you mind if we get 'er out here, so's I can take a better look, eh?"

"Been meanin' to anyway," Pig's Eye Pete said, laughing boisterously. "Cain't leave her sittin' among my liquor in the dark for too long. The fumes might jest set her aglow!"

Hearing the name Pig's Eye sent Brenda's thoughts back to something her father had told her many months ago. He had been talking about a man who sold whiskey to white men, and *illegal* whiskey to the Indians. Her father had called the whiskey trader by the name Pig's Eye Pete, a man known not only because of the whiskey he sold, but also because he had only one eye.

Her father had also said that he had heard that the authorities had been paid well to leave Pig's Eye Pete alone to his whiskey dealing as he saw fit. Brenda's father had even said that he suspected Major Partain was the one responsible for letting the unethical whiskey trader make and sell his wares to the Indians, knowing too well the effects alcohol had on them.

It was just another corrupt practice of Major Partain to add to his list of many!

Towering over her, Pig's Eye Pete grabbed Brenda by her bound wrists and jerked her to her feet. Steadying herself, she was glad when he bent to a knee and released her ankles so she could walk on her own, though she dreaded being pulled into the light, knowing that she was a moment away from Major Partain recognizing her.

She would not be one so easily forgotten by the major. It was she whom had stood defiantly at her father's side so often when he had come to make his outlandish demands. Many times, she had even followed Major Partain from the land, running after him as he rode away on horseback. After making sure she was out of her father's sight, Brenda had defied the major with harsh words . . . words that had not been ladylike to say . . . words she had not been taught from the Bible!

Yes, she knew that he would recognize her once under the bright light. He was soon to know that he had not killed everyone that fateful night of not so long ago, having left one member of the Pfleugger family to reveal the perfidy that was him.

But soon he would also more than likely silence her. This time she would have no way to escape. Between these two men, she could expect to be used, degraded, and only at last murdered.

Fear rippled at the pit of her stomach and her pulse raced as she was shoved from the dark room into a room whose drab walls were filled with shelves of bottles and jugs of whiskey. Two tin cups sat on a simple table, a kerosene lamp reflecting its light into the yellow liquid inside them. The two men reeked of alcohol. Brenda was positioned between them, each looking her over as though mentally undressing her.

"Well? Do you know 'er?" Pig's Eye said, his hands on his hips, his one eye squinting. His face still showed red welts from Brenda's fingernails. He reached for his tin cup of whiskey and swallowed a quick gulp, then wiped his lips dry with the back of his hand. "She's a beauty, ain't she, Major?" he chuckled.

Brenda recoiled as she let her gaze move timidly to Major Partain. A keen hate for him stung her inside as she found herself even more closely scrutinized by the dark eyes beneath his bushy black eyebrows. His thin lips were pursed; the crook of his nose seemed more prominent as he pressed his face closer to hers. The powerful muscles of

his shoulders and wide chest were pronounced in his blue
uniform, its brass buttons shining down the front and at the
cuffs of his coat. His breeches were pressed to perfection.

As he stroked his chin, cocking an eyebrow quizzically,
Brenda's insides rolled with fear. There was no doubt that
he would recognize her. And when he did . . .

"Brenda Pfleugger," Major Partain suddenly blurted.
He took a step backward, a nerve jumping beneath his left
eye. "Well, I'll be damned. If it ain't Brenda Pfleugger."
Again he kneaded his chin. "But *how*? I thought—"

In a flash, courage again returned to Brenda. She took a
bold step forward, her chin lifted. "You thought what?"
she hissed. "That you had murdered me along with the
rest of my family?"

She stubbornly straightened her back. "Well, as you
see, you didn't. I'm very much alive, Major Partain," she
fumed.

She nodded toward Pig's Eye Pete. "And had it not
been for this . . . this whiskey-seller, I would have re-
ported you. I would have surely found at least *one* decent,
honest man in whom to confide."

She tightened her jaw. "If I get the chance to escape
from here I *still* will do what must be done. You must be
stopped. And if I'm not given the chance, someone will
eventually be brave enough to tell of your evil deeds."

Knowing that she had probably said far too much, Brenda's knees and the pit of her stomach suddenly weakened.
Now the major would most certainly see to it that she not
be allowed to escape. But the words had just flowed from
her mouth, propelled by the hate she had carried in her
heart for this man for so long. At least, she reflected, if
she *did* die at the hands of either of these men, she had
said her piece and she was glad for it!

Major Partain's eyes narrowed. He glanced nervously
over at Pig's Eye, then back to Brenda. "You shut your
damn mouth," he growled. "You're talkin' outta your

head. That's what fear does to a woman. Makes 'er talk too much.''

Pig's Eye Pete looked from Brenda to Major Partain. He scratched his brow idly. "What she said," he said dryly. "Is it true? She doesn't seem to be talkin' at all outta her head. Did you kill her family, Major?"

Hope rose inside Brenda. Strange as it would be, under the circumstances of having been abducted by the man, perhaps Pig's Eye Pete would be just the man she had been looking for. Though he *had* wrongly abducted her, maybe he had a thread of decency running through him. If he didn't agree with Major Partain's schemes to rid the land of the settlers—killing them if they didn't abide by his rules—then Pig's Eye Pete could see to it that Major Partain was dealt with!

She watched as Major Partain slowly inched his hand to a belted pistol hidden beneath the long tail of his coat.

"And if I did see a need to do away with them, would that matter, eh, Pig's Eye?" Major Partain mumbled, raising the corner of his coat to reveal the pistol to Pig's Eye. He rested his hand on the pistol, spreading his legs as though readying himself to draw the weapon.

Pig's Eye Pete's face drained of color. He took a step backward, then laughed awkwardly. "Hell, no, Major," he said. "Don't matter none to me *what* you do with them damn settlers. I've had my own run-in with a few over my whiskey-tradin' ways." He lifted his shoulders in a lazy shrug. "Do what you damn want. You're doin' me a favor, too. These damn settlers've got what's comin' to 'em, as *I* sees it."

Brenda's heart seemed to plummet to her feet, despair sorely filling her with the knowledge that her last hope had just been robbed. The cursed, filthy man, Pig's Eye Pete, was no better than Major Partain. He would even let Major Partain *kill* her if he so desired.

Looking on, fear almost stealing both her breath and

heartbeat, Brenda looked from man to man, awaiting her verdict, confident that it would come soon.

Major Partain shifted his feet and dropped his hand away from his pistol. "Now that's more like it," he said, clearing his throat. He glared over at Brenda, then let his gaze rake slowly over her. "What've you got planned for 'er, Pig's Eye?"

Pig's Eye went to a window and raised its buckskin covering and spat outside, then walked heavy-footed back to Brenda. He placed his fingers to her hair and lifted it, letting it tumble a few tresses at a time back to her shoulders.

"Well, now, don't take much thought to figure that out, does it?" Pig's Eye laughed. "You don't find 'em as purty as this every day, eh, Major?"

"She might be pretty but she sure as hell is a feisty one," Major Partain grumbled. He poured more whiskey into his tin cup and swallowed it in three large gulps, all the while watching Brenda.

"Feisty ones are the most fun," Pig's Eye Pete said, guffawing. His pudgy hand cupped a breast through the buckskin of Brenda's dress, making her wince as though she'd been slapped. "I must say this for 'er, she's well endowed. Want to see her with 'er clothes off, Major?"

Major Partain's eyes became dark with lust. He slammed the cup down on the table and stood with his hands on his hips, leering down at her. "Yeah, why not?" he said huskily. "Might as well have some fun before we do away with 'er, eh?"

The words hit Brenda like a cold splash of water in her face. She looked frantically about, desperation for escape so keen she felt dizzy from the rising panic. Her gaze settled on the thin buckskin that hung loosely over the door that led to the outside. If she could just run . . .

"Don't get any ideas," Major Partain growled, following the path of her vision. "You wouldn't get far. And if you *do* try to run, I'd get my pleasure in shootin' *then* rapin' you. Makes no difference to me. Your body would still be warm if I'd hurry fast enough.''

A bitterness rose up into Brenda's throat at his words. Had he no morals . . . no respect for human life at all? Did he merely exist for the pleasures he could seek for himself? He was not only driven by greed but by ignorance as well.

Brenda couldn't understand how such a man could hold such a position of power at Fort Snelling. But maybe she could: he probably blackmailed his way into the position, fear of him securing it for him. She was in misery over her collapsed plans to expose him that had failed. But his kind couldn't go on forever. He would get caught. He would be punished; with luck, he would die!

''One day you are going to meet your match,'' she hissed. ''You will be dealt with properly when that time comes. And it *will* come, Major Partain. Mark my word, it will come.''

Major Partain threw his head back with a fitful laugh. ''And you had thought I had met my match in you?'' he said, sobering as his eyes narrowed again to look down at her. ''You were a mite careless, don't you think, pretty lady? You let yourself get abducted by Pig's Eye. Now no one will even know what happened to you.''

''I'm not alone in the world,''she softly argued, telling a half lie. ''More than one person will come looking for me. And when they do, you will have breathed your last!''

Major Partain grabbed her by the wrists and jerked her to him. ''I always thought you had a big mouth on you,'' he growled. ''Bet your pa didn't know you used cuss words on me those times that you did, did he? He thought he'd raised a genteel little princess, didn't he? Well, your pa ain't here for me to tell now. And I don't give a damn who comes lookin' for me. Let 'em come. I cover my tracks well. You won't be around for them to find. I plan to feed your carcass to the wolves once I'm through with you.''

Brenda blanched; her stomach rolled. ''You won't get away with it,'' she said, her voice trembling. ''You *won't*. You'll be caught. You just can't get away with killing innocent people. Somehow . . . you'll get caught.''

''As far as you're concerned there'll be no proof of what happened to your family,'' Major Partain grumbled. ''You'll be dead and you're the only proof.''

The thundering of hoofbeats outside the cabin drew Pig's Eye Pete to the door. Lifting a corner of the buckskin, he peeked outside, then swung around and faced Major Partain. ''Injuns,'' he said in a loud whisper. ''I clean forgot. The Dakota were comin' to trade today. Best we deal with them first, Major. Don't want to get their dander up. I don't hanker to part with my scalp.''

''Then do your tradin', damn it,'' Major Partain grumbled. He motioned toward Brenda. ''But first get her outta sight.''

Pig's Eye Pete hurried to Brenda and grabbed her by an arm and pushed her into the storage room. ''Now, if you know what's good for you, you'll keep quiet,'' he warned. ''The Dakota ain't ones to fool around with.''

Remembering her experience with the Dakota, Brenda's hopes of getting rescued were dashed. Suddenly, it dawned on her: didn't the Dakota know of her alliance with Striped Eagle? Should they see her here, they might ask to take her away with them, hoping that they might again win many furs from Striped Eagle in exchange for his woman.

It was a risk, but she knew that it was all she had. She would wait for the right moment, then reveal herself to the Indians. She had nothing to lose. She would definitely lose her life at the hands of Pig's Eye Pete and Major Partain if she stayed with them. She could be in no more danger with the Dakota.

Yes, she would give it a try.

"I sorely fear Indians," she said, her eyes innocently wide. "I won't say a word. I don't want them to get their filthy hands on me. Go on. Do what you must. I'll be as quiet as a church mouse."

Pig's Eye Pete's low chuckle drew a mischievous smile to Brenda's lips as he turned and hurried from the dark inner room. She had convinced him well enough. Now she had only to find the courage to reveal herself to the Dakota. They were nothing like the Ojibwa. They, too, were known for their raping . . . their pillaging . . . their murders.

A coldness seized Brenda's inside. There were many different bands of Dakota Indians. What if this was one who didn't know of her relationship with Striped Eagle? Her plan could quickly backfire.

She held her breath and listened as she heard Indians speaking in broken English to Pig's Eye Pete in the next room. If she listened hard she could understand what was being said. But it wouldn't help her to know which Dakota they were, trading for the whiskey. The Dakota who had abducted her hadn't said all that much in English. Sign language had been their preference.

Any way she looked at it, she would again be gambling . . .

Taking wide, bold steps she moved from the back room and into the outer room to find several briefly attired Indians standing around, sampling whiskey from their own separate jugs. When their eyes caught her standing there, the jugs were lowered, Brenda now the center of all attention.

"God . . ." Pig's Eye Pete snarled.

Brenda held her chin high as a stately Indian, lithe and square-shouldered, moved toward her. As his dark eyes carefully assessed her, she tilted her head, studying him in return. She seemed to recognize him, but she couldn't be certain. She had been with them only briefly.

His jaw was set hard, his dark hair drawn back into long

braids down his back. A headband was about his head, two eagle feathers were secured in the loop of his hair at the back, and his brief loincloth revealed the greatness of his outlined manhood. His copper skin shone as though just highly greased, and his muscles flexed as he reached to lift her hair from her shoulders.

"Woman with hair the color of the sunrise," Cloud Rising said. "She is familiar to me."

Brenda felt a thrill race through her at these words, suddenly recognizing Cloud Rising at the moment he recognized her.

Still, she was afraid, so afraid. There was no guarantee that he would in fact trade her to Striped Eagle. He might, this time, want her for himself.

The thought sent waves of sheer terror through her. No other Indian could ever be as gentle as Striped Eagle. Knowing what so many Dakota were guilty of, there was no telling what horrors could await her at their hands.

Cloud Rising swung around on his heel and folded his arms across his chest. "Me want more than fire water," he grumbled. He nodded toward Brenda. "She is what the Dakota also trades for this day." He nodded to one of his warriors. "Get blankets. We make trade. We leave."

Pig's Eye Pete shuffled his feet nervously. "She ain't for trade," he stammered. "Don't you see her bonds? She's my prisoner. She ain't for tradin', Cloud Rising. You've come for whiskey. You *get* whiskey—*only* whiskey."

In two wide strides Cloud Rising towered over Pig's Eye. "She now Cloud Rising's prisoner," he grumbled. "She no more yours."

Pig's Eye Pete inched over to Major Partain. He spoke out of the corner of his mouth. "What the hell are we goin' to do?" he whispered. "Cloud Rising means business."

Major Partain's face was dark with a frown. He looked from Brenda to Cloud Rising. Then a smirk rippled the frown across his brow. "Let 'em take 'er," he whispered back, loud enough for Brenda to hear. "When they get through with 'er, she won't live long to talk to *anyone*. Maybe it's best this way. I can think of no more horrible death than at the hands of Indians. I'll show that little bitch not to interfere in my life."

Brenda recoiled. She knew that he spoke the truth and that by evening she could be wishing to be dead. But she still held out hope that Cloud Rising would see her value for bargaining with Striped Eagle.

Cloud Rising turned and looked at Brenda with fire in his eyes. He grabbed her by the wrists and pulled her along with him as he left the cabin. When he reached his horse he lifted her up and slung her across the animal's back as though she were only a sack of potatoes.

With his warriors whooping and hollering around them, Cloud Rising mounted his horse and rode away, Brenda's arms and legs dangling, the skirt of her dress and her hair flying in the wind.

Twenty-four

The campfire pulsed orange through the forest ceiling, seemingly into the heavens. Brenda sat huddled away from the fire, scarcely breathing as she watched the Dakota Indians lifting jugs of whiskey to their lips. Their increasingly drunken state was what frightened Brenda the most.

For the moment, it seemed they had forgotten her. Some were dancing about the fire, chanting, their heads bobbing in the rhythm of the beat of their feet against the flattened grass on the ground. Others were ripping apart the deer meat they had cooked over the open fire, their mouths shining with grease as they ate.

The aroma of the cooked meat made Brenda's stomach churn hungrily; her mouth watered. She eyed Cloud Rising as he stepped up to the fire and tore meat from the deer and began walking toward her, weaving, his eyes hazed over in his drunkenness.

Brenda recoiled as he lowered to his haunches before her, so close his alcoholic breath touched her face with the force of a blast. She squirmed, inching her way backward along the dew-dampened grass, her wrists on fire as the leather bindings ate into her flesh with every move.

Cloud Rising grabbed her wrists with his free hand and yanked her closer to him. "Eat," he said flatly.

When he thrust the hunk of meat into her face, forcing it against her lips, Brenda's eyes widened in fear. If he force-fed her, she could choke to death!

Turning her face quickly away, she refused him this opportunity, yet the taste of the meat left on her lips was now driving her wild with need of food.

Fingers grabbed her hair. Brenda cried out as Cloud Rising jerked her head around to meet his drunken gaze.

"You *eat*," Cloud Rising said, once more pushing the meat into her face.

Defiantly, Brenda arched her neck and threw her head back. "No!" she cried. "I can only eat if my hands are untied. I must be able to do it myself. Otherwise, I will *choke*."

Cocking an eyebrow, Cloud Rising eased the meat away from her, again impressed by her courage. This white woman behaved as she had the other time he had abducted her. He had never expected this in a white woman! He had only encountered white women who cried and begged for mercy when he had captured them.

Now he understood why Striped Eagle had claimed her as his! She was different, like no other white woman.

Respecting her, Cloud Rising placed the meat on the ground, then clumsily untied her wrists.

Brenda's eyes became wide in surprise that he had actually complied with her request to release her hands. But what could she expect in return for his kindness?

Fear laced her heart, yet she knew not to show it.

Boldly, she swept her freed hands down to the ground and grabbed the meat, wincing as pain shot through her wrists, the blood now flowing more freely through her veins to the tips of her fingers. She ignored the pain, relieved to have her hands free.

Watching Cloud Rising with defiance in her eyes, Brenda

began to eat ravenously. The food at first caused pain in the depths of her empty stomach. But then the pain began to recede in the face of a pleasant fullness. And with this fullness came more strength, sorely needed should she find a way to escape.

An Indian stumbled over to Cloud Rising with a jug of whiskey and thrust it into his hand. The two Indians conversed in the Dakota language, interspersed with leering glances at Brenda and low, throaty laughter.

And then the Indian sauntered away, leaving Brenda and Cloud Rising alone once more. Cloud Rising tipped the jug to his lips and thirstily drank from it. In his drunken clumsiness, golden threads of whiskey rolled from the corners of his mouth and dripped down onto his copper-skinned chest.

Brenda continued to eat in a strained silence, her eyes watching Cloud Rising's each and every movement. And when he suddenly offered her the jug of whiskey, she stiffened and shook her head back and forth.

"No," she murmured. "I don't care for any."

In truth, she was dying from thirst. The deer meat was salty and the grease was unpleasantly coating her teeth and tongue.

But Brenda was not desperate enough to drink the rotgut that Cloud Rising offered her. As quickly as the Indians had become drunk, she suspected there was more to the whiskey distilled by Pig's Eye Pete than mere alcohol. Something powerful must have been added to it. Perhaps some sort of drug . . . ?

But why would Pig's Eye Pete sell such tainted whiskey to the Indians? There could be only one answer. It was cheaper to add something besides pure ingredients to the whiskey. It didn't matter to Pig's Eye Pete that he was driving the Indians mindless! His safety was assured. He was the only one they could go to to trade for the illegal beverage!

Suddenly Cloud Rising placed the jug of whiskey to Brenda's lips. "Drink," he grumbled. He licked his lips and emitted a soft growl. "Good!"

Brenda didn't have time to protest. He grabbed her by the nape of the neck with one hand and tipped the jug to her lips with the other, forcing the whiskey down her throat.

Her eyes wild, Brenda began to choke and tried to push him away. The whiskey was burning a path down her throat. Cloud Rising was pouring it down her throat so fast she didn't have time to swallow quickly enough.

A numbness seized her brain as a rush of blackness swept before her eyes. As she began to lose consciousness the last thing she was aware of was a burst of laughter as Indians circled about her, watching her desperate attempt to save herself from going under.

Drawn from her troubled sleep, aware of the smell of whiskey on her clothes, Brenda slowly opened her eyes. Her hand went to her mouth, feeling the dried whiskey about her lips and on her chin. She ran her tongue over her teeth and swallowed hard, still tasting the bitter sharpness of the drink. Her stomach burned unmercifully. Her throat constricted again as she swallowed.

Slowly rising on an elbow, Brenda looked cautiously about her. Only a few Dakota not elapsed into a drunken stupor of sleep remained about the fire, and these few were scarcely awake, their heads lowered between their wide-spread legs, lolling.

Brenda's heart began to pound as she recognized the possibility of escape. As soon as the remaining Indians fell asleep, she could leave! None would be the wiser. They would be lost in their whiskey-saturated sleep.

Her eyes went to her wrists. They were still unbound. In his drunken state, Cloud Rising had forgotten to retie them!

A warm surge of hope swam through Brenda as she saw that escape could now only be a few heartbeats away!

Trying to wipe the taste of whiskey from her lips, she continued to watch the Indians. One by one they drifted to the ground. Yet some others who had been asleep were now stirring. She tensed when one moved to his knees and crawled to her, his lips lifted in a crooked smile as he ripped the bodice of her dress open and placed a hand to one of her breasts.

Afraid to move, Brenda lay there, dying a slow death inside as the Indian pinched and fondled her breast. Then he crawled away from her and collapsed on the ground beside the others.

Sighing with relief, having expected a far worse encounter, Brenda made a silent prayer of thank-you to the heavens.

But her relief was short-lived. Cloud Rising was suddenly at her side, leaning over her, smirking as he took his turn. He placed his lips to the nipple of the breast only moments ago squeezed by the other Indian.

Desperation rising inside her, Brenda tried to reach the knife beneath the skirt of her dress, but Cloud Rising was in the way. His body was pressed hard against the thigh to which the knife was attached. Both his hands were now on her flesh, exploring her breasts, then creeping lower, across her abdomen.

Brenda tensed, fearing that he would rip the dress completely away from her, revealing her knife to him. But as he leaned away from her, still clumsily groping, she saw a chance to reach for her knife. She must defend herself against what was surely going to transpire in a matter of moments. Rape. Rape! The word flashed before her eyes in its full meaning. She would not let it happen. Not if she had to die trying to stop it!

Placing her hands against Cloud Rising's chest, she gave him a shove. To her surprise he tumbled easily away from her. But his eyes were gleaming, shadowed by moonlight. He was leering, already getting back on his knees to position himself over her. Brenda momentarily froze.

But then the reality of what was just about to happen caused her to shake herself from her fright. With a quick movement of her hand she had her dress lifted and her hand on the knife. Just as Cloud Rising reached her she drew the knife from its protective sheath . . . lifted it in the air . . . and plunged it downward into his chest.

Recoiling, watching the blood surging from the wound she had inflicted, hearing the painful gurgle surfacing from between his lips as he fell back to the ground, Brenda was almost too stunned to recapture her wits, momentarily robbed by the knowledge that she had just taken . . . a man's life . . .

She looked at the dead Indian, and then to where the campfire still flickered. She must escape, and quickly! If anyone awakened and discovered Cloud Rising's body, the whole group of Dakota would answer the alarm and the search would begin for her.

Brenda could only hope that the whiskey would keep the remaining Dakota asleep until morning. By then the village of the Ojibwa could be reached, for she knew that was where she would be safe, not only now, but maybe forever. When Major Partain discovered that she was still alive he would come looking for her!

Knowing that this was not the time to ponder over anything but escape, Brenda wiped her knife clean on the grass at her side and replaced it in its sheath. She then stole silently from the Indians' campsite, finding their ponies grazing peacefully close by.

Choosing a fully-bridled pony, she led it by foot farther into the forest until she could no longer see the glow of the campfire. She then felt it safe to mount the pony and ride away, praying that her chosen route of escape would lead her to Striped Eagle's village. She now knew that he was the only one to help her in her final act of vengeance. She should have asked him long ago. He would have ways to protect his people from the soldiers should they all be drawn into a bloody war.

Twenty-five

Primroses swayed gently in the late afternoon breeze, a carpet of yellow in the valley below. Tired, her thighs aching from constantly gripping the pony, Brenda drew her reins tight and paused to rest. Her fingers raw from the reins cutting into them, she lifted first one to her lips to blow onto it, and then another, all the while trying to gather her wits, unwilling to accept the fact that once more she was lost in this wilderness of Minnesota!

"Now what do I do?" she sighed, shaking her hair so that its perspiration-dampened strands could tumble more freely down her back. "Where *is* Striped Eagle's village?"

Although reluctant, she couldn't help but remember the other times she had become lost. There had been the voyageurs . . . then the Dakota Indians. Would it be the same again. Would she become someone's unwilling prisoner once more?

This time, as in the past, she had been led into danger by the same motive: revenge. In the end, once her revenge was achieved, all her hardships while desperately trying to achieve it would seem worthwhile. She owed it to her

family. She owed it to herself so she could begin life anew
. . . be at peace with herself.

She inhaled a nervous breath, not willing to accept
defeat just yet. Whatever it took to see that Major Partain
was dealt with, she would see that it was done. Now she
must push onward. She must find Striped Eagle at all cost.
Had she known in the beginning that he was her only
answer, how simple life would have been for her!

But she had never wanted to endanger him or his people. She owed him that much for having been so kind to
her. Even now she did not wish to draw him into her
private battle, yet now she had no choice but to do so. She
was weary of carrying the burden alone. She now understood that she was a woman in need of a man's muscle.

Clucking to the stolen Indian pony, reins again in hand,
Brenda urged him down a slope which led her into the
floor of the valley below. She then sent the pony bounding
into a gallop, her hair flying, her chin held high, enjoying
the touch of the wind against her sun-drenched face.

The fringed hem of her Indian dress flipped upward
about her knees, revealing fancy moccasined feet thrust
into the stirrups. The ripped bodice of her dress was a
reminder of her near-rape, but it at least afforded the upper
lobes of her breasts the benefit of the cooling breeze.

With her knife sheathed at her thigh, she felt safe enough,
having proved to herself that she had guts enough to use it.
Though her insides rolled at the thought of having killed
Cloud Rising, it would be a warning to others that she
would not be taken captive so easily again. It would not be
left entirely up to Striped Eagle to rescue her as always
before. She would defend herself, totally!

Now in a full gallop through the primrose carpet spread
out on all sides of her, Brenda shouted to the pony, feeling
too vulnerable in the open space. Her target was the forest
ahead, yet she frowned when she saw that it reached
upward into tall, pine-covered cliffs. Would it be impass-

able? Was she going to have to turn back and try to find
her way back to Mendota?

"No! I shan't!" she shouted, tensing when her voice
echoed back at her.

Pressing her heels into the flanks of the Indian pony,
Brenda rode quickly onward, seeking the cover of the
trees. Alone, she was a target for any man who might
happen along. Was the forest any better, though, where
she was bait for wolves and bobcats?

Not wanting to answer this in her mind, Brenda focused
her thoughts on more pleasant things, taking in the setting
around her. Wildflowers blossomed *en masse,* a sprawling
colorful garden in the wilderness. Besides the primrose,
there were blazing star, goldenrod, prairie phlox, and bird's-
foot violets now visible as she moved closer to the edge of
the forest.

Inhaling, she caught the very identifiable scent of lily-of-
the-valley. Its sweetness overpowered all of the perfumes
she had ever been given a rare chance to smell. The sweet
aroma clung to her now, it seemed, helping to wash away
the scent of death she had carried with her since leaving
the Dakota campsite.

She momentarily closed her eyes, choking when in her
mind's eye she saw Cloud Rising's expression the moment
the knife plunged into his flesh. Could she ever forget how
empty she had felt upon taking a man's life?

But the fact that he was going to rape her helped her
accept the *fait accompli.* And, if put in the same position,
she would do it again. Along the way survival had become
her primary goal!

Fluttering her eyes open again, blanking out all the
recent ugliness of the past evening, Brenda rode quickly
onward. She entered a forest of pine trees, white, jack,
and Norway pines growing together with ash, black oak,
elm, and maple trees.

Wild roses grew in profusion all about her; ferns were

thick at the pony's hooves; trailing arbutus wove in and out of the branches of the trees above her.

The shine of a swift-flowing stream cutting a deep valley into the forest caught her eye. A stream must have an outlet. Perhaps it would lead her to the White Bear River, and then to Striped Eagle's village!

Hope warming her inside, Brenda clucked to the pony and began guiding it in a weaving path around the trees, then alongside the glittering stream. She was tempted to stop and splash her skin clean of perspiration with the fresh, clear water, but the time of day urged her onward.

Peering upward, she caught the dull red glow of the setting sun seeping through the forest ceiling. Too soon she would be challenging another night. Such a thought made goose bumps rise on her flesh. Darkness brought many creatures from their dens. Wolves . . .

Shaking her head, again forcing her thoughts to dwell on more pleasant things, Brenda slapped the Indian pony with the reins and urged it into a gallop. Ahead she saw a break in the trees. Perhaps she had arrived at the White Bear River. Still, she was recalling her worry about the cliffs she had seen from a distance. What if they blocked her entrance to the river? What if the river lay just on the other side and this stream ended ahead?

Brenda prayed softly to herself. "Lord, be with me," she whispered. "If not now, maybe never."

Swallowing back a lump in her throat, Brenda hurried onward. The air was cooling as the sun crept lower in the sky. As she had been the previous night, Brenda was made aware of her torn dress. If she wasn't eaten by some wild creature of the night, she might instead freeze to death! A fire would be required as a deterrent to both her fears. Yet a fire could attract anything she had just cause to fear: the Dakota Indians . . . women-starved voyageurs . . . trappers . . .

"Striped Eagle, where *are* you?" she cried, despair

clutching at her heart. "I should have never left you! Never!"

When she reached the clearing that she had seen, she drew the pony to a shuddering halt. Her hopes waned and insides grew numb when she saw the sharp outline of cliffs that loomed before her. Slowly she let her gaze move upward, surveying the impossible steepness.

Suddenly, she sensed a presence. She was no longer alone. Turning, her pulse began to race. She couldn't believe her eyes! It was Striped Eagle! He was sitting on the very edge of a cliff, his eyes looking toward the heavens, his arms outstretched above him as though in supplication.

A sob of relief tore through Brenda. Her heart raced in her happiness. She raised a hand and began waving. "Striped Eagle!" she cried. "Striped Eagle, it's me, Brenda. Please see me. Please *hear* me."

Striped Eagle was startled from his reverie. He couldn't believe what he had heard. Had his three days of fasting, only eating the barest minimum of berries to keep him strong, made him begin to hallucinate? Yet the voice had been so clear, so close. Surely it hadn't been a figment of his imagination.

Jumping to his feet, Striped Eagle looked downward in the direction from whence he had heard her voice.

"Nee-bin-gee-zis?" he whispered. "Summer Sun?"

His heart fluttered nervously deep within his chest when he discovered that, *ay-uh*, she was real, that she was truly there, looking up at him from a pony. But how? Why? The Great Spirit, Wenebojo? Had he guided her there? Had Wenebojo truly understood his need for Summer Sun at such a time of sadness in his life?

But, yes, that had to be the answer, for she *was* there. She had come willingly. She had chosen to return, surely having seen the wrong of leaving with Morning Flower. His heart was filled with joy. Only his Summer Sun could make him feel this gladness so soon after his father's death. Only his Summer Sun, his woman . . .

Tears welled at the corners of Brenda's eyes when she saw that he had seen her. She rose up in her stirrups and again began desperately waving. "Striped Eagle, please!" she cried. "Please come down here. I don't think I can make it up there either on foot *or* horseback."

Fighting the urge to cry, she blinked her eyes nervously. "I need you, Striped Eagle. I need you," she said under her breath.

She so feared that he would ignore her. Hadn't she shamed him in the eyes of the White Bear Ojibwa by again deserting him? She would understand if he even hated her. Seeing him turning, disappearing from her view, didn't assure her of anything. He might be running away, in a different direction, to avoid her. And wouldn't she understand that?

"I pray that I am wrong," she whispered, dismounting. She secured the reins of the horse beneath a rock on the ground, then began pacing. If Striped Eagle ignored her, then she would have no choice but to turn around and try to find her way back to Mendota. But she sorely feared this. She had altogether lost her sense of direction. She would not know which way to turn to find her way. And she would again not know who to trust, to confide in. So far nothing had worked out for her. If Striped Eagle turned his back on her she would be totally alone.

Stopping to look upward to where Striped Eagle had stood, an emptiness filled Brenda. She heard no sounds of approaching footsteps. He had not spoken to her to assure her that he was coming. He most surely *was* ignoring her. He hated her, hated her!

Pale from worry, from rejection, she walked to the stream and knelt down before it. She watched tadpoles darting around pebbles lying at the depths of the crystalline water. Occasional small gray streaks captured her attention as a school of minnows swam quickly past.

On the opposite side of the stream trailing brambles were interspersed with blooming pink and white lady's slippers, and farther still she saw the bright red berries of raspberry bushes tempting her. But her mind was not on food. It was on Striped Eagle and how he had left her. Wouldn't he be here by now if he had wanted to be? His long legs would have taken him quickly from the heights of the cliff. And didn't he move as lithely as a panther?

Her eyes widened, recalling that he also moved as *quietly* as a panther. Slowly she turned. Just as she did, she found him standing over her, tall and handsome. But now that he was out of the shadows of his perch on the cliff, she saw that his face was strangely blackened! And his eyes seemed even darker this day, as though filled with emotions he did not wish to speak aloud. Were these emotions caused by her, or something else? Why had he been alone, meditating? Had something else happened to sadden him? Why was his face black?

"Nee-may-nan-dum-wah-bum-eh-nawn," Striped Eagle said thickly, his gaze traveling over her. His eyes stopped momentarily on her ripped dress, assuming she had ripped it on her journey through the forest, then again upward, where he locked his eyes on hers. "How is it that you are here, Summer Sun? Why have you come? You have always been so eager to *leave* me. And how did you find me? No one knows where I have chosen to fast, to commune with the spirits and nature."

But again he knew not to ask *how* she had found him. He knew he had Wenebojo to thank. Wenebojo alone had known where he had been since his father's burial.

"Striped Eagle, I've so much to tell you," Brenda said, the keen penetration of his eyes unnerving her. "I had to come to you. But I must know . . . are you so very angry because I was not at your dwelling when you returned after going to destroy the dam?''

She cast her eyes downward. ''I know, Striped Eagle, about the lies. About the deceits. I am . . . sorry. Your sister—''

''*Gah-ween*,'' he grumbled, interrupting her. ''Do not remind me of what my sister did. She was wrong. But she pays now, in her total sadness.''

Brenda's eyes shot upward. Her insides splashed cold. Had Striped Eagle severely punished his sister? Was that the reason for Morning Flower's sadness? Was Morning Flower his reason for being away from the village . . . his heart heavy for having to punish his sister? It *did* all seem to fit into place.

''Why are you here, in such an isolated place?'' Brenda said in one breath. ''Why is your face colored thusly?''

Striped Eagle turned on a heel and placed his back to Brenda, humbly lowering his eyes. She saw the muscles of his shoulders knot and ripple as he clenched his fingers into fists at his sides. Her gaze absorbed the sleekness of his copper skin, yet she was puzzled about the narrow strips of braided buckskin placed about his neck and waist, never having seen him wear this strange attire before. Besides these, he was wearing only his breechcloth and fancy moccasins.

Having seen pain enter his eyes before he turned, Brenda was at first bemused as to what to do, but her heart guided her well as she moved around him and again stood where he could not so easily avoid her. With trembling fingers she reached a hand to his lips, which were set in a firm, straight line. Her pulse raced when she touched them, recalling the many kisses shared with him. The same overwhelming desire of him flooded her senses, and she recognized it as always before as the proof of her intense love for this man, this Indian . . .

''Striped Eagle, please tell me what's troubling you

so,'' she murmured. ''If it's what Morning Flower did, please place your anger about it behind you. She did it for reasons she felt were right. She didn't wish to hurt or shame you. Please let forgiveness enter your heart. You are such a kind and generous and gentle man. And you only have *one* sister. Cherish her, Striped Eagle, for you cannot ever trust tomorrow. It never came for my brother, mother, or father. The pain of loss would be twofold for you should anything happen to your sister while you are still angry with her.''

Two wide strides took Striped Eagle to the stream embankment. Kneeling on one knee, he stared into the water. The reflection thrown back at him reminded him of the ash his sister had placed there. Angrily he dipped his hands into the water and began splashing it onto his face, all the while growling beneath his breath.

''My sister disappoints me not once, but twice,'' he spat. Then he felt shame enter his soul, knowing this was not the time for anger. His father—he must remember to behave kindly at this time. His father would want it.

Brenda settled down on the ground beside Striped Eagle on her knees, facing him. ''I'm sure she is sorry, Striped Eagle,'' she murmured. She watched the black disappear from his face. Again she wondered about why it had been placed there, whether or not it had to do with Morning Flower's punishment.

''Why was your face blackened?'' she blurted, then flinched when Striped Eagle shot a glance at her. But when she discovered that his eyes had again become gentle when he looked at her, she relaxed, sighing heavily.

''You do not know,'' Striped Eagle said. He again looked away from her to splash more water on his face, erasing the remaining traces of black.

''Know what, Striped Eagle?''

''Striped Eagle is now chief.''

His words stunned Brenda. She was rendered speechless. If he was chief, then his father had passed away! She now understood why he was alone . . . why such a withdrawn sadness framed him. She ached to draw him into her arms, to comfort him. Yet she did not know if he would want her to. He hadn't attempted to embrace *her* yet. Perhaps he didn't even want to. The fear that he didn't made her insides feel empty.

"Your father is . . . dead?" she said, oh, so wanting to reach out to him, to touch him.

With a nod of the head, Striped Eagle had again fixed his eyes on her. In them was reflected a deep pain. *"Ay-uh,"* he said shallowly. "My father—the great Chief Growling Bear is now traveling the road to the hereafter." He squared his shoulders. "Striped Eagle is now chief, but a chief with a heavy heart."

His gaze again swept over her, stopping at her eyes. "You have come . . . you were instructed by Wenebojo to come to me, in this, my troubled moments of mourning for my father?"

Brenda's insides quivered, now knowing that her true reasons for arriving could not be voiced aloud to him. Though she hungered to have her vengeance over and done with, had so badly wanted him to help her achieve this goal, she knew that now was not the time. He would not go to war with the white man while mourning for his father. She would not ask him to. And she couldn't find it in her heart to tell him about being abducted again, or the fact that she had killed Cloud Rising. Perhaps later. Now did not seem the time to tell him any of these things.

Her eyes unblinkingly wide, she nodded her head. *"Ay-uh,"* she murmured, speaking in Ojibwa for his sake. "Wenebojo sent me to you, Striped Eagle."

Flooded by keen emotions, Striped Eagle swept Brenda into his arms and hugged her tightly to him. He buried his nose in the depths of her hair and reverently breathed her name.

Twenty-six

The light from the campfire reflected like many moon-beams into the water, spreading its golden glow outward as ripples carried it away. Striped Eagle held Brenda close to his side beside the stream, both seemingly enchanted by the lovely evening, the breeze only scarcely revealing the nip of a chill in its soft caress, the month of June upon them.

The aroma of cooked meat still hung in the air, Striped Eagle having broken his fasting by capturing and cooking a squirrel, sharing it with Brenda who had teasingly said that she had felt close to succumbing because of her hunger.

Together they were sharing a quiet moment, Brenda still determined not to tell Striped Eagle the true reason for her arrival. It still wasn't the proper time. It was not in his best interest to know. It was too soon after his father's death to involve him in her own personal problems. She let him continue believing that his Wenebojo had sent her to him.

"It is good that you are here," Striped Eagle said, breaking the silence. "Striped Eagle was lonely without you. As was the Great Spirit alone in the beginning of time.''

Striped Eagle drew Brenda closer to his side, speaking, yet seeming far away, his thoughts carrying him to another time, another place.

Brenda devotedly listened, knowing that he needed this time to speak to help release him of the sadness inside him. She snuggled close to him, enjoying the feeling that she had gone to another world until now unknown to her.

''In the beginning there was only the Great Spirit,'' Striped Eagle continued. ''He was alone in the universe without form or matter. In his loneliness, he created the earth and the grass and the trees. Deciding the earth needed people, the Great Spirit took a piece out of his heart, near where he had taken the earth, and formed the fragment into a man.''

He paused and took a deep breath. He looked down at Brenda, drawn to her loveliness as never before, yet feeling compelled to finish speaking about what at this moment in time was important to him. The parting of his father had brought him closer to the mysteries of creation and death . . .

''The woman was made next,'' he said thickly. ''But only a small piece of flesh was needed for her. Therefore, it is that the man became great in wisdom, the woman in beauty. To the man was given the tobacco seed so that, thrown on the fire, it might propitiate the messenger-manitos to convey prayers to the Great Spirit. To woman a seed of every kind of grain was given, and to her were indicated the roots and herbs for medicine.''

Striped Eagle took Brenda's hands and held them tightly. ''The Great Spirit then commanded the two to look down,'' he said, almost meditatively. ''They looked down and, lo, there stood a child between them. Instructing the pair to take care of all the children which they might obtain in the future, the Great Spirit created the male and the female the first parents of all tribes upon the earth. Afterward, the Great Spirit created the beasts and the birds for the use of all mankind.''

Hearing Striped Eagle speak of a child made Brenda recall her initial fear of becoming with child by him. Still she was torn. She knew she should be ecstatic to bear him his first child. If everything worked out, perhaps she would be given this opportunity. Wouldn't a child born of their union be a child born of the greatest love? No matter the color of its skin, wouldn't it represent all that was good shared between them?

Pausing, Striped Eagle placed a hand to Brenda's cheek. ''Summer Sun, you are so *bee-sahn*,'' he said softly. He leaned to look into her eyes. ''Are you not *gee-mee-nwayn-dum* that you have come? Do you not understand how you have lessened the pain in my heart by coming to me in my time of sorrow?''

Brenda was drawn from her reverie, glad that he had interrupted her train of thought. Now was not the time to wonder about children. There were still too many barriers in the way. Always there was Major Partain! Should she ever manage to rid her consciousness from him, then she could be free to dream.

Meeting his gaze, she looked at Striped Eagle in wonder, his features sharply chiseled and masculine, his lips firm but sensuous. She would never grow tired of looking upon his handsomeness. Surely even in old age he would be as impressive in appearance. Ah, how she hungered to be with him to see.

Laboring in her mind over the two Indian words he had spoken to her, she finally giggled, placing her hands together on her lap. ''I do not know what words you said to me in Ojibwa,'' she said. Her giggle receded into a soft smile. ''But I am glad you spoke in my language when you said that I have had the ability to lessen the pain in your heart. For that, I am glad.''

She covered his hand with hers. "And I so love your story of creation," she murmured. "Thank you for sharing it with me. It very much resembles what can be found in the white man's Bible."

"As I told you once before, I know of such talking leaves," he said, growing solemn. "I have seen such leaves that carry thoughts and messages over great distances."

"Talking leaves?" Brenda asked, her eyes wide.

"That is what the Ojibwa call those pages of writing found in what the white man calls books," he said, shaking his head matter-of-factly.

Brenda laughed softly. "That's such a lovely way to describe our books," she said, scooting closer to him. Her face twisted into a gentle frown. "But you still haven't told me what were the words you spoke in Ojibwa to me. I'd love to know, Striped Eagle. Tell me."

His eyebrows forked and a smile touched his lips. "It is time for another lesson in Ojibwa for my woman?" He chuckled. "You know the word 'yes' in Ojibwa. So shall you know the words 'quiet' and 'happy.' "

Turning to fully face her, Striped Eagle took one of her hands and placed her fingertips to his lips. "You watch . . . you listen . . . you *feel*," he encouraged "*Bee-sahn*. That is the Ojibwa word for quiet. Now you speak the word, Summer Sun. *Bee-sahn*. Quiet."

Straightening her back, her eyes holding within them the joy she felt at being with Striped Eagle and sharing this light moment with him, Brenda lifted her chin and spoke the Ojibwa word as succinctly as he.

Nodding, smiling at her astuteness, Striped Eagle spoke the other word in Ojibwa, again proud as Brenda responded so quickly, so eloquently.

"Once more you are an apt pupil," Striped Eagle said, laughing. Then his expression changed as her fingers lingered on his lips, stirring the coals of desire inside him.

He took her hand and kissed the tips of each of her fingers, all the while watching her with the haunting darkness of his eyes.

"Striped Eagle would like to test your memory of other skills I have taught you," he said huskily. "Now, my Summer Sun. *Ah-szhee-gwah.* Love me, my woman. When we made love that first time, it was revealed to me that I was the first man with you. I led you into the realms of true womanhood. You followed. Reveal to me that you were as apt a pupil then as now. Let us momentarily leave our sorrows behind, to enter a plateau above, as only lovers have the skill to do."

As though cast into a sudden trance, Brenda rose to her feet before Striped Eagle and began drawing her dress over her head. In one sweep she had the dress thrown aside. She saw a gleam enter Striped Eagle's glittering dark eyes as he eyed her with an amused look. Though he didn't mention it, Brenda thought that he might be looking at her in such a way, seeing so much about her that had changed since the day after that fateful night of her family's deaths. She had matured in many ways.

The one great difference was that she was devoid of shyness, having lost it long ago in Striped Eagle's presence. His gaze burned into her now, branding her, sending a searing flame through her.

Breathless, Brenda removed the knife strapped to her leg, then drifted toward Striped Eagle, obeying the silent command in his eyes as he rose to his feet. In one quick movement he removed his breechcloth and stood perfectly, wondrous in his nudity, awaiting her.

In an almost helpless surrender, she let him draw her to his hard frame of body, leaving no space between them. His lips lowered to hers for a series of teasing kisses; his fingers wove through the red silk of her hair. She clung to him, shaken with this desire only known to her when she was with Striped Eagle.

A sensuous thrill coursed through her veins as he removed his mouth and trailed his tongue across her quivering lower lip. The crazy spinning in her head made her reel with pleasure, his hands now stroking the curve of her buttocks, then the pleasingly, beautifully sensitive inside of one thigh and then the other.

And when he, with his other hand and muscled arm, began lowering her to the ground, she sighed. Her heart beat quickly as he, with his knowledge, led her deeper into the abyss of sensual pleasure. Yes, he had been a skilled teacher, she an apt pupil. She knew quite well what would be next. He would soon fill her . . . marvelously fill her. Together, they would reach that pinnacle sought by men and women in love. The thought drugged her as if she had been given an exotic potion. But his touch, his kiss, was even more powerful than such a potion. His skills at making love were boundless!

Though the ground was now hard against her back, Brenda didn't feel it. It was as though she was on a cloud, floating, as Striped Eagle lowered himself fully over her and eased his manhood inside her. When he started his masterful strokes, Brenda lifted her hips and locked her legs about his waist, then closed her eyes in bliss.

His mouth was fire on her lips, his hand scorching as one hand kneaded a breast, the other the soft roundness of her buttock. Brenda returned his kiss, opening her lips to offer her mouth to his sensual, probing tongue.

Aglow, as if a flame burned inside, she began moving her hands along his flesh, as though memorizing him for future remembrances when they were apart. She trailed her fingers across the sinewy sleekness of his shoulders, down his back, then to the muscled strength of his buttocks. Spreading her fingers on each of his buttocks, they rode with him as he rhythmically thrust himself inside her. When her pleasure began mounting, ready to burst inside her in glorious splashes of warmth, she dug her fingers into his flesh and moaned.

"Moo-shkeke-nay gee-mee-nwayn-dum," Striped Eagle whispered, his breath hot on her cheek. His tongue flicked along the lobe of her ear. "There is only now, my woman. *Mee-ay-tah-goo-ee-oo ah-szhee-gwah.* Fully enjoy as though there is no tomorrow."

Sweat pearling on her brow, the tendrils of her hair damp, Brenda softly nodded. *"Ay-uh,"* she whispered. "Yes. Only . . . now . . ."

Again he kissed her. Bubbles of pleasure danced inside her . . . spreading . . . spreading. And when she became aware of his body trembling in his sensual release, it was as though he commanded her again, for her body responded, matching his pleasure with hers.

They lay together, each breathing hard against the other's cheek, having traveled the road to ecstasy and back again, fulfilled and joyous. Striped Eagle slipped away from her to lie on his side facing her, leaving a hand possessively on her breast as she turned on her side to meet his warm, appraising gaze.

"It was *o-nee-shee-shin,"* he said hoarsely. "In Ojibwa I said it was *good,* Summer Sun. You have proven to be an apt pupil in *all* my teachings."

"I'm so glad you approve," she said, laughing softly. She reached a finger to his lips and traced their outline, so mesmerized by the memory of his kiss. "I do love you so, Striped Eagle. Oh, so very, very much."

"You left before. Will you again?" he growled, leaning on his elbow.

Tensing, Brenda eased her finger from his lip. She moved to a sitting position, suddenly chilled. She trembled as she reached for her dress and slipped it over her head. "No. I hope leaving won't be necessary," she murmured. "Ever again."

Striped Eagle rose to his feet. He drew his breechcloth

on. "What are you saying?" he asked with an air of caution. "Always before you have come, then you have gone. First you give me your heart, then you take it away. Are you saying that is not the way it is to be again?"

Brenda bit her lower lip, still feeling this was not the proper time to reveal all that she sorely wanted to, yet knowing that her silence could be construed as denying him again! And she couldn't take that chance. She now knew that her destiny was with Striped Eagle. She would even willingly give up all comforts that living the life of the white woman could offer. Nothing of the white man's world that she could think of could be as rewarding as to be forever in Striped Eagle's arms. It was not so much a choice given her as it was a choice *made*.

Going to Striped Eagle she splayed her fingers against his wide breadth of chest. "My darling, I give you my heart to keep forever," she said softly. "And, no. I will never leave you again. I have searched and found you this night. *Never* shall I leave you again."

Striped Eagle reached for her wrists and gently eased her hands away from him, whirling to keep from looking into eyes that stole his senses away. He was wary of her promises, though her words had sounded sincere enough. But she had tricked him more than once. His pride could not allow it to happen again. He was now a great chief. No chief could allow being belittled in the eyes of his people!

Stubborn, knowing that she had no choice but to reveal the truth to him, Brenda stepped around to face him. She locked her fingers together behind her, praying that he would believe her, that he would help her.

But he was her life . . . her total being. And she feared it. She knew that he would have to fight Major Partain when he was told that it was he who was still like a sore festering inside her. She hated drawing Striped Eagle into her fight. But now she had no choice. She had done all that was possible alone.

"Hear me out, Striped Eagle," she said softly, her eyes imploring him. "I need your help. I now know that it is impossible for me to achieve my goals alone. But together, Striped Eagle, we might be able to stop Major Partain. Is it wrong of me to ask this of you while you are in mourning for your father?"

Striped Eagle was stunned by her request. Always before she had done everything within her power to keep him separate from her plans of vengeance. Now she wanted him to be a *part* of it!

"Why do you ask this of me?" he said hoarsely. "What has happened to change your mind?"

In a rush of words, Brenda told him about Pig's Eye Pete, Major Partain, and killing Cloud Rising.

Then she eased into his arms, sobbing softly. "I'm so tired of it all, Striped Eagle," she murmured. "Help me to get this all behind me. All I want from life is to stay with you, be your wife. I want you . . . only you . . . from life."

Her words sang inside Striped Eagle's heart. Never before had she vowed to stay with him, to be his wife! In her eyes . . . in her voice . . . he read sincerity.

"My Summer Sun," he said, weaving his fingers through her hair. "Come with me to my village. Sit by my side as my woman. Soon we will celebrate our union. It will be a feast of feasts in our village of Ojibwa. And soon we will make things right for you. My braves will seek out and kill Major Partain."

"I must be allowed to go with you when the hunt for Major Partain begins," Brenda said, leaning away from Striped Eagle, pleading with her eyes as she looked up at him. "Surely you see why I must. The vengeance is *mine*. Not yours. I must have a part in it."

Striped Eagle caressed her cheek with the back side of his thumb, admiring her. "You say you killed the hated

Dakota, Cloud Rising?'' he said thickly. ''My woman, your courage has been proven to me more than once.''

''Then you will let me travel with you and your braves?''

''It would honor me, the chief of my people, to have my woman ride at my side,'' Striped Eagle said, pride thick in his words. ''Does this make you happy, Summer Sun?''

Brenda's face was beaming as she smiled up at him. *''Ay-uh,''* she murmured. ''I am happy. So very, very happy.''

She moved into his arms and snuggled, content. Yet fear was ebbing its way into her heart as she imagined what actually lay before them. Major Partain. And the battle . . .

Twenty-seven

The moon illuminating everything about her, Brenda was beginning to recognize where she was. Striped Eagle had brought her in this direction when he had shown her the sacred quarry. And if she remembered correctly, she should be nearing it now. She could see the outcropping of cliffs, which should stretch downward into the quarry outlined in the darkness. The shadows of pines looked like inverted cones, black against the bluffs.

And then Brenda saw the wavering of orange against the backdrop of the sky. It could only be caused by fire!

Striped Eagle's hand grabbing her reins from her, stopping the pony on which she rode, was proof that he had also seen the signs in the heavens and was startled by them.

"What *is* it?" Brenda asked, suddenly afraid, for in Striped Eagle's eyes she could see a sudden cold hate. "Why have you stopped me?" Her gaze moved back to the sky, still seeing the reflection of the fire. "You see the color of the sky also. It's too bright to be caused by a single campfire. What do you think the true cause is?"

Striped Eagle returned Brenda's reins to her. "*Chee-*

mo-ko-man!'' he growled. ''White man must have found the sacred quarry. The Chippewa do not dig for pipestone at night. Only by day do they!''

''But you told me that no white man knows of the quarry,'' Brenda said, looking puzzled.

''I knew that one day they would. Too many white men in this land now to *not* discover it,'' Striped Eagle said dryly. ''First they take our land and now our pipestone? No. It cannot be allowed to happen!''

Following Striped Eagle's lead, Brenda guided her pony in the direction of the light, fear seeping into her heart. For there to be so much light, there had to be many men. And there was only the two of them to fight for the sacred land. She had only her knife. Striped Eagle had brought no weapons with him to fast and mourn his father's death. The men stealing the pipestone would have to spend only two bullets to be able to return to their thievery undisturbed.

Her breathing shallow, Brenda inched her pony along beside Striped Eagle's stallion, then drew her reins taut when she spied the edges of the quarry within sight. Her insides quivered strangely when she saw many horses riderless at the edge of the quarry, grazing. As she and Striped Eagle drew closer and peered downward into the depths of the quarry, she saw many soldiers holding torches while others dug.

''My Lord!'' Brenda gasped, placing a hand to her mouth. ''It's not just any men stealing the pipestone, Striped Eagle. It's . . . they're *soldiers*.''

And then she recoiled when a torch illuminated a familiar face—Major Partain. He must have been on his way to the quarry when he had stopped to share a few drinks with Pig's Eye Pete! And in his drunken state, Major Partain had forgotten the dangers of stealing from the Indians. He had trespassed into sacred ground! Was there nothing this wretched man wasn't guilty of doing?

Brenda watched Striped Eagle and his horse creep closer

to the edge of the quarry. She could hear him speaking in staccato tones beneath his breath, saying something in Ojibwa as he looked from soldier to soldier.

"They desecrate our ground. They steal from the Ojibwa . . ." Striped Eagle finally said in words that Brenda could understand.

He turned his eyes quickly to Brenda. *"Nee-boo-ah-o-mah-ee-ow-ug-bay-mah-dis-i-gig!* We must ride to my village. *Wee-weeb.* Quickly. We must warn my people. Striped Eagle must bring many braves to stop the evil white men!"

Brenda sighed with relief, glad to know that Striped Eagle was going for help instead of confronting the soldiers alone.

Looking quickly down into the quarry, again seeing Major Partain, her heart began to pound with excitement. Perhaps the time had finally arrived for her to achieve her much sought-after goal! She would return with Striped Eagle and his braves. Major Partain and his soldiers would be cornered! Major Partain might even . . . be slain?

It was perfect! Oh, how long she had waited for the opportunity to avenge her family's deaths! Major Partain had been foolish to let her go with the Dakota instead of seeing that she was silenced. Now she would see to his demise. Once she returned to the quarry with Striped Eagle, she would make herself known to the major just before he was silenced . . . forever.

"Wenebojo, the Great Spirit, will lead Striped Eagle and his braves into victory!" Striped Eagle said, wheeling his horse around. *"Mah-bee-szhon.* Come. Follow me, Summer Sun. We must ride like the wind blows during a storm. *Gee-shee-kah!"*

Brenda nodded. *"Ay-uh,"* she said, an anxiety entering her heart as never before. She had gone through many trials and tribulations to reach her goal of seeing that

Major Partain was rightfully dealt with. Now she could see the end in reach.

She had been taught by her mother that everything in life always had a reason. The fact that she and Striped Eagle had taken this route back to the Ojibwa village had to mean only one thing: it had been *meant* for them to discover the soldiers at the quarry!

Tonight it was possible for her to believe that there was a Great Spirit. For hadn't she and Striped Eagle been led by some unseen force to the quarry to discover the thieves . . . to discover the hateful Major Partain?

Thrusting her moccasined heels into the flanks of the stolen Dakota pony, Brenda rode quickly away alongside Striped Eagle. She bent low over the pony's mane, driven by a vengeful hate. There was no time to waste. They must return to the quarry before Major Partain fled into the night with all that he had stolen.

Now, far enough away from the quarry to feel free to shout to the pony, Brenda yelled at him. She nudged her knees into his sides and flicked the reins. Her hair flew behind her in a tangled mass. Her skirt lifted above her knees. She and Striped Eagle rode hard and long.

The night air was cold on Brenda's face, but she smiled, for ahead she finally saw white swirls of foggy mist and knew that she was approaching the White Bear River. And the White Bear River would lead her and Striped Eagle to the Ojibwa village. Striped Eagle had the task of placing his mourning behind him, now to fully assume leadership of his people. He had his sacred quarry to defend.

"Giddyup!" Brenda shouted, now directing the pony into a thick bunch of bitter cherry bushes which lined the river. She proudly rode alongside Striped Eagle in a fast gallop for what seemed an eternity, winding along the riverbank, dodging low limbs of trees. She was quickly becoming winded from the hard ride.

Then she saw the pulsing glow of the outdoor fires of

Striped Eagle's village only a short distance away. Straightening her back and squaring her shoulders, she rode onward with him.

When they entered the village they didn't stop to dismount. They rode straight to Striped Eagle's wigwam. Once there they swung themselves from their steeds. Brenda followed Striped Eagle into his wigwam, panting hard.

Brenda's breath was almost knocked completely from her when she saw Morning Flower sitting beside the firespace, her face a sudden cold mask of surprised hate at seeing Brenda with Striped Eagle.

Morning Flower rose quickly to her feet, looking angrily from Striped Eagle to Brenda, then back to Striped Eagle. "You bring her here again?" she stormed. "Why, Striped Eagle? Why?"

Morning Flower then went to Brenda and spoke hotly into her face. "Morning Flower took you away," she hissed. "Why not *stay* away?"

Striped Eagle glowered down at his sister. He placed his hands on her shoulders and turned her to face him. "She is here because she wishes to be here!" he stated flatly. "She is here because *I* want her. And this time she stays. You will never interfere again, Morning Flower. Now go to your dwelling. I need no bother of you now. A war party must be formed."

Morning Flower's eyes widened. "War party . . .?" she gasped. "Why *war* party?"

"Many braves must ride with me to sacred quarry. There are many soldiers there digging up our pipestone," Striped Eagle said, stepping away from her. He pointed to the entrance flap. "Go. Do something useful for your brother. Pray to Wenebojo for victory, Morning Flower."

Morning Flower gave Brenda a sideways glance. "And *her*? Do you also ask her to pray? She knows not *how*!" she spat, then stomped from the wigwam.

Striped Eagle sighed irritably, then turned to Brenda, his

eyes lightening when he saw her standing there, so innocent and so lovely. He took her hands and squeezed them
affectionately.

"You make yourself comfortable," he said thickly. His
gaze went to the ripped bodice of her dress, angering
anew at those responsible. The Dakota! But his fight was
not with them. It was with the white man. *He* had handed
Summer Sun over to the Dakota, for soiling!

"When all soldiers are dead, Striped Eagle will return
and give you full happiness!" he added, smiling warmly
down at her.

Panic seized Brenda. She eased her hands from his,
looking disbelievingly up at him. "You said that I could
accompany you when you went after Major Partain," she
said shallowly. "Now you are saying that I cannot? You
have changed your mind?"

"It is different now," Striped Eagle said flatly.

"Why is it?" Brenda asked sullenly.

"There are too many soldiers. I would not fight as
skillfully with you to worry about. And the fight is for the
pipestone. I must concentrate fully on pipestone, not my
woman!"

Brenda's mind whirled. What could she do? How could
she make him realize that she must go with him to the
quarry? She had thought he understood. But he didn't. He
never would, it seemed. But she had come so close to
finalizing her plan. She would not let it go awry again!

Eyeing his cache of weapons against the far wall, Brenda
set her lips in a stubborn line and stomped to them and
grabbed a rifle. Holding it up in the air, she dared him
with her snapping eyes.

"I *will* go," she cried. "Major Partain is there. It may
be my only chance to finally avenge my family's deaths. I
must. And you promised. You promised!"

Stunned by her action, and seeing determination set in
her face and in the stubborn anger in her eyes, Striped

Eagle suddenly recalled all the times she had left him. It had always been with only one motive in mind. Major Partain . . .

Never could she put it from her heart easily. From the moment he had met her it had been her purpose in life to make the major pay for what he had done to her and hers. And somehow they both had been led to find him this night.

As though a dozen arrows pierced his heart, Striped Eagle's thoughts went to the sacred quarry. When he envisioned its grounds being desecrated, he was shaken into action. The soldiers were even at this moment removing the sacred pipestone! Again he was reminded of the dangers to his woman should she go with him.

Hurrying to his weapons, he slung a quiver of arrows on his back, looped his bow over his left shoulder, and grabbed a rifle.

Then he turned and towered over Brenda. "You stay in village," he growled, his eyes searching her face, still unable to agree to her going with him, no matter that he knew how much it meant to her.

But he did understand vengeance. It had driven his people from the beginning of time. He admired his woman for her dedication to family, to self. She would make a perfect Ojibwa wife, for, once this thing with Major Partain was cast from her life, her total being would be Striped Eagle and his people. Her dedication would be to the Ojibwa. It was only right!

Tilting her chin, Brenda challenged Striped Eagle with a set stare. "I will not stay behind while you go to the quarry," she argued. "How can you even think that I would? You know how long I have waited to see Major Partain get his due. I must go with you. I *shall*."

Feeling his eyes following her, Brenda stormed from his wigwam. And then he was there, again before her, blocking her way. "There will be much bloodshed," he grumbled. "It is no place for a woman. You cannot go. I was wrong to ever say that you could accompany me!"

"You still don't understand, Striped Eagle," Brenda said, her voice softening. "And while we are arguing about foolishness, the soldiers are stealing your sacred pipestone."

Striped Eagle's eyes wavered. He placed a hand to her shoulder. "You stay," he said flatly.

"I *go*," she retorted, just as flatly.

Striped Eagle's lips curved into a smile. "In bravery you equal any man," he said. "*Ay-uh*. You go."

Brenda's eyes widened in momentary disbelief. She then flung herself against his powerful chest, half sobbing. "Thank you," she cried softly. "Thank you." Her eyes lifted slowly upward, his eyes golden in the glow of the dancing flames of the outdoor fire. "I love you, Striped Eagle. Oh, how I love you."

"Striped Eagle must alert his braves of the battle ahead," he said, edging her away from him. "A war party must be quickly formed."

His gaze wavered as he looked down at the ripped bodice of her dress. "Go inside. Choose one of my fringed shirts. Use it to cover remembrance of times with the Dakota," he commanded softly.

Brenda felt a blush rising to her cheeks, having forgotten the condition of her dress. "*Ay-uh*," she murmured. She watched him turn and walk quickly away from her, going from wigwam to wigwam, shouting out commands until at least fifty braves were mingling about the large outdoor firespace, already emitting loud war whoops from the depths of their throats.

Heeding the command given her, Brenda rushed into his wigwam and chose a shirt and slipped it over her head, then hurried back outside. Her heart pounded fiercely as her eyes searched for Striped Eagle. And when she found him, she stood back and admired him as he spoke loud and firm, his copper skin glistening, setting off his splendid physique, unclothed except for his breechcloth. His eyes were two points of fire, his muscles rippling as he lifted his rifle into the air, voicing his own war cry.

A war drum with two heads was brought forth and placed on the ground before Striped Eagle. Kneeling on one knee he began to beat with a steady rhythm against the drum, answered by the howls of coyotes on the opposite side of the White Bear River.

As the drumbeats became louder, the braves began a crazed dance about the fire, bobbing their heads up and down. Their fever-pitched voices reverberated about Brenda. Her breathing became shallow. She had never experienced anything as moving before in her life.

"Woo! Woo! Hay-ay! Hay-ay!" the warriors chanted. *"Woo! Woo! Hay-ay! Hay-ay!"*

And then the ceremony stopped almost as quickly as it had begun. The warriors sat down around the fire with their arms folded across their chests, their eyes directed to their leader, Striped Eagle. Brenda stood back in the shadows, silently watching.

A young boy came to Striped Eagle and handed him a long-stemmed pipe filled with tobacco and red willow and decorated with the feathers of the red tanager. Lighting the pipe with a hot coal from the fire, Striped Eagle passed it around to his warriors, then, when it was returned to him, smoked of it himself.

He handed the pipe back to the boy and rose to his feet and made a speech on the honor of going to war against the men with the pale faces and how it must be done *immediately*, for the white man was even now stealing their sacred pipestone!

Striped Eagle raised his arms to the heavens and emitted a harsh and terrible war cry. A distant tom-tom's doleful sound punctuated the air.

And then Striped Eagle ordered his men to their horses.

They scattered in an instant. Striped Eagle turned to Brenda and went to her, his every motion, his every step expressing an inborn dignity at once with a depth of native caution. His moccasined feet fell like the velvet paw of a cat, noiselessly. His glittering, dark eyes implored Brenda as he stepped up to her and stood wordless before her.

He placed a hand on Brenda's shoulder. "Tonight you will prove to my people that you are not only worthy of becoming my wife, but also of ruling alongside me, the chief of my people," he said huskily. "When we return, you will join in the celebration of victory. You will stand at my side. My people will pass by you and smile from their hearts upon you. Striped Eagle will be proud . . ."

A warmth touched Brenda's inside, loving him so. Besides Striped Eagle and her feelings for him, there was only one driving force in the world: Major Partain. Soon she would have fulfilled her need for revenge. And to achieve it alongside Striped Eagle would make her reward twice as rich.

Twenty-eight

꥓ᖀ

Dawn was breaking on the horizon, the sky holding within it a strange sort of yellowish, foreboding cast as the horses' hooves plodded through the sodden ground of the meadow.

Though tired from the long night, Brenda rode straight-backed in her saddle alongside Striped Eagle. Behind them followed the many Ojibwa braves, their dark faces and eyes revealing excitement about what lay ahead of them.

They had taken no time to deck themselves out in warpaint, nor had they had time to decorate their horses with plumes and paint. The dog's head feast had not even been shared. Time had been of the essence since with each passing moment more and more of the pipestone was being stolen by Major Partain and his soldiers.

But each and every brave knew that the celebration of victory awaited them upon returning. It had been too long now since they had had reason to celebrate a victory over the pale-face. Many moons had passed since they had joined in the fight against them. Peace had always been foremost on Chief Growling Bear's mind. And so would it be the same with Chief Striped Eagle! But peace begat peace. And for the moment, it was the white man who had forgotten the true meaning of the word.

When the quarry could be seen in the distance, Striped Eagle reined in his stallion and swung it around, enabling him to face his men.

"My braves, move as does the panther," he said flatly. "And surprise the soldiers only with the silence of your arrows. The boom of rifles arouses every living thing. Even the sleeping ones awaken to prick up their ears, sniff the wind, and watch."

He lifted his rifle into the air. "When the soldiers are alerted to our arrival, only then do you speak with the noise of your rifles!" he ordered.

Low murmurings and grunts were Striped Eagle's response. He waved his rifle in the air, then lowered it in one swift movement, indicating that he was giving his silent command for the braves to move onward to the quarry.

Brenda's pulse raced, fear suddenly becoming trapped in her heart as she continued to ride alongside Striped Eagle. She withdrew her rifle from the gun sling in which Striped Eagle had placed it before their departure from his village. She approached the soldiers' horses still grazing a few yards from the open mouth of the quarry. The soldiers were still there; good. Caught up in their greed, they had not been alerted to the fact that night had drifted silently away and was quickly being replaced by morning.

Brenda's hopes were fueled. By day it would be simpler for her to distinguish between Major Partain and the soldiers working under his command.

The fact that she was soon to have her final revenge made a languorous headiness suddenly sweep through her, fear now replaced by keen excitement. She had waited so long. Could it be that she was near to seeing the end of this long nightmare?

Surely nothing could go wrong this time. Major Partain was soon to become a victim of an ambush. Brenda had to see to it that Major Partain didn't die until he saw her and understood that she had a part in his death! She wanted him to breathe his last with her on his mind . . .

Following Striped Eagle's lead, Brenda drew her horse to a halt and quickly dismounted.

"You must stay close by at all times," Striped Eagle said as he went to her. "While with me nothing can happen to you. I'd die for you, my woman. Remember that."

Her eyes dolefully wide, Brenda's gaze swept over his face, again memorizing his every handsome feature. She so feared for him. She was now questioning her sanity for urging him to come to this place where danger was rife. What if he was killed? Then she would have nothing!

Easing into his arms, she pressed her cheek hard against his chest. "Please be careful," she whispered. "You are my life, Striped Eagle. My life . . ."

He placed his free hand to the nape of her neck and urged her lips upward to meet his. Gently he kissed her, then released her and began moving stealthily toward the edge of the quarry, his glittering eyes scanning every object that appeared within their view, nothing escaping his piercing gaze.

Brenda crept along beside him, holding her rifle erect, out of the corner of her eyes watching as Striped Eagle's braves scattered about the circular top of the quarry.

And then they positioned themselves, aiming their bows and arrows. The sound of the arrows made a low hissing noise as the braves sent volleys of them downward into the midst of the laboring, unsuspecting soldiers.

Brenda watched, mortified, as one by one the soldiers dropped to the ground. She recoiled when the ones not yet touched by arrows drew their pistols and began firing upward at the Indians.

Harsh war cries resounded through the air as the Indians began racing down into the quarry, now firing their rifles, while soldiers began running, trying to flee the wrath of the Indians.

Searching with her eyes, breathless now, Brenda tried to find Major Partain among those who were still living, having not seen him among those who had fallen. But to her chagrin he was nowhere in sight. Her heart faltered. Had Major Partain departed before her arrival? If he had . . .

Brenda's eyes widened. She took a shaky step backward when a figure appeared suddenly before her. Major Partain scrambled to his feet from the edge of the quarry.

"You . . ." Major Partain gasped in surprise, his rifle lowering to his side. "How . . . ?"

Brenda was momentarily rendered speechless. She had not expected to come face to face with the major so abruptly. She hadn't seen him because he had been hiding just below the quarry opening!

She was shaken from her trance when a bolt of lightning suddenly zigzagged across the heavens. Brenda looked quickly upward. She watched the strange phenomenon in wonder. The sky had darkened ominously overhead! The sky was roaring with thunder and the quarry was being lit up by continuous lurid flashes of lightning!

Brenda recalled the time that Striped Eagle had said that the quarry had a spirit of its own and spoke with a voice of thunder. It was true! It was happening! The spirits were angry, and this was their response. The spirits had come to protect not only the sacred pipestone, but also the Indians who were fighting for it. Even the ancient hieroglyphics carved into the far side of the quarry wall seemed to have come to life, appearing to dance in the lightning's reflections!

Major Partain's voice returned Brenda's gaze to him. Her knees weakened when she saw the rifle he held now pointed in her direction. She had been careless again. She had taken her eyes off him for a moment too long.

Scanning the quarry edge with her eyes, she looked for and found Striped Eagle. He was lying on his stomach, firing down into the quarry. He was too absorbed in the battle to notice the danger she was in. Did he trust his Wenebojo so much that he believed she would be safe? She hoped he was right. For she had the most fearful thought that she might be drawing the last breaths of her life!

"You little witch . . ." Major Partain growled, his shaggy brows merging into one as he frowned. "I should've shot you while you were at Pig's Eye Pete's. Well, you won't get away with this—"

A sudden, close bolt of lightning bursting into the side of the quarry startled Major Partain. His rifle clattered to the ground, leaving him weaponless. He swallowed hard, watching as Brenda lifted her own rifle to aim it at his heart.

"For a moment there I became a mite too careless," Brenda hissed. "But it won't happen again, Major Partain. I've waited too long for this moment."

Flashes of Brenda's mother, father, and brother materialized in her mind's eye, but she couldn't seem to control the shaking of her hands. She had already killed one man. Could she kill another, even though it was Major Partain?

She tried to steady her hands, positioning her finger on the trigger . . .

Seeing Brenda place her finger on the trigger of the rifle, now knowing the full extent of her hate for him, Major Partain began moving backward. "No. Don't . . ." he begged hoarsely. "You don't want to—"

Brenda jumped with a start as Major Partain suddenly lost his footing on the loose gravel at the edge of the quarry. As if time had slowed, she saw him slipping . . . slipping . . . slipping. She rushed to the quarry edge and watched him plunge downward, his cry rending the air as the sky again erupted into wild zigzags of lightning.

As though frozen in place, she watched as Major Partain's fall into the quarry chasm was cut short by a ledge jutting out halfway down the cliff face. But he was finally silenced . . . forever silenced.

Nervously blinking her eyes, Brenda continued to stare at Major Partain, his one leg twisted grotesquely backward where he lay sprawled on the ledge, blood a brilliant red as it streamed from his nose.

When solid arms encircled her waist, Brenda turned to Striped Eagle as he drew her into his embrace. Dropping her rifle to the ground, she sobbed against his chest. "You saw?" she whispered.

"*Ay-uh,*" he said, his arms holding her close. "Striped Eagle saw. Striped Eagle proud. Again my woman has proven her bravery."

"It's over," she cried softly. "He's dead. I can't believe it. He is actually dead."

Something drew her gaze back to where Major Partain lay. He *looked* dead. But was he . . . ? He *was* lying so still . . . his eyes were closed . . . and blood still ran from his nose.

He had to be dead!

Striped Eagle wove his fingers through her hair and kissed her cheek. "You are now free," he said thickly.

Brenda looked up into Striped Eagle's eyes. "Am I truly?" she murmured. "Is he truly dead? Look at him, Striped Eagle. Tell me that he is dead. Somehow I can't believe it."

Striped Eagle glanced down at Major Partain's body, then smiled into Brenda's eyes. "He is dead," he reassured. "It is just that you have wanted him dead for so long, you can't believe that he finally is."

"Yes, I suppose that's it," Brenda gulped.

"You are free now to be my woman, my wife," Striped Eagle said huskily.

"*Ay-uh,* yes," Brenda sobbed, resting her cheek in the welcome, gentle warmth of the palm of his hand. "I *am* free. I am totally yours."

Withdrawing from his arms, Brenda wiped the tears from her eyes, aware of the silence enveloping her and in awe of the sky that was now a soft blue as though there had been no lightning, no thunder.

Then her eyes were again drawn downward, past Major Partain. The quarry was strewn with dead soldiers.

"They're all dead," she said shallowly. "Lord, they . . . are . . . all dead."

"As it should be," Striped Eagle said flatly. "They tempt fate one time too many. The Ojibwa show them. The pale-face soldiers no take threats seriously. They take advantage of the Ojibwa peaceful nature. But no more. These pale-faces who worked in alliance with the evil Major Partain are no more. Peace will now be fully restored between those at Fort Snelling and the Ojibwa. You will see. Things will be right again since the influence of Major Partain has been cast to the wind, as was *he*."

Brenda's eyes roamed over the death scene. To her amazement no bodies of Indians could be seen. They had been spared! She felt the closeness of a lingering spirit. Was it because she was becoming more Indian than white, because she loved an Indian?

Bowing her head, she tried not to feel guilty for the deaths of the soldiers. She knew that the Ojibwa had fought for their sacred rights, as she had fought for *hers*.

"It is time to leave now," Striped Eagle said, leading Brenda to her waiting horse. "We will return to my village with many trophies. The soldier horses are now rightfully the Ojibwa's."

"But what about the soldiers?" Brenda said as Striped Eagle lifted her into her saddle. "Won't there be a retaliation when those at Fort Snelling discover their bodies?"

"The bodies will be transported away from the quarry," Striped Eagle said matter-of-factly. "No one will know how they died, or by whose hands. The Ojibwa will be innocent in the eyes of the white father in your village called Washington." He shrugged. "That's how it will be. Do not worry yourself so. You should be happy in your newly found freedom, my Summer Sun."

Brenda smiled warmly down at him, yes, so free she wanted to shout! It still didn't seem possible. It had all happened so quickly. All along she had waited for the moment when Major Partain would be dead, but it happened so quickly, it didn't yet seem all that real to her.

But it was real. Major Partain had paid. He had paid with his life. And Brenda couldn't be happier!

"I will instruct my braves what to do next, then we shall return to the village and spread the news of our victory," Striped Eagle said, squaring his shoulders. *"Gee-mah-gi-on-ah-shig-wah,"* he added, kissing the palm of Brenda's hand. "Follow alongside me. Before we return to the village we must first go and cleanse our bodies of the smell of death. We will go one direction. I will command my braves to go another."

"Cleanse ourselves . . . ?" Brenda murmured.

"It is a ritual that must be performed," he said, then chuckled low. "It will be a most pleasant ritual. I assure you."

Brenda smiled down at him and then let her eyes follow him to his stallion. She was proud of Striped Eagle. This night his courage had been displayed so grandly! And she could see how strong a leader he was in how he now gave his orders to his men as they climbed up from the quarry.

Shaken from her moment of prideful watching by Striped Eagle waving her onward, already riding across the meadow away from the quarry himself, she flicked her reins and followed him. His voice echoed like thunder all about him.

"Aie-eee! Aie-eee!" he shouted. *"Woo! Woo! Hay-ay! Hay-ah!"*

Brenda pressed her moccasined heels into the flanks of her horse and finally caught up with Striped Eagle. Riding alongside him, she tossed her hair back from her shoulders and enjoyed the taste of the wind against her face and the peacefulness of her heart. She lifted her chin, letting the sun kiss her face, *ay-uh*, knowing that she should be so peacefully content.

Yet something still nagged at her consciousness. She would have felt better about Major Partain's death had she felt for a pulse and found none. Somehow he didn't seem all that dead to her . . .

Twenty-nine

The sunshine fell like great needles of light flashing through the high canopies of foliage overhead, dappling the shaded ground with golden shimmerings. Brenda guided her horse among the trees, still following alongside Striped Eagle. Hunger pangs gnawed at her insides; her bones were weary from being in the saddle. It had been so long since she had eaten . . . since she had slept.

Yet she would not complain aloud. Her happiness at finally achieving her goal overwhelmed all other complaints, all other emotions. Now her future could be spent with Striped Eagle in total peace.

She didn't even wonder about her ability to live in the small spaces of a wigwam or to perform as an Indian wife. She had seen the Ojibwa women laboring, but none of them labored harder than Brenda's own mother. Brenda had learned much in the shadow of her beloved mother. She would soon display how well she had absorbed all her mother's teachings to Striped Eagle. After they officially became man and wife she would make him proud of his choice!

Pushing her tangled mass of hair back over her shoulders, Brenda straightened her back, obeying Striped Eagle's lead as his stallion carried him along the banks of the White Bear River, then upward, through a beautiful grove of oak, and finally around and under a very high cliff. The murmur of the river came up from below, peaceful.

Wild pink roses clung to the cliff, reminding Brenda of the other time Striped Eagle had taken her to his private waterfall, lovely in its tranquility. But this was just as tranquil. On the opposite side was a perpendicular cliff from which extended a gradual slope of land clothed with majestic Norway pines. And the scene was not only tranquil. It was impressive, wild, and exotic.

Striped Eagle continued onward, and Brenda followed. He descended the bank until they again reached the water's edge. Nearby, the mouth of an immense cave looked down upon them from above the water, under the cliff. Its opening displayed more clinging rose vines, as if it were a magnificent, giant bonnet worn by the earth it swelled away from. It was so striking in its beauty that Brenda's breath was momentarily stolen away.

But then her attention was drawn back to Striped Eagle as he stopped and dismounted in a grove of cottonwoods and willows and led his horse to the water. He bent a knee to the ground as he placed a rock on his horse's reins to secure them.

Again following his lead, Brenda swung herself from the saddle and guided her horse to graze beside Striped Eagle's. And as if drawn to him by magic, she moved into Striped Eagle's arms to be possessed by his lips.

Twining her arms about his neck she relished his closeness, the sweetness of his lips upon hers, his hands pressing hard into her buttocks, urging her into the curve of his body. His man's strength through his breechcloth now pressed against her body, causing Brenda's blood to grow hot, flowing in sensual torrents through her veins.

Slowly grinding himself against her, Striped Eagle felt

her respond in kind when she moved with him. Almost crazed with need for her, but feeling it was too soon, he eased her from his arms. His lashes were passion-heavy over his eyes; his heart was like a drum being beaten inside his chest.

But fulfillment of their needs must come later. First they must cleanse themselves of the stench of death. Only then could they truly enjoy what was meant to be shared between them! Striped Eagle felt heady with the knowledge that there was no longer any barrier between him and his woman. She was now free to become his wife in every way, not only in heart, but also in mind. She would no longer have reason to leave him. Major Partain was dead!

Without words, Striped Eagle began removing Brenda's clothes; first the fringed skirt, then the dress. He knelt to a knee and lifted first one foot and then the other to remove her moccasins.

And then he rose to his full height and removed his breechcloth and his headband.

As though willed to, Brenda, too, bent to a knee and removed Striped Eagle's moccasins, then stood and took his hand as he offered it to her.

Slowly they entered the water until it reached to their shoulders. Striped Eagle turned Brenda to face him. His fingers swept her hair back from her eyes, then he drew her slowly to him and gently kissed her, locking his arms about her waist.

Breathless from what seemed to be a ritual of meditation, Brenda placed her arms about Striped Eagle and locked her fingers together at the back of his waistline. Birds sang overhead, an occasional minnow nibbled as if in gentle, miniature kisses at Brenda's legs beneath the water, and the sun warmed her shoulders.

And then Striped Eagle took her hands and pulled her beneath the surface of the water. Again his lips sought and found hers, his hands now finding and cupping her breasts, his thumbs and forefingers drawing an invisible circle about them.

Rising back to the surface, a feeling of gentle passion enveloped Brenda. While under the command of Striped Eagle's smoldering eyes, she began to explore his body with the smoothness of her hands. She quivered sensually when she found his ready hardness. Curving her fingers about his manhood she felt his tremor.

Wanting to postpone what they would again sensually share, Striped Eagle urged her hands from him, then circled his arms about her waist. He began swimming, carrying Brenda along beside him. His muscled strokes carried them toward the land where the mouth of the cave towered over them.

When they reached the embankment, he lifted Brenda to the ground, then climbed up beside her. Their bodies shone sleek and smooth beneath the caress of the sun's glow. Striped Eagle lifted his fingers to Brenda's hair and began untangling it, then he pressed a kiss to the hollow of her throat.

Striped Eagle then swept her up into his arms and carried her away from the river. "We have been cleansed of the scent of death," he said. "Now we will rest before we resume our journey back to the village of Ojibwa. We will share a meal of wild grapes. Their sweetness will be enhanced inside our bodies when we make even sweeter love, my woman."

"*Ay-uh*, yes. Sweet . . ." Brenda sighed, then placed her head against his powerful chest and closed her eyes, calm and peaceful inside.

She cuddled against him as he began half running. Without looking she knew that he was carrying her up an incline. She could feel his muscles straining; she could hear his breathing turn harsh.

And then they reached their destination. Brenda opened her eyes and found herself gazing upon the rose-covered cave entrance. Looking around her she saw thick clusters of grapes hanging heavy from their vines.

She placed her feet on the ground as Striped Eagle eased her from his arms. She watched as he began to pluck rose blossoms until his hands were full. When he nodded toward the grapes, she knew to pick them. That was her duty this morning, the first of many before her as his woman.

Proud, she went to the grapes and plucked several rich clusters, then walked alongside Striped Eagle as they moved toward the cave. A coolness exhaled from the mouth of the cavern, touching Brenda's bare flesh with its breath. But as they entered the cave, she forgot her coldness. A feeling of awe encompassed her. It was as though she had stepped into a shrine of nature. Shafts of light admitted by the cracks in the cave ceiling revealed purplish-hued rock formations rising from the floor of the cave and others sweeping down from its ceiling. It had to be the most impressive exhibit of stalactites and stalagmites ever before seen.

A little stream of limpid water trickled down from a spring within the cave like silver threads undulating in the shallow light. The little watercourse served as a sort of natural staircase as Striped Eagle took Brenda's hand and led her upward, stopping where the earth stretched out on all sides in a sort of platform.

Scarcely breathing, so caught up in the wonder of it all, Brenda watched as Striped Eagle began spreading the plucked roses across the ground.

"A bed of roses for my lovely one," Striped Eagle then said, gesturing toward the roses as he completed his task.

Laughing, lighthearted, Brenda settled down on the roses and handed a bunch of grapes to Striped Eagle. "I wish this could go on forever." She sighed. "If there were only you and me forever, Striped Eagle. I need nothing more."

Easing down beside her, Striped Eagle plucked a grape and placed it to her lips. "Our lives shall always be enhanced by such moments as these,'' he said thickly. ''We shall escape often to our private retreats.''

Brenda enjoyed the taste of the grape, savoring its sweetness as she eyed her companion. ''I shall live for those moments,'' Brenda said, accepting another grape as Striped Eagle fed it to her. ''I'm so happy, Striped Eagle. So immensely happy. I had doubted if I would ever be . . . happy . . . again.''

Striped Eagle leaned back on an elbow and ate more. Turning his eyes to Brenda, he studied her loveliness, the satiny texture of her bare skin as she sat unencumbered by clothes. It seemed so natural that they should be there, sharing their nudity, their wildness. It was as though they were the only human beings on earth, perhaps even the first, in their primitive surroundings.

But he knew they were not alone in the world. It was only a fantasy. There were still men like Major Partain, stirring up hate against the Ojibwa, to contend with. Hopefully, for many moons his village of Ojibwa would be spared such hate.

Placing a hand on Brenda's waist, drawing her to his side, Striped Eagle buried his nose in the depths of her hair. ''Summer Sun, you are my life,'' he whispered, forcing troubled thoughts from his mind. He inhaled the heady fragrance of his woman's hair, her skin, stirring his hunger for her.

Brenda trembled with renewed excitement as Striped Eagle's breath touched her neck when he moved his lips against her flesh there. ''As you are mine . . .'' she murmured. She placed a finger to his full, sensuous lips, tracing their outline, so adoring him.

Tossing the grapes aside, Striped Eagle swept Brenda into his arms and lowered her to the bed of roses. The sun slanting through a break in the rock overhead bathed her face in a golden light; her hair resembled a red halo as it

lay about her head. Her lips were barely parted, her eyes
shadowed by her thick lashes.

The merest touch of her set Striped Eagle's fingers afire.
Trembling, he swept his hands down to her breasts to
encircle them. Their softness always amazed him. Dipping
his mouth downward he captured a nipple, feeling it grow
hard against his lips. He flicked his tongue about the pink
lobe, drawing a soft, sensual cry from her.

And then he fit her closely against the contours of his
muscled body, dazzling her senses as he took her mouth
savagely with his, kissing her hard . . . kissing her long.
With a knee he urged her legs apart and positioned himself
inside her to begin his gentle strokes.

Brenda caressed the skin of his back lightly, running
over its soft texture as she swam in a euphoric sea of
rapture. It was an endless spiraling happiness that reached
clean into her soul, this being with the man she loved . . .
had loved from the moment they first looked upon each
other. And he was hers. Totally hers . . .

Soon he would be her husband. There was no longer
anything standing in the way of their complete union. And
though she already knew the bliss of what husband and
wife shared, she knew that these feelings for Striped Eagle
would only grow even more cherished . . . more beautiful.

His hands now stroking her long and tapering calves
made her shiver with anticipation. She flowered open to
him, almost losing her senses as his fingers explored the
satiny flesh of her inner thighs, then crept upward, caressing her most sensitive spot above where he continued his
masterful thrusts inside her. The pleasure was spreading,
touching her everywhere.

His lips moved to the hollow of her throat, kissing her
hotly as his thrusts strengthened and his muscles corded
against the flesh of her shoulders as he pressed into her,
paining her, yet sweetly so.

Striped Eagle felt the pleasant swimming inside his

brain, his peak of passion almost reached. He closed his
eyes, savoring the pulsing warmth that enveloped his manhood as he moved himself inside her. He gave a soft groan
as the spasms began and he felt the total ecstasy that came
from being with his woman, his *Nee-bin-gee-zis,* his Summer Sun.

Breathing hard, enjoying the aftermath of the explosion
of pleasure that momentarily spread through his body,
Striped Eagle did not withdraw himself from her. He knew
that she was still seeking her own release, for she was
clinging to his neck, her eyes glazed with love as he
looked down at her.

Slowly stroking, his mouth slipped down to her shoulder, then to a breast. His lips paid homage as never before.
Brenda's head began crazily spinning, the sensations he
was arousing inside her no longer under control. She was
like a flaming candle, burning higher, hotter.

Then it spread throughout her, momentarily blocking
everything but Striped Eagle and his skills at pleasuring
her from her mind. She closed her eyes and let this sharing, this ecstasy, take hold.

And then it was too soon over, leaving her only to
memories of what had been moments of sheer joy. Spent,
she snuggled in Striped Eagle's arms as he turned her on
her side, facing him.

"Must it end, Striped Eagle?" Brenda murmured, pouting. She traced his handsome facial features with the tip of
her forefinger. "I've never been so at peace as now. I fear
if we leave this place we shall never capture such a
moment as this again. Tell me I'm wrong, Striped Eagle.
Tell me I'm wrong."

Drawing her fully against him, Striped Eagle ran his
fingers through her hair. He spoke meditatively into her
ear. *"Wah-bungh,* tomorrow," he said huskily. "Even
no-goong-dee-bee-kuk, tonight, we will share such bliss
again. In our shared dwelling it will always be the same

between us. We have a special bond, Summer Sun. Our
love is our special bond. Nothing can ever take that away
from us. Just believe in it, then it will be *so*."

"Yes. What you say is right," Brenda said, sighing
contentedly, clinging. "Nothing will ever come between
us again, Striped Eagle. Nothing."

Taking her hands, he helped her slowly from the floor
of the cave. "We must return to our village," he said. "It
is time to celebrate *many* victories. Did I not promise you
a celebration of celebrations when you and I became man
and wife?"

"I believe so," Brenda said, laughing softly as he led
her outside. She laughed again as he swept her up into his
arms and began carrying her back down the incline, back
to their clothes and horses beside the river.

"Then it will be so," he said, his chin lifted proudly.
"We will first celebrate the victory over the pale-face
soldiers. Then we celebrate our union as man and wife."

He placed her on the ground and nodded toward her
clothes. "Dress. Then we ride to my village. We will be
welcomed with much zeal."

Brenda hurried into her clothes, watching him as he
dressed. She wanted to share Striped Eagle's enthusiasm,
and was thrilled with the thought of finally becoming
Striped Eagle's wife!

Yet she was again remembering her doubts. She should
have shot Major Partain! Then she would know he was
dead for sure!

But wasn't she being foolish? As Striped Eagle had
said, she had wanted him dead for so long, she was only
finding it hard to accept that he *was* . . .

Trying to hide her momentary doubts, Brenda smiled
sweetly at Striped Eagle as he lifted her by her waist onto
her horse and then swung himself onto his stallion. She
then rode along beside him, proud, yet her troubled thoughts
having almost spoiled the moments she had just shared

with Striped Eagle. In her mind's eye she was seeing Major Partain falling, falling . . .

Doubts filling her, she rode steadily onward, voicing a silent prayer to God that she could soon forget any ugliness that had marred her life, and pay tribute to Wenebojo, the Great Spirit who guided the Ojibwa's lives. Somehow it only seemed appropriate that she should pray to the Great Spirit, since Striped Eagle's beliefs would also soon be hers.

Thirty

❧ ❧

The new horses grazing alongside those of the Ojibwa made Striped Eagle's face break into a proud smile as he entered his village. The trophies of war well earned! The soldier horses were now his people's horses. It was only right. It, as well as the deaths of the soldiers, was payment for the desecration of their sacred quarry. And it was also payment to his woman, for the suffering inflicted upon her by the evil Major Partain. She would suffer no more!

Glancing over at Brenda as she rode beside him into the village, Striped Eagle was seized by an overwhelming pride of her. She had proved herself in so many ways to him that she was not just an ordinary woman. She was as highly spirited as the wild mustang when first captured. She was brave beyond words!

Chuckling low, Striped Eagle even accepted the fact that she was perhaps the most stubborn, strong-willed woman he had yet to meet. She was even more stubborn than his sister, Morning Flower!

A warmth enveloped his heart. He admired this stubborn nature of his woman. It was a trait no woman should ever be without. In this world of men, it was a woman's true

301

way to prove her strength. If within her mind she held such strength, so also would it be found in her heart. And she shared her heart with Striped Eagle!

Ay-uh, he was proud . . .

Feeling his eyes on her, Brenda turned and smiled at Striped Eagle. She straightened her back proudly and her chin lifted to be entering his village with him in a different capacity this time. This time it was as his future wife. She would no longer be scheming to escape. She had no reason to. Life was going to be good to her at last.

And what she must do to become Ojibwa in the eyes of his people didn't frighten her. Indeed, it thrilled her to know that she would soon learn all the ways of Striped Eagle's people. It was as though she was slowly being transformed into an Indian, even now making her struggle sometimes to remember how it had once been when she had lived with her family in the small cabin on the banks of the Mississippi River. That way of life was becoming vague to her, overpowered by Striped Eagle's presence and what he represented.

But it was hard to completely place her past life behind her. Her love for her family was terribly intense; she would always miss them. It was only their way of life she would not miss.

A sadness momentarily blinded her. She knew what now must be done to cast the black nightmare that had been plaguing her from her mind. As soon as she found the right moment—a moment when Striped Eagle could accompany her—she must return to the scene of the crime. A final resting place, gravestones to mark these resting places, must be erected so that her mother, father, and brother could rest in total peace. It pained her to think of returning, but she must, and *soon.*

Seeing a sadness enter Brenda's eyes, Striped Eagle edged his stallion closer to her horse. "Are you not happy?" he asked, his dark eyes fathomless as he implored her with them. "So much is now behind you. You must not look back in your mind. Do you understand what I say to you, Summer Sun?"

Always in awe of his astuteness, his ability to almost see clean into her heart, Brenda reached a hand to his face. The sunlight modeled the hard, sharp bones—ah, such a handsome Ojibwa Indian, with his smooth, copper skin and high cheekbones! Just touching him made her grow peaceful and warm inside.

"For a moment I thought of my family," she murmured. "There is one more thing I must do for them. Then I can be totally happy, Striped Eagle."

"What is this thing you speak of?"

"I must see to it that they have gravestones. Only then can they rest in peace, Striped Eagle."

Striped Eagle placed his hand on hers. "*Ay-uh*. It will be done. *Wi-yee-bah*. Soon."

"Thank you," Brenda said, almost choking with emotion. Striped Eagle finally understood her. Perhaps he had before, but hadn't wanted to condone what had driven her into an almost insane madness for revenge. But now it was done. And hopefully she would never have the need to desire destruction again.

Moving on through the village, Brenda sensed excitement electrifying the air. Children were racing about, laughing. Women were singing as they prepared meat over large outdoor fires. And tom-toms beat a pleasant rhythm through the village.

"My people have waited many moons for such a celebration," Striped Eagle said, emotion lacing his voice. "Summer Sun, let's not disappoint them. Come. Follow me. Let my people see you at my side. They will know that you are my woman. My woman forever!"

Goose bumps rose on Brenda's flesh as Striped Eagle snapped his reins against his horse and spurred him away from her, guiding his steed around first one wigwam and

then another, emitting loud whoops. She knew that he
meant for her to follow in such a fashion. Was it a test?
Could she? She knew that all eyes would be on her,
watching for her to falter. And she must not let that
happen. So much depended on first impressions!

"*Ai-eee!*" she shouted at the top of her lungs, surprising
even herself at the primeval sound she had brought forth.

She snapped her reins and thrust her heels into the
flanks of her horse. The wind lifted her hair from her
shoulders as she rode after Striped Eagle. She held her
head high as she wove her horse among the same wigwams as Striped Eagle, mindful of the children and dogs
scampering out of the way.

Hearing the gleeful, approving laughter behind her, she
knew that the children were enjoying the merry ritual. It
was good that their chief had chosen to prove his woman
to his people in such a way! And Brenda was soon caught
up in the glory of the moment, knowing that it was only
appropriate that she should be there, with Striped Eagle,
stirring the excitement in his village to an almost fevered
pitch.

As she followed Striped Eagle, the hem of her dress
flying past her knees, Brenda became aware of the drumbeats reverberating about her. She saw the crowd of Ojibwa
following behind her and Striped Eagle, running, shrieking
cries of victory.

And when Striped Eagle finally reined his horse in and
swung around to meet Brenda's approach, she again saw
the smile that she had grown so accustomed to, a smile
that resembled the sunlight breaking a path through darkened clouds, the most winsome that she had ever seen!

And this smile was for her. He approved of how she had
just handled herself. She had just passed her first test as an
Ojibwa!

Trying to conceal her breathlessness, aware of the dampened strands of hair clinging to her brow and cheeks,

Brenda edged her horse beside Striped Eagle's and looked up at him, seeing pride in the depths of his dark, glittering eyes.

And then her head was drawn quickly around when a voice familiar to her spoke Striped Eagle's name . . .

"Striped Eagle," Morning Flower said, running toward him. "Morning Flower so happy for you. There is so much to celebrate!"

Upon first hearing Morning Flower's voice, Brenda was again reminded of Morning Flower's dislike of her. She could be the only thorn in Brenda's newly found happiness. But now, hearing the gladness in Morning Flower's voice, Brenda felt that just perhaps Striped Eagle's sister had had time to think about what she had no control over, and had decided to accept it. She would not show such happiness had she decided to fight her brother's choice of wives!

Dismounting, Striped Eagle met Morning Flower's approach with coldness. He frowned down at her as she swept into his arms and fondly hugged him. Though he was happy to see his sister, he remembered her recent display of stubbornness. Sometimes he found it so hard to forgive his sister for her unthinking ways!

Taking her wrists, he urged Morning Flower away from him. "So you greet your brother with a smile instead of a snappish tongue?" he grumbled. "Why do you, Morning Flower?" He leaned forward and spoke into her face. "As you see, Summer Sun is still with me!"

Casting her eyes downward, Morning Flower placed a knuckle to her lips. Then she boldly lifted her eyes and challenged Striped Eagle with an angry stare. "You shame me, speaking to me in such a way in the presence of our people," she whispered harshly. "Do you not wait for explanations before you scold me, Striped Eagle?"

"And what is it you wish to say?" Striped Eagle growled, folding his arms across his chest, still glaring down at her.

"Morning Flower sorry for bad behavior," she said, blinking her eyes nervously. "It was untimely. You were leaving to defend our sacred quarry and I fuss at you over a *woman*. Do you forgive me? I shall never interfere again. Never!"

Striped Eagle was touched by her sincerity, by her humility. Reaching for her he drew her into hes arms. "*Ay-uh*, you are forgiven," he said hoarsely.

He eased her away from him, lifting her chin with a forefinger. "But remember this moment, my sister," he added. "You have just accepted my woman. Never speak of her wrongly again. To do so would be to anger your brother so much that the word forgive would never be familiar to him again!"

Morning Flower looked over at Brenda. Before she and Striped Eagle had arrived back in the village, many braves had arrived first, speaking openly of Striped Eagle's woman's courage . . . of her bravery . . . of how she had fought alongside the Ojibwa against the pale-face soldiers.

Morning Flower smiled warmly. She was seeing this white woman as never before. She was seeing a strength about her that she had not wanted to see. It would be easy to accept her now.

"My brother and Summer Sun partners in courage?" she said softly, glancing from Striped Eagle to Brenda.

"*Ay-uh*, that is so," Striped Eagle said, laughing amusedly. "I never thought of it that way."

"How then could Morning Flower *not* accept Summer Sun as your woman *now*?" Morning Flower murmured.

His heart singing, his insides pleasantly warm, Striped Eagle drew Morning Flower to one side, Brenda to his other. "From this day forth we shall be linked as one in mind and soul," he said thickly. "So shall it be, my sister, my future wife, my Summer Sun."

And then Striped Eagle stepped away from them both, beaming. "And now it is time to *celebrate*," he said.

"Our people wait!" He offered Brenda one hand, Morning Flower his other. "Come. Let us go and meet our people. Let us dance. Let us eat. Let us sing."

Brenda giggled as she looked from Striped Eagle to Morning Flower, then suddenly sobered. Major Partain. Even dead he haunted her! Why? Oh, why?

Proudly, Striped Eagle led Brenda and Morning Flower into the sunlight. He gave a loud shriek of joy and guided them into the midst of his people, happy.

Thirty-one

The spring fur hunters had been fortunate and the heavy winter had proved productive of much maple sugar for the Ojibwa. The women's patches of maize and potatoes were already sufficiently advanced to use. Wild game had been put away with much care after the hunt in anticipation of such festivity as this day promised. Wild rice and the choicest of dried venison were being laid out in large wooden dishes along with freshly dug turnips, ripe berries, and an abundance of fresh meat, sumptuously cooked and prepared.

The Ojibwa village was filled with much merriment and jubilation as Brenda and Striped Eagle stepped into the center of the dancers whose greased bodies were like light and shadow flickering as they moved. The mourning of one chief had been placed behind the Ojibwa and the new chief who had just proved his prowess was being celebrated.

A raised platform adorned with many furs and blankets awaited Striped Eagle beside the large outdoor fire. He offered Brenda a hand and urged her beside him as he sat down, proud not only of his achievements in war but also to have finally won his Summer Sun as his woman, *ah-pah-*

nay, forever. He had fought for her and had won. From the beginning he had wanted to win her fairly so that she would accept his offer with much gladness in her heart. He offered her not only his heart, but also those of his beautiful people!

Brenda held her chin high, yet quivered as emotion choked her inside. She had dreamed of this moment, when she could freely accept all that Striped Eagle offered her, for so long. The nightmare that had plagued her since that fateful evening had now faded, replaced by, yes, a dream, sweet and overwhelming in its realness! She was happy, so deliriously happy! She only hoped she wouldn't fail Striped Eagle in his people's eyes. What if they would not accept her?

Feeling the strength in Striped Eagle's hand as he closed it about hers, and feeling his eyes on her, Brenda turned and smiled at him. His strength was transferred to her, giving her the courage to look upon his people with confidence that she would be accepted. Their chief had made the choice. They would certainly not argue with his ability to choose!

Her only regret of the moment was that she had not been given time to prepare herself. She still wore Striped Eagle's shirt over her torn dress instead of something primitively beautiful! To be at her loved one's side, she would have much preferred the doeskin dress. But so much had happened so quickly. The dress of the Ojibwa would be a part of her attire forever after this day!

"There will be much dancing, then games will be shared by my braves," Striped Eagle said softly. "You will watch. You will see how Striped Eagle challenges many braves. Then a feast will follow."

He leaned closer to Brenda, his finely chiseled lips grazing a kiss across hers. "And then will be the time to formally introduce you to my people," he said. "We will then join hands. My people will be witness to our becoming man and wife.''

Brenda felt a peacefulness previously unknown to her, realizing that the special moment would soon be upon her when she became Striped Eagle's wife. So often she had felt that this possibility was beyond reach. Yet through all her doubts and dangers he had been there. It was surely meant for them to be together, destinies intertwined!

"I'm so happy," she murmured, feeling the sting of tears at the corners of her eyes. "Thank you, Striped Eagle, for my happiness."

"Mee-goo-ga-yay-ay-nayn-da-man," Striped Eagle murmured, kissing the palm of Brenda's hand. "You are *my* happiness."

The pulsebeat of the drums, the swishing of the turtle shell rattles, and the feverish shouts of the Ojibwa drew Brenda and Striped Eagle apart. Brenda watched as Striped Eagle rose to his feet and joined the dancers. She was in awe of him, watching how his muscles knotted and rippled like a leopard's as his body swayed and his arms tossed first right, then left. He danced about the fire to the rhythm of the drum.

"Hi-ya-ya-ya, hi-ya-ya-ya," he chanted, his breechcloth flapping in the wind, his sleek, black hair bobbing up and down on his shoulders as his feet continued to beat out the rhythm.

Around and around Striped Eagle went in rising frenzy and excitement, followed by his braves. The squaws looked on, their eyes eager, clapping their hands and singing along with the incessant sounds of the drums and rattles. The Ojibwa village was lavishing the greatest praise on Chief Striped Eagle, leader of a successful war party.

As he danced, Striped Eagle was recalling times long ago past, when his father had returned victorious from the distant villages of the Dakota. The highlight of the victory celebration at that time had been a scalp dance. In his mind's eye even now he could see the women dancing about while above their bobbing heads fluttered the new collection of enemy scalps stretched over wooden hoops and attached to five-foot poles. After the feverish dancing those scalp poles had been planted on the nearby graves of the fallen Ojibwa.

It had been long ago, those ways of fighting the Dakota. Now peaceful ways were sought. But Striped Eagle would not place behind him so easily what Cloud Rising had done to his woman! It was good that Cloud Rising was dead! It was good that his woman killed him. Now the Dakota would fear not only Chief Striped Eagle, but also his wife.

Thinking of his wife's courage, of her bravery, enhanced this time of celebration for Striped Eagle. Ah, but this was a time of merriment! Of rejoicing! If only his father could be there to share in it all. That would make it even more perfect! Oh, that his father could have seen Summer Sun at the quarry. He would have accepted her as a daughter with pride in his eyes!

Striped Eagle stopped before Brenda and offered her a hand. *"Mah-bee-szhon,"* he said hoarsely. *"Nee-mee-win.* Dance. *Gi-tchee-eena-kah-mee-gud.* Celebrate!"

A blush rose to Brenda's cheeks and her eyes grew wide. "But, Striped Eagle . . ." she said, glancing from side to side, seeing so many watching her, "I never . . ."

Leaning to clasp her hand in his, Striped Eagle urged Brenda to her feet. "You just *nee-mee-win,* dance," he said matter-of-factly. "Do not be bashful, *Nee-bin-gee-zis.* You have never been bashful before. Do not be bashful *now.*"

Laughing softly, feeling awkward, Brenda felt that this could be another test in the eyes of Striped Eagle's people and knew that she could not fail in any that was offered her. She had to prove herself worthy of being a wife to a powerful Ojibwa chief. She only hoped she did not make a fool of herself in the process!

It seemed as though a sort of hypnotic spell had been woven about her as she looked into the depths of Striped Eagle's smoldering eyes. As his body began to sway, so did Brenda's. And when his arms tossed right, then left, she found it easy, as usual, to follow his lead.

And then her moccasined feet picked up the rhythm of the drumbeats. As she began dancing alongside Striped Eagle, she felt almost above herself, watching, as though she weren't truly there, weaving in and out among the Indians. Lifting her chin, her hair cascaded in fiery reds down her back. The sun kissed her lips; the breeze caressed her face. Never had she felt as free, as happy!

Brenda became even more caught up in the moment of merriment. She spun around. Her hair lifted from her shoulders and swirled with her, a red streak against the backdrop of Indians who were no longer dancing, but who watched.

And then Striped Eagle's muscled arm slipped about her waist, drawing her to him. Looking over at him, Brenda melted beneath his gentle smile. And when he began chanting, forming the words slowly on his lips so she could learn, she obeyed his teaching and was soon chanting along with him. It was a sound almost primeval to her, yet it seemed strangely appropriate that such sounds could be coming from somewhere deep inside her. She belonged! Oh, Lord, she belonged . . . !

"Hi-ya-ya, hi-ya-ya," she chanted, again dancing.

Out of the corner of her eye she saw that the Indians had resumed dancing, chanting low as their heads bobbed. Striped Eagle's embrace tightened, his breath hot on her cheek as he leaned down to speak into her ear.

"Striped Eagle *mee-nah-day-nee-mo,* proud," he said thickly. "You now watch as Striped Eagle competes in games. You be proud of Striped Eagle."

Straightening his back, lifting his hand in a silent command, the drums and rattles suddenly ceased, as did the chants and dancing.

"It is now time for games!" Striped Eagle announced loudly.

This was received with a burst of savage enthusiasm. Brenda watched as everyone left the large outdoor fire and began running toward an open field at the far end of the village.

Striped Eagle took Brenda's hand and led her toward the field. Lighthearted, she followed.

The ground selected for the games was on a narrow strip of land between the forest and the river. It was about three quarters of a mile long and a quarter of a mile in width. The spectators ranged themselves all along the two sides, as well as at the two ends, which were somewhat higher than the middle.

Striped Eagle led Brenda to another prepared platform and when he saw that she was comfortably seated and in full view of the playing field, he left her and went to his braves, dividing them into two squads. His heart beat powerfully inside him, ready for the keen competition among his braves, knowing that each one would strive to excel over all the others. Today would be the best of the games ever, for his woman was present, a witness to all his abilities this day!

"*Wee-wee-bee-tahn!*" Striped Eagle said, accepting a bow and an arrow from a young boy. "*Gah-gway-gee-kah-gee-way!*"

He watched as all his braves were also equipped with a bow and lone arrow. When this was done he fit the notch of the arrow into the tautly drawn string of his bow and pointed it toward the heavens.

"*Ah-szhee-gwah!*" he shouted, shooting his arrow into the air. Before it fell to the ground a volley from the bows of his braves followed. Each was quick to note the direction and speed of the leading arrow, trying to send his own at the same speed and at an equal height so that when it fell it would be closer to the first than any of the others.

A rumble of chants erupted from the crowd as the arrows plummeted to the ground. Laughter and many hand-shakes were shared among the braves, each boasting of his success in the first test of their skills this day, the less strenuous of the games yet to follow.

And then the bows and arrows were left behind almost as quickly as they had been brought out.

Brenda craned her neck to keep her eye on Striped Eagle as he mingled with the others, walking to the far end of the field. A warmth spread throughout her when she saw how he towered over the others, dignified, tall and proud, a handsome Ojibwa Indian. It was as if she was looking at him for the first time, admiring his long, trim torso, narrow hips, and muscular thighs.

His copper skin glistened beneath the rays of the sun, his luxuriant black hair fixed in place by a headband securing a lone eagle feather, which shone because of the deer tallow rubbed into it.

As he cast her a glance over his shoulder, smiling toward her, she felt serene, at peace because of his love for her.

Returning his smile, Brenda shifted nervously on the thick cushion of furs beneath her, wishing to be with him. Yet she knew that she must get accustomed to being separated from him. His duties as chief would most surely take him away from her more often than not. These brief moments of gameplaying would be small in comparison!

She settled in, letting herself enjoy this moment, observing her man from afar. She knew that he was not only enjoying this time with his braves, but was also showing off for her to watch. She could see it in the depths of his eyes, the twinkle sparked because of her!

She watched as the braves positioned themselves for

what seemed to be a race. It appeared that the less powerful men were stationed at the halfway ground while the
fast runners were assigned to the back. It was an impressive spectacle, a fine collection of agile forms almost
stripped of garments.

And then the race began. Striped Eagle quickly took the
lead. His muscles strained and rippled as his powerful legs
lifted and fell. His jaw was tight, his head held high.
Running harder, beads of sweat glistened on his brow, and
his breechcloth flapped in the wind. He reached the far end
of the field first, panting hard, then embraced first one and
then another of his braves as they arrived, praising them
all for their speed.

Brenda watched, curious, as the braves were then separated into groups of two. She clasped her hands together on
her lap when the wrestling matches began. Her face grew
warm with excitement as she kept her eyes on Striped
Eagle and his opponent. Neither struck with the hand, but
it seemed that all manner of tripping with the legs and feet
and butting with the knees was allowed.

Tensed, feeling almost as though one of the participants
herself, Brenda spoke beneath her breath in favor of Striped
Eagle. Her eyes grew wider at every example of his ex-
traordinary alertness and agility; springing like a panther,
now leaping like a deer over his stooping opponent who
tried to seize him around the waist.

Cheers and war whoops became general through the
crowd of onlookers, a show of enthusiasm surely never
equaled before in this group of Ojibwa, as the desperate
struggles ensued.

When one by one the wrestlers fell apart, Striped Eagle
and his opponent still continued. Groans arose from the
two men as they butted each other with their knees. Ojibwa
words were uttered as one stooped and the other leaped!

And then a mighty crash was finally heard as Striped
Eagle tripped his opponent who then lay sprawled on his

back, exhausted, gasping for his breath, yet looking up at Striped Eagle with keen admiration for a victory well-deserved.

Great, exuberant shouts arose from the Ojibwa as Striped Eagle lifted a doubled fist into the air. He smiled toward Brenda. His chest heaved, sweat trickled from his brow, and his body was a glossy sheen.

Then his gaze scanned his people. "*Mee-eewh!*" he shouted. "Enough! The games are finished. Let us now *eat*!"

The crowd began to disperse, but Brenda lingered. She stood waiting for Striped Eagle, but when he began running toward the river, she lifted the tail of her dress and began running after him. Before she could reach him he had plunged into the water head first, then bobbed to the surface and with wide, powerful strokes began swimming away from the shore.

Brenda went to the river embankment and watched as the other braves who had participated in the games dove into the water after Striped Eagle, splashing and laughing. And when Striped Eagle spied Brenda on the bank he swam toward her, playfully splashing her as he stopped at the river's edge to look up.

"This time you are not invited into the water with Striped Eagle," he chuckled. He looked over his shoulder at his braves. "You cannot be shared, my Summer Sun."

Her face warming with a blush, Brenda bent to her knees and reached for Striped Eagle's hand as he reached out to her. "I don't find the water as inviting as you do." She giggled. "I did not run races and participate in wrestling matches."

Clasping her hand, Striped Eagle climbed dripping from the river. "That is so." He laughed. He removed his headband and smoothed his hair back from his eyes, then quickly repositioned it, straightening his eagle feather to stand erect. "But now I am refreshed. Let us go and join my people about the fire. It is time for the feast promised you.''

His gaze shot upward, seeing the slant of the sun's rays through the trees. ''When the sun reaches the horizon and turns the sky in its brilliant sunset the color of your hair, then shall we join our hands and hearts in marriage,'' he said. He placed an arm about Brenda's waist. ''When the moon silvers the treetops, we will be man and wife, my Summer Sun.''

A thrill coursed through Brenda. It was a moment in her life to be cherished, a moment she could hardly believe she was living. She felt a momentary pang of remorse in her heart, oh, so wishing her mama and papa could know that she had found a man who loved her this much. It was a love that compared with that of their own! They would have been proud, would have accepted Striped Eagle as a son-in-law. That he was Indian would not have mattered to them had they known the man, Brenda felt certain. The color of the skin did not change the feelings inside one's heart!

Ah, yes, if only they could share this day with her, then her happiness would be complete!

Brushing her hair over her shoulders with a hand, Brenda walked beside Striped Eagle to the large outdoor fire. Again she sat down beside him, joining him in eating the prepared foods piled high on platters made of oak.

As the dishes were emptied and pushed aside, nearby drums beat a different sort of rhythmic pattern. Brenda's attention was drawn to several small Ojibwa boys who had moved to the center of attention, naked except for moccasins and brief, embroidered breechcloths, their bodies painted in spirited patterns.

On their human canvas some had painted a wild imitation of the rainbow, others a sunset sky. Some had undertaken to depict the Milky Way across their tawny bodies and some had made a bold attempt to reproduce the imag-

ery of lightning. Others had contented themselves with
painting the figure of some fleet animal or swift bird on
their tiny chests.

"We are now to be entertained," Striped Eagle said,
sitting straight and tall. His legs were crossed beneath him,
his hands resting on his knees.

He glanced toward the forest, seeing how the tips of the
trees seemed to be on fire as the sunset colored them in
rusty oranges. His heart thundered inside him, the moment of truth so near. Yet he had learned well the skill of
restraint. He would let the Ojibwa children have their fun,
their part in the most festive of celebrations, and *then* he
would present his Summer Sun to his people, let them be
witness to Summer Sun and Striped Eagle joining together
as one . . .

"What are they going to do?" Brenda asked, leaning
closer to Striped Eagle, having also noticed the lowering
of the sun from the sky. Soon. Soon she would be Striped
Eagle's wife. It would be real. Everything about her life
would again be real . . .

"These young Ojibwa braves are about to perform the
Hunting of the Deer dance," Striped Eagle boasted. "They
will reenact their capture of a deer. Watch. Enjoy."

The drum beat its tattoo as the young braves formed a
circle about the fire, the pulsing of the drum suggesting the
excitement and tension of the hunter and the swift, stealthy
pursuit of the prey. The young boys began to dance around
the fire, then pausing, each shielding his eyes with a hand
as though looking off across the woodland. Then each
stooped, pretending to discover the little pointed footprints
of the deer on the trail.

The pantomime then dramatically, rapidly moved to the
pursuit and the breathless moment when they each aimed
an imaginary arrow and rushed forward to finish off the
stricken deer with their hunting knives.

The dance ended amid a roar of approval from the

onlookers upon the triumphant return from the hunt, the leader bearing the deer hanging on his shoulder. Cheer after cheer greeted the young dancers as they bowed, their faces radiant with happiness.

Striped Eagle rose to his feet. One by one the young braves passed by him for a tender hug. And when this was completed, Striped Eagle turned and held out a hand to Brenda.

Breathless, feeling all eyes upon her, Brenda rose shakily to her feet. Moving to Striped Eagle's side, she felt her face grow warm with excitement, her heart beating so hard she feared that everyone must be able to hear it!

Placing his arm possessively about Brenda's waist, Striped Eagle raised his other hand into the air and began to speak in Ojibwa to his people. Brenda devotedly listened, although she didn't understand anything that was being said. Suddenly, she was aware of movement to her side. When she glanced toward the sound, her eyes widened at finding Morning Flower there, smiling toward her.

Brenda had no time to wonder about this gesture of friendship, or whether or not it was truly sincere—she had so many reasons to doubt her!—for Striped Eagle's words drew Brenda's attention back to him and the fact that he was introducing her to his people.

"My people, Summer Sun is not only *my* woman, but your *tribeswoman* as well," he said in a commanding voice. "She has proven to be as brave as any man. She has proven to be worthy of serving at my side, as my wife."

A strained silence hung over the village, but then one by one the Ojibwa began to come forth, moving slowly with great and solemn dignity, to place their hands on Brenda's shoulder, to silently nod their approval.

Tears threatened to spoil Brenda's moment of acceptance, yet she held them in check until all had passed by her, some even touching their lips first to one of her cheeks, and then the other.

And once everyone had moved back into the circle about the fire, it was Morning Flower who stepped forth to stand before Brenda. Brenda's eyes widened and she scarcely breathed as Morning Flower smoothed Brenda's hair back behind her ears, then placed some snowy white swan's down above each.

"You have been approved by my people, now I make you more beautiful for when you take Striped Eagle's hand in marriage," Morning Flower murmured.

Brenda was surprised and touched by the gesture. "Does this mean that you honestly approve of my marriage to Striped Eagle?" she asked.

"*Ay-uh*," Morning Flower said softly. "Yes. Morning Flower approves. I do not speak with a forked tongue to you, ever again."

Brenda wanted to hug Morning Flower for her kindness but Striped Eagle had already taken Brenda's hand, looking down at her with passion-dark eyes, his lips touched by a gentle smile. Raising Brenda's hand into the air with his, Striped Eagle once again faced his people.

"You are all witness to my *Nee-bin-gee-zis*, my Summer Sun, now becoming my *wife*," he shouted.

Brenda's eyes fluttered nervously, stunned by the abruptness of the ceremony. When Striped Eagle turned to fully face her, now holding both her hands, she questioned him with her eyes.

"It is done," he said thickly. "You are . . . now my *gee-wee-oo*, my wife *forever*, Summer Sun."

Before Brenda could say anything, Striped Eagle swept her up into his arms and began moving away from the crowd toward their wigwam. Her heart seemed to beat in cadence with the thundering of the drums, the chants and applause of the Ojibwa following along after her.

"That was all that was required?" she murmured, looking up into Striped Eagle's eyes. "Those few words?"

"Is it different in the white man's world?" Striped Eagle asked, lifting an eyebrow.

His question reminded Brenda that she was no longer of the white man's world. Forever now she would be of the Ojibwa people! She would not question the right or wrong of their ways any longer. She would just learn, with Striped Eagle the best of teachers!

"It doesn't matter about how white men perform their marriages," Brenda sighed, resting her cheek against his powerful chest. "Your way—*all* your ways of doing everything—is much . . . much more beautiful."

"My woman is not only brave, she is *wise*." Striped Eagle chuckled as he carried her into the privacy of their wigwam.

Thirty-two

The evening was warm and the fire in the firespace had been allowed to burn low, to dying embers. Still, Striped Eagle sat stubbornly by the fire, endlessly carving, as he had been guilty of doing the entire day.

Brenda sat cross-legged across the fire from him, practicing her beading, yet giving him occasional glances, wondering why he was so engrossed in his carvings! He had scarcely spoken a word to her all day, a full day since they had become man and wife. As they had shared the evening meal he had only halfheartedly eaten while between bites he continued to carve. When she had questioned him about what it was that he was making he had merely cast her a half smile for reply!

But now that she saw that he was almost finished, she could make out the shape of what looked to be a sort of whistle. Strange that a whistle could be made from an eagle's wingbone, for that was what he had begun with!

Then she leaned forward, resting her beadwork on her lap, watching him fasten at the end of the whistle a bit of white down from under the wing of the eagle.

Straightening his back, Striped Eagle smiled toward

Brenda. *"Mee-ee-oo,"* he said proudly. "It is *done*." He held the whistle up between his two hands for her to see. "Is it not beautiful?"

Running her fingers through her hair, urging it back from her shoulders, Brenda smiled weakly back at him. *"Ay-uh,"* she murmured. "Quite."

"It is my whistle of love," he said hoarsely. "Do you wish to hear its music?"

"Ay-uh," Brenda said, laying her beadwork aside. She moved around the fire to his side. "Yes. I'd love to hear you play the whistle." She looked adoringly up into his eyes. "Did you make it for me . . . ?"

"It is for you, *ay-uh*," Striped Eagle said, nodding. "It should have been played for you before the wedding ceremony! But many things stood in the way of proper courting rites." He frowned at her. "First you were here, then you were gone. You were a most elusive woman in love."

Brenda covered her mouth with a hand and softly laughed. "Yes, I guess I was," she said. Then she placed a hand to his cheek. "And I'm sorry for that," she murmured. "Am I forgiven, Striped Eagle? Am I?"

His eyes twinkled, his lips lifted into a slow smile. "Striped Eagle forgive you." He chuckled. "Everything *ah-bway-yay-nim*."

Brenda moved to her knees before him, folding her hands on her lap, a lap of doeskin. The dress was as white as snow, its beadwork design elaborate about the bodice and the hem of the skirt. Many strands of beads hung about Brenda's neck, catching the glint of the fire in them.

"And what did you just say in Ojibwa?" she eagerly asked. "I want to learn every Ojibwa word. One day I want to converse solely with you in Ojibwa!"

"In Ojibwa, Striped Eagle say 'forgive,' " he said, then lifted the whistle to his lips and began softly playing it.

Brenda's insides grew warm with love as her eyes looked

into his. While he played a quiet tune, which seemed to evoke a sensual mood, she blushed and smiled softly up at him.

And when he lowered the whistle from his lips and began to sing, Brenda shivered with passion. Her body turned to liquid fire beneath his heated, steady gaze, the words of the song reaching clean into the core of her being.

"Hay-ay-ay! Hay-ay-ay! A-ahay-ay!" he sang. "Listen! You will hear of him . . . hear of him who loves you! Maiden, you will hear of him . . . hear of him, hear of him who loves you, who loves you! Listen ! My maiden! Listen! *Hay-ay-ay! Hay-ay-ay! A-ahay-ay!"*

Brenda grew weak with desire as he placed his whistle aside and drew her into his arms. Twining her arms about his neck she met his lips with gentleness, kissing him long and sweet, overwhelmed by feelings she could only have with him. She trembled as his hands lowered her dress, then her leggings. She emitted a low moan of pleasure as his fingers now moved maddeningly over her breasts, her nipples hardening at his touch.

She eased from his arms and began loosening the leather ties of his fringed shirt. When this was done, she pressed her hands against his bare chest and looked up into his eyes of fire, then lowered her mouth to one of his nipples. Teasingly she nipped at its hard bud, drawing a sensual groan from the depth of his throat.

And then he placed his hands to her shoulders and eased her down onto the cushion of furs beside the fire. While she looked on he stood and disrobed before her. His body was magnificent in its copper sleekness, his desire for her showing in the strength of his manhood. The muscles of his legs rippled as he knelt down over her, his jaw set, his eyes fathomless.

"We will love as never before," Striped Eagle said huskily.

He wrapped his arms about her and drew her hips upward to meet his entrance inside her. With his hands he moved her hips to match his strokes, his lips now fully possessing hers, his tongue hot inside her mouth.

Feverish with desire, Brenda ran her hands up and down his satiny flesh, reveling in the touch of him, his nearness. She closed her eyes and sighed as his lips moved to the hollow of her throat, then again to her breasts. The pleasure was spreading through her body in torrential waves of sweetness. She could feel the peak of her desire swelling . . . swelling . . .

Striped Eagle buried his nose in the soft curve of her neck, the hunger he always felt for her again being fed. He felt the heat of passion spreading inside him. He anchored her fiercely to him as together their bodies spoke to one another of wondrous, joyous, fulfillment.

Slipping from atop her to cradle Brenda in his arms, Striped Eagle spoke gently to her. "Would not a child make our lives perfect?" he said softly. "A child of our union would be so beautiful, Summer Sun."

Brenda's eyes widened. So much had gotten in the way of worrying about becoming with child! She hadn't thought about it for some time now, though at first it had weighed heavily on her mind: to think of having children, not knowing the color of the child's skin.

But now that she had made her full commitment to Striped Eagle, there was no longer any reason to worry about such fears. There was no reason to wonder how a half-breed child might be accepted into a community of white, for she would raise her son or daughter in the Indian tradition, in the village of the Ojibwa!

"Children . . .?" she murmured. "*Ay-uh*. Our children will be very beautiful, Striped Eagle. So very, very beautiful."

He leaned on his elbow and stared into the embers of the dying fire. "A son would be the future defender of his people, whose lives may depend upon his courage and skill," he said hoarsely. "If our child is a girl she would at once be addressed as the future mother of a noble race."

He turned and smiled toward Brenda. "Our son would very early assume the task of preserving and transmitting the legends of his ancestors and his race."

Cupping Brenda's chin he lowered his mouth to press a soft kiss against her lips. "Our daughter will be the mirror of her mother," he whispered. "Brave and lovely."

"You describe it so beautifully." Brenda sighed against his lips. "Oh, so beautifully . . ."

"*You* are beautiful," Striped Eagle said, leaning away from her. His gaze swept over her. She *was* so beautiful . . . and she was *his*, finally his. She was no longer a captive, but so beloved!

"You study me so," Brenda said, lightly touching his cheek. "Why, Striped Eagle?"

"My mind is full of so many things," he said thickly. "The most prominent is happy thoughts. And you? Are you totally happy?"

Brenda cast her eyes downward, not wanting to admit that a part of her was still less than happy. She still had something left undone. And she hoped that she could get it behind her soon, for she wanted to enjoy her new title of wife fully.

Striped Eagle sensed her aloofness. He placed a finger to her chin, forcing her eyes upward to again lock with his. "What is troubling you?" he asked softly. "Do I not make you happy?"

Brenda smiled weakly up at him. "Oh, so happy," she murmured.

"Then why do you look suddenly sad?" he asked, feeling that he was not serving her well enough in the capacity of husband.

"Striped Eagle, it is as I said before. I cannot be totally happy until my parents and brother have gravestones at the site of their deaths,'' she said, swallowing hard at the thought of returning to the origin of her recent nightmarish existence. Even Major Partain would come alive inside her head again! Hopefully she wouldn't relive the night's events all over again in her mind when she was where her family had died.

"This you must do?" Striped Eagle said, gently taking her hands in his. "Then it shall be done. Tomorrow, Summer Sun. Tomorrow."

Brenda quivered inside at the thought.

Thirty-three

The silence along the riverbank was ominous to Brenda as Striped Eagle guided his canoe toward it. The sky was a brilliant blue overhead, the breeze warm. Brenda's breath was coming in rasps, her dread was so keen at what she might see in the next few moments. How had the scene of death changed since she had been there? The last time she had seen it, the cabin had been in flames.

But this was now. She had finally returned. She knew the spot so well, where she had lived with her family. So many carefree hours had been spent on this riverbank, fishing with her papa and Tommie.

The large boulder protruding from the water at the edge of the river was the identifying marker. She had sat peacefully perched on that boulder, alone, dreaming of her tomorrows. She had learned to dive from that boulder under the careful instructions of her papa. She had looked forward to teaching Tommie how to dive this summer . . .

A choked sob rose from inside her. She lowered her eyes and placed a hand to her mouth, not wanting to cry in the presence of Striped Eagle. In the beginning, when they had first met, she had done enough of that. She was now the wife of a powerful Ojibwa chief, and crying was not a show of strength!

Striped Eagle heard the remorseful sound from where he sat in the canoe, his back to her. Though he wanted to turn to her, reach out to his wife to comfort her in this moment of distress, he instead squared his shoulders and looked straight ahead, knowing that she must learn the art of self-control, as *he* had been taught to do, in his first lessons of the Ojibwa.

But it was hard for Striped Eagle. He and his woman were as one. Her pain was *his* pain. Her remorse was *his* remorse. He understood her loss. He had recently had such a loss himself. Silently he still mourned for his father.

With powerful strokes of the paddles, Striped Eagle guided his canoe closer to shore, then jumped into the water and dragged the vessel, beaching it on a spit of sand.

Turning, he went to Brenda and looked at her for a moment, their eyes meeting and holding. Then he swept her into his arms and carried her to the shore and set her to the ground.

Brenda's heart was racing, her eyes wide, mortified at her discovery. Though the leaves of the corn plants in the field were well developed, green and beautiful in their new growth, it was the spot where she had last seen the cabin that drew her full attention.

She ran toward the barren site, disbelieving of what she was seeing. There were no signs of a cabin! Not even ruins from the fire! Everything had been cleared away, even the black ash. New sprouts of grass shot through the ground where at one time stood a cabin that housed a happy, industrious family.

Stopping, numb, Brenda continued to stare at the spot, understanding of why everything had been removed dawning on her.

"All evidence had to be destroyed," she whispered. She coiled her fingers into tight fists at her sides. "Damn that Major Partain. He had to make sure no one would find any evidence of his evil doings!''

Feeling a strong arm around her waist, Brenda leaned into Striped Eagle's embrace. She forced back the urge to cry and slowly lifted her eyes to meet his sympathetic gaze.

"It's all gone," she murmured. "Everything. It's as though . . . as though . . . my family never even *existed*. It's as though that part of my life never happened, Striped Eagle."

"Your life now belongs to the Ojibwa," he said, placing a hand on her cheek. "Do not dwell on the past. Let us leave this place. Now."

Brenda swallowed hard, her eyes blinking nervously. "I have come for a purpose," she said dryly. "I must build some sort of gravestones for my family. It is only right that I do this, Striped Eagle. My papa, mama and brother, *did* exist. Gravestones will attest to that!''

"Striped Eagle will help you," he said, drawing her fully into his embrace, hugging her tightly. "You are a dutiful daughter and sister. That is good."

He lifted her chin with a forefinger and softly kissed her. Then they walked together toward the river and began carrying large stones from the river's edge until three spots were well stacked on the site of where the cabin had been.

Standing over the three marked graves, Brenda could no longer hold the tears back. Her heart was aching so, it was impossible not to let her pent-up emotions spill from her by way of tears.

She looked from grave to grave, forcing herself to refrain from aching too much. It was the memorial that was important. And strangely enough she felt the closeness of her family as she knelt her head in a silent prayer, as though they were there, watching her . . . loving her . . .

She leaned into Striped Eagle's embrace as he again placed his arm about her waist. And when she felt enough prayers had been said, she slipped fully into his arms and openly wept.

"Cry, my lovely one," Striped Eagle crooned, weaving his fingers through her hair, supporting her face against his chest. "Cry today if you wish, for from this day forth, you will have no need to cry. Your life will be filled with much happiness. Striped Eagle will see that it is so."

Sniffing, Brenda slowly felt his strength transferred to her. She leaned away from him and smiled up. "I will be all right now," she murmured. "Thank you for understanding my needs, Striped Eagle. Thank you."

From over his shoulder she caught a glimpse of a thick cluster of purple violets in full bloom only a few footsteps away. She could place flowers on her mother's grave! Her mother had so loved violets!

Slipping from Striped Eagle's arms she began to run toward the violets, but a sound not so far away drew her to a sudden halt. Her spine stiffened when she heard it again. A rush of coldness spread through her. There was no mistaking the neighing of a horse. And where there was a horse, there was usually man.

Spinning around, Brenda questioned Striped Eagle with her eyes. He had heard it, too, for his hand was now resting on the knife sheathed at his waist.

But he didn't get the chance to remove it. The shine of a rifle barrel shimmered beneath the sun's brilliant rays as a man stepped from behind a tree in the dense forest behind where the Pfleugger cabin had at one time stood.

Brenda blanched, a sick feeling invading her insides, as she recognized the man holding the rifle. "No!" she cried out. "It can't be . . ."

Major Partain limped out into the open, his lame leg dragging along beside him as he leered at Striped Eagle and Brenda. His face was heavily whiskered, his uniform spotted with blood. His hands shook as he aimed the rifle at Striped Eagle.

"I knew if I waited long enough I'd catch the two of you alone, away from the rest of the heathen Ojibwa Injuns," Major Partain snarled. "I've been watchin'. When I saw you leave in the canoe I stole one of your Injun horses and followed you. I've been beside you all the way, hidden in the trees alongside the river. Clever, ain't I?"

"You . . . didn't die from the fall at the quarry?" Brenda gasped, remembering how she had doubted that he had, now knowing that she had been right.

"I sure as hell ain't no ghost." Major Partain chuckled. "Jest had the wind knocked outta me for a spell from the damn fall. That's all."

"But Striped Eagle's braves . . ." Brenda continued, fear and hate fusing inside her. "They removed the bodies . . ."

"They only thought I was dead." Major Partain snickered. "When I regained consciousness I nearly died—from heart failure. It's not every day a man wakes up surrounded by dead soldiers. It was like waking up in a grave."

He limped closer to Brenda, glowering at her. "If not for you, none of this would've happened," he said between clenched teeth. "I'd still be in charge at Fort Snelling. Now I must hide like a criminal. I can't go back. I have no one left at Fort Snelling who knows about my schemes. All those who sided in with me died at the damn Injun quarry."

"Thank God," Brenda said, at least glad for that. She glanced over at Striped Eagle. He hadn't said a word . . . only stared coldly at Major Partain.

But his hand was still on the sheathed knife, but not only that. Brenda could tell that while Major Partain had directed his attention fully on her, Striped Eagle had managed to completely circle his fingers about the handle of the knife.

Major Partain's gaze shifted to Striped Eagle. "I wouldn't

try it," he warned darkly. "You're gonna die soon enough. Don't tempt fate any sooner, Striped Eagle." He took another clumsy step toward Brenda, a half smile curving his lips. "First I'll kill your woman, then I'll—"

A flash of light suddenly fell across Major Partain's face. He blinked his eyes nervously, blinded. His footsteps faltered.

Momentarily stunned, wondering where the light was coming from, Striped Eagle then saw the chance he had been waiting for. He moved his hand so swiftly it mirrored a streak of lightning. The knife slashed through the air. Brenda gasped and stared as it went into Major Partain's chest, emitting a strange sound, as though it were a knife entering the flesh of a pumpkin.

Major Partain groaned. He dropped his rifle and clutched at his chest. His eyes roved wildly and disbelievingly as he slumped slowly to the ground.

"You . . . damn . . . Injun . . ." he whispered, then sprawled out at Brenda's feet, lifeless.

Brenda placed her hands to her throat, scarcely breathing. She stared down at the man she had hated for so long, wondering if he were truly dead at long last. She stood motionless as Striped Eagle came and knelt down over Major Partain's body, placing his cheek to the major's mouth.

When Striped Eagle felt no breath on his cheek, he rose to his feet and pulled Brenda into his arms. "This time it is real," he said hoarsely. "He is dead. You have no more to fear from him."

"But . . . before . . . ? At the quarry . . . ?" Brenda murmured.

"Before I was wrong to not test his breath," Striped Eagle apologized. "But this is *now*. My woman, he breathes no more. He is dead."

Recalling the flash of light which had momentarily blinded Major Partain, Brenda let her gaze search about her. Then she, too, caught a shine in her own eyes. It drew them to the cluster of violets that she had seen before.

Slipping from Striped Eagle's arms she ran to the violets. Stooping to her knees she separated the taller grass that grew around them, then gasped. A broken mirror! She quickly recognized what remained of it. It had been her mother's! Brenda had used it herself many times, when she had brushed her hair, lost in dreams of her tomorrows . . .

As she held it, the sunbeams danced in the mirror again as it had done only moments ago, seeking Major Partain's eyes!

Brenda laughed softly as she took it up into her hands. It was fate! Her mother's mirror had blinded Major Partain, had caused his death! In a sense, Brenda's mother had killed him, as though it was her own vengeance sought and now found!

But then something else caught her eye as she looked past the mirror, through the bent grasses around the heart-shaped leaves of the violets. She again gasped, taken aback once more. It was a book!

With trembling fingers she dropped the mirror and reached for the tiny, scorched book. Her heartbeat grew rapid, her knees weak, as she lifted it closer to her eyes.

"My mama's book of poetry . . ." she whispered, her cheeks growing warm with her discoveries. "Somehow it and the mirror survived the fire . . ."

She flicked tears from her eyes, then opened the book, flinching when some of the scorched pages began to flake and crumble in her hand. Yet she could read many of the passages. She recognized many poems that were her mother's favorites.

And then remembrances of something else made her turn back to the inside cover of the book. She sighed longingly when she discovered her mother's signature of ownership still there, the fire at least having spared *that*, was proof that her mother had lived!

Running a trembling finger over the written name, Brenda
felt as though her mother were there, her name on the page
like a soft kiss against her fingertips.

"What have you found?" Striped Eagle said, moving to
her side.

Brenda was shaken from her reverie. She held the book
of poems out for Striped Eagle to see. "First I found my
mama's mirror. It was this which reflected the blinding
sunbeams into Major Partain's eyes. And then I found a
book of talking leaves," she said, smiling softly up at
him. "It was also my mama's. A book of poems. She read
from this book each evening before we went to bed. It was
a special time for the Pfleugger family, Striped Eagle. So
peaceful . . . so loving."

"Do you not see? The Great Spirit spared these for you
to find. You will always be close to your loved ones in
spirit now," Striped Eagle said thickly. He stooped to pick
up the mirror. *"Mah-bee-szhon.* Come. Let us return to our
people."

"Ay-uh, yes," Brenda murmured, clasping the book to
her heart, not even looking toward Major Partain again.
He would no longer trouble her heart. He was dead, this
time forever dead!

"But first I must give my mother a last gift," she said,
smiling up at Striped Eagle.

Plucking several violets, she went and placed them on
her mother's grave. "Mama, thank you," she whispered.
"Thank you for everything . . ."

The breeze lifted Brenda's hair from her shoulders and
the fringe of her leggings as she pushed back to her feet.
She took one last look at each of the graves of her family,
then looked toward the field of blowing, green leaves,
where soon corn would be plentiful. In her mind's eye she
was remembering planting the seed as her father moved
ahead of her, furrowing the land. She had walked in his

shadow. Even now it seemed that he was there, his shadow towering over her, her remembrance of him was so vivid!

Forcing herself to cast such thoughts from her mind, Brenda turned on a heel and walked proudly beside Striped Eagle, accepting his shadow in place of her father's.

Dear Reader:

It is my sincere hope that you have enjoyed reading *Savage Surrender*. This genre is among my favorites, and upcoming books I write will include a passionate sequel to my previously published Indian romance, *Savage Torment*.

I'd be delighted to hear from you all and I will respond to all letters received.

Until my next Indian historical romance, best wishes!

CASSIE EDWARDS
R.R. #3, Box 60
Mattoon, Illinois 61938

Highly Acclaimed
Historical Romances From Berkley

_____ 0-425-10006-5 **Roses of Glory**
$3.95 by Mary Pershall
From the author of <u>A Triumph of Roses</u> comes a new novel about
a knight and his lady whose love defied England's destiny.

_____ 0-425-09472-3 **Let No Man Divide**
$4.50 by Elizabeth Kary
An alluring belle and a handsome, wealthy shipbuilder are drawn
together amidst the turbulence of the Civil War's western front.

_____ 0-441-05384-X **Savage Surrender**
$3.95 by Cassie Edwards
When forced to live in the savage wilderness, a beautiful
pioneer woman must seek the help—and passion—of a fierce
Indian warrior.

_____ 0-515-09260-6 **Aurora**
$3.95 (on sale Oct. '87) by Kathryn Atwood
A charming favorite of Queen Elizabeth's court, Lady Aurora
must act as a spy for the dashing nobleman who saved her life—
and stole her heart.

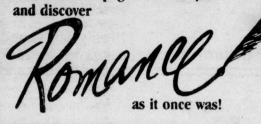